DON'T LET 'EM TAKE THE CHILDREN

R H WILLIAMS

The Book Guild Ltd

First published in Great Britain in 2024 by
The Book Guild Ltd
Unit E2 Airfield Business Park,
Harrison Road, Market Harborough,
Leicestershire. LE16 7UL
Tel: 0116 2792299
www.bookguild.co.uk
Email: info@bookguild.co.uk
X: @bookguild

Copyright © 2024 R H Williams

The right of R H Williams to be identified as the author of this
work has been asserted by them in accordance with the
Copyright, Design and Patents Act 1988.

All rights reserved. No part of this publication may be
reproduced, transmitted, or stored in a retrieval system, in any form or by any means,
without permission in writing from the publisher, nor be otherwise circulated in
any form of binding or cover other than that in which it is published and without
a similar condition being imposed on the subsequent purchaser.

This work is entirely fictitious and bears no resemblance to any persons living or dead.

Typeset in 11pt Adobe Garamond Pro

Printed on FSC accredited paper
Printed and bound in Great Britain by 4edge Limited

ISBN 978 1835740 347

British Library Cataloguing in Publication Data.
A catalogue record for this book is available from the British Library.

For Rachel, Kitty and Idris.

CHAPTER 1

Despite investigating the most haunted sites of my hometown, *Nant-y-Wrach*, the abandoned farmhouse is the first place to genuinely give me the creeps. Even the air seems off. Damp and warm, it tastes bitter, and the smell – when I'm able to sniff it without retching – is like an old-man's vinegary sweat. The building is stuffy and poorly lit, and while the hot afternoon sun warms the air outside, inside, the walls are clammy to the touch like we're trapped in the death grip of a corpse. The shadows are heavy, and trudging through them leaves me drained and glum. All around I sense things hiding that are not of this world and it's like they pull at me to stay, and I say *things* because whatever haunts this place is not alone. There's something about this building – maybe even the ground it's built on – that brings them here, attracts them like a magnet for nightmares. I know it's horror film standard fare, but that's how it is. The house was built 150 years ago and they say the first family that lived in it was massacred – although we couldn't find any details about that. The only information we do have is that no one has lived here since the Second World War, and – by the way – the last owner hanged himself. The house is super freaky and terrifying, and as such, I'm excited and very hopeful that our investigation here will get us some results.

"How many photos have you got left?" I ask Gwyn, my lieutenant and also – perhaps grudgingly – chief photographer of the squad.

He lifts his Kodak Winner 110 pocket camera with his long, skinny arms. "Twelve." He looks back at me with his eyebrows raised and coughs, before reaching into his pocket and taking out his inhaler for two puffs.

I make a snarling sound. "Bloody hell, Gwyn. You've used half the pictures already?"

"I took a few in the parlour – in that dark end of the room," he says, shrugging his shoulders. "Ned, you did ask me to."

"Bollocks," I say. "That means we only have twelve photos left for the bedrooms and the stairs. And you know as well as I do that the stairwell is a popular place for spirit photographs."

"Do I?" he says with a curled lip.

"Well, you should do as chief photographer…" I huff and cross my arms.

"I thought intelligence was my job," he says and clears his throat again.

"Until the squad gets bigger, all of us need to have more than one job. You okay?"

He nods. We've been in the building for an hour and the dust is starting to get to his chest.

Gwyn doesn't share the same beliefs as I do about the mysteries of the universe. He says there's a rational explanation for all of it. I think he lacks an open mind, and we argue about it all the time. I'm pretty sure he never used to be like this. When we became friends in primary school, we only seemed to argue about stupid childish guff – favourite toys and such. Now we're both thirteen, we disagree about all sorts. Top of the list is always the paranormal: hauntings, telepathy, Loch Ness, reincarnation, Mothman, the Bermuda Triangle, et cetera, bloody et cetera. He won't accept any of it. But whatever the case, he still joins me on investigations, and he knows how important they are to me. He may be annoying, but he is loyal. Besides, I see it as my challenge – if our mission leads us to uncovering proof that convinces Gwyn, then I can make a believer of anyone.

Our investigations have nothing to do with the lad at school who went missing three days ago. His case is a separate matter as far as I'm concerned, and we're here, as part of our bigger mission, to uncover the truth about the real mysteries of the town. *Nant-y-Wrach* has a long history of weirdness – from the witch that the town is named after (the name means *Witch's Stream*) to the cursed asylum and the many haunted houses, which include this bloody farmhouse. Could the hauntings have some connection to the witch? I've not ruled it out. She's everywhere here. They teach us about her at school and it's what brings the tourists here. There are brooms and black cats all over. There's a Cauldron Cafe and a Salem Kitchen Furnishings in town, and local buses have black silhouettes of flying witches on their side. On the High Street, there's a second-hand bookshop called Bewitched Books owned by Gwyn's dad and it's where his brother, Rhys, works as well. Rhys is more like me – he's passionate about the supernatural and other mysteries. He eggs on our investigations and knows something funny is happening here. He reckons the *Guinness Book of Records* is going to include the town in next year's 1984 edition as the most haunted town in Britain. He also says that Arthur C Clarke is going to come here to film an episode of *Mysterious World*. Seems farfetched but I do trust Rhys – he's our Q who mans our HQ in the back of the bookshop and researches the places we investigate and provides us with the information we need to carry out our investigations.

Gwyn and I move along the downstairs hallway – I tiptoe carefully while he stomps. I gaze into shadows and run my fingers against the cold walls trying to hear or sense what is there. Behind us, a loud creak comes from the parlour like the house is trying to get our attention and I gesture to Gwyn with my hand for us to head back in there. Military hand signals are an essential skill for squad leaders like me. I learned them from repeat viewings of war films I taped on telly (*The Dirty Dozen* and *The Bridge on the River Kwai* are more like training videos, really).

There are holes in the windows from stones thrown by kids in town. Probably kids we know from school. Horse and his Goons come here sometimes – not today hopefully. The farm is a short hike up the hill outside of town and it attracts attention from anyone wanting somewhere to hang out after school or on the weekend. Older kids come here to have parties and the living room between the hallway and the kitchen is littered with bottles of White Lightning, cans of SKOL, cigarette stubs and torn-up Rizlas.

Next to the window, there are streaks along the walls where rainwater has streamed down from holes in the roof. Any carpets that covered the floors are long gone and patches of the floorboards look rotten. Over the winter months, Welsh mountain weather is cold and wet, and the room is probably flooded most of the time. The walls are covered in faded orange wallpaper that peels and hangs off in places like a peeled banana, or – *gulp* – flayed skin. Life left this house a long time ago.

The dark end of the room Gwyn mentioned is on the opposite side to the window. There is certainly something peculiar about it, and I stare, trying to make out what is lurking there, watching us. Neither of us has any skills in seeing or talking to the dead (that I'm aware of – our experiments went nowhere) but according to *The Hamley Book of the Paranormal*, you don't need to be a psychic medium if the haunting is strong enough. You'll see or hear it anyway.

As I gaze at the back wall, Gwyn strides around the room in a circle, holding up his camera, examining the walls, the ceiling and the floor beneath him. I clench and unclench my fists and wipe the sweat from my brow. The room is muggy but that isn't why I'm sweating – it's the shadows and whatever is hiding there. It all makes me uneasy, and I feel waves of wanting to be sick – the way I did when I had that stomach bug last year. I've never liked the darkness; being unable to see what is out there always takes my imagination to the worst thoughts, and here, as I peer into the gloom, I sense something nasty is gazing back at me.

"Come on, show yourself," I whisper.

"What are you saying, Ned?" Gwyn stands near the window.

"I'm just telling whatever is here, that now is the time for it to show itself."

"Well, if it could hurry up, that'd be great. Fricking air is killing me." Gwyn steps closer and studies the floor. I glance over at him and then back at the shadows.

"You know some of these floorboards are in a really bad state," he says. "We really need to be careful…"

His words are broken by the snapping and roaring of collapsing wood. In the midst, I hear a howl. I turn my head to see that he's gone, and where he stood, there is now a big black hole. I gasp, thinking I've lost him.

CHAPTER 2

I hear his groaning before I see his face as my eyes take a moment to adapt to the half-light in the murky space below. There, he lies on his back on a section of the flooring that has collapsed into the underground room. He appears stunned and both hands still have hold of the pocket camera.

"I didn't know there was a cellar," he says, gazing up at me, wide-eyed before starting to laugh.

"Neither did I." I begin to chortle. "Are you okay? What can you see down there?"

He turns his head and examines the space around him.

"I see the walls under the window on this side. But on the other side of the room, I can't see anything. It's completely black." The look on his face changes. "Ned, I don't like it down here."

"Are there no doors?" I ask.

He shakes his head. That's weird, I think. Gwyn's eyebrows wrinkle as he stares back at me. The whites of his eyes shine in the dark against the void of the cellar. He stands up, sticks the camera in his back pocket, and tries to reach the edges of the hole. I can hear him wheeze again.

"Ned, please, can you help me?"

I rub my chin and scan the room. Frayed net curtains hanging from the windows billow like flying ghosts as the warm air blows through the holes in the glass. I get up and pull on what is left of them. They are strong enough, I think, so I climb up onto the window ledge and pull them off the rings at the top of the rail. Behind me, I can hear Gwyn.

"Ned, where did you go? Don't leave me."

My hands are trembling, but I manage to detach all the material.

"Gwyn, I'm coming," I say.

"Hurry, please," he says. "I don't like it. I can't breathe."

I leap down from the window ledge and carefully tread along the edge of the hole like a tightrope walker to the spot where the broken floorboards are still attached, and they hang diagonally from the remaining wooden flooring. Gwyn is leaping up, trying to grab hold of anything he can to pull himself from the hole, but each jump seems to further lower his energy levels, and then, bent over panting, he tries to catch his breath again.

"Gwyn, here."

I drop the curtain material into the hole. Gwyn looks up and takes a few deep breaths through his mouth. He stands upright and reaches for the makeshift rope. He grabs the end and wraps it around both hands. I begin to pull, hoping the eight-month age gap and the inch and a half of height I have on Gwyn will allow me to get him out. With a tight grip, I hold on to the curtain material and pull backwards with my legs. At the same time, Gwyn clambers up along the jagged face of the stone wall.

"Come on, Gwyn," I yell. "Nearly there."

I pull as hard as I can, my eyes are closed, and I focus all my strength on taking steps away from the hole. Slowly, I reverse, until something gives, and I fall back onto the floor.

"Shit. Gwyn," I say, thinking the material must have ripped.

"It's okay." I hear his raspy voice. He is out of the hole and has let go of the material, sending me flying. He is lying on his front, and I see him struggling to find something in his pocket.

"My inhaler." He glances up at me again before turning onto his back and then pointing into the hole. I rush over to him and examine his face. His lips are turning blue, and he struggles to speak.

"You bloody idiot," I say.

Shit, I think. I'm going to have to go into the cellar to find his inhaler. I look around and there is nothing nearby to attach the material to. But Gwyn could die if I don't do something. I'll have to take my chances getting out.

At the spot where Gwyn emerged, I lower myself down from the broken edge of the floorboards. I hold on for as long as I can before letting go and sliding down and dropping onto the ground below. As I fall, it comes to me that if I fail then we might end up stuck here. We might find proof of the afterlife by becoming ghosts ourselves. I can think of better places to haunt.

I see now what Gwyn described. Behind me – underneath the window – I can just about make out the wall. Ahead of me and underneath the dark end of the room where Gwyn used up half of his film, I see nothing – just a dark screen of mystery. My heart races and I blink repeatedly. Anything could be hiding there, and I wouldn't know it.

"Ned. Please. Find it." There is desperation in his voice – he's suffocating.

I inhale deeply and examine the ground which is covered in a mixture of broken floorboards, dust and rubble. I get down on my hands and knees and begin to crawl around in the area lit by sunlight, but I can't see it.

"Ned…" Gwyn calls out again. I try to remember how he landed when the floor collapsed. He was on his back, and he always kept his inhaler in his front-left trouser pocket. Biting my lip, and on all fours, I start crawling out into the dark. I cannot see anything now. Open or closed, my eyes see no difference. I stretch out my fingers, touching the cool stone floor of the cellar between the rubble as I try and feel for the inhaler in the pitch-black. If something reached out and grabbed my arm right now it would come as no surprise. I could be pulled into the shadows and killed as Gwyn struggles to take his last breath up above. I scurry around in an area away from the light on all fours like a trapped animal – my fingertips reaching out and trying to feel for the damn inhaler. I imagine the hunters in the darkness watching me, enjoying the show as this pitiful trapped creature freaks out, before they decide to move in and end it. Where would it take me, I wonder? What does ending mean, really? Would I join them – the hunters – in the shadows, to wait and hide for more victims to come? Whatever the ending means, I'm not ready and I will fight to survive and get out of this bloody hole. They won't have me today, but my movements are jerky and clumsy over the broken wood and gravel and sweat streams from my forehead. The little finger on my left hand touches something, something plastic. The inhaler is there, and I reach out and grab it before crawling back into the light where I take a few gasps of air and try and stop trembling.

"Gwyn, I have it. Can you reach?"

I hear Gwyn shifting himself around before his hand extends out over the edge.

"I can't reach your hand," I say. "I'm going to throw it to you."

I hold the inhaler up and try to aim the throw, so it drops on or near Gwyn. I toss it up and I hear it land on a soft surface. Gwyn's hand disappears and I hear a series of wheezy gasps. The hand appears again – this time in the shape of a thumbs up.

After an attack like that, I know it takes a few minutes for him to recover. I search around me to see how I might get out of the hole. I reach up but there is nothing there for me to hold on to. I try each side and jump a few times, but it's pointless – there is no way I can climb out of the hole. I sit down and wait for Gwyn.

"Come on, you little bugger," I whisper. "If you're not okay, I'll kill you."

Might there be another way out if he isn't able to help me? That isn't worth thinking about right now. The town will blow up in panic if more children go missing.

My eyes have now got as used to the darkness of the cellar as they ever will. Away from my position in the spotlight of the sun shining through the broken window, I still see nothing. I gaze at the black wall and will whatever is there to show itself. I reach for a piece of wood and hold it up, ready to defend myself.

"Show me," I say. "Come on, I'm ready for you. I don't care how many of you there are."

From the shadows, I hear scratching. I turn my head towards the noise and listen. I close my eyes and try to concentrate on the sound. I'm certain I can sense something there – I hear distant chattering like someone left the television on in the next room. I try hard to listen in on what I'm hearing but it isn't normal sound like you hear through your ears – it's all around and inside my head. I suddenly leap back against the wall as something touches my hair. I stumble over broken timbers trying to regain my balance and bumping my head in the process. Leaning against the cold stone, I look up and see the curtain material has been dropped down into the hole.

"Shit, Gwyn. You scared the piss out of me."

"Use that." Gwyn's head pops over the edge.

"You can breathe?"

He nods.

"Can you pull me out?"

"You can pull yourself out." He points across the room. "I've tied the other end to the doorknob."

"Is the curtain long enough?" I ask.

"One isn't, but there were two curtains."

Clever lad.

"Right." I peer back into the quiet void and start to doubt what I experienced; was there anything there? For a moment I believed I sensed something, but there's no way we can stay any longer. Haunted or not, I must get Gwyn out of the house.

I pull on the material to make sure it'll hold my weight. Then I grab it more firmly, fill my lungs with air, and pull hard to lift myself off the cellar floor. I use the jagged stone wall and the remaining pieces of attached floorboards to give me footing and allow me to step up the side as best as I can. It works and when I reach the top, Gwyn grabs my shoulders and we both fall to the floor.

"Okay?" he asks.

"Yep." I point to his filthy dust-covered clothes. "Your mum won't be happy."

"She never is." He laughs a tired laugh and smacks his knees to try and clear the dirt from his skinny brown cords.

"We should probably get going," he says. "I haven't got much puff left after all that. We don't want another attack."

I bite my lip and take one last look in the hole. "You made me shit myself in there. Literally."

"You mean figuratively," Gwyn says, deadpan. "Had you literally shat yourself, you'd reek even more than you do right now."

"Alright, thanks, wise guy," I say. "Let's get out of here before I throw you back in."

I breathe a little easier knowing we're both safe but as I push Gwyn ahead of me, through the parlour door, I let out a deep sigh. Another failed investigation with no proof of anything, but I feel we were close. Really close.

CHAPTER 3

We leave the farmhouse through the same open window that we used to get in. I go first – climbing up onto the sink in the kitchen. As I step into the metal bowl, I hear tiles under my feet cracking. The old window frame screeches like an angry old man as I push it open, and I crouch as I go through before dropping and tumbling onto the overgrown courtyard outside but stopping myself before I roll further down the incline. The outside air tastes clean and – despite the summer heat – fresher than the vile air of the old farmhouse. I get up and hold the window open for Gwyn, who drops onto the ground and tumbles and rolls dramatically. I offer my hand and pull him up to his feet. He nods a thank you and we make our way around the building to the front where we left our bikes leaning on the stone wall. There, we stop and both stare at the place.

"Anything?" Gwyn asks.

I start shaking my head. "Sod all – unless we got anything in the photos. It's depressing. I really thought we were close."

He smirks but I don't bite this time; he doesn't believe yet – but he will.

"I – we – will get there," I say, puffing out my chest. "I'm confident of it."

Gwyn purses his lips and blows. "I'm just glad to be outside. Haven't had an attack like that for ages."

I put my hand on his shoulder. "You okay now?"

"Chest is still tight," he says, "but I'll be okay."

I nod and start to wheel my bike out of the front garden.

"Thanks, by the way," he says with a pained look on his face.

I glance over at him. "For what?"

"You probably saved my life."

"Never leave a soldier behind." I give him a military salute with my right hand, and he grins.

As annoying as he can be, he plays an important part in operations. He's our intelligence guy because he's great at analysing problems and coming up with answers to tricky questions. He isn't a man of action. Those are the skills I bring. I watched all the Bruce Lee films on Channel 4 last year and I've watched the dodgy copy of *First Blood* we have at home seven times. I have a good knowledge of war films and can handle myself in most situations, I reckon, with solid nines for strength and agility (based on my own scoring). I'm not sure about my weaknesses. I'm sure I have some but they're not obvious – not to me at least. Gwyn would be a two and a three on strength and agility, respectively. He does well at tests, but you wouldn't want him to back you up in a fight – with his small body and thin arms and legs. Overall, I'd give him an eight for analytical skills and a seven and a half for intelligence. Right now, he'd get a five for his photography skills. Maybe when he learns not to waste pictures, he'll get a higher score. His main weakness is his asthma.

As I push my bike away from the farmhouse, I turn my head to see the hills behind me grow like a bunch of huge earthy-coloured creatures standing up straight and reaching their heads into the skies. The seven mountain peaks that surround the town are called *Y Cewri* – after the Seven Giants of legend. According to the story, a king once lived here, and he was tormented by a *cythraul* – a demon – that would not leave him or his family alone. The *cythraul* killed the King's firstborn child, strangling the little girl in her bed, and the King was distraught. When his wife became pregnant with another, he realised he needed to act. He visited a local witch and asked for her help. She told him there was something she could do but he would need to give up his lands and move elsewhere. All the King had to do was speak some words and then be ready to leave. So be it, he thought, and he returned to his castle and readied his family and his people. When the time was right, he spoke the words and a thunderous sound erupted across the land. From the sea, there emerged seven huge giants that were as tall as the skies. They walked from the coast and made their way to the castle and each of them sat down around it. The King and his people started to leave and the *cythraul* tried to follow them, but the giants stopped it and trapped it in the space between them – they had it surrounded. The giants remained where they were, and over time, grass and trees grew on them – as they became the seven mountains that now surround the town. The *cythraul* was never heard of again but it stayed where it was – never to leave the area.

Staring at the *Cewri*, it's not surprising that people used to think they were giants. They form a thick rocky wall around the whole of the town and the only way in or out is along the main road that winds its way between them. People here have always taken comfort in the way the *Cewri* provide a wall of protection around the place – keeping all the nastiness of the world out. But the way I've always seen it, they do the opposite; they keep the world outside safe by trapping the evil forces of the town right here.

We walk our bikes downhill along the farm lane, which is full of holes and half covered in grass making it difficult for us to ride. Gwyn guides his BMX while I push my Chopper. His bike is much newer, but I prefer mine because the seat is comfier, and it has a back that I can lean on. Also, it has a gear stick like a car. Meanwhile, Gwyn's brakes are squeaky and in dire need of some oil.

We're both silent as we walk. I'm disappointed at another failed investigation while Gwyn looks like he has something on his mind. Experience tells me it's better to ask him rather than let it fester. Jeez, I think, it's like we're married.

"What is it?" I say.

"Some of the lads from school are going to the cinema tomorrow."

Right, I think. It'll be one of these again.

"Okay," I say. "To see what?"

"*Return of the Jedi*. Matinee showing. Fancy it?"

"Oh, is that out already?" I gasp and feel a flutter in my stomach.

"It is – the final part of the trilogy," he says. "Dying to know how they follow up *Empire* – that ending was so dark."

"Yeah, can't believe Vader was Luke's dad all along," I say. "And Han getting frozen was nuts..."

"So, you in?"

Gwyn stares at me expectantly. Part of me would like nothing more than dropping everything and going to see the film, but thinking about it, I realise it would just be a distraction, and I find myself grinding my teeth. "I can't. There's no time for that now."

"Right." Gwyn sighs.

I start to breathe harder through my nostrils. "Go on, what is it?" I say, stopping my bike.

He faces me but his eyes look away. "Don't you think we need a break from these investigations? It's all we've been doing since the start of the holidays and to be honest they're not so fun any more. You know, I could've died in there."

I cock my head to the side. "You think I'm doing this for fun?" I sigh loudly. "Look, I know the asthma's a problem so maybe you should sit out some of the investigations?"

Gwyn stares at the ground. "Ned, I can't let you go to these places alone. Maybe you should sit out a few as well? Take a break and try to enjoy the summer."

I feel my chin lift as my neck tightens. "It's not about having fun – our mission is bigger than that. We're close, Gwyn. Close to uncovering something huge. I can feel it. We just need a bit of luck."

He shakes his head slowly. "I don't know. Maybe it's getting a bit too serious. I know why you're doing this, but I honestly think it's a waste of time. It's like you're looking to pick a fight with something that isn't there."

"Picking a fight with something that isn't there? That's a new one from you. And why do you suppose I'd be doing that, eh?" I cross my arms.

"So you can beat it and keep everyone safe," Gwyn says. "That's what you want, isn't it?"

"Well yes, I suppose. But what is wrong with that?" His argument is starting to confuse me now.

"How can you fight something that isn't there? Meaning, what if there are no monsters? How will you defeat them if they're not real?"

"I don't want to get into that again," I say. "You know what I saw."

"The night your mother died – right. But whatever you think you saw, you know it wasn't your fault and none of this will help bring her back."

His words hit me somewhere, hard, and I raise my hand and stick my index finger in his face. "Just leave it." I turn away and shake my head. "Go to the bloody cinema with your friends. I know what I plan to do tomorrow."

He drops his head, leans over the handlebars, and takes a deep breath. "It's just that..."

"Leave it," I say again, the words erupting from inside me like hot lava bursting from a volcano.

"Okay. But you know they're also telling kids to stay away from places like these," he says, nodding his head in the direction from where we came. "Terry being missing and all. There may be some nutter out there wanting to hurt kids."

I look Gwyn direct in the eye. "I'm not stopping, okay? Up to you whether you join me or not. But I intend to keep going."

"Suit yourself." He nods and we both continue along the track, neither of us saying anything further on the matter. My hands tremble as I grip the handlebars tight. He's probably my best friend but man, can he push my buttons.

CHAPTER 4

Without saying a word to each other, we reach the end of the lane and get on our bikes. The route continues downhill so, after a single push of the pedal, we both freewheel down the road; me slightly ahead of Gwyn. As the air blows through my hair and we get further away from the farmhouse, my teeth stop grinding and the muscles in my arms and legs seem to relax like the anger is seeping out, dripping on the road the way Dad's van leaves a trail of oil behind it. I remember that Gwyn means well, annoying as he is. I brake slightly and look over at him.

"You don't know everything, you know," I yell over at him.

"Yes, I do," he says, smiling and pulling on his brakes, which screech their agreement.

"Need to get those fixed, mate," I say.

"They're not broken," he replies.

"No, but they're bloody annoying." I am smiling now as well.

The warm summer air glides past my face like invisible fingers stroking my skin. It's the end of the day and we ride past green fields on our way into town. It doesn't get dark until much later this time of the year, and the sun is still high in the sky. The night could be months away and in the bright light of the evening, the scary things hiding in the darkness and the shadows seem like they belong in a different world. From across the fields, we hear farm machines going about their business. The smell of cut grass is strong reminding us it's bailing time. For the tiniest of moments, I forget about the mission and all the crazy nightmarish spookiness and enjoy just being on my bike.

That moment passes, and as I've dropped behind, I pedal a little to get alongside Gwyn. I've had a thought.

"What these investigations need is someone who can talk to the dead," I say. "I reckon that would give us the edge we need."

"A medium?" he says. "Bloody hell, mate. While we're recruiting nutters, why don't we invite Horse to join us as well?" Horse is a local bully and all-around psychopath who Gwyn knows would be the last person in town that I would invite to join the squad.

"Don't be a dickhead," I say. "You said you'd keep an open mind."

He sighs. "What about that Traveller girl in school?" Gwyn asks. "The one who's only here half the year."

"You mean Rebecca?" I say. "The Gypsy girl in the year below us?"

"I think they prefer to be called Travellers," he says.

"I've heard them called far worse," I say. "What's the deal with her?"

We both swerve our bikes to dodge a squashed pheasant on the road.

"They say she can talk to the dead. Rhys told me a lady from our street went to visit her so she could *speak with her late husband*." Gwyn changes the tone of his voice when he says these last words to make it very clear he's not sold on her skills.

"She's a medium?" I ask.

"Something like that. Whatever she does – she gets paid for it."

This news is like a light switching on in my brain. I'm not sure if it's excitement or an opportunity I sense but it's a good feeling.

"We should go talk to her – find out more about her skills." I drop one hand to my side and hold on to the handlebar with my other hand. I sigh. "We're not making much progress with the investigations as it stands. Is she still around?"

"Yeah. They're usually at that site from summer until the end of the year."

"Imagine having that skill in the squad," I say. "I've got the strength and action skills. You're on analysis and intelligence."

"And photography, it seems," he says.

"Yes, photography as well," I say. "I'm also the leader of the squad."

"You would be if there were more than two of us," Gwyn says.

He brakes again so as not to pull ahead. His BMX has bigger wheels so tends to speed up more quickly than my Chopper.

"I'm working on it," I say. "But no one else gets it – the other kids aren't interested."

"Fancy that." Gwyn scoffs but I ignore him.

"We explore the shadows and investigate the bigger mysteries, so they don't have to." I like my explanation. Being the boss of the squad, it's important I can think of things like that to say. Sometimes leaders must inspire their troops when the chips are down.

Gwyn sighs. "There's also Rhys," he says. "He's kind of like our third member."

"Yeah, but he doesn't join us on investigations, does he? He's not operations. He gets us ready for missions, which is great, but sometimes it would be good if there were more than two of us in the field."

"I don't think he'd want to," Gwyn says. "He's comfortable in the shop surrounded by books. He gets nervous when he spends too much time outside."

We're a good team right now, I think. There's a decent balance of skills and experience. If we could only unlock the damn mysteries and find something in the investigations.

CHAPTER 5

As we near town, our bikes begin to slow as the slope flattens and I change my gear to a lower one and start pedalling. We start passing lamp posts covered in the face of the missing lad, Terry Rowlands. In the photo, he looks happy, and he stands in a goal wearing the junior school team's goalkeeper kit. Terry hasn't been seen since he went out on his bike to take some shopping to his *nain*. Of course, he didn't make it to her house and his bike was found behind the church and the shopping was scattered on the floor. Gwyn and I look up at the first of the posters before glancing at each other. Neither of us knew Terry that well but knowing one of our own is missing in action feels weird.

"A lot more posters up now," I yell over at Gwyn.

"Mmm," he says. "No progress either. No one has a clue where he went."

"They'll have to decide what happens with the *Gŵyl Awst* festival soon," I say. "It's getting close."

Every summer, we celebrate the witch's death with the *Gŵyl Awst* festival. People of the town run around with horse skulls on. Not like the *Mari Lwyd* puppets they use to celebrate Christmas and New Year in other parts of Wales – these are actual masks worn over the face. It sounds weird – and probably is – but it's an ancient tradition and something they've done in these parts for thousands of years, since long before the witch trial. The grown-ups get shit-faced, and the children stuff themselves full of sweets. It's great fun. It's like a summer Halloween and they say ghosts escape the spirit world during this time and get to party on the streets with the living. The festival should be happening soon, but no one knows whether it'll go ahead because of the missing boy. It's a hot topic around town and people are talking about it a lot. Some think it should be cancelled while others get angry at such an idea. I usually enjoy the festival but this year – in all honesty – I'm so focused on the mission that the party would just be a distraction.

"You think it'll go ahead?" Gwyn asks.

"Not unless they find Terry alive," I yell back. "Can't see the town being in much of a party mood as things stand right now."

"That's what I thought," he says. "Bloody shame. First time I made an effort with my costume... Dad got us horse skulls weeks ago." He clears his throat. "But you know, it's unlikely they'll find him alive."

We both move onto the pavement to avoid the traffic.

"What – why do you say that?" I say, a little shocked.

"It's been three days. Do you know how likely it is to find a kid alive after they've been missing for seventy-two hours?"

"How likely?" I ask.

"Chances are zero to very low," he says.

"Bollocks," I say. "Look at the space we have around here." Hide and seek and manhunt games in the surrounding mountains have to be restricted to certain areas otherwise they could go on for days…

"Besides," I say, "he could be anywhere, and the warm weather means the nights are pretty mild. What if he fell and broke his leg?"

"Ned, his bike was left, and the shopping dropped on the ground. He wasn't out exploring. He was taken."

"He could still be out there," I say. "Maybe the search parties haven't found him yet."

"Search parties have been stopped," Gwyn says.

"What – why? Thought his dad was organising groups to go out searching?"

"He was, but the police stopped that soon afterwards. Uncle Len told me it was doing more harm than good. Chaotic townsfolk wandering around the *Cewri* in the dark. Some guy fell while searching and got hurt, so police said to leave it to them and the other services."

"Jesus," I say. "If that was my kid…"

Gwyn stops his bike suddenly with a loud screech and his face becomes pale, and he points across the road.

I turn my head to see what he's looking at. "Bloody hell, is that…?"

On the other side of the road, we see a woman, barefooted and wearing a dressing gown. Her hair is a wild crow's nest, and her arms are crossed as she stares at one of Terry's posters.

"Yeah," Gwyn says. "It's his mum."

"What's she doing out here?" I ask, glancing over at Gwyn. He shakes his head.

The woman is frozen to the spot. She doesn't move an inch as we watch her.

"We should do something," I say.

"Like what?" Gwyn bats back.

"We can't leave here like this, can we?"

"She doesn't look well," Gwyn says, leaning on his bike.

As we watch Terry's mother stand on the corner of the street at the edge of town looking like she's just got up, we hear the roar of a speeding vehicle, and both turn to see a panda car approaching. It screeches to a halt next to the woman. Inside are two coppers. Sergeant Gatsby – Gwyn's Uncle Len – leaps out of the car and rushes over to her. He puts his arm around her and says something before guiding her into the car. He opens the door at the back and forces her to sit down like he's one of those television detectives arresting a New York hooker on the side of the street (I assume hookers are criminals, but I've never been told what they do to break the law; I did ask Dad once whether there were hookers in *Nant-y-Wrach* but he just shook his head sheepishly, so that didn't help).

Gatsby jumps into the front of the car and slams the door, and we see him chatting with the other police officer, who gestures in our direction. They both look over and Gwyn raises his hand to wave. Gatsby gives us both a forced smile and nods. Then he mouths the word 'home' and points at us before the car takes off.

"I guess that's that," I say. Had the situation not been so sad, it would've been the coolest thing we'd seen all week.

"Yeah." Gwyn turns to face me. "I better get back," he says. "Rhys will be home from work and if I'm not with him, there'll be trouble."

Gwyn lies to his mum when he's out with me, so she doesn't worry. Says he's at his dad's bookshop or around town during the day. I guess his dad never mentions anything. In my case, I don't have to lie. Hannah is not my parent. And Dad, well, Dad is often distracted nowadays.

"Right," I say. "Let's get going."

"Poor woman," Gwyn says as we set off. "Can't imagine what she's going through…"

I try to respond but end up mumbling something about *hookers*, unsure of what to say.

CHAPTER 6

After leaving Gwyn at the usual spot, I cycle past a row of stone terraced houses down my road. At the end is our place, *Imladris*. All the other houses have a number but ours has a name, which was something Dad insisted on. On the street is a row of parked cars and they move around each day as our neighbours come and go to work. Dad's white transit van, however, has been in the same position for months. Below it, an oil leak has stained the ground leaving a shadow that I suspect may never fade.

I stop in front of the house then push my bike in through the gate and around the back to a spot where it's sheltered from the rain. I open the back door and go into the kitchen where I see Hannah standing by the stove stirring something in a pan. I can't tell what it is by smell as the stink of burnt toast fills the kitchen. Behind her – on top of the fridge – the small black and white television is showing *Crossroads*. From the way she is dressed it looks like she hasn't left the house today.

"Have you been out on your investigation until now?" she asks.

"I've been out," I say awkwardly.

"You know they're warning kids to stay close to home and keep in groups if they do go out," she says.

I huff. "Why though? They don't know what happened to him."

"They just want everyone to be careful," she says, frowning.

"You know there's stuff I need to do," I say.

"Yes, but if there's someone out there who hurts children, then maybe exploring derelict buildings and the darkest corners of the town might not be the best idea?"

I sigh and take out a bottle of milk from the fridge, remove the foil lid and slurp it down. Hannah glares at me – I know this really annoys her.

She clears her throat and pushes the glasses she wears only at home – or when absolutely needed at school – up the ridge of her nose. "Did you find anything at the farmhouse?"

"Dust and rubble." I go and sit down at the table and turn my attention to the television.

"Well, you know it's been empty since the war."

"Yep," I say.

"They say the last owner killed himself. And there's that story about the family…"

"I know. We always do our homework."

I stare at the telly trying to work out what is happening. The only character I recognise is Benny because of his silly hat. Fancy setting a programme in a stupid little hotel – how boring is that?

"And it's probably not safe," she says, and I glance up at her. "Some of the older boys at school go there to have parties. They say the roof is about to collapse."

"And the floor," I say under my breath.

"What was that?"

"It's a bit of a tip," I say with a louder voice.

She points the wooden spoon in my direction. "You should be careful when you go to old buildings like that."

Hannah opens the fridge door and peers in. As she bends over, she looks up and down at my clothes.

"I see what you mean about the dust and rubble."

"You're not Mum," I bat back.

"I know, but somebody needs to watch out for you," she says.

"It shouldn't have to be you," I say.

"It is what it is right now." She grabs the butter and returns to the stove.

I take another sip of milk and wipe my mouth with the back of my hand. Hannah is fifteen. Two years older than me and what is she doing for the summer holidays? She's stuck at home taking care of her little brother and her dad. She's a pain in the arse but deserves better.

"What are we having?" I ask.

"Beans on toast," she says. "We need to do some shopping."

"Right. Is Dad in his usual spot?"

"Where else?" She glances past me. "Can you go get him? Dinner's almost ready."

I nod and go out into the garden. Dad is in the shed. It's where he hides most days. As I get closer, I hear the clacking of his typewriter and I reach for the handle and open the door of the shed. The typing stops.

"Jesus wept, Ned." He turns around and holds his hands in the air. His hair is wilder than usual, and he has dark circles around his eyes. "What have I told you about knocking?"

I look down at the floor. "Sorry, Dad. Hannah told me to let you know supper's ready."

"You know I need space when I'm working," he says. "When I'm in the flow of things, I must keep going otherwise I'll never finish."

"Hannah says it's time to eat," I say again, before turning on my heels to leave. My foot catches on a stack of paint pots and brushes, knocking them over and making a group of creepy crawlies homeless. Behind me, I hear tutting.

Hannah and I sit down at the kitchen table. On the television, the weatherman is telling us that July 1983 is going to be the hottest month on record.

"You hear that?" Hannah says. "Hottest month ever."

I shrug my shoulders. I've spent most of my days over the holidays so far inside. Sunny weather at least means I don't get wet as I cycle between investigations. Other than that, it doesn't make a lot of difference. Thinking about it, the hot nights make it difficult to sleep, so it's more of a pain, really. Hannah insists we hold off eating while we wait for Dad.

"Can we not start?" I ask. Then we hear the back door open and in he walks. He stops at the kitchen door and nods us both a greeting.

"Dad, you've got cobwebs in your hair," Hannah says. He combs it with his fingers and grins.

The three of us sit in silence eating the beans on toast. In the middle of the table is a small plate piled high with extra toast.

"Ned was up at the old *Cartref-Y-Gwynt* farm today, Dad," Hannah says, her eyes smiling.

I frown and give her daggers. She pulls out her tongue at me. Dad doesn't rise to the bait. He just nods, eyes still fixed on his plate.

"That's nice," he says, chewing and staring at the table.

"Hannah's going back there later for a party with the older boys," I say, and I hear her gasp.

"That's a good idea," Dad says.

Hannah and I make eyes at each other again; neither of us is smiling. I decide to change the subject to see if he'll respond to another topic.

"How's the writing going, Dad?"

Hannah shakes her head.

This time, the response is different. Dad stops, bites his lip, and places his knife and fork down next to his plate.

"I made some progress today, I think. I had to revisit the first act because the narrative drifted too much after the inciting event. After that, I was on a good run – until I was disturbed of course." He turns his gaze over at me and narrows his eyes.

"And what's it about?" I ask with a mouthful of beans and Hannah sighs. "The story you're writing."

"I don't want to share too much," he says, "but what I can tell you is that it's set in ancient times and describes a war between a single country and a powerful alliance of nearby nations."

"That doesn't sound fair," I say. "Why's it happening?" I am curious this time.

"There's a long history to it. I try not to get too bogged down in revealing the background details at the start. But the story really gets going when the capital city of the country is under siege, and the King sacrifices his son – the prince – in full view of the enemy forces."

"What? That's horrible," I say. "Why would he do that?"

"Well, that is a key part of the story. Everyone tries to figure out why the King did it. But it works. The alliance forces are horrified, and they retreat."

"I bet it freaks them out," I say. "Where did you get the idea for such a story?"

"From the Bible. Old Testament. King Mesha of Moab sacrificed his son, the prince, on the city walls when they were under siege from the armies of Israel, Judah and Edom."

I feel myself frowning. "When did you read the Bible?" I ask.

He gives me a knowing smile. "It was a story I heard growing up. Something my father told me, I think. A lot of clever people have tried to work out why the King did what he did but perhaps only he really knew why he did it. Maybe he thought it was the only way of defeating a superior force. He made the greatest sacrifice to save many other sons from his country."

"Very interesting, Dad," Hannah says, holding her knife and fork up like they're weapons. "What about the day job? Will you be decorating any houses again soon?"

Dad hisses like a snake before shaking his head. "I'm – erm – not sure I'm ready yet, *cariad*."

"Right, well this came today." Hannah reaches for an envelope from the windowsill behind her. She holds it out for Dad to take and he stares at it for a moment before taking it, reluctantly.

"Water bill. A final reminder," she says.

"Don't you worry," he says. "I'll sort that out." He places the envelope on the side without opening it.

"That's what you said last time, Dad."

"No, I will, honestly this time. You know how forgetful I can be."

"Dad, I've seen the bank statements. I'm not sure how long we can survive without any money coming in."

"Hannah *bach*, you're a child. That is not something you need worry about."

I drift away during this exchange and think about the cellar of *Cartref-Y-Gwynt* Farm. I can see myself back there, staring into the darkness. The spoon I hold begins to tremble and my mouth becomes very dry, so I reach for the water and take a sip.

"Dad, if we don't have the money then we need to find it somewhere," Hannah says.

"I know, I know. I just need some time." Dad is now leaning on his knuckles with his face down towards the table.

"How much time do you need though?" Hannah's voice is rising. "Aside from money to pay the bills, and for food shopping, Ned and I will also need to pay for school stuff in a few weeks with the new term."

"We'll be alright by then, I promise." He remains in the same position with his eyes closed.

"Promises don't pay the bills, Dad. Mum isn't here any more to do all this for you. We need to sort it out between us. We can't ignore it."

Dad looks up but doesn't make eye contact with either of us.

"Thanks for dinner, Hannah. Delicious." He does a chef's kiss and stands up and places the plate in the sink. "I'm just going to go finish in the shed. I think I can do another chapter or two before bed."

Hannah and I look at each other.
"He can't keep ignoring this," she says.
I nod along but my thoughts are elsewhere.

CHAPTER 7

After dinner, I wash the dishes and Hannah goes into the living room to watch *Top of the Pops*. We are out of washing-up liquid, so I use soap from the bathroom. With my hands sunk in the cold soapy water of the washbasin, I gaze out through the kitchen window. In the glass, I see my reflection: dark curly hair and wide-set brown eyes, like Mum. I try to look beyond the glass. In daylight, there would be nothing to see but the hedge that runs along the side of our house. But now, at night, it's a black wall of nothingness. I find myself staring into the void, biting my lip as I think about my mission to uncover the evil that lurks in the town.

"What the hell are you?" I whisper. "I know you're there. Why won't you show yourself, you coward?"

Shocked, I hear a voice calling my name. But then I turn my head as I realise Hannah is shouting from the living room. I dry my hands with a tea towel and drop it on the side before stomping through.

"What is it?" I say, rubbing my neck.

Hannah points to the television. "'*Give it up*', KC and the Sunshine Band." Oh, she was on to me.

"What? I hate this song."

"I've heard you sing along to it many times on the radio," she says with a big smile on her face.

I snort and grin. I know better than to protest. I go and sit down next to my sister on the sofa. I start humming and by the time we reach the next chorus, both Hannah and I are howling along to the lyrics.

Afterwards comes Elvis Costello and Bananarama, before Paul Young finishes the programme again at number one in the charts.

"This video does my head in," I say with my arms crossed. It's been number one for the last few weeks, so I've watched it a few times.

She turns her head and looks over. "Why?"

"The song is dull and the whole story doesn't make any sense."

"The story is the best part," Hannah says with a confused look on her face.

"I don't get it," I say again and bang my fist on the side of the sofa.

"I think you have to listen to the lyrics to make sense of the story," Hannah says.

"You think?" I'm not convinced.

She opens her hands and gestures to the television. "He's talking about always being on the road and his home is wherever he leaves his hat."

"I still don't get it."

"It means he doesn't want to settle down. Maybe it means he doesn't want to commit to one woman either."

"Like he's having an affair?" I say.

"Kind of…" she says, and her grin widens.

I point at the screen. "And that's why the brunette shoots him?"

Hannah shrugs. "Maybe?"

I open my mouth but cannot think of the words. Hannah starts to laugh.

"What is it?" I say, smiling.

"These are the same arguments that Mum and Dad used to have."

"Are they?" I say, trying to think back.

"Don't you remember? Whenever they watched a film or a programme on the telly, Dad would complain if there were plot holes or things about the characters that didn't make sense. Mum would wind him up about it."

I do remember and I think about it. "You're saying I'm more like Dad and you're more like Mum?"

Hannah smiles and I jokingly bare my teeth and throw a cushion at her.

"I suspect you don't agree with my theory," she says, and we both laugh.

There's a moment of silence before Hannah speaks again. "I miss her."

I take a deep breath. "Me too. Do you think Dad's okay?"

"He's dealing with stuff in his own way," she says, and she sounds annoyed.

"We need him to start working again though, right?"

"Yes."

I stroke my chin with my hand. "You know, for a moment, I thought we had something today. But in the end…" I shake my head.

"You thought you had a real ghost?" Hannah half-smiles.

"Something like that."

She clears her throat. "Just be careful."

"Don't start this again," I say, slapping my hands on my thighs.

"Try not to get carried away," she says. "It's just a laugh, isn't it?"

I sit up as my whole body becomes tense like a plank. "God, not you as well. A laugh? Is that all it is to you? Just some kids having a laugh?"

"I didn't mean it like that…" she says, stroking her hair.

I get to my feet and shake my head. "Bloody hell, Hannah. I thought you understood."

"Oh, come on." She rolls her eyes.

"This isn't just a childish hobby. This is serious stuff. There is something very wrong with this town – an evil and nasty force that lives here. I need to find out what it is before someone – someone else – gets hurt."

"Where are you getting these ideas from?" Hannah rubs her forehead.

"I know you don't want to believe me right now but trust me..."

"Trust you? Ned, I'm not even sure I understand you."

I put my hands on my hips. "Whether you believe me or not, I know there is something out there. I can feel it in my gut. And if I don't stop it, then people here will be in danger. You and Dad will be in danger."

"Is this about Mum?"

I ignore the question. "We'll find proof, Hannah, and we'll show you. Your little brother and his little squad are going to find answers to questions that people in this town have always been too afraid to ask. Then we'll see who thinks this stuff is fun. I'll show you – we'll be the heroes of this bloody place."

Hannah stands up and looks me in the eye. Her smile is gone, and she looks fed up.

"Right, I understand. Good luck with that."

She walks over to the television, switches it off, and raises her hand to wave. "I'm going upstairs to read. See you in the morning."

"Goodnight," I say flatly, staring at the ground. I watch as she leaves the room and then drop down to my knees and start punching the sofa. I push my fists down hard against the back and then go down into the space behind the cushions where my fingers touch fluff and crumbs that have gathered there. My fingertips on my right hand feel something hard and I grab it and take it out. Gazing down at my hand I see a faded fifty-pence piece. It raises my spirits slightly and I pop it into my pocket.

I'll show Hannah, I think. I'll show them all. There's something out there and we'll find proof. We'll figure out what the dark cloud that hangs over this town really is and then we can destroy it. But for now, the investigations carry on.

CHAPTER 8

I wake up around eight, asleep on top of my bed covers. I slept in my pants (again) with the window open. The night was hot and sticky, and I struggled to sleep after my argument with Hannah. But today is a new day and right now I can hear birds chirping outside and the sound of a car engine turning over. My lips and mouth are dry and crispy, and my throat makes a sound like I'm choking so I reach and grab for a glass of water on the bedside table. As I drink, I look down at the book I was reading before I fell asleep, *The Hamley Book of the Paranormal*. I've read the whole thing once, already, and now I'm rereading sections. They say it's the bible for ghost hunters and it covers everything – and I do mean everything – about the paranormal. Last night I read the section about mediumship again. Some mediums can hear and talk to spirits directly, and they may have a spirit guide who helps them with this. Others allow spirits to control their body and speak through them using their voice or by writing messages on paper. Those who have the power must be trained carefully as the whole thing can be dangerous. Not all spirits on the other side are friendly and sometimes evil or angry spirits or even demons can cross over if the medium is unprepared or unskilled. I wonder how the Gypsy girl does it – I really hope she's willing to help us. I can't see any other way forward for these investigations.

I grab the book and put it on my bedside table before getting up and scanning the room. There's a bunch of model soldiers that Gwyn and I painted still set up in their battle formation next to the window. This was a made-up war scene we worked on a while ago, but it's been so long that I've forgotten who the goodies were and who were the baddies. I pick up one of the army men and examine him having not touched any of them in months. Part of me wants nothing more than to sit down, forget about all the crazy, spooky stuff, and just go back to painting soldiers, arranging them in formation and playing out the scene. Maybe Hannah and Gwyn have a point about me taking these investigations too seriously, but I must keep going. There's something terrible out there that needs to be destroyed. No matter how hard it gets.

I look closely at the plastic soldier's face. It's like he's urging me to rejoin him in the battle. "Maybe, once I've defeated the enemy," I tell him.

I place him carefully back in his position, get dressed and go downstairs. In the kitchen, Hannah is sipping a cup of tea and leaning on the kitchen windowsill that looks out over the garden. Her uncombed hair tells me she hasn't been up that long either.

I say nothing to her and go to the cupboard to get some cereal. I slam the door closed. She turns around and glances at me before peering back into the garden. I open the fridge to get the milk and close that door as well with the same energy.

"I get that you're pissed off at me," she says. "But don't take it out on the poor kitchen." She turns around and smiles.

I sigh and sit down at the table and start to eat my Sugar Puffs.

"About last night," she says. "Maybe I don't really understand why you're on this mission, but I do get that it's important to you. I'm just trying to watch out for you. You know that, don't you?"

"Mmm." My focus is on the sweet cereal.

"I just need you to be careful in case there is a maniac out there. I couldn't bear losing anyone else…"

This is a message I understand fully.

"Alright," I say. "Just leave it. I get it – I'll be careful."

Hannah raises her hands and turns around to carry on looking out of the window. I reach over and turn the television on to see *Good Morning Britain*. Bollocks, too early for cartoons.

I glance back at Hannah. Maybe I need to be nicer to her. She's just trying to help. Besides, she doesn't really know why I'm on my mission. Maybe I should tell her what really happened to Mum. Not yet. When I'm ready. Dad's the problem here right now.

"Is he in there already?" I ask before shovelling another spoonful in my mouth.

"Been in the shed all night, I think," she says.

"He slept in there?"

"I doubt he slept. He came in before for a brew and he looked well rough."

"Flipping heck." I shake my head.

Hannah turns and comes to sit down. She's wearing her pink dressing gown and fluffy slippers that look like she has a sheep on each foot.

"What are you up to today?" she asks.

I chew on the Sugar Puffs and keep my eyes fixed on the television. "Meeting Gwyn down the bookshop."

"Is Rhys working there all summer?"

"Meant to be but all he does is sit around and read." And get us ready for missions.

"That's how he was at school this last year. Doesn't say much to me. The only one I've seen him talk to is Brian Roberts."

"Brian Lemon-face?" I say, trying not to smile.

"Yes, that Brian." Hannah shakes her head disapprovingly and sips her tea.

Rhys is the same age as Hannah. On weekends and holidays, he works at the bookshop. They have a section in the back for rare books – many of which are on mysteries and the unknown. Forteana, they call it. Everything from ghosts and the paranormal to UFOs and the occult. They have a few Alister Crowley first editions apparently, but they are kept in a locked cupboard under the stairs and Mr B won't let us see them. Perhaps because Rhys is often a little too willing to lend books out to his friends (my copy of *The Hamley Book of the Paranormal* is one of theirs).

I sense her gaze like she wants to ask me something.

"What?" I say.

"Will you be doing any of your investigations today?" Her voice has softened, and her eyebrows are drawn together. I put my spoon down and cross my arms. "That's not the current plan."

"Just remember what the police are saying about not going off alone. If you stick around town with Gwyn and Rhys, that's okay."

I purse my lips and blow a raspberry.

"I know, I'm not Mum. But someone needs to watch out for you."

"That someone should be watching out for us both." I glance towards the window.

Hannah's eyes move in the same direction. "Yes, well…" she says, trailing off.

She clears her throat and the expression on her face changes. "I just remembered – Auntie Val gave me a twenty-pound note for some shopping. She says if there's any left over, we can get some fish and chips. How about it tonight for a Friday night treat?"

"Yes," I say giving her a thumbs up.

I get up and take my bowl to the sink. *HTV Wales News* comes on the television. I hear the theme but don't pay much attention until our town is mentioned.

"And in *Nant-y-Wrach, Gwynedd*, search continues for missing schoolboy, Terry Rowlands, who has now been missing for four days. Terry was last seen leaving his home to take some shopping to his grandmother on 18th July. Last night, police confirmed that no new developments were made in the investigation."

Hannah and I glance at each other. The news programme cuts to Detective Alwen Thomas speaking to the camera.

"We are doing everything we can and using all available resources to find Terry…"

Next to her are Terry's parents. They look like they're suffering.

His father holds up the photo we've seen plastered across town and tries to speak about his boy. "He is such a kind and happy lad." His voice is slurred and sorrowful. It's not easy to watch. I notice he says *is* and not *was*. Seems his parents are more hopeful than Gwyn about Terry's return.

"… Always helping us out around the house. We never have to ask him to do any of it. He was taking some shopping to his *nain* when he… *went missing*."

He struggles with the last words. I point at the telly with my spoon. "Gwyn and I saw his mum in town last night. She was in a bad way. Hadn't even got dressed yet. Gatsby and that other plod came to pick her up."

Hannah's hand goes to her mouth. "Must be a nightmare for her. For both of them."

I watch for a little while, but no one has anything new to share and all the sad dramatics makes my stomach turn, so I decide to head out.

"I've heard enough," I say. "See you later."

"Remember what I said. Be careful."

"You too," I reply and realise my tone is not friendly.

"I'm serious." Hannah points to the television with her hand. I roll my eyes and leave the house.

CHAPTER 9

It's good to get out of the house and away from my controlling sister. All the warnings and questions are starting to annoy me. I cycle along the usual route – to the end of my road, through Bryce Estate and Hanging Gardens, past the church, and down to the end of the High Street – the home of Bewitched Books. It's early in the day, so the air is a little fresher, although still warmer than what we're used to. A police car passes, and I stare at the two plods inside – neither of whom I've seen before. There's been a lot of coming and going from the police station over the last few days.

I notice that Terry's posters are all dry and undamaged and realise it hasn't rained for weeks. I wonder if that helps the investigation. It usually pisses down here for the whole summer – one of the joys of living in the mountains. *Nant-y-Wrach* is not a huge town but because of where it is, it needs to be quite self-sufficient. Aside from the bookshop, the most important sites of the High Street are the newsagent, which has the finest collection of penny sweets this side of the River Conwy, and the fish and chip shop – where a delicious fish supper costs less than a quid. There's a library, a cinema, a Woolworths and a chemist, and a few other shops as well but I don't take much of an interest in them unless there's a haunting – of which, I might add, there are quite a few.

The most famous ex-resident of the town was a woman called Mari Evans who lived here in sixteen-something or other and was convicted of being a witch and hanged in a field that is now a park near the church. Before she died, she placed a curse on the town, promising that each future generation would face great suffering. I'm not certain whether what I am searching for is related to the witch, the ghosts, or something else, but it does seem odd for it all not to be connected. It's one of a few working theories I have.

Rhys knows all about the paranormal. In fact, he has answers for most questions I have – whether they're related to local matters or general knowledge on the subject. He and Hannah were friends in primary school but at secondary school – and as they got older – he started spending a lot more time alone. She says he prefers the company of books to other people. When I ask him questions about ghosts and the occult, he seems to like that. He encourages Gwyn and me with our investigations but never joins us. In fact, I don't remember the last time I saw him outside of the shop. As our Q, he makes sure we're prepared for our missions. Although annoyingly, he doesn't have any gadgets. His main skills are knowledge of the town and its history and general research. His weaknesses are shyness and physical strength. Much like his brother, I would not count on him in a scrap, but that's okay for his role in the squad.

Before the holidays, we met at the bookshop most Saturdays. Now it's the summer, we're in there most days. Before and after investigations, we always meet at the bookshop. It's our HQ.

Cycling down the High Street, I see Mrs Jones from the newsagent standing outside speaking to someone. She's run the shop for years and years and before that, her father was the shopkeeper. She smiles at me and points to the door and rubs her tummy on the front of her blue tabard. I grin back; she doesn't need to work hard to get me in there. It's exactly where I intend to go later in the day and spend the fifty-pence piece that I found down the back of the sofa.

I rest my bike outside as I always do and enter the bookshop. Gwyn and Rhys's dad, Mr B, is sitting behind the counter with a folded newspaper in one hand and a pen in the other. He looks like an older, more feral version of Gwyn. Without looking up, he speaks.

"Shopkeeper sounds ruder."

"Sorry?" I say and cock my head.

"Shopkeeper sounds ruder. Six letters. Sounds means this must be a homophone. It's probably asking for a synonym of shopkeeper. One that sounds like a synonym for ruder."

"Ah." He's doing his crossword.

"Ha, of course. Grosser. It's a synonym for ruder. And grosser sounds like grocer. So that is our answer."

I just stare at him.

"Sorry, Ned, cryptic quiz in the paper today. I thought they had me for a second with that one. But they need to get up pretty early in the morning to fool me."

I smile at him and point to the back of the shop.

"Yeah, go on through," he says. "See if you can get him to do some stocktaking if you can."

I nod and grin before walking between piles of stacked books and gazing at the full shelves. I love the special stink of the place – a sweet and bitter smell that makes its way into the nose and just stays there. It reminds me of chocolate. It's no wonder I enjoy spending so much time here.

I step through a doorway with a sign above that says, '*Rare and Forteana, this way.*' The sign has a pentagram on it as well. The back room is a more extreme version of the rest of the shop. More books, more chaos and stronger smells. A lot of these books are much older. Some have interesting symbols on their spines and titles that wouldn't sound out of place in horror films: *The Necronomicon, The Book of Shadows, The Sixth and Seventh Books of Moses, Dragon Rouge*.

"Ned, my lad," speaks a voice from behind a wall of books. I peer around and see Rhys with his long hair draped over his shoulders. He's wearing his black Hawkwind T-shirt and sits on the floor with his back against the wall.

"Alright," I say. "What are you reading?"

He turns the cover around, looks at the front, and then back at me.

"It's about secret societies."

"Which secret societies?"

"All of them," he says, frowning.

"But what are they?" I narrow my eyes.

Rhys closes the book and gets up off the floor. "You never heard of secret societies? Knights Templar? Freemasons?"

I shake my head.

"Conspiracies and funny handshakes? Mysterious temples and weird rituals?"

"Not on my radar." Although he has piqued my interest.

He puts his hand over his mouth. "And I thought you were into all this?"

I shrug my shoulders. Rhys folds his arms and gives me a confused look. "What do they teach you at that school?"

"Same shit they taught you, old man," I say.

He smiles and hands me the book. "I'll lend you this when I'm done."

I scan the cover. There are weird symbols on the front, plus a group wearing strange costumes, JFK in the car before he was shot and medieval knights at the edge of a battle.

"These are the people in charge, Ned. Powerful secret groups with fingers in many pies. Behind some of the biggest conspiracies and cover-ups known to man. And they've been linked to all sorts – devil-worshipping, Jack the Ripper, fake moon landings…" He taps his finger on the cover. "Even JFK's assassination."

"Bloody hell." I look up. "Gwyn not here yet?"

"Dad sent him to the post office." Rhys claps his hands and rubs them together. "And there's lizard people…"

"Huh?"

"Blood-drinking, flesh-eating, shape-shifting extraterrestrial reptiles that some say are running the world."

"Wow." I'm unsure of where to start with my questions.

He taps on the table in front of him like he's knocking on a door. "Even the royal family may be lizards."

"Maybe we should investigate them," I say.

Rhys stands upright and rubs his chin – I think he's considering it.

"How did it go yesterday?" he asks.

My head drops. "Sod all. Thought I sensed something, but we got nothing really. Unless anything was picked up by the photographer."

"We're not having much luck, are we?" he says, crossing his arms. "Weird happenings have been reported at all the places you've investigated but you've seen nothing yourself, have you?"

"No." I sigh.

"I wonder if there's anything we can do differently," he says and his eyes scan across the books on the shelves like he's looking to them for answers.

"I did have one thought," I say, and he glances back at me.

"Get that Gypsy Traveller girl from school – the one with the medium skills – to join us."

"That's not a bad idea if you can. Her help might be exactly what we need. Do you think she'd do it?"

I shrug my shoulders. "Need to ask. I don't really know her. Was thinking of going today. These investigations are going nowhere."

"That's great, I agree," Rhys says. "Strike while the iron is hot, why don't you. Let's recruit her. Use her skills to get the spooks out of the woodwork."

"Maybe we can revisit some of the old places we've looked at," I say.

"I know of somewhere else as well. A source tells me there've been disturbances at the library," Rhys says.

"Disturbances?" I repeat.

"Yeah. Floating books and orbs," he says. "Some of the workmen there have heard a woman crying as well."

"What workmen?" I ask.

"Haven't you seen the scaffolding at the back of the place? They're converting the storage space into a museum, of sorts. Found loads of old artifacts and objects in the cellar of the old courthouse that they're going to put on display. A lot of it is related to the witch."

"I didn't know. Not been there in ages. What kind of artifacts?" I lean on his table and scan over the books he's been reading. So much for stocktaking…

"Horseshoes, weird statues, witch bottles."

"Witch bottles?" I repeat. "What are those?"

"Old glass bottles filled with things like nails or hair that were meant to protect people from witchcraft. Evil spirits and nasty spells would get trapped inside."

"To protect against the witch's curse?" I ask. "How do they work?"

"Not entirely sure. Think we have a book somewhere that would explain." His eyes look over at the witchcraft section.

"It's not important now," I say. This was a typical Rhys conversation. Tangent after tangent – starting with alien lizards and ending with witchcraft. Usually, it was worth listening to because it led to some interesting insights. But as a rule, I tried to keep him focused on the right topic.

He turned back to face me. "Imagine they would've tried anything to stop it. Anyway, probably worth a look when it's finished. Our local lord is funding the project and they're planning to rename the place, the Robham *Nant-y-Wrach* Library and Heritage Centre."

"That's a mouthful," I say.

"Yep—" Rhys opens his mouth to respond but his head turns when we hear the shop doorbell ring.

"Too early for customers. That'll be our other member," he says enthusiastically.

We hear Mr B mumble something before Gwyn raises his voice. "No time for your crosswords now, Dad."

He rushes into the room, panting.

"What is it, Lassie?" Rhys says.

Gwyn gently sneers at his brother. "Press conference now," he says, tongue hanging from his mouth. "On steps. Outside police station. Open to everyone. Updates about Terry." He grabs his inhaler from his pocket and takes two puffs.

"Outside?" I say. "What is this – Gotham City?"

Gwyn leans on the nearest bookshelf and wipes his brow with his arm. "Too hot inside. Health and safety, apparently. All the telly and newspaper people are gathered outside."

"How do you know this?" Rhys asks.

"They're all talking about it down at the post office."

I glance over at Rhys and then back at Gwyn. "We need to go see this," I say, and the three of us leg it out of the shop.

CHAPTER 10

It's not far to the police station, so we don't bother with the bikes. It's on the same tree-lined road as my school so I'm very familiar with the route. Rhys and I sprint ahead – he for some reason still with the conspiracies book in his hands – and Gwyn follows behind, panting and puffing. We arrive to find the small car parking space outside is full of people with television cameras, microphones and notepads. They're all waiting for someone to come out of the building. By the doors – at the top of the steps – there is a podium with three microphones.

At the back, we join a few kids and neighbours of the police station who are clearly not there on behalf of the news.

"It's like we're waiting for the commissioner to come out and tell us the Joker's escaped from Arkham Asylum," I say.

"I've never seen anything like this here before," Rhys says, looking around. "It's peculiar."

"I guess a missing child is not an everyday thing," I say.

I hear heavy breathing behind me and turn to see Gwyn has caught up with us and he's searching his pockets for his inhaler.

"You think it's just about the heat?" I ask.

"I don't know," Rhys says. "If I was paranoid, I'd think there was more to it than this." He fans his face with the conspiracies book.

Gwyn shakes his head. "If you were paranoid…"

This makes me chuckle. The sun is higher in the sky now and aside from the sycamore tree across the road, there is little shade here outside the police station.

We hear murmurs from the crowd in front followed by the clicks of cameras and look up to see four people coming out of the building. At the front is the detective I saw on television earlier. Behind her is a man in a suit.

"She's the detective running things," I whisper to Gwyn and Rhys. "She was on the news this morning. Who's that with her?"

"That's the local MP, Pierce Chelmsley," Gwyn says, pointing to the suited man with carefully styled hair who stands to her left.

"Tory gobshite," Rhys says. "Thatcher loves him, you know. They reckon he might be in her next cabinet. Fucker lives in Surrey and only visits here for photo ops. Doesn't give a shit about the people here or the place."

"Maybe he's a lizard?" I say and Rhys nods his approval while Gwyn looks on confused.

Behind them are two men – one of whom we are very familiar with – Sergeant Len Gatsby – a relative of the brothers and the most senior police officer at the local station. The other man has a funny look about him.

"Who's the guy with the gnarly moustache next to your uncle?" I ask.

"You don't know who that is?" Gwyn says, his eyebrows raised.

"Why would I ask if I did?" I snap back.

"That's Lord Archibald Robham," Rhys says. "Our esteemed local dignitary."

"He looks rough," Gwyn says.

"That's Lord Robham?" I say. The lord is someone I am very aware of. Everyone around here knows of him, although I can't ever remember seeing him in person before. Gazing at the man, I see Gwyn is right; his eyes are bloodshot, and his face is red like a big, fat tomato. Robham's name is everywhere around town, and his family and the history of the place are twisted together like the cords of a twine. If it wasn't for the witch, I reckon the place would be called *Nant-y-Robham*.

"Why are they all here, do you think?" I glance at the two brothers and they both shrug their shoulders.

The detective stands at the podium shuffling papers. She looks up and lifts her hands, requesting the crowd be silent.

"Thank you for gathering so quickly," she says, her face heavy and serious like she hasn't smiled for weeks or slept for days. To her left, the MP tries to keep a straight face, but he winks at someone at the front like he can't help himself.

She scans the crowd and takes a deep breath. "Today is day four since Terry went missing, and we continue to examine every possible avenue in our search for him. We are scouring the town and the surrounding area. Search and rescue continue to examine the surrounding hills and mountain range and police divers have searched local lakes, ponds and rivers…"

"They've got nothing," Gwyn whispers, leaning in between Rhys and me.

"Then why all the theatrics?" I ask.

"They have to update the locals on what's happening," Gwyn says.

"No reason for the MP and Lord what's-his-face to be here though, is there?" I say.

"Chelmsley doesn't need much of an excuse to get in front of the cameras," Rhys says. "Don't know about Robham though."

An old woman standing next to us with her corgi leans in with her finger to her mouth and hushes us, and Gwyn rolls his eyes. We all look back up at the detective.

"We've spoken to a few key persons of interest," she says. "And although this has not yet led to any arrests, we haven't excluded any of these individuals from our lines of enquiry."

A voice nearer the front speaks up and the detective cocks her head as she tries to see where the question came from. The man repeats it louder and this time we hear what he says. "Is Terry still alive?"

Before the detective has a chance to respond, the MP leans in and gives the man a painful, false grin. "James, I know you're keen to get to the pub. But please be patient – we'll be taking questions shortly, but not at this moment."

The man then repeats his question again more loudly and the detective holds her open palm up to Chelmsley.

"Really," she says in a voice that has a million times more sincerity than the old bloody politician, "I don't know. But we will find him. We will find him." As she repeats her words, her voice begins to crack, and her eyes start blinking.

"This is really getting to her," Gwyn whispers into my ear.

There are more murmurs in the crowd, and we hear cameras clicking again.

Chelmsley puts his hand on the shoulder of the detective, leans in to say something and she pulls away, looking annoyed by his attempt to comfort her. She steps aside and he moves closer to the microphone.

"Thank you to Detective Thomas and her team, who've been working tirelessly around the clock for the last few days to find the boy."

"The boy," Rhys says. "Twat doesn't even remember Terry's name."

The crowd is now yelling and loads of questions are being thrown in the direction of the MP. He responds by lifting his hands and making downward motions as he tries to quieten them down.

"As I said, you'll have your chance to ask questions."

He turns his head and looks at Robham and Gatsby and the sergeant gives him a little nod of encouragement. I glance over at Gwyn and see that he noticed that as well. Chelmsley turns back to face the crowd.

He grabs the podium tight with both hands. "The other matter we need to discuss is more for the local media, so sorry to the national press for having to sit in on this." He pulls up a big cheesy grin across his face.

"As I'm sure many of you are aware, over the last few days there has been some debate in town regarding the planned *Gŵyl Awst* festival, which is due to go ahead this coming week. This is of course a huge event – and probably the biggest date in our calendar here in *Nant-y-Wrach*. However, given what is happening with the ongoing investigation, town leaders – particularly Lord Robham – feel that going ahead with such a day of celebration is not appropriate at this time, therefore the event has been put on hold until further notice. That is the official decree of the town leaders – the festival is postponed." There are flashes and the clicks of cameras and whispers among the people around us. He stops and licks his lips.

"Perhaps when the boy is found," he says, "it may be an opportunity to celebrate." He lifts his cheeks into a forced smile with these last words and my stomach turns.

I glance over at Gwyn and Rhys and see raised eyebrows. This – at least – is new information.

"Shame," Rhys says, "but you know…" and he shrugs his shoulders.

"Guess we finally have our answer," Gwyn says. "Odd way to tell people though."

"We can use our costumes next year," Rhys says.

I continue to watch the stage. Chelmsley has his hand over the microphone and is speaking to Gatsby. Robham looks down at the ground and doesn't say a single thing. What is going through his mind, I wonder? The detective, meanwhile, stands at the side with her arms crossed, appearing at odds with the other three.

The MP turns back, pinches the skin on his neck, and leans into the microphone. "Now, we'd be welcome to questions. Who's first?"

"Bollocks to this," Rhys says, "I'm going back to the shop."

"Yeah," Gwyn says, "let's leave before they share any more bad news. Ned, are you coming?"

I sigh. "Yeah, let's go."

As we withdraw from the spectacle, Rhys strides away while Gwyn grabs my arm and freezes like a zebra that's just seen a lion. He nods his head in the direction of the sycamore tree on the other side of the road. Stood, leaning against it with his two goons, Shag and Pablo, is Horse.

No more than a couple of years older than Gwyn and me, Horse is a lad with a reputation for trouble with a capital T. Some might call him a bully but those who know him are aware he's far more than just a local ruffian. Horse's key skills are deviousness and criminal intelligence. He's like a council house Lex Luther, with a little bit of Yorkshire Ripper thrown in.

I hadn't seen him for a few weeks. He'd been quiet since his recent fame in the local paper after saving a parish councillor's dog. Said mutt had gone missing, and Horse had achieved fame by discovering the poor animal stuck to a barbed wire fence on the edge of a field, up in the hills. For this – of course – he was treated like a hero. *Local Lad Saves Pedigree Chum* – that was the headline. The reality of what happened was likely quite different. Many people in town – those who know him anyway – didn't believe any of the story. The other version was that he and his Goons had kidnapped the dog, hidden it somewhere for a few days, and then returned it later – starved and having hurt it to make it look like it'd been caught on barbed wire. Was he crazy enough to do something like that? You bet your ass. And from the stories we'd heard about him, he was capable of a lot worse than just torturing a dog.

Gwyn and I cannot help but stare and unfortunately Horse notices, but he doesn't move an inch from the tree, he just raises his eyebrows and waggles his fingers to wave. Seeing us, Pablo leans and whispers something into Horse's ear, but Horse shakes his head and moves his eyes back in the direction of the podium, where the MP is still answering questions.

"He's not interested in us," I say to Gwyn.

"Not right now," Gwyn says, "but let's not wait for that to change."

We both move away from the station with our eyes focused on Horse. Reaching the end of the street, and with a bit of distance between us and the sycamore tree, I sense we're both a little calmer. Gwyn sighs.

"What is it?" I ask. "We're clear of Horse now."

"It's not that – it's just turning into a bloody depressing summer."

"Have some perspective, will you?" I say. "That family's lost one of their kids."

"I know, it just feels like a dark cloud has descended onto this town recently," Gwyn says.

"I think you'll find that dark cloud has always been here," I say.

"Hmm, right," he says and huffs.

I look around. "No sign of Rhys – he must have legged it."

"That Chelmsley dick makes him angry," Gwyn says. "He's probably back at the shop with his head buried in his books."

"Right," I say. "You know, before you came, we were talking about my idea of recruiting a new member. He agreed it was a great suggestion and that it could turn our fortunes around this summer."

Gwyn sighs. "You're still thinking about that?"

"Yep, and you know something? We should do it now. Our investigations are going nowhere."

His head drops. "Is it really that important to you?"

"You know it is," I say. "You don't agree?"

"I'd just prefer a bit more rationality and a bit less delusion in the squad."

"You, my friend, just need the right experience," I say. "Let's go see this Gypsy girl and see what skills she can bring to the squad."

"What makes you think she'll want to join us?" he says, rubbing his chin.

I purse my lips and blow. "We'll see what she wants. I have a good feeling about it, and we've got to try something."

CHAPTER 11

The Travellers' site is on a lay-by between a road and some fields where strawberries are grown at the edge of town. In the summer months, the Travellers come here to work in the fields. For the rest of the year, they are elsewhere – somewhere on the other side of the mountains. A lot of people in the town aren't fond of them. There's no obvious reason for this from what I can see. People don't seem to like them because they're different. They live in a way that the townsfolk don't understand – travelling between different homes and not wanting to settle in one place. They don't have normal jobs like the people in town do. They make money by picking strawberries, fixing machines, and, well, talking to the dead.

"What do you know about Rebecca?" I ask Gwyn as we cycle across town, riding side by side. I am on the pavement, and he is on the road.

"Not much. She lives here for half of the year and goes to our school during that time. She keeps to herself in class but does surprisingly well for someone switching schools so often."

"What do the other kids think of her?" I ask.

"They mostly stay out of her way," he says. "Probably scared of her."

"Talking to the dead is a skill that scares people, I guess."

"It makes me nervous."

"A lot of things make you nervous," I yell, as we go our separate ways around a phone box. "Hang on, I thought you were a sceptic?"

"I am," he says defiantly. "But look at it this way – she either believes this madness herself or she makes it up in order to take money from people."

I see two elderly women up ahead chatting outside the butchers, so I swerve onto the road, to be back next to Gwyn. "You're too cynical," I say and shake my head. "But who was it you said had been to see her? A neighbour of yours?"

"Mrs Roberts from two doors down. Her husband died last year."

"Right. I bet helping people to talk to their dead relatives is worth a bit more than picking strawberries," I say, as we cut across the pavement to avoid red traffic lights.

"I'd rather pick the fruit myself." Gwyn's brakes shriek as he swerves to avoid a dog-walker.

As we leave town, the streets open onto pastures surrounded by dry-stone walls. In the distance, the yellowing grass tilts upwards – where its colour changes to green as the field begins to rise up into the skies as part of the *Cewri*. I hear farm machines droning away in the distance and turning my head I see a tractor pulling a bailer in the furthest corner of the field, and a few large bales are scattered along the edge. It looks like the farmer hasn't been out too long yet. We slow down our bikes and watch the big machines rumble onwards eating up the line of cut grass and turning it into big, round hay boulders. We continue along the road until the wall becomes a hedge and the hay meadow becomes a crop of green plants – strawberry plants. We can't see the fruits from the road but there are a few people walking between the green rows carrying boxes filled with punnets.

A narrow lane hidden by thick trees leads away from the road. In between the greenery, are the white, grey and brown of caravans and other machines.

Gwyn stops his bike and turns to face me. "How do we do this?"

"Huh?" I say.

He holds out his hands. "Do we cycle in there and tell them we want to speak to Rebecca?"

"I guess so," I say, shrugging. "Any other ideas?"

He bites his lip. "Well, no. Do you think they'll be weird with us?"

"Why would they be?" He has me confused, now.

"You know," he says. "They're different."

"Bloody hell," I say, "you're the one who keeps telling me not to call them Gypsies. Come on."

I cycle ahead of Gwyn and stop when I reach the first caravan. He is right behind me. There are ten or so caravans in total; most of which have seen better days. Also, an old double-decker bus and a lorry. Between the vehicles are all sorts of rubbish and scrap; rusty trolleys and old televisions and enough battered appliances to fill a kitchen. There are gas canisters and piles of tarpaulin, wooden pallets and old furniture.

Gwyn wrinkles his nose like he's sniffing the air. His asthma means he's sensitive to breathing in anything that could bring on an attack. He's like a sniffer dog, and thinking about it, maybe it's another of his key skills. I make a mental note to give him a score for it.

"Over there." He points to the far end of the site where smoke rises, and the ground is black and covered in ash. "Looks like they had a bonfire last night."

From behind we hear creaking. We both turn our heads and see two piercing eyes staring back at us – a man with jet-black hair and a thick shiny beard is glaring at us through an open window.

"Watcha want, you little fockers?" he says.

Gwyn nods at me – gesturing for me to respond. I shrug.

"We're here to see Rebecca," I say.

"Lil' Rebecca? Why do you want to see Rebecca?"

"We're in school with her."

The man examines us both with thin eyes. He reaches out his arm and points to another of the caravans. I mouth *thank you* and the arm and the face pull back behind the curtains. We approach this other caravan and look it up and down. I knock on the door. I prepare myself for another peculiar encounter, but the door is opened by a girl. She has striking green eyes and the same black hair colour as the man who greeted us, pulled back into a ponytail.

"What are you doing here?" she asks.

"I – erm…" My mouth freezes and my voice fails. I realise I've never spoke to her before, and other than Hannah, I don't talk to many girls. Thankfully, Gwyn steps forwards.

"We're in school with you."

"And?" She has her hands on her hips.

I clear my throat. "We need your help. We really need your – erm – skills."

"Skills?" Her eyes narrow. "Help with what?"

I take a deep breath. "Talking to the dead."

"What do you know about that?" she asks.

"You helped one of his neighbours talk to her husband. Dead husband." I look over at Gwyn.

He rolls his eyes. "Mrs Roberts, *Stryd-Y-Cythraul.*"

She pinches the skin on her throat and scrutinises us both. I can see she is thinking about it. She nods before stepping back and pushing the door of the caravan open.

"Right then, come in."

I enter first and Gwyn follows. The caravan looks cosier and more homely than it did on the outside. I try not to act surprised as I glance around. The place is filled with the strong smell of honey mixed with citrus.

"You live here alone?" I ask.

"Father and I," she replies. "He had an early start on the fields."

"Right." I tap my legs nervously with my fingertips as I anticipate what comes next.

Rebecca points to a fixed table next to the window. On it is a jam jar filled with honeysuckles. Gwyn and I sit on one side while Rebecca sits on the other.

"So, what do you want?" she asks.

I clasp my hands to keep them steady and place them on the table and take a deep breath. "We believe there is an evil supernatural force haunting this town." I pause to see how she reacts. Rebecca bites her cheek and tilts her head. The cogs are turning.

"Gwyn and I are on a mission to investigate places where paranormal things have been known to happen, in order to find the real source of the evil."

A wry smile appears on her face. "Okay, and how is that going for you?"

"Honestly?" I say. "We're struggling. Found nothing yet. Done investigations at most of the haunted sites around this town and we've found diddly-squat. We've seen nothing, heard nothing. I believe I may have sensed something in a couple of places but nothing more. We've found no proof. It's depressing really."

She starts to laugh. "That's all you've got?"

Gwyn and I look at each other.

"What more do you want?" I tap my fingers on the table like I'm playing an invisible piano.

"I thought you might have something more solid. Something significant to report. All I'm hearing are two little boys playing make-believe."

"Excuse me, we are both thirteen," Gwyn replies in a serious voice and Rebecca smirks.

"Our age is not important here," I say. "We are deadly serious about this. I saw your face when I mentioned this town. You know the stories about this place. Our mission is to find proof. To make people believe. Uncover the truth and force this nasty, horrid thing – whatever it is – out into the open."

"And then?" she asks.

"And then," I say, "we destroy it to make sure it can never hurt anyone else again."

She takes a deep breath. "You're playing with fire, you know. The answers to your questions are likely nastier and uglier than anything you can imagine."

"We're prepared," I say.

"I doubt it," she says.

"We're a team," I say. "It's not just us – there are more."

Gwyn clears his throat and gives me a look – I know I'm stretching the truth, but we need her.

"And…" I bang my fist solidly on the table, "…we are very dedicated to this cause."

"I bet you are." She glances out of the window and crosses her arms. "So how exactly am I supposed to help you?"

I take a deep breath. "We need someone with your skills to make sure we're in the right place at the right time. We're trying so hard, but we're just chasing our tails right now."

She sits forward and places her crossed arms on the table. "You know I don't do this for fun, don't you?" She glances at each of us in turn. "I do have a gift, but I use it to help support my family."

"That's very nice," I say.

Gwyn elbows me. "She means we have to pay her."

"Oh, right. So – erm – what's the going rate for your services?" I ask. "We're not that flush right now."

"Hmmm." She looks out of the window. "There is something you can do for me."

"What's that?" I ask.

"I won't do anything illegal," Gwyn adds, and I glance over at him frowning.

"Something was taken from me," she says, "and I need it back."

"What?" I ask.

"My grandfather, *Taid*."

"Your grandfather?" Gwyn repeats, loudly. "Was he kidnapped?"

"No, he's dead."

"Someone took his… remains?" Gwyn wrinkles his nose.

"Kind of," she says. "He was wrapped up in a purple velvet cloth. If you can get him back for me, I'll help you."

This is not what I expected but – hey – I appreciate we need flexibility with the mission.

"Who took it?" I ask. "Sorry, who took him?"

"Do you know of a boy they call Horse?"

"Oh God, no." Gwyn puts his head in his hands, and I feel my heart flutter.

"Horse and his Goons took your *taid*'s remains?" I ask.

"Yes. They came to the site a few weeks ago looking for work. Father told them there wasn't enough work for them. Then, when everyone was out, they sneaked around the site and had a look through some of the caravans. As far as I'm aware, *Taid* was all that was taken."

"Didn't you tell your dad?" I ask.

"If I did, there's a good chance he would kill Horse. And then me."

"Why you?"

"Because *Taid* was supposed to be locked away, but I left him out accidentally after a consultation…"

Consultation? Is this how she talks to the dead? I rub my jaw and see Gwyn frowning.

"Having him around helps, I guess. He helps me to connect to the other side."

"Right, of course." I look to Gwyn. "I reckon we probably know where your *taid* was taken."

"Jungle?" Gwyn says through gritted teeth.

"Jungle," I repeat, looking over at him and then back at Rebecca. "It's where his den is, *The Eagle's Nest*. An old stone hut in the centre of the woods. It's where he stashes all the stuff he's stolen."

"So, you can get *Taid* back?" she says with a hopeful look on her face.

"It's risky but I reckon so," I say. "We'll need to plan how we get in there without being spotted. He and his Goons are there a lot of the time – especially this time of year."

Rebecca lays her hands out – palms facing down – on the table like she is committing to the negotiation. "If you can get him back then I'll help you in whatever way I can."

"Leave it with us," I say. "We'll get the job done."

I notice Gwyn is rubbing his temples with his fingertips.

"It's the only way forward," I say, glaring at him.

CHAPTER 12

As we cycle back to the shop, I can see Gwyn is thinking about something.

"What's bothering you?" I ask but I think I know.

"Why does it have to be Horse?" Gwyn's voice is high-pitched when he's worried.

"Because he's the biggest psycho in town," I say. "And that's how things roll for us."

"I didn't need an answer but you're right," he says. "It's weird that we saw him this morning."

"He loves that kind of stuff though, doesn't he?" I say, and it crosses my mind that maybe Horse and I may share certain interests.

"Wouldn't surprise me if he was involved in Terry's disappearance," Gwyn says.

"Maybe he's moved on from kidnapping animals." I move ahead and to the side of the road as a car goes past.

"Town hero, my arse," Gwyn says, looking away across the fields. "You know they say he stabbed his dad in the leg with a screwdriver?"

"I heard that story," I say. "Used to fiddle with him and one day Horse snapped."

"And afterwards," Gwyn says, "rather than report him to the police or get angry with him – his dad gave him a beer and said he was proud of him."

"Bloody weird family." Makes my dad seem normal by comparison.

"Ned, what if he did take Terry?" Gwyn's brakes screech like his bike is shocked by the suggestion. "What if he got a taste for fame with the dog and now, he's going through the same motions, but with a child? They say serial killers follow cases and stay close to crime scenes because they want to be close to the action – it would explain why he was there this morning."

"He wouldn't be that stupid," I say. "Would he? There's no way people would believe him again. Plenty here who didn't believe the dog story in the first place."

"But he wouldn't do things the same," Gwyn says. "There would be a different plan. He's a clever bastard."

"I know but I seriously doubt it," I say, although Gwyn's got me really thinking about it now.

He clicks his tongue. "I hope you're right, but I don't trust him. If he catches us there tonight, God help us."

That, I agree with; whether he had taken Terry or not, we wouldn't want to be caught by Horse and his Goons at his den. We had to be one hundred per cent clear about our plan for the Jungle. Our best option would be to approach at night. We'd have the cover of darkness and not even Horse would be there the entire night, or so I would hope.

The other thought is what exactly we're looking for. Ashes are usually kept in a box or one of those vases with a lid, I think. What are they called? Urns? Yes, urns. I guess we're looking for an urn wrapped in purple velvet. Why would he steal someone's remains though? Could he have thought it was something else? Maybe it was the only interesting thing he could find at the Travellers' site. Maybe he wanted to piss them off.

At the shop, Rhys gives Gwyn and me a look that tells us he's ready. Stood in front of the map with his arms in the air, and with open books all around, he looks like an orchestra conductor just before the music starts.

"The Jungle," he says with a firm voice. "Ready?"

Gwyn glances over at me. I nod.

"The Jungle sits at the south-west edge of town, between the *Maes Athen* estate and the hillside route up to the old asylum. From the main road, the best way to approach so as not to be spotted is over the stone wall, here." He points to the map and moves his finger over the paper. "You make your way around the Jungle to this point, where you enter."

"Rhys, we've done this a million times," Gwyn says. "We know where we're going."

"We need to be clear about the details, Gwyn," I say, crossing my arms. "We can't afford to get anything wrong. Remember who we're visiting."

"Let's just hope he and his Goons are elsewhere," Rhys says before pausing like he's expecting us to argue.

I nod. "Go on."

Rhys taps on his watch. "The sun will set at twenty-one thirty-nine hours. I'd go after ten to be sure."

"We'll be there after midnight," I say.

"Why so late?" Gwyn frowns as he looks over at me.

"To minimise our chances of running into anyone." Three persons specifically.

"It'll be a really dark night," Rhys says. "Weather forecast says it will be overcast and there's no moon, so make sure you take your torches."

"Right." The darkness will make it spookier, but it will help, I think.

Rhys points to the map again. "After entering the Jungle, here, follow the dry stream until you get to this point. Anyone coming or going at that time is unlikely to take this route in or out. They'd more likely take the farmer's path."

I lift my head and narrow my eyes. "What do we know about the Eagle's Nest?"

Rhys makes a dramatic pointing gesture at me. "Good question. It's an old stone hut used in the past as a shelter for woodcutters. Horse named it after Hitler's secret mountain headquarters."

"Nice," Gwyn says.

Rhys nods. "My intel tells me Horse and his gang have kitted the place out with old furniture and stuff they took from the dump."

It crosses my mind to ask Rhys where he gets his intel. He probably wouldn't want to say – intel is one of his main skills, and he doesn't like to reveal his sources. But chances are, it would be Brian Lemon-face – a big lad who gets his nickname because of the shape of his head. According to Hannah, Rhys isn't close to anyone else at school.

"Any idea where the object might be kept?" Gwyn asks.

"Well, that is the one good thing about Horse. He treats the things he steals like trophies. It won't be hidden away. Expect to see a trophy area where the object is on display."

It makes me wonder what other trophies he's acquired from around town. Hopefully, no body parts…

"What are the chances that someone will be there tonight?" I ask.

"Difficult to say," Rhys says. "This time of year, they do tend to be out and about rather late. If they're awake, I suspect they'll be on the prowl looking for trouble, but I can't make any promises."

We can't be spotted, I think. "We'll need camouflage."

"Army clothing?" Gwyn says. He wants to wear his army kit, I bet.

"No, black clothing. Shoe polish for our faces. Need to make sure we're not seen. Rhys, are we done here?" I have visions of my disguised head rising from a river like Captain what's-his-face in *Apocalypse Now*.

"Yep. For now." He stands back and clasps his hands to tell us his job's done.

"Right, good," I say. "Gwyn, shall we get ready?"

"Yes, let's go to my house for a bit and find what we need." Gwyn leaves the room to have a word with his dad. As I follow, Rhys grabs my arm and gives me a serious look.

"Be careful out there. I don't need to tell you Horse is a nutter. But there may be someone even more dangerous out on the prowl. You watch out for yourself and my little brother."

"I will," I reply. "You can always come with us, you know? Extra pair of eyes might come in handy."

He shakes his head. "No, you know I prefer to leave the operations to you two…"

"Even out of shop hours?" I say.

"Nope," he says firmly and lets go of my arm to return to his books.

His response doesn't surprise me but it's good to ask him occasionally. I pause and take stock of what we need to do tonight. This would be our riskiest operation yet, but it must happen to get the Gypsy girl on board. There really is no other way to move things forward.

CHAPTER 13

After we source our supplies and pack our kit for the operation, I return home for family dinner – fish and chips as a Friday night treat courtesy of Auntie Val. Hannah and Dad fight briefly about his work, or more accurately, lack of work. She keeps making comments about how lucky we are to have Auntie Val helping us, which doesn't help. I manage to polish off my saveloy and chips without saying much of a word. My mind is focused throughout on the Jungle and the Eagle's Nest.

After the meal, I go upstairs to read and think. I tell Hannah that I'm tired. But far from it, my mind is racing. I'd struggle to sleep if I had to. I have no intention of telling Hannah that I will be sneaking out just before midnight to go and meet Gwyn. She would just worry. Rightly so, maybe. Dad, on the other hand, will be lost in his own world with his typewriter.

I look at the clock and see that it's time. Dressed in a mixture of black and navy-blue clothes, I open the door of the bedroom and check the hallway. The landing light is off, and no sound comes from Hannah's bedroom. My face is covered in black shoe polish. If she does come out of her room, then it's a good test for my camouflage – how I explain it is another matter.

Down the stairs I go, and in the kitchen, I see light coming from the shed. I ignore it, not expecting to run into Dad at this time, and leave through the back door with gentle, slow movements. I push my bike out, down the path, through the gate, and halfway down the street before I get on and cycle to my rendezvous point with Gwyn.

We have planned to meet at the bus shelter on the corner of *Goedwig* Street. I am the first to arrive, so I hide my bike behind the shelter and sit down on the bench in the shadows. The last bus went by over an hour ago so I'm unlikely to run into anyone.

I hear the screech of brakes coming down the road. When it comes nearer, I step out from the bus shelter and Gwyn nearly falls off his bike.

"Fricking Jesus, Ned, what are you doing surprising me like that?"

"You knew we were meeting here," I say.

"Yes, but I didn't know you'd appear from the darkness with a blackened face like some fricking ghoul."

"Oh, right. Sorry." I open my bag. "Come on – you need to put some on as well."

We are now both covered head to toe in dark camouflage. We get on our bikes and head along *Lôn Werdd* away from the Travellers' site. Beyond the Jungle, this route carries on to the old asylum. Further still, it goes up into the hills until it reaches *Cartref-Y-Gwynt* and then comes back down past the secondary school and the police station.

I remind Gwyn about his squeaky brakes as we get nearer to the Jungle. Here, we are away from the streetlamps and the night is a thick block of nothingness. We reach the stone wall and slow to a snail's pace to make sure we don't miss the entry point. Gwyn drags his feet on the ground, and I can hear the scraping.

"Here," I say.

We drop our bikes into a dry ditch on the other side of the road, where they are out of sight. I leap up onto the dry-stone wall, taking care as I do this. Pulling or stepping down too hard at the wrong spot will pull large chunks of rock down. I land in the field and the ground is hard since it hasn't rained for over a month. Next to the wall, I squat for a moment to take out my torch and turn it on. I am careful to keep it pointing down to not light up the field around us. Gwyn lands beside me and we are on our way. From our position, the Jungle looks like a dark chunky mass in the night, like a black hole might appear in space to astronauts.

We leg it across the dry field, reach the perimeter of the Jungle, and walk around to the other side where we climb under the barbed wire fence and step into the dry stream bed. There, we turn our torches off and take a moment to try and let our eyes get used to the dark. I squat and touch the ground beneath us. I feel pebbles and soil on my fingertips and can make out the edge of the stream. The air among the trees is fresher than in the surrounding field and the smell reminds me of the little tree-shaped air freshener that hangs from the mirror in Dad's van.

"We follow the riverbed to the hut," I whisper to Gwyn, recapping the plan, and I hear him grunt his agreement, although I cannot see his face.

As we follow this curvy route further into the woods, our surroundings seemingly become blacker like we're getting closer to the rotten core of this place. I rub my stomach as a fluttering feeling comes to me.

"Your breathing is fast," Gwyn says.

"Just the pace," I say, but that's not it.

I stop and notice everything around us is completely still. The only noises are the snapping of twigs and crunching of leaves under our feet. I am suspicious of the darkness and what it hides but the mood here is different to that of the farmhouse cellar. I don't sense the same presence I did there. Here, my nerves are more grounded and what scares me has a person's face. Does that make it more dangerous than the evil that hides in the shadows? I don't know.

The Jungle is like a dartboard. The outer layer is made up of evenly spaced older, taller trees like oaks and sycamores. The middle layer is made up of younger trees that form a dense layer filled in between with brambles and thicket. In the centre – the bullseye – is a small clearing where the hut is. As we move from the outer to the middle layer, I stop and Gwyn bumps into me from behind. I reach my hand out of the stream and feel the dense thorn-covered branches on either side. Thankfully, the stream cuts through this wall and the recent dry weather allows us to use it to access the clearing in the centre. When it isn't dry, the farmer's path is the only way in or out of the Jungle, and for anyone unfamiliar with the forest, getting lost inside is easy.

The night around us is as black as – well – night. I can't think of anything else to compare it to right now. In Welsh, we say, *tywyll fel bol buwch*, which means *as dark as a cow's belly* but that just seems strange. How would anyone ever know how dark the inside of a cow's belly was? In *Empire Strikes Back,* Han Solo makes a comment about the smell when he cuts open a *tauntaun* before sticking Luke in to keep him warm, but he says nothing about how dark it is on the inside. Maybe Luke would if he was conscious? Whatever the case, maybe I should stick with a *raven's wing,* or the *ace of spades,* or the *midnight sky*? When I look up at the heavens, there are no stars or moon to speak of. But when I stare long enough, I can make out the branches of trees against the sky and they look like clasped skeleton fingers, and the further into the woods we travel, the closer they get, like death is bringing its fingers together to trap us inside.

Beyond another bend in the dry riverbed, I spot something else and my stomach drops – a dull, small light flickers to us like a lighthouse across the seas. I blink repeatedly to make sure it's not my eyes playing tricks on me. But they aren't, and after another five minutes or so, up ahead, we see it: a space without trees and in the centre, a small grey shape where the light comes from. Gwyn taps me on the shoulder, and I turn to see the bulging whites of his eyes, full of fear. I imagine his face would be pale right now if it wasn't covered in shoe polish. This is it – the Eagle's Nest.

We get closer and see the round stone hut that Horse has made into his den. It has a curious shape – like an igloo made of rock with its rounded roof. The light emerging from inside isn't enough to light up the forest but after five minutes of trudging our way through the dark woods, it's bright enough to shock the eyes. We can make out the shapes of the doorway and two narrow windows on either side. I hold my fist up in the air to tell Gwyn to stop. We sit on the ground for a moment and watch the hut for activity. There's no movement or sounds coming from inside and the trees and the woods remain silent all around.

"There has to be someone in there," Gwyn whispers in my ear; I nod my agreement, but we can't tell from out here.

"Let's push on," I say.

Gwyn bites his lip, and I can hear gentle wheezing on his chest.

"Inhaler?" I ask.

He nods, takes out the little plastic object and sucks hard on it twice.

We step out of the stream and crawl along the edge of the clearing to try and approach without being seen by anyone who may be in the hut. At the back of the small building, I hold my right hand up, and with my fingers I count to three before we dash across the clearing to the wall. We tread carefully around the side of the stone building – me first – until we reach one of the narrow windows. Gwyn taps my shoulder and points to the ground, which is littered in crushed, empty beer cans.

I crane my neck and look in through the window. The light is coming from an old paraffin lamp in the corner of the room. I must stretch on my tiptoes to see the floor. I gasp and put my hand over my mouth when I see the heads of Horse and his two Goons on the ground, lying on an old mattress. It looks like they're asleep, and next to them, are more empty cans and sleeping bags that have been kicked off. Thankfully, I see no kidnapped children or dogs or other creatures.

I look at Gwyn and point to myself and then to the door. His eyes become wide like flying saucers and his forehead wrinkles. I turn away and tiptoe past the window and peer in through the door. Lying on the battered mattress on the ground – completely still – is Horse and his two Goons. I gasp and take a step back when I see Shag isn't wearing any pants or trousers and his bare white arse shines like a full moon in the lamplight. Horse wears only underpants and a vest, and Pablo is topless. What the bloody hell have they been up to, I wonder, and my eyes don't know where to look. Something pinches my shoulder and I realise Gwyn is stood behind me and has grabbed me as he sees the spectacle inside. I turn my head and see his eyes popping; he mouths the words, *what the fuck*? I shrug and put a finger to my mouth. If Horse knows we've seen this, he'll kills us – that, I have no doubt about. I close my eyes and take a deep breath. Okay, I think, keep calm. I open my eyes and examine the room. On the opposite side of the wall to the lamp is a stone shelf of sorts. On it are a mixture of strange items – the trophies, as Rhys called them – that I assume Horse and his gang have stolen from all over town. There is a brown metal statue of death, a black leather-bound book and a few trinkets in the shadows that I cannot see. I bite my lip when, at the end, I see an object wrapped in purple cloth. That's it – Rebecca's *taid*.

I stare at the three half-dressed sleeping beauties on the mattress and watch for any sign of them waking up. I glance at the beer cans and back at them. I hope the skinful they've had means they're out for the count. My heart is racing, and I really would be happy to be anywhere else in the world right now, anywhere but here. If only I could leg it far from this psycho and his two henchmen, but I can't. But my mission is going nowhere. I need Rebecca and the only way I can get her to join us is if I go into the hut and get that bloody purple thing.

I imagine my body to be as light as a cloud and that I can float into and out of the hut without making any noise. I glance at Gwyn and his terrified face does nothing to calm the nerves. Then, like I'm diving into a cold lake, I take the first step, and with all my body tense, I tread around the mattress, all the while watching the three half-naked sleeping trolls. The hut stinks of piss, beer and something else – something very fishy – and between that and the warm air, it makes me want to vomit. I glance over at Gwyn and see sweat dripping from his forehead. He reaches for his inhaler and takes a couple of quick puffs. I put my finger to my mouth and try to hush him.

Pablo – who always has a fag in his mouth when he's awake – releases a booming cough from his throat. I freeze, still, against the wall like a rabbit in headlights, though it doesn't make any difference. If any of them wake up I would be the first thing they saw as they opened their eyes. And what would they do? Murder me or force me to join in with their weird sex stuff? Thinking about it, perhaps death might be the better option.

Pablo's breathing settles and he turns over to his other side. Then it's Shag's turn and he reaches his arm around and scratches his bare arse before shifting and pointing his floppy penis in my direction. I blink and remember the saveloy I had for dinner and put my hand to my mouth. I wish pictures in your brain could be deleted in the same way you can record over a video tape.

I move further along and after a couple more steps I reach out and grab the item wrapped in purple velvet. I pick it up with both hands to make sure I don't drop it. I'm like Indiana Jones reaching for the gold statue at the beginning of *Raiders of the Lost Ark*. I haven't brought a replacement weight though, so I really hope Horse hasn't rigged the place with traps.

The material is smooth and feels gentle on my fingertips. The velvet is very thick, so it's difficult to make out what the item inside actually is; some of it is round but there are parts that feel sharp and jagged. I am unable to turn around, so I step backwards, tracing the same route I took on the way in. This, however, is a mistake and I fail to see an empty beer can and I slip. I fall against the wall and manage to keep upright but I drop the package between the occupants of the mattress. It bounces and unwraps. My jaw drops. There, next to Shag's penis, is a skull.

I hear a gasp from the doorway. I turn around and dramatically mouth the words, *shut up*. Luckily, my small accident has not woken any of them and Rebecca's *taid*'s bloody skull appears content to rest there next to Shag's willy. I can't leave it, of course. I still must have it. I bend over and reach for it like I'm one of those grabbing games at the fairground, although I hope for more luck than I've had with those machines. I cannot fully grab the skull, but I can hook my finger into the eyeball socket and lift it up. This action brings me closer to Shag and his body parts than I ever would have wished for. I pick up the velvet material with my other hand and wrap the skull in it. I leap back and kick another can.

"Oi," yells a gravelly, slurred voice. "Who's fucking there?" I glance over at Gwyn and he gestures for me to get out of there, pronto. But before I can get away, I realise someone has hold of my leg. I look down and see Pablo's grabbed it with one hand and his other hand is flailing around trying to push himself up.

Horse glares at me with one eye open and points. "Gonna fucking cut you."

Shag is in an even worse state and struggles to sit up. He puts his hand over his groin and seems to be looking around for his clothes. I struggle and Gwyn grabs my arm to pull me away.

"Fuck's sake. Get him," Horse says, and I manage to kick at Pablo's arm, so he lets go of my foot and without a second thought we leap out of the hut. Gwyn heads in the direction of the stream from where we came but I pull him back and point towards the shorter, direct route out of the Jungle. From inside the hut, we hear commotion – yelling and panic – but we don't wait to find out what's happening. We both dash along the overgrown farmer's path between the trees and thicket. Gwyn takes out his torch and guides the way. My fingers hold on to the skull tightly like I'm a rugby player frantically dashing towards the try line. The route brings us out on the road, and we run the short distance down to where we left our bikes. As Gwyn gets them out of the ditch, I turn to see lights moving about in the Jungle.

"Bloody shitsticks, they're coming, Gwyn."

I drop the package in my rucksack and off we both go. We peddle hard until our legs burn. I keep turning my head to look at the Jungle, but beyond the dancing lights among the trees, I see no one emerging. They usually go everywhere by foot, and I hope this is not the day they took some innocent soul's bike and are able to follow us and catch up. As the road dips and we get out of sight, Gwyn slows, and I hear his wheezing.

"Keep going," I yell at him.

He nods and continues to hold up his torch and guide our journey back in the direction of town. After a few minutes of mad, tired peddling and constant watching, we find ourselves back under streetlights. We exchange glances, and Gwyn gives me a relieved look; he takes out his inhaler for three puffs, but we carry on without slowing too much, until we reach the High Street. There, I stop and turn my head in all directions like I'm expecting them to pounce, but we're alone.

"I think we're okay now," I say with massive relief.

"What the fricking hell was that?" Gwyn says.

"I don't know. Is Horse… into that kind of thing?" I'm not sure how to describe it but I'll certainly not forget it.

"I've heard stories…" Gwyn says.

"Yeah, guess we've all heard stories." Stories about Horse and certain tendencies. Habits he may have picked up from his dad, but nothing I want to think about now.

"And a fricking skull, Ned. A fricking skull. It wasn't her *taid*'s ashes they took. It was his head."

"Bloody nuts," I say, and I wipe the dripping sweat from my forehead.

"Do you think they recognised us?" Gwyn asks.

"I don't know," I say. "They were shitfaced and half asleep. Maybe they won't remember. Plus, the shoe polish may have helped disguise us."

He takes a deep breath and rubs his head. "I hope you're right. If they did recognise us, then we could have a big problem…"

I rub my chin and decide it's best not to imagine being in Horse's bad books.

"But – erm – even if he didn't recognise us, I suggest we don't mention what we saw back there. They might find out if we tell people and stories spread…"

Gwyn purses his lips and blows. "Right. Very happy to forget about it."

"Anyway, the important thing is the operation was a success." I pull out the skull and remove the velvet cover, and we both stare at it.

"That was some proper Indiana Jones shit back there," Gwyn says.

"I don't remember any bare-arsed Nazis getting in his way," I say, and we both laugh like madmen but he's right about the comparison and I'll take it.

"So, this is how she does it?" I examine the skull. "This thing helps her talk to the other side?"

Gwyn looks away and sighs. "I'm sure it adds to the theatrics."

"I have so many questions for her," I say.

"Bet you do," he scoffs and shakes his head.

As I place the skull back in the bag, we hear commotion and we both look at each other. It sounds like a mixture of clapping and animals braying. We hear it coming from one of the side streets and we push our bikes along towards it. Outside the Black Cat pub, a small crowd is gathered.

"Talking of theatrics…" Gwyn says.

"Looks like they had a lock-in," I say.

Outside the pub, a man in a flat cap plays a fiddle while two people wearing horse-skull masks over their heads and black cloaks over the rest of their bodies dance around. It reminds me of the festival and the weird press conference we watched earlier in the day.

"Is this because of today's news, you think?" I ask.

"I'm sure these folks are gutted the festival's not happening," Gwyn says. "Maybe they've decided to go ahead with it anyway."

"It'll be a quieter summer without it." I lean on my handlebars as we watch the spectacle. One of the men wearing a cloak and horse mask takes a tumble and the music stops, and the others start laughing and cheering.

"Hardly graceful, are they?" Gwyn says.

"Nope," I say, gently chuckling and I start to rub my eyes. "Let's get going. It's late, and there's lots to do tomorrow." I feel myself start to crash after the drama of the Jungle.

"I'll head this way," Gwyn says, pointing to the next road.

"You okay getting home?" I ask.

"Yeah, fine. So long as I can sneak back into the house without being caught. Tomorrow, we return that thing to Rebecca?"

"Yep. Then we see how she can help us."

"Right," Gwyn says, nodding slowly, and he turns his bike and cycles away. "See you at the shop."

"First thing," I say.

"Night," he calls out.

"And what a bloody night it's been," I say to myself.

CHAPTER 14

It's just after two in the morning when I get home. I sneak in through the back door and listen for a moment as I enter the kitchen. The only sounds in the house are the humming of the fridge and the ticking of the clock in the living room. Speaking of the fridge, all the rushing about in the darkness has made me thirsty. I take out a bottle of milk, pull the foil top and gulp down half the bottle. I look out of the window and see that the light is still on in the shed. *Bloody hell, does he ever sleep?*

I sit down in a chair next to the table and sigh. What a night it's been. I was lucky. Had I not been able to get away, it wouldn't have ended well. But I delivered the goods – I acted bravely and did the right thing – and it worked out in our favour. We took back Rebecca's *taid* – well, his head, anyway – and having her on side would be a gamechanger for our mission. Hadn't really figured how that would work yet but it would work. Maybe she could guide us to the most active haunting sites? Maybe she could tell us more about the nature of the evil thing that haunts this town?

Lost in thought, I fail to notice the light brightening outside as the shed door opens.

In through the back door walks Dad and he makes me jump. He has a confused look on his face.

"Have you been down the mines, son?"

Shit, my face is still black. I try to think of a response, but Dad takes little interest in me. He strides past, over to the kettle, fills it with water and puts it to boil. As he waits, he turns around and crosses his arms.

I make a swallowing action and then it comes to me. "I was at a fancy-dress party."

Dad shrugs his shoulders. I get annoyed. "It's late, you know. Doesn't it worry you that your son has been out in the middle of the night?"

"You were out until now?"

"Yes."

"Do you want me to tell you off?" he says matter-of-factly.

I think about the question for a second. "No, but, you know, they're saying there might be someone dangerous out there."

"Who is?" he asks.

"People," I say. "Because of the missing boy."

"So why were you out then?"

"Because I had things to do."

"But what if there was someone dangerous out there?"

"What? I just told you about that." I don't know what else to say. He turns around, pops a teabag in his mug and then pours hot water over it.

"I'm sorry if you think I'm not strict enough with you," he says, all the while staring at his tea. "Your mum was always so good with that kind of thing." He reaches for the milk and pours a little into the mug. "Let's talk about it again when I get through some more of the writing. I'm just very productive right now and want to get as much down as I can before the creative juices dry up. You understand, don't you?"

I shrug my shoulders.

"There's a good lad." As he heads for the door, he stops for a moment and turns to look at me with a stupid smile. "I do hope you'll be heading to bed soon, son. It's very late."

I fake a smile, nod and watch as he goes back to his hideout. As the door closes, I grit my teeth and my throat makes a growling noise. I throw the milk bottle into the sink where it smashes and fires out pieces of glass across the room.

Screw it, I think. Tonight was about our victory. Dad will not spoil that. I get up and head to bed. Tomorrow will be an interesting day – plenty of work to be done. We'll return the skull, get our newest recruit onboard and plan our next investigation. All I need now is a good night's sleep and rest ahead of the next part of the mission. There would be lots to do in the morning.

CHAPTER 15

I've been lying in bed for about an hour trying to sleep but it's impossible. The room is hot, yes, but it's been like that for the last week or two and it hasn't been a problem for me before. My brain is in overdrive, but not because of thoughts. It's like the buzz of a detuned radio on full blast. It reminds me of when Gwyn pushed the speakers from his dad's record player together and he dared me to put my head in between them and listen to Mr B's opera LP on full blast. Of course, I couldn't back down from the challenge. But I was unable to put up with it for more than a second – not because of the awful fat man howling on the record but because of the pain it caused my ears. Any longer and I'm sure I would have gone deaf. When the music was turned off, my ears were filled with this loud buzzing sound like the radio sounds between channels. That is what my brain is going through right now but it's not because of a loud noise that I've heard recently – this thing sounds like it's in my head.

I sit up in bed and wipe my brow with the back of my hand. My head drops and I sit forwards with my arms crossed. Maybe I'm ill, I think. Maybe I've got one of those tropical brain parasites that makes you go mental. No, I think, I've never been to a jungle – not a real one that is – or a swamp so this must be something else. I look up and over at my rucksack on my desk. It occurs to me that only one thing is different about my room tonight. I have Rebecca's *taid* with me. The bloody skull. Could that be it?

I turn my bedside lamp on and leap out of bed and approach the bag. I reach in and take out the covered object and place it on my desk. I pull off the velvet and stare. Strangely, at exactly the same time, the detuned radio sound stops.

I crouch down and stare at the spooky bone face.

"Are you the one keeping me up, eh?" I say, before scoffing and shaking my head. I'm talking to it like it's a puppy that needs attention. A thought comes to me, and I grab *The Hamley Book of the Paranormal*. I look up skulls and find a page about screaming skulls. *A screaming skull*, it says, *is a haunted object that causes those around it to feel dread or hear sounds that lack an obvious source or origin.* It describes the case of the Bettiscombe screaming skull of Dorset, which was believed to belong to an African slave who died desperate to be buried in his homeland. When the skull was buried somewhere else, the skull's screams were heard by lots of people nearby.

"Bloody hell," I say, looking back up at Rebecca's *taid*. I know I should be scared but I'm not. I feel okay being around this haunted skull. Maybe even a little excited. Is that weird, I wonder? I've got so used to hanging around graveyards and haunted houses that it's become normal. I didn't use to be like that. But I can't help it now, and I can't stop thinking about such things. Something inside keeps pushing me to find out more and – ultimately – complete my mission.

"What do you think, *Taid*?" I say aloud. "Have I gone mad or is this what it takes?"

I sit back on my bed and yawn. This time I feel sleep getting closer.

"Are you going to let me rest now?" I ask. There is no answer.

I switch off my bedside lamp and lay my head on the pillow. I carry on staring at the skull on the desk – which now is just a dark shape against the wall – like I'm expecting it to do something.

"I really hope you and Rebecca can help us," I say, and my words become softer and slower. "I've tried so hard… but had no luck so far…"

I close my eyes, and as I drift away to sleep, something shifts on the desk, and I sit up instantly like a rake that's been stepped on by a cartoon character. I turn the light on and leap over to the desk and examine every detail. The skull has not moved. In fact, the only thing that has is my rucksack, which has toppled over.

My eyes narrow and I gaze into *Taid*'s socket holes. "Was that you?"

But there is no response and I lie back down on the bed and stare at the desk. I dare not turn my light off, in case I miss anything, but from then on in, the night is completely still and quiet.

CHAPTER 16

I wake up with a startle in daylight and the first thing I do is look over at the desk. *Taid*'s skull is still there. I'd half expected it to be on my bedside table, or even balanced on the pillow right next to my head – that is how it would happen in horror films.

It's later than I would have liked so I rub my face and leap out of the bed before sluggishly moving around the room putting clothes on and heading to the bathroom. Despite scrubbing my face the night before, there are still traces of black around my ears that need a further scour to remove. I pick up my rucksack and place the wrapped skull inside before making my way downstairs.

There is no one in the living room or the kitchen. Hannah must be out, and Dad – I assume – is still in the shed. I stop at the sink. The broken glass has been cleared up. I'll pay for that later, no doubt. But there's no time to dwell on anything, so I pop a couple of slices of bread in the toaster and polish off half a pint of milk that's in the fridge. After buttering the toast, I leave the house and jump on the bike, eating my breakfast as I cycle along. It's about half ten. I told Gwyn I would be at the shop for opening time. Maybe I should have been more realistic. It doesn't matter – there are more important things to worry about right now.

Cycling along, I think about the skull and Rebecca. What does it do for her, I wonder? My night-time experience tells me there's definitely something weird about it. But how does it enable her to connect to the other side? And is it just about the skull or is it more about her powers?

Whatever the case, having her onboard will be great and will really complement our current skillset. Between us, we have brains, brawn and a boss (me) but none of us can talk to the dead. Having Rebecca as part of the squad will change everything. There are a few haunted sites around the area that we haven't investigated yet – like the old asylum – but I also hope we get a chance to visit previous places: *Cartref-Y-Gwynt, Pen Cawr* crossroads, the churchyard... These were sites I held so much hope for but delivered nothing. Maybe all we needed were the right skills.

I open the door of the bookshop and prepare myself for the usual puzzle discussion with Mr B, but to my surprise there's no sign of him. The front of the shop is empty. In the backroom, I find Gwyn sipping tea and Rhys reading.

"Alright, gents," I say. "How are we doing?"

"Tired," Gwyn says.

"Where's your dad?" I ask.

"Nipped to the chemist," Gwyn says. "Rhys is in charge, apparently."

"Working hard," I say with a grin.

"Working hard or hardly working." Gwyn chuckles.

"Hey," Rhys says. "My role here is critical. Someone must be the knowledge keeper."

"You mean sitting on your arse all day with a head in a book?" Gwyn says.

"I'm familiarising myself with the merchandise," Rhys says. "I build my expertise for the benefit of the business."

Gwyn looks at me and shakes his head, and I can't help but laugh before taking the rucksack off my back and taking out the skull.

"I had a bloody crazy night with this thing in my bedroom," I say.

"You slept with the skull?" Gwyn says, giving me a disgusted look.

"In my room, I said. It wasn't in bed with me."

"Let's have a look at this thing," Rhys says, reaching over and taking the object.

"There was this constant noise in the room," I say. "Like a tuned-out radio. I just couldn't sleep. Then I went into my bag and took this guy out and it stopped."

"Weird," Rhys says.

"I reckon your mind was too active after our crazy mission," Gwyn says.

"Looked it up in the *Hamley* book," I say. "Sounds like one of those screaming skulls."

"Like the Bettiscombe screaming skull?" Rhys says. "Cool."

"So, it's not the only screaming skull then? Wonderful," Gwyn says.

Rhys turns *Taid* around in his hands and examines the skull. "Gwyn told me about your mission," he says. "Quite an eventful night?"

"You could say that," Gwyn says, biting on the nail of his thumb.

"But we were successful." I try and stress the positive outcome of the mission, hoping it makes the images seared into our minds worth it.

"I just hope those nutters didn't recognise us," Gwyn says.

"No sign of them about this morning?" I ask.

"Probably biding their time," Gwyn says, and he sips on his tea.

Rhys holds up *Taid*. "Whether or not Horse comes after you, I tell you one thing, this object could really help our investigations."

"I hope so," I say, leaning my hands on the desk and blowing through my lips. "We're getting nowhere."

"I would've expected something from *Cartref-Y-Gwynt*," Rhys says. "Kids at school who go there are always on about the weird things that happen there."

"Your brother almost died there…" Gwyn says.

"Died?" Rhys sits up in his chair. "Don't you be offing yourself while out, dickhead. Mum will kill me."

"Oh, he's being dramatic." I leaf through pages of the books on Rhys's desk.

"Had an asthma attack," Gwyn says. "After falling into the cellar."

"Cellar?" Rhys says. "The farm has a cellar?"

"Pretty creepy vibes," I say. "Whole place did, for that matter. Felt like we were being watched." I make binoculars with my hands and pretend to scan across the room.

Gwyn blows a raspberry.

"He wasn't convinced," I say.

"When will you get the photos?" Rhys asks.

"Next month," Gwyn says.

"Why the wait?" I ask. "Boots is now doing one-hour developing."

"Yeah, but it's bloody pricey," Gwyn says. "I'll have to wait for next month's pocket money. And I certainly won't be paying for one-hour developing. This photography business isn't cheap."

"Right," I say, stroking my hair with my hand. "You know I'd help if I had the cash…"

"I know," he says.

"By the way, fuckwad, you still owe me for the last prints." Rhys turns to face his brother and holds out his open palm. Gwyn offers him the empty teacup and Rhys shakes his head.

"The ones from the churchyard?" I ask.

"Yeah," Gwyn says. "Dad should have them when he comes back from the chemist, actually."

"Today?" I ask.

Gwyn nods and I rub my hands in anticipation. "Great."

These photos were the first ones we'd taken on an investigation. Gwyn had received the camera a few weeks earlier for his birthday and it was an exciting development, although maybe not as exciting as getting the skull and recruiting its owner.

I clear my throat. "*The Hamley Book of the Paranormal* says the best piece of evidence you can find is a nice clear image of something supernatural." I straighten and begin pacing around the room. "Photos are very difficult to fake and can be very convincing to the sceptic." I look at Gwyn with narrowed eyes.

The two brothers nod in unison, having heard the same words a few times, I suspect. But I am very excited about the possibility. The Brown Lady of Raynham Hall, George Adamski's cigar-shaped UFOs, the surgeon's photograph of Nessie – these images are now infamous and provide serious evidence that many strange things can and probably do exist in this world. Although we are limited by Gwyn's camera and photography skills (and our budget), I still see this as our best chance of proving the existence of the supernatural infestation of this town. Decent evidence would help increase support for my investigations – and maybe allow us to grow the squad – plus, if we could sell a photo to one of those big papers then we could better fund what we do. Maybe even get a better camera. All we needed was one decent picture.

I stop pacing and turn to face the brothers. "How long do you think your dad will be?"

"God knows," Rhys says. "He's only gone to the chemist, but you know how he tends to stop and talk to people on the High Street."

"Shall we wait for him?" Gwyn asks.

"No, let's deal with the other matter first," I say, perhaps even more excited about this than I am about getting the photos.

"Time to return this?" Rhys says, handing me back the skull.

"Yes." I wrap it up in the purple velvet. "Let's do that now and then we can come back and have a look at those photos."

Gwyn purses his lips and blows before putting the mug down on the table and getting up.

"Don't look at them until we're back here with you, okay?" I yell back at Rhys as we head out towards the door, and he gives me a thumbs up.

CHAPTER 17

The Travellers' site is busier than the last time we were here. We get off our bikes as we arrive and push them between the various folk who are coming and going. It must be near lunchtime and the workers are back from the fields. Gwyn looks nervous, so I lead the way. A group of men glare at us; one of them says something and the others laugh. Three women stride past carrying piles of plates and cutlery. They are chatting away about something Isaac did, whoever Isaac is. The bearded man we saw last time is sat in a camping chair sipping a drink from a tin cup. He stares off into the distance like he's thinking about something important. The place smells like fire and cooked meat.

Sat on the step of her caravan door is Rebecca. She has hold of a pack of cards and she repeatedly – and skilfully – shuffles them from one hand to the other. Her eyes widen as she sees us approach and she gets up and gestures for us to follow her into the caravan. Gwyn and I lean our bikes against it and go inside to find her pacing around and rubbing her hands.

"Did you get him?" she asks. "Did you manage to get him back?"

"Him?" Gwyn replies.

"Yes, we got him back," I say and open my rucksack and take out the velvet-wrapped skull. I hand it to her, and she grabs it – him – with both hands. She glances out of the window and then takes the cloth off.

"Oh, *Taid bach*," she says. "I'm so sorry I let them take you."

She kisses the skull like we've returned her teddy bear. Gwyn rubs the back of his neck and looks away, awkwardly.

"We got him back for you," I say. She doesn't take much notice. "It wasn't an easy operation."

She hugs her *taid* and closes her eyes tight.

"And there may well be hell to pay for it," I say. "So now it's your turn to help us?"

"Hello?" Gwyn yells.

She frowns, nods and lowers the skull. "What do you need?"

I sit down at the table and gesture with my hand for the other two to join me. Gwyn sits next to me and crosses his arms. Rebecca sits opposite and places the skull on the table in front of her.

I take a deep breath. "There's something evil here in this town."

She glances at Gwyn and then back at me. "Why do you say that?" She cocks her head to the side.

"I saw something." My hands start sweating and I start to rub them together and then against the table. "Something I can't really explain. But I know it was very bad. It did something terrible."

She furrows her brow. "What did it do?"

"Just trust me. Something terrible." I hope this works – I really don't want to revisit what happened.

She looks over at Gwyn again and I see he's now staring out of the window. He knows it's a difficult subject for me.

"Right." She starts stroking the skull like it's a cat. "People come to me all the time for help. Usually, questions about what their dead relatives think about new things in their lives – hairstyles, boyfriends, wallpaper."

She takes a deep breath. "I'll take your word for it. For now. But the more information you can give me, the better help I can give you."

I nod.

"Can you at least tell me what you think you saw?" she asks.

I shake my head slowly. "I don't know for certain. Not a living thing – that's for sure. I don't think it was a ghost. It was nasty and its intentions were bad, very bad. Maybe a demon or the witch. I can't tell you. But it isn't just about that one thing in that one place. It's the whole town. I'm sure you know the stories, but don't you feel it too? There's something deeply weird here. Something evil at work. That is why we're here. To try and piece the puzzle together, bit by bit. We need to find out what this thing is and stop it before anyone else is hurt."

"Anyone else?" she repeats and narrows her eyes.

"It's why we need your help," I say.

"You should know it won't be easy," she says. "Doing what I do takes a lot of skill, and it can be very dangerous." As if to emphasise her point, she turns the skull to face us.

"And what exactly do you do?" Gwyn leans forward, places his elbows on the table and rests his chin on his clasped hands.

Rebecca looks across the two of us. "What do you two know about *Annwn*? The place beyond death."

"Like heaven and hell?" I say.

She shakes her head. "No, none of your Sunday school nonsense. *Annwn* is a word that was used well before the time of Jesus and the New Testament. It's an old word for the Otherworld."

That isn't in *The Hamley's Book of the Paranormal*, I think.

"You're connected to this *Annwn* place?" I ask. "Can you speak to those who are there?"

"Not exactly. See, *Annwn* is not a physical place. Not like a house or a town. Thousands of years ago they used to think of it as an island or a place underground. But for those of us who've experienced it, it's something we know is all around us."

"The dead are all around us?" Gwyn scoffs and wrinkles his nose.

"They're there but they're not as well. For most people, the barrier between our world and *Annwn* is like the walls of this caravan. There's no way through it. If you're in here, all you know is this world. There is no other space outside."

"What about you?" I say. "Do your skills allow you to see through the window?" I point to the glass.

"Not exactly," she says. "It's more like..." She leans over to the window and breathes on the glass until a patch of it becomes foggy.

"It's like condensation?" Gwyn asks.

Rebecca rolls her eyes. "We call the barrier, the *Ffordd*. The *Ffordd* is foggy, unclear. When you look, you can sense the presence on the other side but it's difficult to fully connect until the conditions are right."

"And what if they are right?" Gwyn asks.

"Well, then..." Rebecca wipes the glass to remove the fog and just at that moment the face of the big, bearded man who we met before appears, and we all jump.

"Oh Ronnie, piss off. You big feckhole," Rebecca says. He lifts his cup like he's toasting us and moves away laughing.

"Sorry," she says. "He does that sometimes."

After almost jumping out of my chest, my heart's thumping returns to normal. My brain on the other hand is going crazy. "Your skill is to see through the *Ffordd* to the other world, through the foggy glass?"

"Not exactly. People like me have always been called *klewmeirw*. They say we hear the dead. Truth is, it's a bit of a mixture of seeing and hearing."

"Whoa." I'm lost for words.

"Why's it dangerous though?" Gwyn asks.

"Huh?" Rebecca turns to face him.

"You said before it was dangerous," he says. "Why so?"

"The *Ffordd* attracts all sorts on the other side. Often the most active and powerful entities are not well intended."

"What can they do from the other side, though?" I tap on the window to emphasise my point.

"If they're strong enough then they can reach through and hurt you; they can even grab hold of you and pull you through."

"You mean they could kill you?" Gwyn says.

"Yep," she says.

"Jesus, how do you...?" I'm unsure of how to put it.

"How do I avoid that?" she asks.

"Well, yeah," I say.

"I've been well trained. And I have *Taid*. In life he was a *klewmeirw* priest. In death, his spirit guides me and keeps me out of danger."

"Couldn't do much to stop Horse though, could he?" Gwyn says, in a mocking tone.

"His strengths are limited in this world," she says. "But in *Annwn*, he's very powerful."

I sit back and rub my hands. I glance at Gwyn. He's not buying any of it. That's okay – we'll make a believer of him. With Rebecca onboard, we'll make everyone a believer.

"I've never read about any of this," I say.

"You won't," she says. "This knowledge is passed down in my people through bloodlines. *Taid* shared it with Ma and Ma shared it with me."

"Where's your ma now?" I ask.

"No longer with us." Her eyes drop slightly.

"Oh," I say. "Sorry."

She looks up and taps the table with both hands. "Anyway, you still want my help?"

Gwyn shrugs and looks over at me. Of course, I don't need to think about it.

"I've never been so certain of anything in my life," I say. "Your skills are incredible, and I think they'll really help our mission."

"When do we start?" she asks.

"We need to plan our next investigation back at HQ," I say. "How about tomorrow? We'll figure out our plan and come back to get you. We'll be here early."

"Alright," she says. "Tomorrow it is."

We get up to leave and as Gwyn steps out ahead of me through the door of the caravan I turn back to see Rebecca wrap her *taid* up in the purple velvet.

"How do you sleep with that thing around?" I say. "He was a noisy bugger last night in my bedroom."

"You heard him?" she says.

"Yeah, wouldn't stop screaming or buzzing or whatever it was until I took him out of my bag and unwrapped him."

"You heard him," she repeats. "That's interesting."

"Is it?" I say.

Gwyn lingers outside by the door, and he looks uncomfortable. "Come on, Ned. It's time to go."

I'm curious but I raise my hand and wave to Rebecca before Gwyn and me head over to our bikes and return to town.

CHAPTER 18

Back at the shop, we enter the backroom to find Rhys with his nose deep in the conspiracies book again. The underside of his Doc Martens are in view as his feet rest on the desk.

"We're back," Gwyn says.

"I can see," Rhys says without moving an inch. "Any luck?"

"She's in," I say with some pride like we've just recruited a new top agent, which in many ways we have. "It's time to plan our next mission."

"Right," Rhys says slamming the book closed and taking his feet off the desk. "I'm glad to hear it. So, where to next, boys?"

I notice Gwyn looking at something and he points at the desk in front of Rhys. "Is that what I think it is?" he says.

"Oh yeah," Rhys says. "Forgot to say. Dad brought them back from the chemist before."

"The photos," I say. "Have you opened them?"

He shakes his head while Gwyn takes out the prints and carefully lays them out on the table. Rhys and I both step closer.

We examine the first one and see two gravestones – each surrounded by lush green grass. In some of the photos, we can see the wall of the church as well. Gwyn takes all the photos in turn and lays them on the table. The three of us examine each one. A few of the first ones are fuzzy.

"Really need to work on your photography skills," I say.

"Thank you for the feedback," he says in a tone that suggests he really isn't thankful.

"What was the strategy here?" Rhys says leaning over the desk. "Take as many pictures of graves as you could?"

"Basically, yeah," Gwyn says.

"It was the shrouded figure we were after," I say. A kind of white cloud that a few locals had seen moving between the graves. That was the purpose of the investigation, but we discovered nothing and saw nada.

"No luck," Gwyn says. "No, wait. That's odd."

Rhys and I move closer to Gwyn, and we try and see what he's staring at.

"Curious," Rhys says.

"Shit," I say.

In the photo, there are three graves. The one in the middle is larger and made of a dark grey colour with a purple tinge – slate, I think. Right over this grave – as clear as day – is the face of Terry Rowlands. It's the same picture that's plastered across the town, but here the image is a faded white colour. It stands out against the rest of the picture with its different colours and textures.

"That's freaky," I say.

"It's Terry, right?" Rhys looks at us both, wide-eyed.

"Yeah, same photo as the poster," I say.

"It looks like a double exposure to me," Gwyn says. "But it can't be. This photo was taken like three weeks ago. Terry's only been missing four days. And the posters only went up yesterday."

"That's not possible," Rhys says. "Is it?"

"There must be some meaning to it," I say.

I take the photo from Gwyn, place it on a stack of books and examine it.

"Hey," Gwyn says.

"It's definitely him," I say. "Do you think that means he's…" I'm not sure I want to finish the sentence.

"Wait a second. Jesus. Is that…" Rhys leans over the photo, pushing Gwyn and me out of the way.

"God, it is." He looks up. "That's Henry Blythe's grave."

Gwyn and I glance at each other.

"Who?" I say, with my hands raised.

"For goodness' sake, guys, you really need to read more."

Rhys zips away and goes over to a bookshelf near the till. He searches for a moment before reaching up and pulling down a book.

"We did have another book about him – written by some local author – but it's not on the shelf. I'll need to check with Dad whether it was sold. But anyway, for now, look at this."

Rhys opens the book in front of us and searches through the pages until he finds a black and white photo of a serious-looking man dressed in a dark suit.

"Sir Henry Blythe was a rich Victorian spiritualist who moved here in the 1870s. His wife and daughter died a few years before in a fire and he became obsessed with the paranormal, or spiritualism as they called it then. He moved around Britain spending time in places known for hauntings and ghost stories. Eventually, tales of the spooky Welsh town in the mountains made their way around these isles. Old Henry heard about them, and he came here."

"But the grave," Gwyn says, "he died here as well?"

"Yes. I don't know much about his death."

"Did he ever find anything with his investigations?" I ask.

"There's no mention of it here." Rhys taps on the book.

I stare at the picture. On the page around it is a brief description of the man's life. I close the book a little to see the cover. The title, *Local History of Nant-y-Wrach and the Surrounding Area*, is written in a large white font and beneath it are smaller images of the town and its landscape.

"Look here," I say. "This photo was taken in 1879."

Gwyn examines the photograph again. "On the grave, it says he died in 1881. Seems like he died well before he got old."

"That wasn't so uncommon in those days," Rhys says. "Before antibiotics, a little cold might have killed you."

"Doesn't say anything about his death here," Gwyn says.

"How weird for Terry's image to appear on this guy's grave, given his history and interest in the paranormal," Rhys says.

That is when the penny drops, and I gape at the two brothers. "This is no coincidence," I say, pointing at the book. "This is the proof we've been looking for."

"Is it?" Gwyn asks.

"It's a bloody message from Henry Blythe to us. Terry is out there, and we're meant to find him."

"But he's been missing for five days now," Gwyn says.

"Doesn't mean he's dead, though," I say.

"Maybe…" Gwyn glances at Rhys, and he looks uncertain.

I begin nodding as all my thoughts fall into place like my mind is quickly piecing together a jigsaw puzzle at a hundred miles an hour. "Yes, think about it. Why would we capture a picture of Terry right now and in this way? Henry Blythe is on our side and he's trying to get our attention."

I turn around the room and look up. "Well, Henry, you've got our attention. Now what do you want?"

"Don't you think we should take this photo to the police?" Gwyn asks.

"Nah, they'll just laugh at you," Rhys replies.

"We're going to need it, anyway," I say.

"For what?" Gwyn asks.

"It's time to begin a new investigation. With the help of Henry Blythe, we're going to find Terry Rowlands."

"Okay," Gwyn says. "But where do we start? When do we start?"

"We start now. We don't know what kind of danger Terry's in. Our best bet is to go back to the graveyard and carry out another investigation there. And we should go now."

Gwyn picks up the photo and stares at it with a concerned

look on his face. Rhys gives me an approving smile followed by a wink.

Before, I wasn't certain whether Terry's disappearance was connected to the wider dark mysteries of this town, but it looks almost certain like it is. Our mission has become a missing person's investigation. We hadn't connected the dots, so Henry Blythe came to help us do just that.

CHAPTER 19

"Right, *Nant-y-Wrach* churchyard." Rhys yells like he's stood in a chapel pulpit ready to deliver his sermon. Gwyn and I glance at each other.

"You've had a mission briefing about this place before. The church dates back to the thirteenth century. The oldest gravestones are from the 1850s or so, but they've been burying people on the site for a lot longer."

All three of us stand around an open map of the town; the same map they give to tourists who visit the place each summer. It's like we're planning military manoeuvres. To us, we may as well be. We need to be thorough, and Rhys has good knowledge of the area. Map reading and planning are definite skills of his; probably deserving scores of eight or nine. We want to be prepared and ready for whatever challenges we might face along the way.

"The oldest graves are here on the west end of the graveyard – behind the church." Rhys points to the map. "In terms of hauntings, you know about the ghost candles that are often reported here at night. When these lights are seen, they say a funeral procession is likely soon to follow. Near the south wall, by the road, a shrouded figure has been spotted on a few occasions. From the church itself there have been reports of hymn singing coming from inside when the place is empty."

"What do we know about Henry Blythe's life here?" I ask.

"Not much," Rhys says. "All the information we have is on those two pages." He points to the open book nearby. "There is another book about him, which I'll try to track down. I'm sure we had a copy here somewhere but maybe it was sold."

"We sell books here as well? They're not just for reading?" Gwyn says with a smile and Rhys gives him daggers.

I examine the photo again and bite my lower lip. "Has anything weird ever been noticed near his grave?"

"No reports that I'm aware of," Rhys says.

"If he's trying to make contact with the living for the first time then we need to find out why," I say.

Gwyn sighs, while Rhys nods enthusiastically. It is time. As we leave the shop, I am almost running. Gwyn follows a few steps behind, as he always does. I am excited. This photo is proof of something. Proof of what – I'm not sure. Maybe with our updated squad and refreshed skills, it's my chance to finally take on the evil of this town. Maybe this time I can stop it. I can stop the monsters before they hurt Terry. Maybe if I can find a way of keeping him safe, then I can keep everyone safe.

Within a few minutes, we're at the churchyard. It's now later in the morning but not yet midday. We push our bikes through the gate and lean them against the wall. The graveyard forms an L shape around the building. Only a few graves at the end of the L are visible from the road. Most are hidden behind the building. Around the edge is a thick line of trees – many of which are yew trees that hang low over the graves. Knowing about trees is not one of my skills, but I have come to learn a little about them during investigations. Here – for example – I know that yew trees are commonly found in graveyards because they grow well in soil full of dead bodies; in other words, they like to feed on the dead. Their branches hang low and hide the sun and look like they're reaching down for their next feed.

Newer graves are dug in a green space where the churchyard was expanded a few years ago – a portion of Hanging Gardens that the council gave up to the church to make room for more bodies. That is where Mum is buried. I haven't visited the grave since the funeral. I really don't want to go there now while I have other important stuff to deal with, but knowing she is near makes my chest ache.

I clap my hands and try to focus on the operation. "Where is Henry Blythe's grave again?"

It's not a huge space but there are enough tombstones to make finding one grave difficult. Plus, I'm not in the mood to spend ages searching for it.

"It's around the back of the church." Gwyn takes out the photograph and holds it up. As he walks along, he compares the picture to the graves we pass.

"Here," he says.

"Ah yes."

We both approach and examine it. *Henry Blythe, born 1838, died 1881.*

"He was forty-something when he died," I say.

"Forty-three," Gwyn says, before reading the words underneath. "*Whoever sows injustice will reap calamity, and the rod of his fury will fail. Proverbs twenty-two, eight.* Not the lightest verse."

"Sounds like a warning," I say.

We both stare at the huge slate headstone, which hasn't lost any of its colour – although the side of the crypt-shaped box that covers the ground – beneath which, Henry's skeleton now lies in the dirt – is covered in lichen.

"Don't you think it's odd he was buried here alone?" Gwyn says.

"What do you mean?" I say.

"Well, presumably his wife and daughter were buried near their home in London. So why would he be here?"

"I don't know." I stroke my chin as I think about it.

Gwyn steps away and scans the nearby graves, and I rub my fingers along the rough, indented letters of Henry's headstone and whisper to him, "What are you trying to tell us? Why did you show us Terry's picture and why now?"

I sit down on the dry ground with my back against the next grave – a large stone box-shaped crypt you'd usually see in horror films being opened by a vampire hunter before he sticks a stake in the undead creature just as it opens its eyes. Gwyn approaches and sits next to me.

"Now what?" he says. "I can't be taking any more photos. Not until my next pocket money comes in at least."

For me the timing is almost perfect. "Time for Rebecca and her *taid*…"

Before I can finish, there's a scratching and squeaking like someone is writing on a blackboard with chalk. We both glance at each other.

"What the hell is that?" Gwyn asks.

I peer around the side of the grave and signal for Gwyn to join me. From our position, we see an older woman kneeling in front of a headstone – about five graves down – and she appears to be writing or drawing on the grave with a large piece of chalk. Despite the warm morning air, she is dressed in a wax jacket and wellies, and her hair is covered by a headscarf. She looks like a widow visiting her husband's grave, but something about the way she acts is strange. My heart beats faster and above her, I notice a yew tree branch looming down on her like the tree is accusing her of something.

"Who is that? What's she doing?" Gwyn whispers.

"She's drawing or writing something, I think?" I say.

"Can't tell from here," Gwyn says.

Whatever she is doing doesn't take long and she gets up and moves along – towards us – to the next grave. Here, she scrawls again but now she makes noises with her voice. I find myself breathing faster – in short, sharp gasps.

"Ned, are you okay?" Gwyn asks. "You sound like you've got asthma."

"I'm fine," I say, but inside, I'm not. There is something about this woman that makes me very nervous.

"Is she singing?" Gwyn asks.

"It's more like she's reciting poetry or…" I turn to face Gwyn, "… chanting." We've both seen enough horror films to know this is weird.

"Shit."

She moves on to the third headstone – closer to us again – and repeats this action.

"She's coming this way," Gwyn says with raised eyebrows. We shouldn't fear a lone older woman like this, but I can't help the feeling of dread that's come over me. I can smell her perfume. It reminds me of *Nain*, and I try and remember her and what she looked like. I pull my head back and sit up against the stone crypt. The chanting stops and we hear her chalk against the gravestone. I am desperate to see what she is drawing or writing, but my body wants me to get away from the place and go wherever she is not. Gwyn continues to stare.

"Is she coming closer?" I ask, between gasps. In my mind's eye, I expect her to discover us hiding, and she stands over us, sneering and her face changes into something monstrous.

"She's got up," Gwyn says. "She's stepping back and examining the graves she's marked. Checking out her handiwork. Wait, she's doing something else…"

"What?" I ask.

I peer around the side of the grave again and see her take out a plastic bag from her pocket. She opens the bag, dips her fingers in and flicks something on each of the graves she marked – a red liquid.

"Jesus, she's flicking blood on the graves," Gwyn says. "Why would she be doing that?"

"Why would she be doing any of this?" I say.

After reaching the furthest of the graves, she ties a knot in the plastic bag and returns it to her pocket before turning and striding away. The further away she moves, the calmer I feel. We watch from our position until certain she's gone. We both get up and dash over to the nearest of the marked headstones. We stare at each one in turn. On the graves she drew the same thing – a picture made up of a single central circle overlayed with five other circles. Each one crosses each other and touches in the centre.

"Is that some kind of flower?" Gwyn asks.

"I suppose it could be." I survey each of the graves. "It's the same pattern on all of them." I look up at Gwyn. "Do you have that notepad and pencil?"

"I know the drill, Captain. Capture all evidence."

As he copies the flower image, I get down onto my knees and run my fingers on the dry grass. I feel something wet and sticky and see my fingertips are smeared in red.

"It is blood," I say, wrinkling my nose.

"God, clean your fingers, man," Gwyn says with a look of disgust on his face.

I rub my fingers on the grass. I scan some of the other headstones nearby. "She only marked some of the graves, Gwyn. What on earth was she doing?"

"Hang on," Gwyn says. "Look at the dates. The deaths on all these happened in 1943. Autumn, 1943, in fact."

I furrow my brow and notice the others from 1943 marked with the flower shape.

"Could it be to do with the war?" I ask.

We check the other headstones and find another three that have been marked: two from early 1904 and one from November 1863. Each grave has the same pattern scrawled on it, as well as traces of blood on the ground.

Gwyn crosses his arms and rubs his jaw. "How did she do this without our noticing?"

"I guess we wouldn't have paid her much attention when we came in, if she was here that is. Why would we?" And my weird feelings started when we saw her marking up the graves.

"Right. Do you think the photo and all this weirdness are related?" Gwyn taps his notepad.

"Has to be," I say. "But why these graves? Is it about the year of death?"

"Three timepoints – each forty-ish years apart," Gwyn says.

Gwyn's eyes dart across the graves again in turn. "Hang on," he says. "There is one thing. Look at the birth and the death dates."

"Huh?" I cock my head to the side.

"They were all children," he says.

We move quickly past each of them again and examine each headstone in turn.

"Blimey," I say, gaping. "You're right – all kids." The youngest was three and the oldest eleven.

"We should go back to the shop," Gwyn says. "See if Rhys can help us."

"We're going to need those research skills," I say.

"I'll write down the names and dates," he says. "He can look up local history. Also, need to see how this symbol is connected." Gwyn holds up the notepad.

"Right, let's do that. After that, we come back here with our new squad member and see what info her skills can get us." I rub my hands together; we may have finally found the thread we were after.

CHAPTER 20

Inside the shop, we find Mr B stood with a clipboard examining books on a shelf labelled *Supernatural Thrillers*. He seems to know that it's we who've returned without turning around.

"If I'd known you were coming back, I would have saved you some clues."

"It's alright, Dad," Gwyn says. "Wouldn't want to spoil your fun."

We move past him quickly into the backroom, where we're greeted by Rhys. For once, we find he's not reading, but dusting the shelves.

"Bloody hell, you're working," Gwyn says.

"Mum came by before," he says. "Moaned that Dad and I never do anything in here."

"Gave you both a talking to, did she?" I say.

"Meh," he says and shrugs. "Find anything at the churchyard?"

"We have homework for you," Gwyn replies, taking out the notepad. Rhys lifts his head and gapes at us both, eyebrows raised.

He listens intently to every detail of what happened in the graveyard before grabbing a pile of books from one of the shelves and dumping them all on the table in the centre of the room.

"Got to be witchcraft-related," he says, full of excitement. He lifts a book called *A Brief History of Witchcraft in Britain* and skims through the pages.

"That's what I thought," I say. Although in actual fact I hadn't thought of that until this moment.

"You think she was a witch?" Gwyn asks.

"Not necessarily." He drops the book and then picks up another. The title of this one is *Witches and Demons of England and Wales*.

"Those symbols look familiar," he says. "I'm sure it was one of these books." He flicks through tens of pages at a time, then stops. "Yes, yes. Fuck, yeah. Of course. I knew I'd seen them somewhere." He looks up at us both.

"What?" I say. He points at the page and shows us the pattern the woman drew on the headstones. Gwyn grabs the book from his brother's hands and examines it.

"Witch marks," Rhys says. "Symbols or patterns scratched or drawn onto surfaces that are meant to protect against witches and witchcraft. They'd often scratch them into the wooden frames of new buildings – near the doors or windows – to keep the evil out."

"It says blood and animal parts were used as well," Gwyn says before looking up.

"You mean she was protecting the children buried in the graves?" I ask.

"Most likely," Rhys says. "Any idea who she was?"

"Not seen her before," I say. I also fail to mention the weird feelings that came to me as she approached.

"What about those dates?" Rhys says. "Tell me those again."

Gwyn turns the page on his notepad. "Three from the autumn of 1943, two from early 1904 and one from November 1863."

"Any idea?" I ask.

"No. I'll need to do some digging in some historical texts." He taps his fingers on the table like he's thinking. "Maybe visit the town archive."

"How long will that take?" I ask.

"Let me see what I can find this afternoon," Rhys says. "Dusting may have to wait."

"Good. We need to move quickly." I glance from one brother to the other. "There's too much weirdness for it all to be unconnected."

"Yep, leave it with me," Rhys says as he grabs the ladder and pushes it from one shelf to another.

"Cool. I'm going to head over to the shop to get some penny sweets – I'm starving. You coming, Gwyn?"

He shakes his head, unsurprisingly. His mother isn't keen on him eating anything unhealthy, which for some reason includes sweets. She is very protective of him. Presumably because of the asthma. I, however, need an energy boost for the operation and maybe some fresh air – still feeling a little odd and drained after the experience in the graveyard.

CHAPTER 21

I only have a fifty-pence piece in my pocket but that will be enough to buy a decent selection at the newsagent. When I arrive at the shop, I find Mrs Jones stood behind the counter with a big smile on her face. She has a newspaper open in front of her but thankfully not on the crossword page.

"I was wondering when I might see you today, Ned. Hot out there, isn't it?"

I nod and lick my lips. Being a newsagent, you can buy newspapers and magazines, but it also sells lots of other stuff like bread and milk and odds and ends like stationery and birthday cards. But it's the sweets that bring the kids in. As soon as you enter the shop, you can almost taste the sugar in the air; you can certainly smell it. Fruity sweets, mints, bubble-gums, Parma Violets. The aromas are enough to raise any spirits.

I turn my head slightly to see most of the newspapers on the rack have headlines that mention Terry. Mrs Jones sees me looking and her smile drops, and she wrinkles her forehead. "Don't think there's anything new in the papers."

"Right," I say. I have updates, I think. But I certainly won't be sharing any – not with her, anyway.

"But, you know," she says, "wherever he is, I'm sure he's well taken care of. He's very important to all of us, and we all want to ensure his well-being. What can I get you, Ned?"

Mrs Jones has an odd way of saying things, but I pay it little attention and focus on the current objective. On one side of the counter are several rows of trays full of penny sweets. These are covered by a single large glass panel, which raises on the side nearest the old woman and stops customers from helping themselves. Many have tried to see if there is a way around it, but there isn't. Mrs Jones watches those sweets like a Fort Knox guard. She holds a paper bag in one wrinkly hand and lifts the glass cover with the other. I look across the many small boxes, all full to the brim with tasty treats.

"I'll have five fizzy cola bottles, five fried eggs, five flying saucers, three cherry bon bons, two lemon bon bons, three milk teeth, three Black Jacks, four jelly babies, one packet of Parma Violets and two of those marshmallow twists. How much is that?"

"That's forty-five pence, Ned."

"Then another five fizzy cola bottles, please."

"No blackcurrant pencils today?"

I shake my head. My mouth waters as I see her pick out the sweets and with full concentration pile them in the bag before twisting the end. I hand the fifty-pence piece over and grab the bag. Feeling its weight in my hand makes my insides jump for joy. The world is a better place with that bag in my hand. I take out a fried egg and put it in my mouth. In the newspaper rack on the other side of the shelves, something catches my eye. It's a picture of Terry on the front of one of the rags. *North Wales Boy Still Missing*, it says. It's the same picture that appears over Henry Blythe's grave in the photo. I stare at it and chew on a fried egg.

The bell above the door rings as it opens and someone steps in. I gasp and almost choke on the sweet when I see it's the woman from the graveyard. I leap behind the shelves and duck down. I freeze, expecting the panic to come again. But this time, with a few deep breaths, the terror holds off. A bit of clear thinking helps me realise that if I don't move, I may miss out on something important, so I step closer and lower my head, and try to remain out of sight. I can see through the gaps in the newspaper rack that she's buying sweets. They both speak nice words to each other. There's smiling. Bloody hell, Mrs Jones knows the woman. She buys three big bags of mint humbugs and causes some kerfuffle when she hands over a twenty-pound note, and Mrs Jones must empty her cash register to give her the change. Beyond that, nothing seems out of the ordinary about their chat.

As soon as the mysterious lady leaves, I rush over, trying my hardest not to act suspicious. Mrs Jones is emptying out rolls of coins into the tray of the register.

"Who was that?" I ask.

"What's that, Ned?" she says without turning her back.

"The lady who just left. Who was she?"

"Why do you ask?" she says matter-of-factly.

"I know her from somewhere," I say, clearing my throat. "Just trying to remember where."

"I can't tell you," she says. "That's a secret."

"Huh?" I look to the door and back to the shopkeeper.

Mrs Jones turns around with a wide grin on her face.

"I'm just pulling your leg, boy. You don't know who Mrs Astley is?"

"Erm no, should I?" I say with my mouth wide open.

"Maybe not. But she's the housekeeper at Lord Robham's house."

"Housekeeper? What – like the cleaner of the house?"

"More than that – she takes care of the lord and his home. She manages the household and makes sure all the staff there do their jobs properly. She's had quite a job to do since his wife left him. Been in quite a state from what I've heard."

"State?" I say, unsure of what she means.

"Oh nothing." She leans on her counter with her hands clasped.

She takes care of the lord and his big stately home. Why would she be drawing witch marks on the graves of children who died years ago? How does it all fit together? Bloody hell, is the lord involved in this thing as well?

"Ned *bach*, you look like you've seen a ghost."

"I'm okay." I raise my hand to say goodbye and leave the shop.

I lean on the wall outside gazing across the street. Mrs Astley is long gone, and I look at nothing in particular, but my mind is buzzing. Maybe it's the sugar or maybe it's my brain making connections between all the new pieces of information. Unless his housekeeper is up to something that he's not aware of, Lord Robham must know what's going on as well. Could it be related to his appearance at the weird press conference this morning? Might the whole thing be connected to the festival?

Also, if Mrs Astley was trying to protect the souls of those children from witchcraft, wouldn't that be a good thing? Why would it be a secret if she was doing a good thing? Why did I hide from her, twice? Is it because, inside, something tells me she isn't up to good and on detective programmes they always say you need to trust your gut?

I twist the end of the paper bag and pop the sweets in my pocket before returning to the bookshop to tell the guys what I've learned. I have some answers but an awful lot more questions.

CHAPTER 22

I stomp back into the backroom of the shop, where I find the two brothers with their heads down, looking intently at something on the table.

"Wow," Gwyn gasps and I bound over to see what they're staring at.

"Developments?" I ask and they both look up.

"Something strange," Gwyn says.

"What?" I clap my hands together.

"Those years," Rhys says. "In each of those years there was some kind of disease outbreak in the town."

"Disease?" I repeat and step nearer.

Gwyn drops his head and examines the book again. "Flu in 1943 and 1903, and diphtheria in 1863."

"So those children died from those diseases?" I ask.

"Possibly. Probably," Rhys says.

My eyes narrow. "What does that mean for our investigation?"

They both shake their heads.

"Right. Disease," I say. "In and amongst the curses, hauntings and missing children. Now there's this."

"Wait," Rhys says. "There's more."

"More?" I'm not sure my brain can handle any more discoveries today.

"Nearly every forty years going back to the seventeenth century, there is some outbreak." He looks down at the book. "1822, typhus. 1783, cholera. 1743, smallpox. 1702, cholera. 1663, bubonic plague."

"That is odd," I say. "Just those years?"

"Those are the only years listed here," he says and rubs his chin.

"Nothing happened before 1663?" I ask.

"Well, there was one thing forty years earlier," Rhys says. "Remember what happened here in 1623?"

"Mari fricking Evans," Gwyn says.

"Bloody hell," I say. "Could her death be connected to all this?"

"Witch marks," Rhys says, shrugging.

"But why only mark those graves?" Gwyn says, turning to face his brother.

"Well, the churchyard graves only date back to the 1850s," Rhys says. "Maybe they're the only graves that she could mark."

"If only there were older graves," I say. "Maybe we'd see the same pattern."

"Well, there's the Mud Chapel," Rhys says.

"Mud Chapel?" Gwyn repeats.

"That old chapel up in the mountains," Rhys says. "Some of the graves there date back to the 1660s." He leans over the book and taps his fingertips on the table. "It is of course possible that all of this is a coincidence. A lot of these diseases would have come and gone in this area over the years. This forty-year cycle could be nothing more than a random series of events."

I bend over and look down at the page. I see the dates listed in the book. It's all there in black and white. All the evidence is mounting up. It's not what I expected but does suggest something weird is happening here.

Just as I consider this, I remember the shop and excitedly lift my head and slam my hand on the table. "I forgot – there's something else. I know who the witch-mark lady is."

After I explain what happened, the three of us stand silently and stare at each other, digesting the day's events. Both brothers are wide-eyed and full of nervous energy; in Gwyn's case I think it may stem from worry, while for Rhys it could be excitement. For me, it could be Christmas morning.

"So, what next?" Gwyn asks.

"I reckon we've got time for one more investigation today," I say, grinning.

"The Mud Chapel?" Gwyn asks. I nod and look at Rhys.

"Operation brief?" he says. I nod again.

CHAPTER 23

We cycle past our school and then the police station, which is now quiet and free of the dramatics we saw yesterday. Beyond, at the end of the street, is a cul-de-sac where the biggest houses in town can be found and there is a stile where you can climb over the wall to reach a path that goes up into the *Cewri*. Gwyn and I lift our bikes over the wall so we can hide them from the road. The land is dry, and we can just about make out the trail in the yellowing grass leading up the incline, although the chapel is out of sight.

The hill air is quiet, thick and warm. All I hear is Gwyn's panting and the odd caw of a crow. There are no sheep to be seen – likely taken in for shearing, as is often the case this time of year. The trail becomes steeper the further we go. I've been meaning for us to come here to carry out an investigation. A 350-year-old chapel and graveyard seems like a perfect site for hauntings but because no one ever comes here, there's never any mention of ghosts or paranormal activity, so we've prioritised the places where people have seen or heard things.

"Odd place for a chapel," I say, getting out of breath myself now as well.

"There were chapels everywhere in Wales back then," Gwyn

says. "Plus, there were a lot more people living here when the mine was active."

The trail curves around the hill before flattening out in an area full of large rocks and boulders. Here is where we find the chapel. All the glass in the windows is gone and half the roof has collapsed. The graveyard is overgrown. There are green blackberries everywhere. Come September, this spot will be a goldmine for the juicy ripe ones.

"Wow," Gwyn says. "Never been here before."

"I know," I say. "Kind of forget it's here."

We walk on towards a hole in the wall where the gate used to hang. During the mission briefing, Rhys told us it was a Baptist chapel. There's a stream on the other side where they did the baptisms, meaning a minister would splash water on the faces of those who accepted God, Jesus and the rest of it.

"What years are we looking for again?" I ask my lieutenant.

Gwyn examines the writing on the back of his hand. "1822, 1783, 1743, 1702 and 1663."

"Right, let's get to it."

We move branches and twigs aside to see the dates on the graves nearest the entrance. They are old and the newest graves we see are from the 1900s. Then, as we move further between the crypts and headstones and battle through the thicket, I hear Gwyn call out.

"Ned, there, right there," he says in a shrill voice.

"What is it?" I say.

"There, right there. God, it's fricking disgusting."

I can't see Gwyn fully, but I can hear his groaning and retching. I follow the direction of his pointing to a small slate grave. Pushing the brambles aside with a stick, I see – sat atop the headstone – a white jelly ball, leaking like a runny egg over the gravestone, rotting and covered in flies. It smells like death, so masking my nose and mouth, I bring my face close and see the clouded stare of the dead thing.

"It's a fricking eyeball," Gwyn says.

"Bloody hell," I say. "Why would that be there? Hang on, what year is the death on the grave?"

Gwyn squints at the headstone. He hugs his mouth and nose with the inside of his elbow.

"1783," he says and looks over at me, wide-eyed.

I read the name. *Elen Angharad Williams. Born 1777, died 1783*. No surprises, beneath it is a bloody witch mark – drawn in the same way as the churchyard.

Gwyn moves away and further into the trees.

"There's another one over here. Another eyeball and a witch mark. This one's 1822."

I follow him into an area where the brambles are replaced by ferns. The openness makes it easier to see across the graves. We can see fifty or so more of them here, mostly slate, but a few stone ones as well. There are eyeballs on quite a few and the warm air holds on to the putrid stench and the whole place is pungent and disgusting. Gwyn looks green but carries on with his arm over his face, counting. I examine each of the eyeballs in turn. They're big – probably from a cow or a pig. The other possibility crosses my mind, but I dismiss it hopefully as too gruesome.

Gwyn returns and clears his throat and wrinkles his nose. "There are fourteen graves here with eyeballs and witch marks on them. All of them are the graves of children who died in these years." He points to the numbers written on the back of his hand. "Well, apart from that stone one. The letters are really worn down but I'm fairly certain it says 1663 on it."

I stand up straight and put my hands on my hips. "This proves it. There's definitely something connecting these dead children with what is happening now. If we can figure out what that thing is, then we might be able to save Terry."

"Do you think we should be worried?" Gwyn asks. He points to the graves around us. "Whoever did this is weird."

"Maybe but there's no avoiding what we must do. We have to carry on – otherwise Terry will be lost forever. And whatever this is, may be just the tip of the iceberg. I have a feeling that what comes next may be weirder still. But we must go on. This evil must be stopped."

I am finally on to something. There really is a sinister force at work in this town. Something old, bitter and nasty and I am on to it. This realisation brings with it a mixture of feelings – relief that I was correct, fear at what we might discover, and anger at what really might be happening. I must keep going. The only way to protect my family and friends is to drive this thing out of the darkness and bring it into the light.

"Alright," Gwyn says. "I just think we need to be careful."

"Right." I nod and breathe out heavily. "Let's get out of here before I throw up."

CHAPTER 24

Today has given us so much. I want to keep going but Gwyn and Rhys must head home. I will also face the music if I'm back late, so we hit pause until tomorrow. With a new day we will start early and see what Rebecca can do to help us. At home, I plan to study the *Hamley* book for any information that might be of use.

When I get back, in the kitchen I find Dad and Auntie Val talking. Dad is sat by the table and Auntie Val rests her back against the cupboard. There's an odd mood in the room, and I feel I've just walked in on something heavy. Dad has a sheepish look on his face. Auntie Val's nostrils are flaring.

"Ned *bach*," she says. "Have you been out with the Bowen lads until now?"

"Yeah – you know – hanging out at the bookshop, mostly."

"I hope you're being careful," she says. "Still no sign of that Rowlands boy."

I clear my throat. "Oh yeah, we don't stray too far."

"I'm glad," she says. "You don't know what kind of perverts may be out there."

I nod. If only she knew the truth of the matter. I reckon we're closer to finding Terry than the police are.

I leave them to it and run upstairs to go for a piss. When I come out of the toilet, I almost topple backwards down the stairs when I see Hannah sat in a dark corner of the landing.

"Bloody hell, Hannah. You gave me a heart attack. What are you doing there?"

She puts a finger to her mouth and tells me to sit down.

"I can't hear anything," I whisper.

I remember the milk bottle I smashed last night and expect it to be brought up, but Hannah remains quiet. She's trying to listen to the discussion downstairs, and she says nothing until we hear the back door close.

"Right, she's gone," Hannah says, sitting up.

"What did you hear?" I ask.

"Auntie Val was giving him a talking to."

"About what?"

"I told her he spends all his time in the shed working on his book. I told her I was worried about money and that he seems to have no interest in working."

"Oh." I look down at the carpet.

"It's six months since Mum died," she says. "We've been living on her insurance money since then and it's almost all gone."

I start shaking my head. "You shouldn't have to be worrying about this stuff, Hannah."

"I shouldn't but someone needs to. Dad needs to. He needs to be working again. If writing is what he wants to do, then fine. But he needs to keep earning otherwise we're in trouble. He can't forget about everything else. He can't ignore his responsibilities."

I don't know what to say. Hannah is leading this mission on her own. I have my own secret operation to complete. One that is more pressing and is an actual matter of life and death. I pat her leg, get up and go into my room. I pick up *The Hamley Book of the Paranormal* and see what it says about witchcraft.

I finally know that my mission is a real and necessary one. I was right about the evil all along. I know for certain it is here. And although I don't know what it is or what it looks like, I know that it must be defeated, or Terry is a goner.

CHAPTER 25

It is the next morning, and I am back at the Travellers' site. Unlike the day before, I'm up early and raring to go. I can't wait to see what new information Rebecca might help us uncover. I have a speedy breakfast with Hannah before heading off in a flash. Dad has not yet emerged from the shed but that's okay.

"You weren't kidding about being early," Rebecca says as she opens the caravan door.

"Ready?" I ask.

"Just give me a minute." She disappears back inside, and I look around to see a few bleary eyes around the site. Others are coming and going – getting ready to start their day. As I wait, a tall man with long black hair and green eyes that are the same colour as the stained-glass grass under Jesus's crucifix in the church window, comes out holding a mug of something that has steam rising from it.

"Morning, boy," he says. It looks like he's just come out to speak to me.

"Good morning – erm – sir," I reply and forcing an awkward smile.

"Sir? Ha. Call me Abraham."

"Abraham – erm – alright."

Interesting name, I think. Important character in the Bible? Don't see these folk going to chapel or church so wonder how he got this name.

"So, you're wanting to use my daughter's talents with the dead, are you?" The man speaks in a way that is different to everyone I know. His accent is a mixture of Welsh and something else. Irish, maybe? I'm not sure.

"She's helping us with some research. Erm – local history."

"Local history, is it?" he says, with a slight scoff. "And some very dark local history you folk have in this town."

"You mean the witchcraft?" That's the usual connection people make.

"Yes, and the rest. You be careful what you get yourself into. Those forces can be strong on the other side. Particularly in a place like this. You talk to the dead too much and sooner or later you'll attract the wrong type of attention. That's very difficult to shake off and you'll bring a shitstorm of terror down on yourselves."

"Right." My palms are sweating but I'm also thrilled by what he says.

He looks at me briefly with a serious and frightening look and for a moment he grows even taller and becomes a giant next to me. Then, in an instant, his face changes, and he gives me a big smile. One of his front teeth is replaced by shiny yellow metal.

"Don't worry though," he says. "You're in safe hands with Becca. She's been doing this for years and has been very well trained."

"Good to know." I can't help but wonder what the training would be like…

"To be honest. I'm glad she's making friends here. The way we come and go often makes that difficult and she spends a lot of time by herself."

I grin. "That's – erm – good."

"You do one thing for me, though," he says. "Anything goes skewwhiff with your activities, and you come back here to me, right?"

"Okay," I say.

"You promise?"

I nod. "I promise."

The caravan door opens, and Rebecca steps out carrying her satchel.

"I hope Abe hasn't scared you," she says.

"Abe?"

"Father."

"Oh. Not at all," I say, a bit flustered.

"We were just chatting about your history project," Abraham says.

"Right, we need to get going," she says. "I'll be back for dinner, Father."

We begin walking away from the caravan and turn to see Rebecca's father raise his mug in our direction.

"What did he say?" Rebecca asks.

"He's interested in what we're up to," I say. "Warned me about the dark forces here. What did he mean? Demons? Poltergeists?"

"Kind of. Certainly, there are the dead who are not as well intended. The spirits of those who suffered in life and took the pain with them. But there are also darker entities out there – creatures that have roamed these lands for aeons." The tone of her voice surprises me – she could be talking about schoolwork or the weather.

"In these lands or the *Annwn* place you talked about before?"

"They're here as well," she says. "Some of them crossed over from *Annwn*, while others have always been here."

"Is that what witches are?" I ask.

"Witches get a bad press. A lot of them were just innocent women with – let's say – exotic interests…"

"What about Mari Evans?"

"Her, I don't know about. It's possible she was nothing more than an innocent victim…"

"Or?" I say, stopping and turning to face Rebecca.

"Or she may have been the human form of something far older and far nastier."

I cross my arms and find myself nodding. I may need to tell Rebecca about my experience. But not now. I'll do it when the time is right.

She cocks her head to the side. "It's important you know that there are scarier things out there than the haunted stairwells and spooky stories you read about in your kiddy ghost books."

"I don't read kiddy ghost books…" My voice becomes deeper as if I'm trying to stress my point. She grins, and I clear my throat and also cock my head to the side. "So, what happens if you encounter one of these dark entities? Is it possible to defeat them?"

She shrugs. "Perhaps. If you know what you're dealing with." She walks on ahead and leaves me pondering.

"Where's your bike?" I ask as we approach my Chopper.

"Sorry, forgot to mention that." She shakes her head.

I realise I'll need to be a taxi driver. "Bloody hell, right." I step over to my bike and point to the seat. "You okay with a backie?"

She nods and lifts her leg over and sits back.

"Just hold on to me," I say, and her hands grab my side. I feel a little odd and my heart beats a bit faster and another part of my body tingles. Thankfully, I face away from her, otherwise she would see my cheeks redden. I'm not used to being so close to girls. Other than Hannah. Or before that, with Mum.

"I have done this before," she says.

"I just don't want you to fall off," I say, clearing my throat.

"I won't so long as you keep it steady."

CHAPTER 26

The ride is uneventful and we arrive at the churchyard a few minutes later to find Gwyn waiting for us.

He steps towards us with his arms crossed. "You made it then?"

"I said I would, didn't I?" Rebecca says and she places her hands on her hips. I sense a little tension between the medium and the sceptic, so I step between the two. "So, how do we do this?"

Rebecca surveys across the churchyard. "First things first, show me his grave."

"And then what?" Gwyn asks.

"And then you leave it to me."

Simple enough, I think. "Follow us."

We get to the grave and Rebecca looks around. "If we are in the right spot and he wants to communicate with you, then it should be possible to make contact. It's all about making sure we have the right means of hearing him."

"And how do we make sure of that?" Gwyn asks.

"That's what I do." She gives Gwyn a wink.

I scan the area. There is nothing out of the ordinary to report as the sun shines and birds call out from the branches of the green leafy yew trees above us. It's no different than the day before, apart from the Astley woman not being there. Rebecca takes out the skull from her bag, strokes it and then turns it towards her face like she's looking him in the eyes. Of course, the eyes are long gone. She whispers something and brings the skull close to her ear. She nods like it – he – is talking to her. I feel Gwyn grab my arm.

"This is fricking nuts," he whispers. But for me, it's the main event.

Her hand holding the skull drops to her waist and she turns to face us both.

"Right, we'll do it like this." She flicks the velvet cloth open and lays it out on the flat surface of Henry's grave like she's setting up a picnic. She places her *taid* in the centre and puts her hands around it. She leans over the skull and whispers something. I look over at Gwyn, and he rolls his eyes.

Rebecca lifts her head. "Henry. Henry Blythe. Are you there? Talk to me. We know you want to speak with us." She pauses and strokes the skull again. This is amazing to watch – to see somebody really trying to connect to the other side. I am aware of Gwyn trying to get my attention with his glances, but my eyes are fixed on what Rebecca is doing.

"Henry?" Her head lifts again. "No, I'm looking for Henry Blythe. Not you, sir. Madam, sorry, no. Henry, is that you?" She appears to be staring into the distance. "Henry, I sense you're there, but I can't hear your words. There's too much noise. Please, everyone be quiet. I need to speak to Henry."

I glance around and it's still just the three of us and the skull. There is no visible sign of a haunting, but the mood has changed. The birds have stopped singing and the trees above are filled with silent crows glaring down at us. The luscious leaves have faded, and the stark bony branches loom closer. My eyes connect with Gwyn's, and I point upwards, but he shakes his head unphased and unconvinced.

"Henry, please come to me. I can see you," she says. "Please, let him through. Stop pushing. I can listen to you all another time but right now I need to speak with Henry. Please stop pulling me.

Get away. Get away now. Ouch." Rebecca yelps and drops back onto the ground.

I bend over and put my hand on her shoulder. "You okay?"

She looks up at me and nods, but my mouth falls open when I see three long scratches have appeared on her face. "Bloody hell."

She appears shaken but remains calm. I glance over at Gwyn and see him staring with a dazed look.

"Are you okay to carry on?" I ask, my voice trembling.

She pushes me away and puts her fingers together to form a circle shape around the skull.

"*Taid*, please help me – I can't get through. There are too many voices. Too much anger and frustration. Please help me, *Taid bach*. You can give me the strength."

She leans in to look closely at the skull. "What – not here? Why not? Where then? Too dangerous – why?" She stops and turns her head to face Gwyn and then me.

"There's no use doing it here," she says. "Too many spirits in this place, and some of them are vicious and most of them are too full of beans."

"Full of beans?" Gwyn repeats, looking bewildered.

"Henry's voice is not strong enough. *Taid* says it's a lost cause. There's no way we'll get through."

"Damn it," I say. "Where can we get through to him?"

"*Taid* says there is a place."

Before she can tell us where, we hear another voice – one that gives me more dread than a hundred haunted houses.

"Oi oi, what fuckery is this? Having a little seance, are we?"

I turn around to see Horse and his two Goons ambling towards us. His torn jeans billow like curtains in a haunted house and his exposed thick arms swing furiously from his black T-shirt like they're powering his forward motion.

"See, lads, I told you it was these little gayboys who stole from us."

I look over at Gwyn and see the veins in his neck throbbing. At least we now know whether Horse had recognised us in the Jungle.

Horse's spikey hair looks wild, like he's been sleeping in the Eagle's Nest for the last few weeks. Pablo, the skinnier of his two Goons, has a cigarette in his mouth. Shag is like a big bear and – as thankful as I am that he's fully dressed this time – I'll never shake the image of his naked parts lying next to the other two.

"What do you want, Horse?" I ask.

"You pair of homos trespassed in my lair to help this little Gypsy bitch steal our skull."

"You had no right taking him," Rebecca says.

"Him? Fuck's sake, boys. For us, it's a trophy. But for the Gypo, it's a friend. Take *him* to bed at night, do you? Let him kiss your sweet spot?" He purses his lips and makes smooching noises.

"It's her *taid*, actually," Gwyn says.

"What the…?" Horse doesn't appear sure of how to respond.

"What are you doing here?" I ask, again.

"You cock gobblers spoiled my party; trespassed in the Eagle's Nest and took a possession of mine."

"It didn't belong to you," I say. "You stole it first. We took it back."

He stops smiling and steps closer. "I want it returned. Give it back, right fucking now."

I cross my arms and hold them tight against my body as I try to stop trembling. "You're not having it."

Horse gazes into my eyes. Despite being two years older, he is the same height as me. My hands have tensed into fists, like cement becomes stone, and I ready myself for the attack. I try to hide the terror I feel from being in the spotlight of his reptilian gaze.

"I'll have that skull whether you give it to me or not," he says. "Now the question you should be thinking about is not whether I take it. It's how severe my punishment will be for you and your little boyfriend here for trespassing in my lair and spoiling my party."

"Party?" Gwyn squeaks.

"You're not taking it," I say again.

"Get out of my way." Horse knocks me to the floor with the back of his hand, dipping me in darkness like a brush into black paint and I return an instant later to push myself up from the ground and taste blood in my mouth. I focus my vision and turn my head to see him lunge towards Rebecca. Gwyn – on the other side of the grave – has not moved an inch.

As he reaches over to grab the skull, Rebecca screams in a way that would deafen banshees; the loudest ear-piercing scream I've ever heard, and Horse freezes and turns to his Goons.

"I told you, boys," he chuckles. "These Gypos are full of spirit."

The three of them laugh like mindless hyenas, and he turns his attention back to Rebecca. "That is why I want the skull – I'm a huge fan. If I can't have that one, then I'll be needing another." He winks and Shag cackles behind him.

I wipe my mouth and see red streaks on the back of my hand. Deep inside, something tells me to run. We must get away or more blood will flow. But unexpectedly, somebody else makes themselves known by clearing their throat. Having just emerged from around the other side of the church is Sergeant Gatsby on his morning beat.

"Ahem," he repeats, and everyone looks over. "So, I hear screaming coming from the churchyard and surprise, surprise, who should I find but Mr Robert Chandler, and his two Goons entertaining. Are we all right here? Gwyn, aren't you supposed to be at the shop?"

I watch Horse's face and see him turn from monster to choirboy. Gwyn does not respond, and Horse is first to speak. "Sergeant Gatsby, so great to see you as always. I was just saying to the boys here, earlier, how lucky we are to have a brave and honest protector of the town like yourself."

"Horse, charming as always. What are you up to, eh? Searching for missing dogs, perhaps?" He looks to Rebecca. "Miss, are you okay? What happened to your face?"

"Yes, fine." She touches the scratches on her cheek. "We were just going, actually." She puts the wrapped skull away in her bag and starts walking.

Gatsby spies the object. "What've you got there?"

"Just a game," she replies. "Not important."

Gatsby's eyes dart across all of us and he frowns. "Right. Just an innocent playdate in the graveyard, was it? With Horse and his Goons?"

"Something like that." Rebecca turns her head. "Ned, Gwyn, are you coming?"

Gwyn follows her and I get to my feet and stride after them.

"Don't forget," the policeman calls after us. "There's still a child missing. You be on your guard in case there's someone dangerous out there."

The three of us nod, force smiles – painful in my case – and wave. Gatsby carries on speaking to Horse and the Goons. As we turn a corner around the side of the church I glance back and see Horse glaring at me with his teeth exposed. He winks and I know we haven't heard the end of this story.

None of us says a word until we get to the bikes.

"That was a good move, Rebecca," Gwyn says.

"We should get going," she says. "The copper won't keep their attention too long."

"We hadn't finished with Henry," I say. "You were about to tell us what your *taid* said to you."

"It was too busy here. Too many spirits competing for attention. Some of them, desperate. Dangerous." She reaches up and touches the scratches on her face. "Very hard to focus on one voice. We need to go somewhere else, where things are more focused, and we stand a better chance of connecting with him."

"Do you have somewhere in mind?" Gwyn asks.

"Yes," she says firmly.

"Alright," I say. "Let's get back to HQ and you can tell us where our next operation will take us."

CHAPTER 27

Mr B excitedly welcomes us into the shop when he sees we're not alone. "Oh, hello. You two have company now. Does this young lady like puzzles?"

"Dad, we don't have time…" Gwyn says before Rebecca responds.

"I do, actually," she says, shrugging her shoulders.

"Good. How's this: 'Cook a chop another way', five letters?"

"Can I see that?" She grabs the paper. "Cook a chop another way. Ah yes, it's 'poach'. It's an anagram of 'a chop'."

"Ha, indeed, it is. Indeed, it is." Mr B gives me a big smile. "Your friend here…"

"… Rebecca…"

"Thank you. Your friend here, Rebecca, is very welcome in future. As you are of course, Ned."

He cocks his head slightly and points to his cheek. "What happened to your face there, Rebecca?"

"This?" she says.

"She ran into a low-hanging branch before," I say and push her away from Mr B.

I bring my mouth next to Rebecca's ear. "I'd like to hear the answer to that question myself."

Gwyn follows us in, and I hear him telling his dad she's fine.

In the backroom, Rhys looks up from his book as we enter, while Rebecca's eyes open wide as she scans the full shelves.

"So, this is our new member?" he says peering over at Rebecca.

"Rebecca has amazing skills," I say.

"Fantastic," he says. "Finished at the churchyard already?"

I glance across at Rebecca. "Yeah. Ran into some difficulties…"

"Oh?" Rhys says.

"Seems the dead weren't playing ball and then Horse and the testicle twins turned up," I say.

"Oh," he says again.

Rebecca glances over while running her fingers over the spines of books in the Demonology section.

"This is Rhys," Gwyn says. "My brother."

"He gets us ready for investigations," I say, not certain whether she would know who Q was.

"I've heard about your research skills," Rebecca says, and Rhys sits back with a pleased look on his face. "You have some very interesting books here."

"Absolutely. Best collection of occult books in Wales," Rhys replies.

Rebecca picks up a few and turns them around to examine the back cover. She pulls out a book titled *The Book of Lies* and mouths the word *wow* to Rhys. He gives her a thumbs up. Meanwhile, Gwyn taps me on my shoulder. He seems nervous.

"What do we do about Horse?" he says. "He won't leave it like that."

"I know," I say. "But not much we can do about it now. There's no way he can have the skull back. Maybe we can make it up to him somehow. Or perhaps if we're lucky he'll forget about it."

"He won't forget about it," Gwyn says and rubs his chin. "You okay, by the way? For a second, I thought he had you out for the count."

"For a second, I think he did," I say. "Anyway, let's see where part two of the investigation will take us."

I look over at Rebecca and Rhys who are still discussing books and clear my throat. "Rebecca, we need to get planning," I say. "Where are we going next?"

"Right," she says. "We're going to *Cartref-Y-Gwynt*. It's an abandoned farmhouse in the hills. Do you know it?"

Gwyn and I glance at each other.

"Yes, we're familiar with the place," I say.

"Good."

"Why there, though?" Gwyn asks. "How is it better than the churchyard?"

She closes the old book in her hands and licks her lips. "I don't know why but there's something about that house. Whether it's the land on which it was built, the stones they used to build it, or something that happened there, I can't say. But what I do know is that many people in my community know about it. I went there a while ago with Father for a visit."

She stops briefly and seems lost in thought. Her gaze focuses up into the upper corner of the room.

"What do you mean, *there's something about that house*?" I ask.

"In the churchyard there were many voices – some of them desperate for attention. Lots of energy – more than I expected. Some of them were angry. It was difficult to hear one lone spirit amongst them. That wasn't just because we were in a place where many spirits had gathered, it was also because graveyards and cemeteries are often located in places where the barrier between this world and *Annwn* – the *Ffordd* – is less clear. More opaque, I guess."

"Like frosted glass?" I say.

"Yes, like frosted glass," she repeats. "You can make out many spirits on the other side, but the barrier makes it difficult to see or hear any of them clearly. Because of this, they used to think the spirits would be less likely to make direct contact, and therefore more likely to rest in peace. That was the belief, but I'm not sure it's that simple."

Having never heard this before, it blows my mind. Gwyn strokes his chin, thoughtfully, probably sceptically, while Rhys sits forwards and rubs his hands excitedly.

"You're saying graveyards are located where it's easier for the dead to stay dead?" Rhys says.

"You could put it like that," she says.

"But if the barrier is more difficult to cross, how could they hurt you?" Gwyn now crosses his arms.

"I guess some of them were strong enough," she says, stroking her hair. "The energy levels everywhere are crazy right now."

Gwyn nods slowly and fires me a look of disbelief but I ignore him.

"And the farmhouse, how does that compare to the graveyard?" I ask.

"The farmhouse is the opposite – a magnifying glass. There, the energy and will of the spirits can be amplified, be more focused. The right connection can be strong and crystal clear…"

"What if you make the wrong connection?" I ask.

Her face drops. "Let's just try and avoid that if we can."

CHAPTER 28

We arrive at the farmhouse after pushing our bikes up the hill and gaze at the mysterious building. I felt certain there was something strange about the place when we were here last, but Rebecca's explanation has blown me away. It's near twelve and all three of us are sweating heavily in the midday sun.

"Come on," I say, gesturing to the other two. "We'll show you the way in, Rebecca."

"You said you've been here before?" Gwyn says.

"Yes, last year," she says. "But that was in the autumn. It was cold and dark."

"It's fricking grim enough in summer…" he says.

"Why did you come here?" I ask.

"Abe wanted to try and speak with Ma," she says with a wistful smile.

"Abe is her dad," I say.

"Oh." Gwyn glances between the two of us awkwardly.

We arrive at the window at the back of the house, and I point to it. "Who wants to go first?"

"I'll go," Gwyn says.

"Do you have your inhaler this time?" I ask.

He pads his pocket and nods.

As he climbs through, I turn to Rebecca. "There's definitely something odd about this place."

"I know," she says. "For the *klewmeirw*, places like these can be intense. You should know."

"What do you mean, *I should know*?" I ask.

"You have some *klewmeirw* in you, I think?"

"I don't – I don't know…" She's caught me off guard. I'm not sure what to say.

"I think you do," she says, smiling. "It's why you see and feel things that other people don't."

My jaw drops and I'm unsure of how to respond but we're interrupted by Gwyn.

"Are you two coming or not?" he yells through the window.

"I'll go," Rebecca says.

She is nimble and leaps up onto the frame and in through the window in no time. I hear cracks as she steps in the sink, then it's my turn. Inside, I find Gwyn and Rebecca staring into the hole in the parlour. She glances in my direction as I enter the room.

"You had quite an adventure here," she says.

"Yep," I say. Since entering, I've started feeling weird – dizzy may be more accurate – and I feel the shadows calling out to me but not with sound, with something else, maybe some unseen line that connects us; hooks stuck in my flesh and they're trying to reel me in. I keep thinking about what Rebecca said. Could I have some of her abilities? None of our experiments before suggested I did but maybe we were doing them wrong. Anyway, for now I'm keen for us to get going with this investigation so I stay in the light.

"How will you connect with Henry if the connections are strong here?" I ask.

"Well," Rebecca says, "if he's reaching out to connect like you say he is then it shouldn't be too hard. It's like tuning a radio until you get a clear signal."

"So, you need the right frequency?" Gwyn asks.

"Kind of," she says.

"You don't need to go down there, do you?" I ask, pointing into the hole.

"No, shouldn't need to. The space at the end of the room feels strong enough." She opens her bag and takes out the skull. "What do you say, *Taid bach*?"

She glances at Gwyn and then me. "Just give me a moment here, will you?"

Gwyn and I wander off. We go up the stairs and see if there is anything new to report. We're both careful with where we stand to make sure the floorboards are solid enough.

"What excuses do you think she'll have for us this time?" Gwyn asks.

"What do you mean?" I say.

"Bit convenient that things didn't happen this morning, wasn't it?" he says.

"But we were interrupted by that psycho," I say as I stroke the bedroom wall with my fingertips.

"You heard her," he says. "She was giving up before he turned up. No doubt it'll happen again here."

"Don't start this now, Gwyn. She's no faker…" Before I finish, we hear a howling from downstairs.

"Rebecca." Gwyn turns to me with wide eyes, and we leg it back down the stairs to the parlour.

She is sat cross-legged facing the wall in the dark end of the room. We cannot see her face, but we can hear her whimpering. I bound over to her and see her staring at the wall. She looks petrified and she holds the skull tight in her hands.

"Shit, what's wrong with her, Ned?" Gwyn asks.

I shake my head and touch her shoulder. Her whole body is trembling – vibrating almost.

"Rebecca," I say. "Rebecca, are you okay?"

She doesn't respond. I move forward and kneel next to her. I wave my hands in front of her eyes and then click my fingers, but she continues to stare ahead.

"Rebecca, come back to us." I grab her shoulders and try shaking her, but her body is tense and frozen in its position. "It's no use. Something's got her."

I hear Gwyn wheezing and look up to see him breathing hard. "Oh no, not you as well."

He holds up his hands and takes three puffs on his inhaler. "I'll. Be. Okay." His words are staggered across the deep breaths.

"Oh, this bloody place," I say and glare at the walls like I'm keen for the house to know how I feel. From the dark end of the room, I hear a muffled thundering rumble from the shadows.

"Do you hear that?" I say.

"What?"

"It's like a high-pitched waterfall. It's like…" I don't finish what I say but what I hear sounds like screams from many voices in the darkness. "Doesn't matter…" I shake it off and turn my attention back to Rebecca. I clap several times until my palms are stinging.

"Try grabbing the skull," Gwyn says.

When I do, it's like touching an electricity wire and I feel a surge of something attack my hand leaving it numb.

"What happened?" Gwyn says.

I shake my head and rub my hands together. I try again and grab her wrists – trying to pull them away from the skull without touching it, but they're fixed like they're glued to it. Him. Whatever.

Gwyn bends over next to me. "Her face is white, Ned. Like she's seen a…" He doesn't end his sentence.

"I can see."

A tear streams down her cheek over the scratch she got this morning.

"We need to do something," Gwyn says, his voice quivering. "She's suffering. Whatever it is, it looks real. She… she can't be acting."

I know what we must do.

"We have to go and get her dad," I say. "He'll know what to do."

"From the site?"

"Yeah." I place my hand on her shoulder and squeeze gently.

"We can't leave her," Gwyn says.

"You can't go, mate," I say. "If you have another attack…"

"I know," he says.

"Will you be okay staying with her?" I ask.

"Yep – go." He crosses his arms and holds his body tight. I give him a slap on the arm, turn on my heels and leg it out of there.

CHAPTER 29

I almost fall out of the window on my way out. I bounce my bike down the bumpy track of the farm lane – falling off a couple of times. I pedal as hard as I can when I hit the road. Through town and across the High Street, I swerve around cars and vans. On Lôn Werdd, I overtake a tractor pulling a trailer stacked high with small square bales and hear the farmer yell something at me through the cabin window. I pedal until my legs are burning red-hot pokers. When I get close to the Travellers' site, I begin to worry that her father might not be there, and I might need to head out across the strawberry fields to search for him. Gwyn would panic if I took too long, and when he panicked, his asthma became worse. I need to get back to the farmhouse, pronto. It's entirely possible that both their lives depend on it.

It's quiet at the Travellers' site. I try and see the strawberry fields in my mind's eye in case I need to go searching. As I dump my bike, I see a wild-looking old man sat on a tractor tyre telling stories with his hands to three young children; it looks like he is scaring them, but they seem to be enjoying it. I run over and – between breathless gasps – ask him about Abraham. The children appear annoyed as I interrupt their story. The old man points to a place behind the bus and I follow his directions. On the other side of the huge vehicle, I find three cars – each with their bonnets open. I can see someone has their head in one – and I recognise his grunts – Abraham. I run over, slowing as I get near and start to wonder how he will react when I tell him what's happened. I clear my throat but before I say anything, he turns to look, and I can tell he knows instantly that something is up.

"Is it Rebecca?"

"Yes," I say, rubbing my hands nervously.

"At the farmhouse?"

I nod. "It's like she's in a trance."

He takes his head out from underneath the bonnet of the car and grabs a rag from the side. "Ah bollocks, she's stuck. We'd better get going. Come with me."

I point to my bike, not sure exactly how he intends for us to return to the farmhouse.

"You can leave that here. Come on, this way will be quicker."

I follow Abraham between the cars, and we dash along a path lined with stinging nettles on each side. We reach a small open space where four motorbikes are lined up.

"This one," he says, striding over to the bike on the end, which has *Triumph* written on it in a dull silver lettering. He climbs on and pushes the bike forward to release the stand. He turns a key and kicks down on his foot causing the engine to roar to life.

"What are you waiting for?" he says. "Get on."

I stare at him for a second before remembering the urgency of the moment. I reach over and pull myself onto the back.

"You have to hold on to me now, tightly, alright?"

"Okay," I reply gently and too quietly for him to hear.

"Hold on," he repeats more loudly, and he turns the throttle. It feels like the bike is taking off and I grab the man's waist more firmly. In seconds, we are on the road. We take a route through the backstreets and avoiding the centre of town. I wonder whether we should be wearing helmets and how badly hurt we'd be if we came off the bike right now. Then, I see people glaring at us from the pavement and I put my head down, hoping that no one I know sees us. Hannah wants me to keep a low profile, and I doubt she'd consider riding around the town on a vintage motorbike with a scary Gypsy man to be keeping a low profile.

The track up to the farm is bumpy as Abraham weaves in and around the holes, but it's more fun than trying to pedal my Chopper up this route. By the time we reach the farmhouse, I am sore and glad to get off the motorbike. We head to the back of the building, and I climb in through the window first. Right behind me is Abraham and he seems familiar with the place as well.

"This way," I say inside.

"Ned, is that you?" Gwyn calls out.

In the parlour, I see that Rebecca has not moved an inch since I left. Gwyn sits in front of her; he has his inhaler in his hand. His face is ashen, and his eye are bulging like huge golf balls.

"Thank fuck you're back."

"Everything okay?" I ask. I see his hands are trembling.

He shakes his head and opens his mouth, but before he can say anything, Abraham has pushed me aside and is crouching down next to Rebecca.

"Dear Lord, girl. You know better than to get yourself stuck."

"Stuck?" I say.

"Yeah. The signal to the other side is strong here, and something has pulled her in so she can't get away. It's got hold of her tight."

Abraham looks closely into his daughter's eyes. "For people like Rebecca, the dead are like magnets. They try and pull you close when they connect. Places like these are tough for the *klewmeirw*."

That certainly explains a few things, I think. "What do we do?"

"I need to get her out of this house. Her breathing is already very shallow. If she doesn't leave this place soon…"

"Then what?" I ask.

"Then she might never leave."

He looks at Gwyn then me, each in turn, like he's assessing what we make of all this madness. He tries to pry the skull from Rebecca's hands. Rebecca holds on tight to the object, but he persists, and he strains until it is released, and he puts it in her satchel.

"Right, lads. I'm gonna need your help now."

Abraham lifts Rebecca in his arms and stands up. He beckons us to follow him. At the kitchen window, he stops.

"You two are going to have to climb outside ahead of me and be there to receive her."

"What?" I say.

"I'm going to pass her through to you," he says.

"I got that," I say. "I just don't know how we're going to carry her on the other side."

"You are strong lads," Abraham says. "You can do it."

We both climb through and stand outside the window nervously. Gwyn rubs his hands together and takes another puff on his inhaler.

"What happened in there?" I ask.

"I – erm – saw something…" he says. His tone reminds me of the mayor of Amity Island in Jaws when he speaks to Chief Brody at the hospital and he's full of remorse and confusion about having kept the beaches open and allowing the shark to eat the man in the dinghy. I, however, cannot contain my excitement.

"Oh shit, something paranormal? What? What did you see?"

"I don't…" he starts but again we are interrupted by Abe who taps on the glass of the window. He's sat on the sink, with Rebecca leaning on his legs.

"I want to hear everything," I say. "But for now, you hold the window open. I'll guide her down onto the ground."

This is what we do. Her dad strains and holds on tight to her upper body. He lowers her down and – below – I try and hold her up and cushion her fall. I wrap my arms around her legs, but she is heavier than she looks.

"Have you got her?" Abraham yells as he tries his hardest not to drop her.

"I'm trying," I say, through gritted teeth. But the weight grows too quickly. "Gwyn, can you help a bit?"

Gwyn tries to keep the window open with his elbow while grabbing onto Rebecca's clothes and sharing some of the load.

Abraham is now hunched over and hanging out of the window. "I can't hold on much longer, lads," he grunts.

I try and get a good hold of her legs around her knees as I sense she is dropping faster.

"She's coming down," Abraham yells.

"Grab her arms," I say to Gwyn.

"I'm trying," he says desperately.

"I'm losing her," Abraham says, and Rebecca falls through my arms down onto the grass and pulls down Gwyn and me with her. Somehow, we all drop like skittles and end up rolling down the incline away from the house. At the bottom of the small hill, we all stop. To my side I hear groaning and look over and see that Rebecca's lips are moving.

"Rebecca." I jump up and lean in close. Her eyes are shut but she whispers something. From the house I hear Abraham huffing and puffing as he scrambles out of the window. I close my eyes and focus on her soft voice – breaths barely shaped into words. I hear what she says and cannot believe my ears. I move closer to her mouth and hear the same words again.

"Terry's alive," she whispers.

I glance at Gwyn. "She says Terry's alive."

"What?" His mouth opens so wide I can see his tonsils.

I can hear more words and drop my head again.

"Under... the... bridge," she whispers.

"Say that again, Rebecca?" I say.

"Under the bridge," she repeats before falling silent. Her eyes have opened but she's not with us yet. I sit back as Abraham arrives and examines her.

"What is it?" Gwyn asks.

I rub my hands and take a deep breath. "She said, *under the bridge*. Must be something there. What if it's him? We need to go."

Gwyn silently nods and Abraham strides over and scoops up his daughter in his arms.

"Will she be okay?" I ask.

"Yes, but I need to get her home now."

"We have to…" I start to speak but Abraham cuts across.

"You lads do what you need to, but I'm taking my girl home."

Gwyn and I glance at each other, and we follow Abraham over to the motorbike. He places her up in front of himself on the bike and then places the satchel strap around her to keep her close. Before he starts the engine, he looks over to us.

"Did she help?"

"Massively," I say.

"Good."

"There's more," I say. "I mean, we have more questions. She couldn't tell us much."

He raises his hand. "Right, but maybe give her some time to rest, okay?"

"But things are moving fast…"

"She needs to rest." Abraham speaks with a firmer voice this time.

I nod and bite my lip.

The engine on the motorbike starts up and they both leave. We watch as they carefully navigate around the potholes and grassy mounds of the dirt track.

I turn to face Gwyn. "Now tell me. What the hell did you see in there?"

He starts shaking his head again. "I'm not sure, Ned."

"Well, what happened?" I ask. "Tell me everything."

"Not much for the first few minutes after you left," he says. "She was quiet, and nothing changed."

"And then?" I ask impatiently.

Gwyn crosses his arms and holds them close to his body like he's trying to keep himself warm. "She started moaning and her body started shaking like something was grabbing her and moving her about."

"And what did you do?"

"I put my hands on her shoulders and tried to hold her still," he says. "She stopped for a moment, and I thought it was okay. I got up and walked around her slowly, trying to calm myself down. That was when…" He pauses.

"What?" I ask with my arms up in the air.

"This huge dark figure – like a man's shadow – came out of the wall fast like it leapt out and stood over Rebecca and it reached out its hands and had them over her throat. She started choking. Ned, this thing was trying to kill her."

"Bloody hell," I say. "What did you do?"

"I tried to push it away – I waved my arms at it, but they just went through it, like I was punching smoke. I was panicking. There was nothing I could do. This thing had hold of her and I could hear her gasping and choking and there was nothing I could do."

"What happened?" I ask, gaping.

"That's the craziest part. Suddenly, a beam of bright light comes from the skull – *Taid* – and it's aimed directly at the shadow figure. It's like a torch has been switched on. This light somehow pushes the shadow away from her and back until it fades into the wall."

"Shit," I say. "Then what happened?"

"Then, it was calm. I checked on her and she seemed okay. Well, the same as before. That is how you found us."

I bend over and hold my head in my hands. It's almost too much to take in.

"Gwyn, you had a bloody paranormal encounter. You saw a ghost. Or something."

"Did I?" he says, unsure. "I don't know. Could it have been something else?" He stares at the ground, looking shocked and confused. The mayor of Amity Island is with me again and he's seen the bloody shark with his own eyes.

"The sceptic is now a witness," I say.

Gwyn shakes his head in disbelief. He'll need time to get his head around this. I look back at the house and remember we still have an investigation underway. "I know this is all nuts, but we need to get going," I say. "Are you okay to go?"

He takes a deep breath. "The bridge?"

"Yes, the bridge." I look over at Gwyn's bike. "Shit, my bike's still at the Travellers' site. You're going to have to give me a backie."

Gwyn half stares at me confused and dizzy like he's just climbed out of the washing machine. I realise he's in no state to be cycling. "Actually, let me give you a backie," I say. "We need to go now. If Terry's alive then this is huge, and we might be the only ones who can save him."

CHAPTER 30

Betws Bridge is where the A52 crosses the Gwion River. To reach it we fly through the town centre and down to the end of *Tangwlyst* Street. I pedal hard and Gwyn holds me tight, so he doesn't fall off but also, I can't stop thinking that maybe he's in shock – maybe he's scared. Usually, he'd be more vocal but what he saw seems to have affected his tongue. I won't slow down though. Seeing Terry's face on lamp posts, I know his life is in our hands. It's up to us to save him, wherever he is.

We get to the busy main road, and I stop the bike. Cars fly by in both directions, and I realise there's no way we can cycle any further. We both get off and I hand Gwyn his bike. We stride ahead, staying as close to the edge of the road as we can. On the near side of the bridge, I gesture with my hand. "Down here."

Through the trees I can make out the white rapids of the river. Between passing cars, I can hear its rumble. Gwyn drops his bike next to a tree. There is no path here so we must carefully tread through the underbrush, scrambling over broken branches and avoiding prickly thorns.

"Slow down, Ned," Gwyn says. I look back and gesture to him to hurry up. He still looks pale. The barbs scratch my legs and arms as I push through, but I won't stop. Away from the road, the sound of traffic begins to fade, and the river's roar starts to fill my ears. I climb over a fallen tree and pull off some bramble branches that have become stuck to my arm before turning to see the river. I glance each way and scan across the area ahead. The route through the trees has taken us away from the road and right up to the water.

"See anything?" Gwyn yells as he approaches.

"Nothing yet." I point along the river in the direction of the bridge. "This way."

Gwion River moves fast. The water comes down from the mountain, passes under the main road and then snakes its way along the edge of the town until it reaches Ogyn Lake. We climb through the branches and over boulders along the riverside trying to stay out of the thicket as best we can.

"Been meaning for us to do an investigation here," I say. "Well, up on the bridge. People have seen a hitchhiker who disappears after being picked up. A girl was hit by a car when she was walking home. She fell down here."

Gwyn nods and bites his lip. Does he believe now, I wonder?

"They didn't find the body for weeks. She was carried all the way to Ogyn Lake."

Gwyn doesn't say a thing.

"You okay?" I ask. "You know, what you saw in the farmhouse was bloody cool. You shouldn't let it freak you out."

He shrugs and points down the river.

"Okay," I say, and we carry on.

Through the trees we see the darkness of the underpass nearing between the branches. The entrance is lined with thick shrubbery.

"Shit, I thought it would be easier to get in from this side," I say.

I examine the wall of green ahead of us, searching for a way through.

"There," I say. Near the ground, right next to the water, is a small opening.

"Bring your shrinking pills, did you?" Gwyn finally speaks up. I give him a wry smile and then lower myself down. I inspect the gap and can see a way through of sorts.

"We can do it," I say. Gwyn sighs.

To get through I get down on my front and start to crawl. My legs are sore from bramble scratches, and I have stinging-nettle rashes on my hands. A voice in my head is telling me to stop and go home but I cannot yet. We're close to finding something very important. As I wiggle my way through, the back of my T-shirt catches on something, and I reach around to release it so I can move on.

"Almost there," I yell. "Keep yourself low and you'll get through no problem." It may even be easier for Gwyn and his smaller, skinnier frame.

A large thorn-covered branch blocks my way out of the opening. I try and push it with my fingers without spiking myself but each time it springs back like it wants to smack me in the face. I pull it down towards me so that I can snap it but it's far too thick and I'm unable to get a good grip because of the thorns.

"Why have you stopped?" Gwyn asks.

"Cos there's a bastard tree in my way." I grind my teeth. "Bugger it," I yell and push the branch down and climb over it. The barbs pull on my flesh and I see a bunch of thin red lines appearing on my arms. Then they stick into my body, and I yelp in pain. "Bloody fricking bushes."

"Ned, are you alright?" Gwyn calls out.

I take a deep breath. "Almost."

I get most of my body over it and find myself slowly coming out. On the other side, the ground under the bridge is covered in small pebbles, soil and patches of grass. But crucially, there's no more of the thicket.

"It's all clear on this side," I say. "There's nothing here. Absolutely nothing." I look back at the hole where Gwyn will shortly emerge from. "Hang on, stay where you are for a sec. I need to do something."

I look around and spot a large rock. I kneel next to it and start to push. My hands screech at me in pain, and I see that my fingers and arms are covered in scratches and open cuts. I take a deep breath before starting again. I push the rock up against the gap in the bush. Then I grab the end of my enemy branch, careful to avoid the thorns, and pull it back over and around the rock. I let go and the heavy stone holds it in place.

"That seems to work," I say. "You can come through now."

I turn on my heels and examine the space. Overhead, I hear the rumble of traffic crossing the bridge. Underneath, it looks like the area was cleared of all greenery a long time ago. The soil under the pebbles that cover the ground is hard and dry. On the other side of the river, the space is the same. Between, the river runs fast and forms rapids around a large pillar in the middle of the water. That is when I see it.

"Is that what I think it is?" Gwyn says, now standing next to me.

"It's a bag," I say. "A holdall bag."

One of the red handles is caught on the edge of the pillar and the pressure of the water pushes against it, holding it in place.

"Looks like a HEAD bag." Gwyn turns to face me. "That's what Terry had."

I nod. This must be why we were sent here.

"What's it doing in the river?" Gwyn asks. "He disappeared by the church."

"Someone must've dumped it," I say. "What better place is there to make something disappear in this town? You toss it in the river and then it's carried off into the deepest, darkest parts of the lake, like that girl's body."

"Whatever the case, it's not going to be there for long," Gwyn says.

"We're going to have to grab it somehow," I say.

"Whoa, what?" Gwyn glares at me with his arms crossed. "Why don't we go and tell the police?"

I walk over to the water's edge and look down. "How long did it take us to get here? By the time we make it there and back, the bag will be long gone, and chances are we'll never see it again."

"Ned, there's no way we'll get it."

I turn to face Gwyn. "What if it has evidence on it? Fingerprints or fibres or something?"

"Shit, Ned. That's crazy."

I can see that Gwyn knows I've made up my mind. He sighs. "You can't swim there – you'll disappear in the current."

I glance around the place, searching for ideas. "What we need is a rope. There's no way I can jump it – that's like four or five yards."

I notice Gwyn is staring at something near the other end. "What about a bridge?"

"Huh?"

"Come with me." Gwyn dashes off, and I follow behind.

"Look," he says. On the floor are three long plastic pipes. "Our bridge."

I can feel a grin rising on my face. "Gwyn, you're a genius."

Each pipe is over six yards at least in length and made of thick, strong plastic.

"Water company must have left them here," he says. "You'll need two of them at least to climb across on. You'll never balance on one."

They're heavy, and it takes both of us to drag each one over to the water's edge. The pillar is stone and the central base splits where it emerges from the water forming two separate columns. If we're lucky, the space in between will not only support the two pipes out of the water but it'll also hold them together so I can climb across.

"Right," I say. "You start pushing it out over the water. Try holding it down so it doesn't topple in the water. I'll use my belt to try and lift it as much as I can."

"Okay."

I take off my belt and loop it around the pipe. I grab both ends tightly and turn my head and nod to Gwyn to start pushing it out. Slowly, Gwyn starts feeding it out over the water. I pull on the belt and after it extends out a yard or so, I start to feel the weight.

"We okay, Gwyn?"

"Yep," he says.

"Keep going."

Another yard and the weight now pulls hard on my arms. Gwyn sits on the pipe and tries to edge it out slowly, using his weight to try and provide a counterbalance and stop it from dropping into the river.

"We're halfway there," I say through gritted teeth.

"I'm not sure if we can hold it," Gwyn says spitting his words.

"Just keep going," I say.

As we make another yard, my arms tremble under the stress. Gwyn continues to push.

"One more yard to go." I take a deep breath. "Push it. Push it now or it's lost." The pipe makes it all the way over the water and drops onto the pillar. We both collapse onto the floor, panting.

"You okay?" I ask.

Gwyn pulls out his inhaler, takes two puffs and then nods.

I give him a minute or so. I stand up and rub my sore, bloody hands together. "Ready for round two?"

He closes his eyes and nods. We start the same process again, but this time realise that we can place most of the weight of the second pipe onto the first.

"That's it," I say. "This way is easier. Take your time and I'll keep it balanced."

I need to keep it steady and be ready to take the weight fully at any moment. We push all the way until it lands firmly with a satisfying thud onto the area between the two columns, next to the first pipe. The narrow space nicely wedges them together. I give Gwyn a thumbs up and a smile. He is breathing heavily.

"I didn't think that would work," he says.

I chortle, which turns into a cough. "Now comes the fun part," I say.

I tie my belt tightly around both pipes so that they hold together.

"You're going to crawl over?" Gwyn asks.

"I think it might be easier to sit on it and push myself along," I say, staring at the makeshift bridge.

"Are you still sure you want to do this, Ned? You can't fall in the water."

I look down at the rushing white torrent below. "I must. There's no other way."

He nods and bites the inside of his cheek.

I crouch down and test the strength of the pipes before sitting on them and letting my legs dangle off the side. I hear the rushing water underneath and take a deep breath. My thoughts turn to the hitchhiker and a strange feeling comes to me: somehow, I know she wasn't killed by the car – she drowned in the river and her last breath was taken in the cold foam beneath me. I shake my head to try and forget so I can focus on crossing the river, but she won't leave me, she's still here, I'm certain of it, and it's lonely here.

"Can't stop now," I say aloud, and I speed up.

Edging myself along is easy enough – both pipes are smooth. Too smooth in fact, and I realise how easy it would be for me to slip over into the fast river. I can swim, of course. I got my twenty-five-metre badge last year at the leisure centre, so as a skill I would give myself a six. But this water would take me if I fell in. I'd likely disappear in the current and be lost in the lake like the hitchhiker. I'd join her here forever.

I gaze at the bag as I move along the pipes. Grabbing it could mean the difference between finding Terry alive and – well – not finding him at all. There's no way I can lose it. I sense the pipes bending under my weight. I turn around and glance at Gwyn and he looks worried, but he often does. He says something that I cannot hear over the roar of the water but makes an okay symbol with his hand and I carry on. I'm getting near now and I start to move faster.

As I reach touching distance of the pillar, I stretch and grab one of the concrete columns. I pull myself up onto the pillar base and look around. There's a narrow ledge around the bottom. The bag has become hooked on the concrete block in a spot where it has split and part of it sticks out. I move my feet carefully along the ledge. The bag is caught on the other side, so I slowly make my way around one of the two columns. This proves difficult as the ledge is wet and slippery. I move at a snail's pace and think through every tiny movement. The bag is now right next to my foot and all I need to do is reach down and grab it. I stop for a moment. I cannot see Gwyn's face, but I imagine he is holding his wheezy breath and barely able to watch what I am doing – the worrywart.

I hold on tight to the column and lower myself. My left hand lets go and I reach below and touch the cold, wet handle of the bag. I crane my neck to see how to release it. It's hooked on the jagged rock, and I should be able to gently shuffle it off. I take another look and push it further away until suddenly – there it is – I have the strap fully in my hand but as this happens, the water takes it, and the bag pulls me into the freezing water. The shock of the cold snaps my teeth closed, and I howl. Somehow, as I slip down, the hand that I had around the column lands onto a metal handle on the concrete. I still have hold of the bag but it's pulling hard on me. I'm fighting with all my strength. It wants to take me with it to Ogyn Lake. I cannot let go of it – it's too important – but I don't know how long I can hold on. I am like a chain link that is slowly being loosened and will soon break.

"Ned, up here." I hear Gwyn call out from somewhere.

I turn my head and see he is above me on the pipes having crawled across.

"Let go of the bag," he yells.

"No." I shake my head in the water.

"It's taking you with it. Let go of it." Water streams around me but I still hear his anger.

"No. Only... connection... we have. Must... help... Terry." Talking is a chore as the cold water leaves me breathless. I try and pull on the bag, thinking that if I can only get it over to Gwyn then he can take it, but I can't. The only strength I have left is keeping me from being swept away by the river.

"Keeping everyone safe is not your job," he says. "Let go of the bag and take my hand." Gwyn now leans over and tries to reach down to me.

"No," I say again. "I. Just. Need. To. Pull. It. Close."

"Let go of the fricking bag before you drown." Gwyn is screaming and I see the terror in his eyes. I am now at breaking point. I either hold on to the bag and get washed away into the darkness or I let go of it. I remember the hitchhiker again and I'm overwhelmed by a feeling of suffocating in a cold and black twisting torrent. I feel what she felt in her last moments. She's giving me a warning – let go or face the same end as she did and stay here with her in the freezing loneliness. Wait, does she mean let go of the bag or let go of the metal handle? Does she want to save me or is she after company?

"Ned!" Gwyn howls my name. "If you drown, who will save Terry?"

That's it, I let go of the bag and my roar echoes underneath the bridge. I swing my arm around and grab Gwyn's hand. As he pulls me in underneath the pipes, I realise the metal handle I had hold of is a rung on a ladder. I let go of Gwyn's hand and point to the ladder. I get my feet up onto the other rungs and step up. The ladder is directly beneath the pipes, so I reach up onto the ledge and then onto our home-made bridge. As I lift my leg over the pipes, and sit down, Gwyn puts his hand on my shoulder.

"Alright?" he asks.

I nod. I am shivering, numb and exhausted, but I am okay.

"Let me go back first," he says. "I'm not sure these things will hold both our weights. Try not to drown while I'm gone."

I keep nodding. I look down the river to see where the bag has gone. There is no sign of it. I sigh.

"Your turn," Gwyn yells across the river.

I start to push myself back along the pipes. Being soaking wet means I slide along them more easily. I hold on tight and move across quickly. When I reach the riverbank, Gwyn grabs me and pulls me off the pipes and onto my back. We both lie quietly next to each other. After catching my breath, I look over at Gwyn. "Why the hell did you do that?"

CHAPTER 31

Gwyn stiffens and moves his hand to his chest. "Do what?" he says. "Save you?"

"Make me let go of the bag." I punch the ground. "I had it. I had it in my hand."

"The fricking water was taking it away," he says, "and you with it, dickhead. There's no way you could've kept hold of it."

I shake my head desperately. "Bloody hell, Gwyn. It was our only chance. The only thing Rebecca told us, and we bloody well lost it."

"Ned, you could've drowned."

"And what about Terry," I say. "What happens to him now?"

Gwyn cocks his head to the side. "Why are you being like this?"

"Because you screwed up our only chance." As soon as I've said this, I regret it.

He grits his teeth. "Me? I'm the one that saved your obsessed arse. I'm the one who follows you around on these stupid investigations."

As he speaks, his nostrils flare and his hands shake like he doesn't know what to do with them. "I'm the one who stayed with Rebecca and watched her get attacked by some fricking

I-don't-know-what. Today has been one weird fricking thing after another, and I'm done with this shit." He gets up and heads over to the hole at the bottom of the thicket from where we came in. I get up and kick the pipes and scream. My voice makes a satisfying noise as it bounces off the walls of the underside of the bridge. The edge of the pipes slips off the riverbank into the water, and I lose my belt.

I crouch down and stare into the water. I've definitely lost my belt.

"Shit," I say and purse my lips and blow.

I look over to the thicket where Gwyn is huffing and puffing and swearing loudly as he tries to crawl through. Poor lad is freaked out after the farmhouse. I shouldn't blame him for trying to help. I approach him slowly and look down at his feet, which are sticking out from under the bush.

"Are you stuck?" I ask.

"What gave you that impression?" he scoffs and wriggles around roaring. "I hate this fricking tree."

I rub my face and kneel next to him. "I shouldn't have blamed you," I say. "I just really wanted to get that bag."

He sighs. "We'll find another way," say the feet.

"Yeah. Maybe." I stroke my chin. "You're really stuck down there, aren't you?"

He kicks the ground with both feet and stops. "Can you help?"

We make it out from underneath the bridge eventually and follow the route back out of the woods onto the main road where we find Gwyn's bike. We walk along the side of the busy A52 back onto *Tangwlyst* Street. There, we stop for a second and Gwyn turns to face me.

"What do we do now?" he asks.

"We need to see Rebecca again," I say. "But her dad probably won't let us near her."

He puts his hands on his hips. "Do you think we should talk to the police?"

"What do we tell them – that a dead Englishman told a Gypsy girl with ancient superpowers and a talking skull that Terry's alive?" Would that be too long a title for a horror film, I wonder?

"Right. What about the bag? That's more – erm – believable."

"Chances are we've lost it in that bloody lake," I say. "No one will ever see it again."

On the way back into town, Gwyn gives me a backie this time. It seems much later in the day and we're both flat and tired. Gwyn must return to his dad's shop before he can head home, and I tell him that I'll walk from there. Before he goes in, he stops, and we stare at each other. I need to ask him something and I think he knows.

"Crazy day," I say and Gwyn nods and glances at the shop.

"So, do you believe me now?" I ask. "About all of it? What I saw and what's out there?"

"I don't know," he says. "I didn't ever doubt you. I just thought what happened to your mum maybe influenced what you believed. Like you convinced yourself there was something there because you had to blame something."

"I didn't," I say. "There was something real and you saw something similar today."

He shakes his head. "I just don't know what to make of that yet."

"Gwyn," I say. "You saw a ghost. You saw a bloody evil phantom and you saw it trying to kill Rebecca."

He closes his eyes and rubs his forehead. "Ned, it makes no sense. How could anything like that exist? There's no place for it in a rational world."

"We don't live in a rational world," I say. "We live in a haunted world – in a town that's possessed by something nasty. Something that'll do harm to the living at any chance it gets."

"I just can't get my head around it." He looks up and I can see tears in his eyes.

"Maybe you need time," I say. "But work on it. We have a mission to complete, and a kid's life depends on it."

He nods and takes a deep breath. "Just don't get yourself killed in the process as well."

"I'll try," I say and force a smile.

Gwyn's dad taps on the window and gestures for him to go in. He raises his hand and I wave back.

"We'll talk about this again tomorrow," I yell, and I watch him saunter inside with his head down and his shoulders hanging low.

CHAPTER 32

I get home and enter the kitchen to find Hannah stood by the stove stirring something in a saucepan and Dad sat by the table. The television is on, and both are silent.

"Why are you wet?" Hannah asks.

"Long story," I say.

She stares at me, and I look over at Dad then back at her with a confused face. I point to him and then extend out my hands. She shakes her head. I walk out of the room on my way upstairs and Hannah follows me and taps me on my shoulder.

"He's feeling sorry for himself after the telling off from Auntie Val." She speaks softly, almost whispering.

"Has he stopped writing?" I ask.

"Lost his mojo, it seems," she says.

"Mojo? What do you mean?" I cross my arms.

"He's lost his inspiration. His creativity. Whatever you call it, he's been feeling sorry for himself and has sat there for most of the day."

I sigh. "Right."

"To be honest," she says, "I preferred it when he was in and out of the shed. This browbeaten behaviour is even more annoying than the obsessed writer."

I pull the T-shirt away from my chest. The warm air is making my damp clothes feel uncomfortable. "What do we do then?" I ask.

"I don't know. I'm tired of giving pep talks. I wish he'd pull himself out of this and start being a dad again." She looks at my shirt and narrows her eyes. "Why are you wet?"

"I, erm… Horse was pelting passers-by with water balloons, and I got hit."

"Horse was? You need to stay out of his way. That lad and his Goons are trouble."

"You don't need to tell me." I turn on my heels and carry on in the direction of the stairs.

"Dinner will be ready in five minutes," she yells. "Come back down as soon as you've changed."

When I return, both Dad and Hannah are sat at the table. There is steam rising from the bowl next to my empty seat.

"Tomato soup and buttered toast," Hannah says.

"Mmm." I lick my lips.

Dad stares at the television. I glance from him to Hannah.

"Dad's not been writing today," she says.

"Oh," I say, blowing on my soup. "Why's that, Dad?"

Dad does not answer. His head turns away from the television and then he looks down. He lets out a deep, low rumble.

"I have fallen down," he says. "Down a very dark and bottomless hole."

Hannah and I exchange glances

"I am alone and without a voice or any light or spark of creativity." He raises his head and gapes at both of us. "Until I can find my way out of this hole, I fear there will be no writing."

"You could always go back to work while you wait for the inspiration to return," Hannah says. "A change of scenery and a different focus might help." She clears her throat and the tone of her voice changes. "And – erm – you know that we need the money."

He pinches the skin on his throat and nods. "Yes, I know it's all on me to deliver. I am the workhorse here, aren't I?"

"No, you're our parent," Hannah says. "Our only parent and we need you, Dad, to get back on your feet."

"Get back on my feet," he says and stands up. "You're right, *cariad*. And that is what I will do. Let's see if I can pull myself out of this hole. Sitting here will help no one."

He picks up his spoon and bowl and walks out of the back door leaving Hannah and I sat in the kitchen with both our jaws dropped.

"That man…" Hannah stands up and strides over to the kitchen window. She shakes her head and bangs her fist on the sink. I'm tired of thinking so I turn my attention to the television and see the local news is talking about Terry again.

"If only they knew…" I murmur.

CHAPTER 33

I stand next to Rhys in the backroom of the bookshop as he sorts through a pile of books and makes a note of all the titles. The shop has just opened, and Gwyn has not arrived yet. I – however – was waiting outside, raring to go. I am fired up by our experience yesterday and excited to plan next steps. I've just explained what happened to Rhys as it seems Gwyn mentioned none of it.

"Well, that would explain things." Rhys wanted to sit down and chat, but his dad has insisted he get off his arse and do some work for once – clearly still fired up by the telling off from Mrs B. He tells me he's stocktaking – meaning checking on recent arrivals and tracking inventory in a logbook.

"Explain what?" I ask.

"He was quiet all evening. Didn't say a word – even at dinner." He drops one book and picks up another and reads the title on the spine.

"It definitely freaked him out," I say.

"He was able to handle the scary stories and haunted houses by rationalising everything. Not believing was his shield. But seeing what he saw yesterday, I don't know how that would've affected his brain."

"A headfuck alright," I say. "But a necessary one. It's better he knows the truth."

"Maybe." Rhys lowers the book and takes out another from the box.

"Where is he, anyway?" I ask. "He should be here by now."

"Think he slept late," Rhys says. "No sign of him at breakfast. Heard him banging about in the middle of the night like he couldn't sleep."

"I hope he wasn't possessed by that thing." I rub my chin.

"Maybe he's gone mental," Rhys says in a deadpan voice, and I can't decide whether he's joking or being serious.

"Well, I hope he gets here soon," I say. "My bike's still at the Travellers' site. He needs to be my taxi."

Rhys writes a note in the log and places the book he has hold of in one of four piles on his desk. He reaches for another, but this time his eyes open wide when he sees the cover.

"Shit," he shouts.

"Language," yells a voice from the front of the shop and Rhys shakes his head.

"What is it?" I ask.

He lifts the book and shows me the cover: *The Life and Times of a Victorian Spiritualist*. "Henry shitting Blythe," he says. "It's the book I was on about the other day. I knew it was here somewhere."

"That was here all along?" I ask.

"These lot were in the back. Been meaning to sort through them for ages."

"Let me have a look." I flick through the pages. There's a bit about his life in London; the death of his family and his struggles afterwards; his interest in spiritualism and the paranormal investigations he conducted across Britain.

Rhys peers over my shoulder. "Anything useful?"

"I'm not sure," I say. "It's the story of the man's life."

"What about his death?" he says curiously.

I turn to the end of the book to see pictures of *Nant-y-Wrach*. I scan across the words until I find the right spot, and there, I find it.

"Bloody hell," I say.

"What?" Gwyn says.

"He was committed to the asylum," I say. "That's where he died. The haunted bloody asylum."

"Whoa." Rhys claps his hands together excitedly.

I point to the page. "This is important information. I'm not sure why, but my gut tells me this is very important."

As I wait for Gwyn, I skim through the rest of the book and search for more information that might help our investigation. Throughout, Rhys hovers, half trying to do his job and half trying to see what I'm looking at. The details of the man's paranormal research around the country are interesting but less relevant to what we're doing right now. I focus on the pages that describe what happens in *Nant-y-Wrach*. Here, things become weird, and I become so focused that the world around me fades into silence. Suddenly, an unexpected voice chimes in.

"What've you learned?" Gwyn asks.

"Jesus, Gwyn," I say.

"You can just call me Gwyn," he retorts.

I can't help but smirk. "When did you get here?"

He purses his lips and blows. "Not that long ago but you seemed so engrossed in your reading that I left you to it."

"Right," I say. "So – erm – how are you doing today?" My attempt to not sound awkward fails completely.

"I haven't gone mental – not yet anyway – despite what my brother thinks. Still a bit weirded out but hey ho."

"Good, I guess," I say. "We've got lots of work to do."

Rhys is craning his neck as we speak – trying to see the pages in my hands. "What did you find out?" he asks.

"He made a name for himself with his investigations. The stories of what happened to him across Britain are wild. But things change when he gets to *Nant-y-Wrach*. His investigations here were not popular. He was at odds with those in charge – people in power. He kept pushing them, telling them there was an evil presence here. Something that was responsible for the deaths of the children. They said he was mad, and he was committed to the asylum where – eventually – he died."

"There's got to be more to it than that," Rhys says.

"There is one thing," I say and both brothers lean in with the same concentrated look their dad has every morning when he has his head in the paper.

"It's only mentioned right at the end. The author says Henry was the victim of a huge miscarriage of justice at the hands of a secret group; a secret group that has run this town for hundreds of years. It suggests he was silenced because he posed a threat to them."

"They killed him?" Gwyn says. "Jesus."

"Wow." Rhys looks excited. "I told you – the whole world is run by these bastards. Secret societies and cabals. They're fricking everywhere."

"What else?" Gwyn asks.

"That's it," I say. "The only mention made of this conspiracy to silence Henry by the secret group is in the last paragraph. It's weird."

"Bloody author's looking to get a sequel in," Rhys says, and he grabs the book from me.

"What the frick…" Gwyn says.

"We need to find out more," I say and point at the book. "What do you know about the author?"

"Gerald Edwards?" Gwyn says. "He lives nearby – just outside of town. Written lots about local history. He's been in here in the past for book signings. Got quite a colourful history, I believe. Trouble with the law in England when he worked there as a reporter. Don't know for what exactly."

"Do you think he'd be open to visitors?" I ask. "Maybe school kids, doing a research project on local history?"

"I reckon there's a good case to be made for his help," he says. "We'll have his details here somewhere. I'll find them."

"Okay, good," I say. "Let's see if we can visit him today. We're kind of running out of leads right now. Until Rebecca recovers."

"Or until her dad lets us near her," Gwyn says.

"Let's pop in to see her on the way," I say. "Walking everywhere is a pain and I want my bike back, anyway."

"It's a plan," Rhys says and Gwyn shrugs.

CHAPTER 34

As we get close to the Travellers' site, I have a strange feeling. I'm not certain what'll be waiting for us there, whether Abraham will be angry with us (me), and what state Rebecca will be in after the thing at the farm. It's near lunchtime and the site is very busy. There are people sat around eating and drinking and Gwyn and I receive some stern looks as we approach.

"Not the best time to arrive here," Gwyn says. "They're all back from the fields. If they wanted to hurt us, now would be a perfect time."

"Don't be silly," I say as Gwyn leans his bike against the wall near the entrance. "They're our friends now. Abraham is on our side. He gets what we're doing." I really hope he does, anyway. I'm pleased to spot my bike is still where I left it.

We enter the middle of the site, heading towards the caravan that Rebecca shares with her father. I glance to my left, stop and turn my head slightly. Then I tap Gwyn's shoulder. "Look."

Rebecca is doing a handstand against a double-decker bus. There are younger kids around her, cheering her on. Gwyn and I approach. She is smiling and then her eyes turn to us.

"Oh, hiya, boys. I thought I might see you today."

She drops her legs and then brings herself upright. She has

a scarf around her neck, despite the warm weather. The children continue to watch like they're expecting another trick.

"You okay?" I ask.

"Yes, didn't take long once I was away from that place." She waves to the kids and steps away in the direction of her caravan.

"What... what actually happened to you?" Gwyn asks.

"At the farm?" She stops and crosses her arms.

"Yeah," he says. "I was with you the whole time. It was scary."

"Gwyn's – erm – never seen anything like that before," I say. "Neither have I, to be honest."

"Something was trying to hurt you." Gwyn's voice trembles as he speaks.

She stares into the distance like she's thinking. "Being stuck is like being so focused on something, you can't look away. Something grabs your attention and pulls you in. The forces in *Annwn* are very strong right now. There are more spirits around and the energy here is high."

"But what attacked you?" I ask.

"Some of them are nasty," she says. "Angry. Hateful. They rage against the living and given half a chance they'd bring you into their world."

"But why are you not more freaked out?" Gwyn asks. "That thing tried to kill you. Didn't it hurt?"

"Oh, it did." She pulls down the scarf and shows bruises on her neck that look like handprints. I can hear Gwyn gasp. "But I was protected by *Taid*. You may only see him as a skull but in *Annwn* he is a powerful, ferocious warrior. A force of great power. His energy protected my body and mind. So long as he's with me, I have fewer fears about my safety."

"If you say so." Gwyn looks unsettled.

"That is utterly... awesome." I can't think of anything better to say. "Having a bloody dead warrior priest as a bodyguard."

Rebecca shrugs, gives me an eyebrow flash, and continues walking. Gwyn looks over at me and shakes his head.

"Anyway," I say, following her. "Do you remember speaking to us while you were stuck?"

"What did I say?" She turns her head and narrows her eyes.

"You told us Terry was still alive. Then you said *under the bridge* like there was something there that would prove he was alive."

"Right. Yes, I think I remember that. Something told me Terry was still with the living and he was in distress. He needed something and it was under the bridge. Did you find anything?"

Gwyn shakes his head.

"Did you manage to speak to him then?" I ask. "Henry Blythe, I mean?"

"I saw him, but I was overwhelmed by the dead before we could talk."

"Again?" I say. "I thought that place was meant to be better for connecting?"

"He was clearer but so were the rest of them and they're not normally like that. Something's got them riled up."

"The dead are riled up?" Gwyn's face becomes even paler.

She reaches the doorway of the caravan and stops before stepping up inside. "Yeah. There's something big going on."

"Like what?" I ask.

"No idea," she says. "*Taid* says he's only seen it like this one other time, many years ago."

Gwyn and I look at each other.

"We found something out as well," I say. "Henry spent the last couple of years of his life at the asylum. Something happened to him there. We're going to speak to someone who can hopefully tell us more. Someone living this time."

"Do you want to come with us?" Gwyn asks.

She turns her head, and I can see she's interested. "I'd like to. Let me check with Dad. When are you going?"

"Right now," I say.

CHAPTER 35

Gerald Edwards lives a few miles outside of town, on *Lon y Mynydd*, which takes us up a long uphill journey and neither Gwyn nor I can pedal all the way – him with his bad chest and me with my extra passenger. Rebecca's dad was nowhere to be seen but she reckoned he'd be happy for her to join us – so long as *Taid* stayed at home, and that she avoided any conversations with the dead. That was not our plan, for this day at least.

Along the way, we pass the entrance to *Cartref-Y-Gwynt* Farm, where we all look at each other silently without stopping. The air is still, and the sun does a good job of reminding us that it's still with us.

"This might be the hottest day yet," Gwyn says. "Whose idea was it to do this journey today?"

"It couldn't wait," I say. "Terry's been missing for eight days now. We need to do everything we can to save him."

"If we can save him," Gwyn says, and I glance over at him with a frown.

"What do you think this author can tell us?" Rebecca asks.

"Not sure," I say. "All I know is that Henry Blythe is the key to this mystery and this Edwards guy wrote a book about him. He's gotta know something."

The road flattens and looking back we can see the whole of the valley from where we stand.

"You know, in spite of the dark history, this town is still pretty nice," Rebecca says.

"How does it compare to your other home?" I ask.

"That place is alright, I suppose. It's away from the mountains so the land is flatter."

"I'd settle for somewhere flatter right now," Gwyn says, panting, and Rebecca and I chuckle.

After another mile, we find crossroads surrounded by three houses.

"It should be one of these," Gwyn says.

"What was his house called again?" I ask.

"*Plas y Rhos*," he says, exhaling.

"There," Rebecca says.

Painted on a sign hanging from a stone post, we see the name. We enter through a white iron gate and follow a path around the house to a garden where we find an old man with a white beard, wearing a flat cap, sat in a chair facing a rose bush. In front of him is an easel covered in green and red.

Gwyn clears his throat and there is no response. He does it again, but the man still seems to hear nothing.

"Mr Edwards," I say loudly, trying not to shout.

The old man turns his head and examines us all with thin eyes.

"We're from the secondary school," I say. "For the summer project?"

"Of course," he says. "I've been expecting you. Come inside."

He leads us into his dark house and sits us down at a table in the dining room. He offers some orange squash and we all – thirsty as anything after the journey – take him up on the offer. Rebecca clears her throat to get our attention and nods in the direction of the opposite wall, which is covered in interesting artwork. There's a drawing of a pentagram and a painting of a witch burning. In one picture, a group of people wearing animal skull masks are dancing around in a circle, hand in hand. There is also a print of a famous painting called *Salem*, which shows a Welsh lady with what many say is the Devil's face in her shawl.

"Seems we have similar interests," Gwyn says.

Edwards returns with a trayful of glasses filled with an orange drink. "Here we are," he says. "Now, as I said to your teacher, I can't believe they're giving children homework to do over the summer holidays. Seems cruel to me."

I neck half the glass and gasp before speaking. "Something they're trying out."

"You knew the missing boy?" Edwards asks before sitting down next to us.

"We know him," I say, purposefully changing the tense. "He's in the year beneath us."

"Right," Edwards says, sounding unconvinced. "Very sad. Don't suppose there's much hope for him now, is there?"

"Who knows?" I look to Gwyn, and he looks to Rebecca.

Edwards places his clasped hands on the table before him. "Now, what can I help you with? Your teacher said it related to local history – which of course is something I am very passionate about – so when he phoned, I said I would be delighted to help. What is it specifically that you're interested in?"

I glance at the other two before answering. "We're doing our project about a person you wrote about – Sir Henry Blythe."

The old man's face drops. Gwyn takes out a copy of the book from his bag and places it on the table. Edwards picks it up and flicks through the pages. "Well, well. I haven't seen a copy of this in years. It's not an easy book to get hold of. May I ask where you got it from?"

"Gwyn's dad runs the second-hand bookshop on the High Street," I say.

"Ah," he says with a sparkle in his eye. "I do like that shop. This old thing has been out of print for a fair few years and I wasn't aware of any copies still circulating."

"Dad specialises in rare books," Gwyn says.

"Yes, of course. I did a signing there once." He takes out glasses from his shirt pocket and puts them on before inspecting the pages. "Fascinating character, Sir Henry. It's all in here. His whole life. He faced tragedy and turned it into something positive, travelling around the UK trying to help families affected by grief."

"Then here, he ends up being committed," I say. "Your book doesn't say much about that."

"Well, I wanted to focus on the important parts of his life. He deserved some dignity after all the good he did." Edwards lifts the open book and examines the pictures.

"But what happened to him?" I ask. "Why did he end up at the asylum?"

"Your book mentions a secret group," Gwyn says.

Edwards shoots glances at each of us. His brow is wrinkled. "Hmm. The answer to your question depends on who you ask."

Gwyn cocks his head and Rebecca leans forward with her palms on the table.

"The official word is that he lost his mind from grief. The effect of losing his family finally caught up with him and he became too obsessed by the paranormal and the occult. He was a danger to himself and others around him, so they had him committed."

"And what was the unofficial word?" Rebecca asks, rubbing her hands together.

Edwards closes the book and reaches for his orange drink. "He discovered something sinister about this town and powerful local persons decided to silence him."

"What sinister thing?" I ask. "Is this the secret group?"

Edwards licks his lips. "You need to be careful with what I am about to tell you. You may want to give some thought to writing about it in your school project. I can tell you – from experience – that people don't want to hear this story."

"What story?" Rebecca asks.

"The story of the people who run this town." He places the glass back on the table.

I clear my throat. "Who are they? Are they like the Freemasons?"

Edwards appears to think carefully about his answer. "Similar in ways, I suppose, but far more secretive. And dangerous."

"Dangerous?" Gwyn repeats, his eyebrows raised.

"How does it relate to Henry Blythe?" I ask.

"This group goes back hundreds of years. Back to the days of Mari Evans. You know that name, don't you?"

All three of us nod.

"Henry Blythe discovered their existence and threatened to expose them," he says.

"And they had him committed?" Gwyn asks. "Why?"

"That is where my knowledge ends," he says, and he sits back in his chair. "I've been told it relates to Mari Evans; connected to witchcraft. Whatever they stood for – stand for – it was enough for Sir Henry to want to risk his freedom and maybe even his life to expose them."

"Stand for?" I say. "You mean this group still exists today?"

He shrugs. "I've heard rumours..."

I lean forward. We're hanging on his every word. "What's the purpose of this group? Are they Satanists?"

"Or are they a coven?" Rebecca asks.

"We've seen weird stuff," Gwyn says.

"Like what?" Edwards asks.

"Weird markings," Gwyn says. "Animal parts placed on graves."

Edwards crosses his arms. "The honest answer is I don't know. Witchcraft is everywhere here. It's part of the heritage and the town character. It entertains the tourists who come here and it's very likely that many of them and those here still practise wicca and pagan rituals. But it's all harmless."

"What about the secret group?" I ask. "If it's related to Mari Evans then they must be into all that stuff. You must know more?"

"I'm sorry, I don't."

"Where did you hear all this?" Rebecca asks. "Who was your source?"

"There are people out there who make a hobby of tracking these underground groups." He nods slowly as he says this.

"And they know about this town's secret coven?" I ask.

"To be honest, they're mostly crackpots," he says blowing through his lips. "They're the same people who believe that Freemasons and the Illuminati are controlling the world, and that the Queen is a shape-shifting reptile."

I think back to my earlier conversation with Rhys.

"Reptile?" Gwyn repeats.

"Look," Edwards says. "Your project is about local history, isn't it?"

"Erm, yeah," I say.

"In that case, I suggest you stick to the facts and the evidence. Sir Henry was a fascinating character who lived a very rich and colourful life. Tell his story – the grief and the sadness; his investigations and the obsession with the supernatural that led to his madness. It's a sad tale but it touches on many of the key themes of the time."

"But what about this secret group?" I ask. "We can't ignore it."

"All hearsay," he says. "If you hadn't seen it in the book, you'd be none the wiser."

"Why did you give up on it?" Gwyn says. "You describe it as an injustice. It sounded like you cared."

His eyes look down and I sense a sadness in him.

"I wrote that book many years ago," he says. "Poured my heart and soul into the damned thing. For what? So that it disappears from circulation until school children take an interest in it because of the spooky stories?"

Gwyn stares at the ground while Rebecca bites her lip.

I drop my fists on the table. "What if this secret group is

behind the missing boy? We've seen the graves of children marked by symbols of witchcraft. Is this what they're after?"

Mr Edwards stands up. "Right then. You must have enough by now for your project? If you don't mind, I'd like to get back to my painting."

He stands behind the chair and grits his teeth like he's faking his smile. We each glance at each other and get up.

"Thanks for your time," Rebecca says as we leave.

He walks us to the gate and stops. "If I were you, I'd put that book back on the shelf and hope some customer takes it away."

He looks at each of us in turn, tips his hat and turns on his heels. "All the best with your project. I hope you find time to enjoy your summer holidays – especially before this glorious weather leaves us."

We all watch as he strides back across his garden.

I storm away from the gate, furious.

"Bloody hell," I yell and grab the book from Gwyn and throw it to the ground. I crouch and rub my forehead. Breathing helps me to calm down. I'm aware of Gwyn's and Rebecca's gaze.

"This is all so bloody frustrating," I say.

"We'll find another way." Rebecca puts her hand on my shoulder and gently squeezes.

"Come on, mate," Gwyn says. "Let's go back to the shop."

CHAPTER 36

Rhys bounds around the backroom clapping his hands and pulling books off shelves. He's determined to find out more about this apparent secret group that runs this town. Rebecca sits behind the desk; she is amused by his enthusiasm. He climbs up a stepladder that's leant against the tallest shelf and starts throwing books down to Gwyn who dances from side to side trying to catch them all. I am on the floor leaning against the wall in the corner, feeling deflated.

"I've spent years reading about secret societies from all around the world," Rhys says, "but I didn't see the one right here, right in front of my face. Tell me exactly what he said."

"Not much more than what is in the book," Gwyn says piling the books he's caught onto the desk nearby. "Henry uncovered this secret group, and they may have been responsible for him being sent to the asylum. But he froze at that stage. Told us he didn't know any more."

"Why would he tell you that much and then nothing after that?" Rhys asks as he descends the ladder.

"Maybe he realised he'd said too much," Rebecca says. "He wasn't comfortable talking about it. What do you think it means?"

"I don't know," Rhys says, stopping at the bottom step. "I need to get reading. Did he tell you anything about this secret group?"

"That they'd been around for hundreds of years," Gwyn says. "Since the time of Mari Evans."

"You think it could be a coven?" Rebecca asks.

Rhys shifts the stepladder across to another section before striding up. "That would be the obvious answer," he yells.

"What actually are covens?" Gwyn asks.

Rhys stops and turns around. "Groups of witches who come together to combine their powers. They meet in groups of thirteen."

"You think this group could be a bunch of witches?" Gwyn's jaw drops.

"Not necessarily," Rhys says. "Maybe they worship witches. Like Satanists worship the Devil."

"Maybe they worship Mari Evans?" Rebecca says.

"Oh, bloody hell," Gwyn says. This reaction catches my attention.

"What?" I say, glaring at Gwyn.

"Do they make sacrifices?" he asks.

"Sometimes," Rhys says. "I think."

"Maybe that's what Henry discovered," Gwyn says. "He found out they were worshipping Mari Evans and sacrificing children in her name?"

"But Terry's still alive," Rebecca says.

"Maybe they're preparing to kill him," I say, and everyone looks over at me.

"We really should tell the police," Gwyn says.

"And tell them what exactly?" I get up onto my feet. "That the secret group of witches who run this town have taken Terry and plan to kill him?"

"How do you know the local police aren't in on it?" Rebecca sits forward and claps her hands together. "Edwards said powerful people were in this group, didn't he?"

I see Gwyn and Rhys making eye contact. They're thinking about their uncle.

I stamp my foot on the floor. "Damn it. What can we do? We've run out of leads."

"We do have one more place to explore," Rebecca says.

"The asylum?" Gwyn says with a horrified look on his face.

"Your dad would murder us if we took you on another investigation so soon," I say. "Besides, we haven't got your *taid* with us."

Rebecca reaches down and digs around in her bag. She lifts out an object with a rounded top covered in a purple velvet blanket.

"Oh wow," I say. "Are you sure?"

"I don't think it's a good idea," Gwyn says. "It's too soon."

"We've got to," I say. "We're running out of options and it's becoming very clear that Terry is in terrible danger."

Rebecca nods and Gwyn rubs his face with his hands.

I point at Rhys. "We need a mission briefing, pronto."

CHAPTER 37

We cycle past the Jungle, Gwyn on his bike and Rebecca catching a backie from me. We've haven't cycled up this far along the road before. It's slightly uphill but not as steep as the road up to the *Cartref-Y-Gwynt* farm. There are tall trees on either side and the road is marked with their shadows. They all point in the direction of the asylum like they're telling us that is the way we need to follow.

"Have you been to this place before?" Rebecca asks.

"No," I say. "It was on our list, but we didn't get around to it."

We reach the entrance to the hospital, get off our bikes and push them along a lane where the concrete has cracked and filled with weeds.

"It's weird this place only closed down twenty years ago," Gwyn says. "My dad remembers coming here when he was a kid to visit a relative who'd been committed."

"What happened to them?" Rebecca asks.

"No idea."

To our right, the hedge lowers and, in the distance – over the fields – we can see the Jungle.

I turn to face Rebecca. "How should we do this? We don't want you getting stuck again."

"I'll be alright," she says. "The *Ffordd* here isn't so clear."

"How are you so willing to go somewhere like this so soon after last time?" Gwyn asks, nervously.

"Honestly – and this may seem odd – but connecting with *Annwn* makes you feel good. It's difficult to explain. Although the experience itself is horrible, you soon forget about it. And not long after you want to go back." She looks in my direction and I feel she's saying this to me.

"That's what they say about childbirth," Gwyn says. "Still fricking freaky."

"Also, *Taid* will be doubly careful after what happened at the farmhouse," she says.

"Just don't take any risks, okay?" I say. "You're a key member of our squad now and we don't want you in harm's way."

Rebecca quietly nods her head in response.

As we get nearer, beyond the twisting path, we see the huge abandoned building. Rhys told us it was built in the 1840s, when the population of the town was three times what it is now. This was when the lead mine was active. Many who worked there became ill with what they called the *miner's madness*. The Robham family owned the mine, and they knew what caused the illness but because of the money it made them, it was better to ignore that and treat those affected when they could, so they built this place and continued mining the lead. Many said it was cursed because of the number of deaths that happened here. But cursed or not, the deaths were mostly due to heavy metal poisoning.

As we get nearer, we see the full scale of the place. It looks like a forgotten prison. The stone walls are covered in ivy and the windows are smashed. The grounds are overgrown and there are sheep wondering about where the car park used to be.

"This place is seriously spooky," Gwyn says.

"Perfect place for an investigation," I say.

"Is that the entrance?" Rebecca asks.

"Yeah. Let's go in," I say, picking up the pace.

The door screeches as I push it open. Ahead I see a long corridor. Paint has peeled from the walls, and it now covers the floors. Halfway down is an abandoned wheelchair with rusty wheels. The place smells sick and stale. My head starts to spin and when it stops, for some reason, pictures of Mum spring up in my head and a heavy weight grows in my chest.

"You okay?" Rebecca asks.

"Yeah," I say. "Must be the air in this place…"

"Mmm."

I take a deep breath and look around. "What do we do? Search the place until we find something?"

Rebecca takes out *Taid* from her satchel and removes the velvet cover. "Let's head that way and see how we get on."

We reach the wheelchair and I give it a push with my hand and the wheels give out a whine. Gwyn jumps and frowns at me. He turns to Rebecca. "Do you sense anything?"

"A lot of pain," she says. "A lot of suffering."

"Stay with us though, okay?" Gwyn says.

"It's not strong," she says. "More like echoes bouncing off the walls. Minds without direction and not anchored to anything. Really chaotic thoughts."

"Let us know if you hear from Henry," I say.

"I will."

As we walk, Rebecca holds out her *taid* like he's a gun in her hands. I can't tell whether he's meant to protect her or guide her. We reach the end of the corridor, and we all jump as pigeons take off through gaps in the wall where windows used to be. There are several rooms along this section. We enter one room and see three rusty bedframes and piles of tiles that have seemingly dropped from the walls.

Rebecca stops at the door. "I can't come in. The energy here is making me woozy."

"Woozy?" Gwyn says.

"Lots of ups and downs," she says. "Like riding a roller

coaster. This whole corridor was full of very sick and confused people."

"Most of the people in this section were poisoned at the mine," I say. "It made their minds sicker than their bodies, but security wasn't much needed."

"Where did they keep the dangerous ones?" Gwyn asks. "You know, the proper headcases."

"Underground," I say.

Gwyn and I step out of the room. I look up and down the corridor. "Where are you, Henry? We need your help now more than ever."

Rebecca grabs my arm and her jaw drops. "I can hear him."

"Where?" Gwyn asks.

"This way." She moves ahead of us down the corridor and to the end of the block. We push through two doors where we find a stairwell. Up appears bright, probably from an opening in the roof. But the steps down head into a black pit.

"We're going to have to go down, aren't we?" Gwyn says.

"Yep," she says.

"Fricking underground." Gwyn shuts his eyes and shakes his head.

Gwyn and I take out our torches and down the stairs we go. We tread carefully. The steps are covered in the same mixture of peeled paint and old rubbish that we've seen everywhere else. Some of it is slippery and falling down the stairwell here would be easy.

We reach the bottom and Rebecca gasps like she's in pain.

"You okay?" I ask.

"Yeah," she says. "We're going in the right direction."

"Stinks," Gwyn says.

"Smells like something died down here," I say. Inside, I know many things have died down here.

Rebecca leads us along another corridor. We enter through a pair of very thick doors that look like they should be locked.

"This area is different," Gwyn says. "Much older."

There are only a few rooms on each side, and each door has bars over their windows – not glass. They are also thick and made of a heavy wood lined with metal.

"Did they really keep people down here until the sixties?" Gwyn asks.

"That's why they closed the place down," I say. "Its reputation was bad. Patients were kept in these dungeons, and it was far too old-fashioned. They realised it would cost less to build a new hospital than refurb this building."

"It's like something from a horror film," Gwyn says.

"There was a lot of pain here," I say.

"There still is…" Rebecca says, and Gwyn takes a step back and holds his upper body tight.

"Hush," Rebecca says, raising her hands. "I can hear him again." She points away from where we stand, and we move slowly in that direction.

Gwyn puts his arm to his nose and mouth. "That smell is getting worse."

"What are you hearing, Rebecca?" I ask.

"Henry's voice is weak. He's trying his hardest to reach us but he's struggling."

"Are we going in the right direction?" I ask.

"Oh yes," she says. "He's down this way."

"Do you think this is where he died?" Gwyn asks.

Rebecca nods. The area where we walk is now black like space without stars. Without our torches, we see nothing. The place feels heavy and the sadness I felt earlier keeps swirling around me like a storm I can't escape. The air is thick with death and illness – a place where the sick living and the recent dead existed side by side for years, decades and now forever. Wounded bodies and rotting flesh and meat and bones and death and dust come together and there is no separation between one and the next. I shine the light around me and see dirt hanging, floating, moving softly through the tunnels and the cells of this dungeon.

"How's your chest?" I ask Gwyn.

"Fine, for now."

"Tell us if it starts to get bad and we need to get you out."

"I will."

Rebecca stops next to a doorway and looks in. I march forwards past her. "Is he in here?"

Rebecca grabs my shoulder and pulls me back. "You don't want to go in there."

"Why not?"

"There's something very bad in there. It's desperate for you to go in. But if you do, I'm not sure what might happen."

"What do you mean – something really bad?" Gwyn asks. "Why would it want us?"

"It likes them young," she says.

"Likes them young?" Gwyn repeats.

"The younger the better," she says. "In life it – he – hurt them. He did unspeakable things to them. More than people know." She puts her hand to her mouth. "Just please, stay out of there."

Gwyn and I look at each other. "Okay."

Rebecca turns her head like she hears something. "I've got him." She dashes ahead down the corridor into the darkness.

"Slow down," Gwyn calls out.

We both stride ahead behind her. Rebecca runs to the end of the corridor and turns into the last of the rooms on the right. Inside the room, we see her crouching on the floor.

"This is where he spent the last days of his life," she says.

"Bloody hell," Gwyn says.

"Can you hear him? Sense him?" I ask.

"I can. But it's not his spirit like at the graveyard – it's like a recording of his spirit."

"It's like the stone tape," I say. "I read about it in the *Hamley* book."

"What's that?" Gwyn asks.

"He died in agony," Rebecca says. "Locked away here

from the world. The only company he had was his grief. It was dreadful."

"His suffering imprinted onto the stones of the walls and room around him," I say. "It remembers him."

"That's right." Rebecca looks over at me and I see her eyes are welling up. "It was horrible. He lay here on the floor, waiting for the end to come. Eventually he took things into his own hands."

"He killed himself?" I ask. Rebecca nods.

"Wait, there's more," she says. "A lot of rage. He was very angry." I feel it as well.

"Don't blame him," Gwyn says.

"Do you know why he was here?" I ask.

"No, only that he felt it wasn't fair. A huge injustice."

"Why? Tell us everything," I say.

"Wait," she says. "There's something coming."

"What?" I ask.

"That thing – from the other cell," she says. "It got out. Our presence here let it escape. It clung itself to us and it's coming this way."

"Shit." I glance over at Gwyn and then back at Rebecca. "What do we do?"

"Close the door," she says. "*Taid*, we're going to need your help."

I leap over to the cell door and pull as hard as I can, but between the rusty hinges and the shit on the floor, it won't budge. "Gwyn, help me."

He rushes over and together we pull like our lives depend on it. At first it won't shift but as we rock it to and fro, it begins to screech and starts to move.

Rebecca gasps.

"Oh God, what now?" Gwyn says.

"I see Henry," she says. "There's a surge in energy coming from somewhere and it's opening the *Ffordd*. It's like our worlds are getting closer."

"Great, tell us everything," I say.

"I can see Henry, but I also sense that thing out there." She turns her head in the direction of the door.

We feel the door pull away from us and Gwyn and I look at each other.

"Should we stop?" Rebecca says and for the first time I see a worried look on her face.

"No, keep going," I yell. "Need to know what happened. Pull harder, Gwyn." He and I roar as we battle against the thing on the other side.

"It's too strong," Gwyn shouts.

"We can't let it in," I shout. We're both using our weight to pull the door shut but all we can do is just about keep it from opening.

"Rebecca," I say through gritted teeth. "Do you see Henry? What's happening?"

"He's sat on the floor and he's writing in a book. He's dipping a pen in a small bottle of ink and he's writing in a black book." She leans in. "I think it's a bible. He's stopping. He's put the pen in the bottle and now is taking the book over to that corner."

"Why? What's he doing there?" I ask.

"Ned, fricking focus, will you?" Gwyn's mouth is wide open, and his eyes are welling up.

"He's pulling the stone away from the wall," Rebecca says, "and he's placing the book behind it. Now he's returning to where he sat and he's picking up the pen. He's… oh no." Rebecca turns away and puts her hand to her mouth.

"What?" Gwyn says. We both gape at her, awestruck.

"He stuck the pen in his throat, and it's started bleeding."

Before I can process the scene she describes, the force we battle against overwhelms us and tears the door away and we both fall – Gwyn toppling to his side and I onto my front as I am dragged by the door. I now sense whatever was outside the cell coming in and after I fall, I hear a deep voice making a sneering sound, and I scream as something steps on my hand and traps it. I can sense the evil, putrid malevolence above me, and I almost have a fit as it touches my back and starts stroking me, and I cannot move, my fingers trapped, holding me to the floor as the hands that feel like claws move down my back lower, stroking and pinching my flesh like it's playing with me. I see faces flash in front of my eyes: scared children trying to hide, running away but failing, being caught by it – him – and then pinned down and he touches them in a way that they know is wrong, and I can't look away; my mind's eye is open wide and cannot be shut from the horrors I see – the anguish on little faces that experience unspeakable horrors.

"It's bloody with me; it's touching me," I yell and scream. "End it."

"Oh Jesus," Gwyn whimpers.

"*Taid*, it's time." Rebecca turns in my direction with the skull and a bright flash of light fills the room like a firework has just gone off, and a rumbling growl shakes the walls as the evil presence fights back. It doesn't want to return to its lair – it desperately wants to stay here with us. It tries to hold on to my skin and my flesh and I howl as it holds me tighter. Gwyn's jaw opens wide, and he looks like the entrance to a ghost-train tunnel.

"It's holding on to me." I spit my words as the pain becomes overwhelming. "Do something."

"*Taid*, help him," Rebecca urges, and she shakes the skull.

A constant and intense white light engulfs the room, destroying the darkness that has ruled this hidden place for decades and wiping out every murky corner, killing shadows and expelling all that hides in them. The brightness is so intense that I must shut my eyes tight and let the power wash over me, making my body vibrate as it cleanses the space around me, and the evil presence releases its grip and I hear its vile moans inside and outside my head as it retreats and the dread seeps out of the room quicker and quicker until finally it is snapped back into its cell.

"What the...?" I turn around and see Rebecca, with eyes shut, holding her *taid* up in the air with trembling hands. She bites her lower lip. Gwyn is pinned against the wall with his arms over his face.

"What... what happened?" Gwyn asks.

"*Taid* has pulled up the drawbridge," Rebecca says. "He needed a second push. That thing was strong."

"I saw things," I say. "Things it did." I shake my head and squeeze my eyes shut.

"But it's gone?" Gwyn asks.

"Yes, *Taid* shut the *Ffordd* completely."

"And Henry?" I ask.

"Gone as well."

Gwyn crawls over and puts his hand on my shoulder. "You okay?"

I nod and try to take a few deep breaths and will myself up from the floor.

"I preferred our investigations when they were boring," he says.

Rebecca examines the stones of the wall. I step over to her. "Where did he put the book?" I ask.

Rebecca moves her hand across the stones and stops. "Somewhere here."

"There's no way that book will still be there," Gwyn says.

I kneel and push the stone and it seems firm. I try to pull it with my fingertips, but it doesn't move. I try to get a firmer hold around it and find an area where I can pull.

"Maybe, if I..." I stop. "Gwyn, come here, will you? See if you can pull on that side."

Together, we both use our fingernails to grab onto each side.

"It's fricking moving," Gwyn says. It is, and slowly, together, we're able to pull the stone out of the hole and it drops to the floor with a thud, blowing more dust into the air. I drop my head and shine the torch into the hole.

"Holy shit," I say before reaching into the gap in the wall and pulling out a small black leather-bound book with a gold cross on the cover. "It's the bible."

"Wow," Gwyn says and Rebecca gasps. I rub my dirty fingers on my clothes and then open the book carefully. Inside, the printed text is surrounded by scribbles. I squint as I bring the torch closer and try and read the handwriting.

"What does it say?" Gwyn asks.

"I don't know," I say, skimming through the pages. "The handwriting is difficult to read."

"Can you not make out any of it?" Rebecca asks.

"Wait," I say. Near the end of the book, I find words printed in large letters. "There's one sentence I can read. It's written in print, and it's repeated over these final pages."

"What does it say?" Gwyn asks.

I look up at them both. "*DON'T LET 'EM TAKE THE CHILDREN.*"

CHAPTER 38

Rhys studies the book through his large magnifying glass like he's Sherlock Holmes. I am impatient but despite my best efforts I have failed to read most of Henry's notes.

"We have a copy of the 1851 edition of the King James Bible covered in – mostly illegible – handwritten notes." Rhys lifts the closed book to the light and examines the cover. "Very nice condition, given where you found it. Quite rare. Might be worth a penny or two."

"Get on with it," I say, pacing around him, and Rhys frowns at me before placing the book back down on the surface of his desk and opening it.

"Chill, guys," he says. "What's the rush?"

"You have no idea what we had to go through to get that thing." I rub my hand, which is still sore after our encounter at the old asylum and glance over at Gwyn who holds his arms tight against his body and Rebecca who breathes into her clasped hands like she's trying to warm them up.

"I know, you explained," Rhys says. "Let me just get my bearings."

"Can you read his handwriting or not?" Gwyn asks, shortly.

"It's not easy," Rhys says.

"It's possible that some may be gobbledygook," Rebecca says in a calmer tone. "I sensed that his mind was very confused in those last days. Lots of incoherent, angry thoughts."

"A lot of it does appear to be scribbles," Rhys says.

"Might the handwriting and words they use be any different then?" Gwyn asks.

"Not this much," Rhys says.

"Could it be a different language then?" I ask. "Maybe something old-fashioned like Latin?"

"I did consider that, but I don't think it's the case. I can't seem to see any defined letters, let alone Latin words. Saying that, it is strange how some of these names stand out the way they do."

"Names – what names?" I bound over to him and examine the pages he refers to.

"You didn't see the names?"

"No, we went through it a few times," Gwyn says.

"Evidently not enough it seems." Rhys bends down and points to the book. "Here," he says. "*MARI EVANS TRIBUTE PREVENTS PESTILENCE.*" He flips through a few pages. "And here, *ROBHAM FAMILY RULES THEM. ROBHAM FAMILY RUINS THEM.*"

"Lord Robham," I say and Rebecca and Gwyn both glance over at me wide-eyed. They both step closer to see the pages for themselves.

"And there's this. *STOP ROBHAM. STOP THE* – what's this word? Oh yes – *STOP THE APO–TRO–PAIC CUSTODIANS. STOP THEM. STOP THEM AT ALL COSTS.*" He turns the page and looks at the other side. "*Stop them* is written dozens of times all over these two sides."

"Stop Robham," Rebecca repeats, thoughtfully.

"Stop who else?" I ask. "What were those other words?"

"Apotropaic Custodians?"

"Yes, what does that mean?" Gwyn says.

"Well, a custodian is a person that takes care of, or protects, something. But the other word, I'm not sure." Rhys moves his head around like he's searching for something. "Where's that dictionary?"

"Why don't we ask the human dictionary in the next room?" Gwyn says, and he grabs the book and takes it to the front of the shop.

"Odd," Rhys says. "I usually have it to hand."

"Maybe your dad took it for his crosswords?" Rebecca says.

"No, he would consider that cheating. He wouldn't dare."

Gwyn returns. "Dad says the other word," he stops and reads it again, "apotropaic, is something designed to ward off evil or bad luck."

"This group protects the town from the evil?" I ask. Have we been looking at this picture the wrong way?

"Can't be a coven then, can it?" Rebecca says.

"No, I suppose not," I say.

"You're saying they protect the town from her curse?" Gwyn says.

"It's different to what we thought it was," Rebecca says.

"You mentioned pestilence," I say. "Could that be the curse?"

"I reckon so," Rhys says. "Pestilence is an old-fashioned name for disease outbreaks. It's used in the Bible." He points at the book in Gwyn's hands.

I see the graves of the children in my mind's eye…

"And what about Robham's role?" Gwyn asks.

"Our resident lord and his family must lead this secret group," I say.

"That would explain their longevity," Rhys says.

"What do you mean?" I ask.

"Keeping a secret group like that going for hundreds of years can't be easy," Rhys says. "You need continuity. You need traditions and practices to be maintained over generations. And what better way than for a single family and their bloodline to keep things going?"

"Fricking hell – that makes sense," Gwyn says, his eyes dropping to the floor.

"But how does this connect to Terry and the children that are taken?" Rebecca asks.

"Sounds like they might be the tribute. The Mari Evans tribute," Rhys says. "A gift from the town."

"A gift?" Gwyn leans on the desk with his face in his hands. "Like a sacrifice?"

"Would they sacrifice children to keep the town safe?" Rebecca furrows her brow as she says this.

"Maybe it's a price they're willing to pay," I say.

"And what about Mrs Astley and the witch marks," Rhys says. "Why would she be marking up those children's graves and covering them with animal parts?"

"The children died in years when epidemics hit the town," I say. "Maybe the pestilence did come." I lean on the desk and tap my fingers on the wooden surface.

"Meaning the tribute failed in those years?" Rebecca asks.

"Perhaps they did something different those years." Rhys rubs his chin.

"Maybe they missed the tribute," Gwyn says.

"That doesn't make sense," I say. "I'm sure they would keep this up over the years."

"Can we not check?" Rebecca asks. "There should be some record of missing children across those years."

"That did cross my mind," Rhys says, sitting back in his chair. "Most police stations like ours were set up after the County and Borough Police Act in 1856. That means there were no real records before then. Archives only detail births and deaths – so disappearances and crimes are more difficult to track down. We only have the years between 1863 and 1943 to consider."

"That would be enough, right?" I say, making eye contact with the three of them.

"It would," Rhys says. "But there are two main problems.

Firstly, the police station burnt down in 1943. All records and documentation before that time were destroyed."

"Shit," Gwyn says, crossing his arms.

"And the second problem?" I ask.

"In lieu of police records, an alternative source might be old newspapers."

"Why is that a problem?" I say, raising my hands.

Rhys raises his finger in the air. "Because, my dear boy, newspapers at the time were fairly focused on coverage of that minor skirmish going on across the world."

"World War II," Gwyn says.

"Yep. At least that's what I saw when I checked what they had at the town archives. To do a more detailed search, we'd need to go to Aberystwyth and look through the records at the National Library of Wales." Rhys sits down and puts his hands on his knees.

I shake my head. "We don't have time for that."

"Do you think the fire at the police station was related?" Rebecca asks.

Rhys shrugs. "Who knows?"

"Bit of a longshot," Gwyn says. "But we can always ask someone who was around then? They might remember something?"

"I did already. Mrs Jones at the newsagent," Rhys says. "Her family has run that shop for over a hundred years. She mentioned something about an English boy who went missing around the time of the *Gŵyl Awst* festival in 1943, but she couldn't be certain because there was a lot of coming and going at the time. Evacuees were sent here from the cities because of all the bombings that went on there."

I rub the side of my head. "Need to be careful. This could end up being a bit of a rabbit hole. Whether the tributes happened in previous years or not, they don't really help us right now."

"True," Rhys says. "Reality is, if the Custodians have Terry, then he is in grave danger."

"Yes," Rebecca says. "We need to do something."

"We should go to the police," Gwyn says.

"Do you think that's wise?" I ask. "These Custodians. Aside from the lord and his family, we don't know who else may be involved."

"Look at what happened to Henry Blythe," Rebecca says.

"We can go to Uncle Len. We can trust him." Gwyn has an earnest expression on his face. He's desperate for his uncle not to be involved. I can't blame him.

"You sure?" I look from Gwyn over to Rhys.

"There's no way Len is involved," Rhys says. "He's as straight as a ruler."

"We haven't got much evidence," I say. "What influence could we sway based on an old bible covered in the scribbles of a mad man?"

"Don't know," Gwyn says, "but the police are desperate for leads."

"They'd have to look into it," Rhys says. "If any of this is true and they were shown to ignore it then it'd be a huge scandal."

"We need more proof," I say.

"We've got to think of what is best for Terry," Rebecca says. "He's still alive for now. But for how much longer, I don't know…"

I sigh, realising it's risky. "But if we do expose them, do you think they'll just release Terry without any effort? I wouldn't bet on it."

"Then let's talk to Uncle Len," Gwyn says. "If we can find him while he's out on the beat then we can talk to him in secret, without that Detective Thomas finding out."

"Then what?" I ask.

"Then he can get our message out," Rhys says, "to Scotland Yard or wherever the proper police that can be trusted are based."

I look around at all three of them. Rebecca nods her approval. "We have to try," she says.

I take a deep breath. "Okay. Let's go and find him."

Rhys glances at his watch. "He should still be out on his afternoon beat."

CHAPTER 39

Gwyn and I have no luck finding his uncle, so we return to the shop to find that Rhys and Rebecca were more successful. In the backroom, they hover on their feet nervously as Sergeant Gatsby and Mr B are seated and sipping tea. There's a mixture of smiles and curious expressions in the room. The policeman appears to be telling a story. "So, your mother yells, get down from the tree, *the dog is gone*, and I drop and end up breaking my leg. And she had to carry me home and I never heard the end of it."

Sergeant Gatsby and his brother-in-law are laughing but Rebecca and Rhys appear tense. They stare at Gwyn and me as we walk into the room.

"Dad, come now," Rhys says. "Give us a moment – you know we need to speak with Uncle Len."

"Okay," Mr B says. "I've got work to do, anyway. See you later, Len." The copper gives him a nod and Mr B lifts a newspaper that he was carrying under his arm, folded open on the crossword page.

Sergeant Gatsby looks around at each of us and he can see the mood in the room has changed.

"Well, this is interesting. What is it, children?"

I nod to Rhys to get the book out.

"Uncle Len. We need to tell you something," Rhys starts.

"Rhys, my boy, I've told you before, the Queen is not a lizard." He smiles.

"You won't believe us at the start," I say. "But do please hear us out."

He narrows his eyes and gives us all a puzzled look.

"We were tipped off by someone that we might find clues about what happened to Terry at the old asylum," I say.

"Terry? Tipped off?" He sits up.

I nod. "We went there and found something. An old bible hidden in the walls."

Rhys places the book in front of Sergeant Gatsby. His eyes widen. I watch his face and study it as I share the information. I want to pick up on any signs of guilt or that he knows more about what I am talking about.

"This book was hidden in the walls by an old resident of the asylum," I say. "Sir Henry Blythe. An English spiritualist who died there just over a hundred years ago."

Rhys opens the book in front of him.

"His notes talk about a secret group that exists in this village. One that takes children and sacrifices them to Mari Evans."

Gatsby almost leaps out of his seat. "What?" His face is torn between laughter and worry. "The witch?"

"This secret group is run by the Robham family," I say.

"Lord Robham?" he says, and his head is knocked back like I've just punched him in the face.

"Yes, the lord," I say. "They've been keeping it going for over 350 years."

"We don't know why yet," Gwyn says. "But it relates to Mari Evans's curse."

"Her curse?" he repeats.

I step closer to the policeman. His face is ashen. "We saw Mrs Astley – the lord's housekeeper – drawing witch marks and putting bits of dead animals onto the graves of children who died in years when disease hit the town."

"His housekeeper?" he says. I see his leg is shaking.

"Yes."

Gwyn steps closer to Sergeant Gatsby and crouches down in front of him. "We know this sounds absolutely nuts, but it all checks out, Uncle. It all fits together and makes sense."

The policeman leans forwards and inspects the old bible that's been placed in front of him. He squints and bites his lip as he examines each page.

"My dear children," he says. "This is…" He pauses and we all hold our breath.

"This is all so very creative." He looks up and smiles at each of us. "I know you've been busy with your investigations over the last few weeks, and I must commend you on this story – a conspiracy. Fantastic."

"But it's not…" I start before he talks over me. He's nervous, I think. Flustered even.

"Though you really shouldn't be talking about your school friend like that. Especially to the police about it. Some people would take such claims very seriously."

"Uncle Len, this isn't a joke," Gwyn says, sternly.

"Of course it is. How could any of this be true?" He signals to the book. "I mean look at this. The scribbles make no sense at all. Did you really find this book at the hospital? This book should be on the shelf here for sale. And by the way, you really shouldn't be going to places like that, as things are now. We have no idea what happened to Terry and the working theory is that some loner took him. So, there is a possibility that there might be someone dangerous out there."

"Sergeant Gatsby," I raise my voice. "This is all true."

He turns to look at me. "Oh Ned, I know you've had a rough year, so I'm pleased the lot of you have a hobby but there are serious matters underway in this town right now. Something very bad may have happened to your school friend. You are very close to the bone on this one." There's something in his voice I don't like but before I can respond, Gwyn steps in.

"We're not making this up," Gwyn says. "Our source believes the same thing."

"Your source?"

"Gerald Edwards," Rhys says, before I can tell him to shut up.

"Ah, the troubled author," he says with a knowing smile. "Another man with creative ideas. You know about his history, don't you?" Gatsby's eyebrows are raised as he speaks.

"History?" I repeat.

"I won't tell you the details of his deviancy, but I'd be careful in his company."

Gwyn stands in front of his uncle with his fists at his sides. Is he sad or disappointed? I can't tell.

Sergeant Gatsby stands up and puts his helmet on his head. "Now, joking aside, I don't need to remind you that Lord Robham is a very kind and decent person. He does a great deal for this town and local charities. His family – in fact – have been faithful friends of *Nant-y-Wrach* for hundreds of years. They've contributed an astounding amount of money to make this place the special home it is to us all. Now don't you forget that." He lifts his finger in the air and moves it around like he's threatening us with a magic wand. "Do not share your little stories with anyone outside this shop. I understand the fun of it but it's not nice to be making things up about the lord or your missing friend."

"Uncle Len, you're not listening to us," Gwyn says.

"Gwyn, I've listened to you enough. Now I must get back to work."

He puts his hand on Rhys's shoulder. "Thank you for the cup of tea, boys. Oh, and madam." He looks over at Rebecca. "You try and keep these boys from getting carried away with their investigations."

Rebecca smiles awkwardly and nods to the policeman before he walks out of the shop. I notice she didn't say a word during the conversation. Gwyn roars and pushes a pile of books off the nearest desk. Rhys stands silently and stares at the ground with his mouth open. I look over at Rebecca and I know she's thinking what I'm thinking.

"He was lying," she says.

"He wouldn't – would he?" Gwyn turns to Rhys with a worried look on his face.

Rhys shrugs his shoulders. "I never thought he would. But there was something off about his behaviour, wasn't there?"

Gwyn shakes his head. He's fighting it but I can see he's unsure. "I don't believe it. He loves this town. There's no way he would stand for something like that…"

"Unless…" Rebecca says.

"Unless what?" I ask.

"Unless this is the real face of the town," Rebecca says. "The face behind the mask. And it's very different to what we see every day."

"He was there with Robham at the press conference outside the police station," I say. "We knew there was something odd about it. Maybe the Custodians planned it."

Gwyn crosses his arms and starts shaking his head. "No chance. He knows right from wrong – I'm certain of it," Gwyn says.

"He may well do," Rebecca says. "But if this place is in his heart and in his bones, his view of what is right and what is wrong may be different to how we see it."

"Love is blind," Rhys says.

"Whatever the case," I say, "we're still in the same position as where we were before."

Gwyn takes a deep breath. "Right. So, what do we do next?"

"I think we've ruled out the police," Rebecca says.

"We certainly can't approach them with what we have," Rhys says.

I take large steps around the room trying to think of other options. "What about someone else? Like that detective on television? She's round here a lot, isn't she?"

"We'd need more evidence," Rhys says. "What we have now doesn't amount to a hill of beans."

"So how do we get that?" I ask, scratching the back of my neck. I notice Gwyn is facing away from us. He's laid his hands on an empty shelf and he's tapping his fingers as he thinks.

"Where is the evidence?" Rebecca says.

"We know what family would know," Rhys says, clapping his hands together. I realise he has it.

"Could we get into Robham House?" I ask.

"They do tours there," Rhys says. "Every day."

"Then we take the tour and investigate the place," I say. "Can we go tomorrow?"

"I might need some time," Rhys says, rubbing his chin and scanning the shelves around the room. "I don't know much about the layout of the house and the grounds. Need to get those details right."

"We don't even know if the Custodians are keeping him there." Rebecca crosses her arms.

"Where else could he be?" I ask.

Rhys turns around and grabs the town map from behind him. He opens it up and drops it onto his desk and scans over it. "Of all the questions I would expect to have an answer for, this really is the one I thought I could respond to, but honestly, I don't know."

I step over and point directly at the map. "Has to be Robham House."

"Yeah," Rhys says. "The only other place we don't know much about is the mine. But there's no way in or out so His Lordship's house is the only obvious location."

"Why do you say that?" Gwyn turns around and seems to be back with us.

Rhys signals to the map. "Look at it. Where else is there where people can come and go with any anonymity? Everyone knows each other here so to run a secret group without any notice – and for hundreds of years – takes organisation and infrastructure. At Robham House, they can host parties and gatherings without anyone in town noticing."

"And we've got good knowledge of the other places," I say. "*Cartref-Y-Gwynt* Farm, the churchyard, the library, Ogyn Lake, the Jungle, Mud Chapel, the bridge, the asylum…"

"Could they be somewhere else?" Gwyn says. "Another village or town or somewhere nearby?"

"I suppose they could…" Rhys says, unconvinced.

"But that wouldn't make sense, would it?" I say. "Their purpose is to protect this place, this town, and the people here. Their base needs to be here."

Gwyn looks up at me and nods slowly. Rhys lifts his head as well and makes eye contact with me and then looks over at Rebecca who glances at each of us, moving her eyes while keeping her head still. We all know what we need to do next.

CHAPTER 40

I am knackered when I get home. The place is quiet – no one in the kitchen or living room – so I head upstairs. In my bedroom I collapse onto the bed and stare up at the ceiling. I stroke my sore hand and fingers. Having Rebecca with us has changed everything – there's no way we'd be where we are without her – but the encounters we've had are nuts. Both Gwyn and I have seen, heard and felt things we couldn't have imagined only a few days ago. What's more, it seems that even when she's not there, I'm sensing things more strongly than I did before. I could feel the hitchhiker in the river with me yesterday and it was only Gwyn and me there. Maybe I do have some of the skills she has. Once all this is over, I'll have to reassess skills within the squad. And that thing today – thinking about it makes me grab the quilt and pull it over me despite the room being warm – that was on another level of nasty and I can only hope it is trapped in the asylum – trapped inside its small cell even. I really don't want to think about what I saw – what I felt – when it came after us. I started this mission, knowing evil was out there, but maybe the truth of what the evil looks like is a million times worse than what I imagined, and I can imagine a lot. Kids really are not safe here; in fact, that thing enjoyed hurting them. Hurting them in ways that make me feel weird and want to throw up all my guts. For a second, I was with it – inside its dead head – and I knew what it liked, what it really liked, and those thoughts now burn my brain. It didn't want to be with a lady and have a wife or a girlfriend, what it wanted was to be with little boys and girls. That's the only thing that made it feel right and *he* hurt them so that they stayed with him. And they're still with him now.

I turn on my side and rub my eyes – trying to get rid of thoughts from my head. I kick off the covers as I'm sweating and find myself trembling and I can't say whether it's anger, fear or excitement, but I'm deadly tired. Lying on the bed, my breathing becomes heavy, and my eyelids slide down, bringing darkness to my world.

I'm asleep but awake somehow. I cannot see anything. I'm lying on my back in a black void. I could be in space or at the bottom of the darkest lake.

"Down here," a familiar voice calls out.

"Terry, is that you?" I yell back and my voice echoes.

"Yes, I'm here."

"You're alive?"

"I think so."

I try and move my body, but my limbs are frozen. My right leg aches but the pain is dull and comes in waves like the water at the edge of Ogyn Lake. My hands lie at my side and my fingertips tap the ground beneath me – it feels like cold rock.

"I can't move," I say. "Where are you?"

"Here. It's where they put me. Can't you see me?"

"No, it's too dark."

"Don't give up on me, will you?" Terry sounds afraid.

"I won't," I say. "But where are you?"

"I don't know," he says. "Just please help me."

"Every time we get close," I say, "something blocks our way."

"But you're really close now," he says. "You know where I am."

"We don't," I say. "We're guessing. Searching is all we can do."

"Please keep searching. I'm alone and so scared." Terry's voice softens.

"I'm losing you," I say. "Just stay strong. We're doing all we can. We'll find you."

"I don't have long left, Ned." Terry's voice becomes faint and the next words I hear are the last. "I don't have the strength…"

I wake up to find my room is between day and night; sunlight is almost all gone, and the time of darkness is here. There's someone in the doorway.

"Mum?" I call out.

"It's me." Hannah steps into the room from the dark of the hallway. "You were yelling."

"I must have fallen asleep," I say. "What was I yelling?"

"You were talking to Terry."

"A dream," I say and pause. "You know, when I saw you in the doorway, I thought it was Mum."

Hannah steps closer and sits down on the edge of the bed. She strokes my hair. "Just me, I'm afraid. What were you dreaming about?"

"I dreamt I was talking to Terry. That I'd found him."

She stops stroking my hair. "You've been searching for him?"

"I think we know where he is," I say.

"Where?"

"You wouldn't believe me."

She shrugs her shoulders. "Try."

"He's been taken by a secret group of powerful people that run this town."

Her eyes become narrow. "Of course."

I sit up. "I knew there was no point telling you."

She scratches her head. "Okay, so who's in this secret group?"

"They're called the Apo-something-or-other Custodians. They've been sacrificing kids to the witch for the last 300 years."

"Three hundred years? How's a secret group survived so long in this town doing something like that? You can't get new curtains without Mrs Jones in the newsagent finding out…"

"I don't know," I say. I see how she's looking at me and I'm not sure if she's playing along or having a laugh. She doesn't believe me – that's for certain.

"Look, I know you're sceptical but don't make fun of me. This thing is serious."

"Right, well, if it's serious, you should talk to the police. They're on every news programme begging people to come forward with anything. Anything at all."

"We have, actually," I say. "We spoke to Sergeant Gatsby."

"And?" Her face tightens when her tone gets like this, and it usually comes before an argument.

"He didn't believe us."

"There's a surprise."

"But we have proof," I say and raise my voice.

"What proof?" There's a dull attempt from her to look surprised.

"Notes in an old book we found at the old asylum."

Hannah's jaw drops. "You've been to the asylum? What did I tell you about staying away from those places?"

"Hannah, we had to. So many things are guiding us right now. We've seen and heard too much for all this not to be true."

Hannah turns away and I grab her arm. "Terry's alive, Hannah. I'm sure of it."

"Ned, he's been missing for over a week. If this secret group really has him, why would they be keeping him alive for so long?"

"That, we don't know," I say. "But we're certain that if we don't help him soon then he will be a goner."

She shakes her head. "A secret society in this town – of all places – I don't know…"

"It's true," I say.

"Do you know who's in it?" she asks.

"Lord Robham for one. His family has always run it. Maybe some of his staff as well. Other than that, we don't know. It's not a good sign that Gatsby lied to us."

"He lied about believing you?"

"Definitely," I say with some emphasis. "We're sure of it."

"Oh God," she says and pinches the skin on her neck. "Just try and stay out of trouble, will you? Hanging about in derelict buildings is one thing but winding up the local police is not good."

"We're careful," I say. "We're thorough – you know that."

"But if there is a secret group out there snatching children, don't you think you're in danger as well? Why would they stop at Terry?"

I shake my head. "We hadn't really thought about that."

Hannah stands up and puts her hands on her hips. "I'm tired of being the only parent in this family. Do whatever you want. Have you had dinner?"

"No, I fell asleep as soon as I came back."

"You hungry?"

I nod.

"No sign of Dad since you've been here?"

I shake my head.

"Come on then – there's fish fingers in the freezer, I think."

We both leave the room and I follow her down the stairs.

"Where were you before?" I ask.

"Went to see Jenny. Needed to get out for a bit. You know her brother is in hospital with this bug that's been going around."

"Bug?" I ask.

She stops and turns to look at me as we enter the kitchen. "It's like a bad flu – fever and terrible coughing," she says. "They reckon he got it from a lad at Scouts who's also in hospital."

"You gonna warn me to avoid Scouts now as well?" I can't help smirking a little as I say this.

"Would you listen to me?"

I shrug and sigh. "You know if you want to get out more, you can always join us on our investigations. We always need more skills in the group."

Hannah puts her hands on her hips. "What skills do you think I could bring?"

"Logistics," I say.

She cocks her head and gives me a funny look. "Where did you hear that word?"

"War film," I say. "Can't remember the name."

"Logistics," she says. "I suppose running this house is a complicated operation. Right now, our mission is dinner."

CHAPTER 41

After an early briefing at the shop, we've arrived at Robham House. There were two interesting developments in the briefing: Firstly, Rhys told us there's an old secret passage that leads beneath the house, which has now been closed off (and we'll be trying to find out more about this in today's operation). Secondly, to help distract the attendant, our very own Q would be joining us out in the field on this operation, so quite a turn-up for the books, which sounds like a good joke because he usually does nothing but read books, but I don't think that was the original purpose of the saying.

Gwyn and I arrive at Robham House ten minutes or so after Rebecca and Rhys. After cycling up the gravel lane we leave our bikes resting against the side of the building. Before entering, we both inspect the grounds. On one side, the hedge curves around to a small wooded area that leads around the gardens to Ogyn Lake. The water barely moves in the warm, still air. Beyond the water, we see the old windmill that sits above the lead mine on Plum Mountain.

"Does the Robham family still own the old mine?" Gwyn says.

"Think so," I say. "Why?"

"Just wondering."

We enter Robham House and get our tickets from the attendant who stands by the door. We've coordinated our timings so that Rhys and Rebecca will start asking questions exactly five minutes after we arrive. We won't let on that we know either of them, so they have no reason to think that the two groups are together. In addition to the four of us, there's also an elderly couple wandering around. That's good, I think – more distraction. We walk through the main hall, past the grand stairs, in through the drawing room and around into the music room. From there, we have visibility of the library, and we see Rhys and Rebecca have positioned themselves in front of the mural.

Gwyn looks at his watch. "It's almost time," he whispers.

We see the attendant entering the library on her rounds. Rebecca nudges Rhys with her elbow and Rhys turns to ask the attendant something. From where we stand, we can't hear them speaking. I glance over at Gwyn and nod and we both follow our route back to the main hall. There, we stop and look around before Gwyn ducks under the barrier at the bottom of the stairs and heads up. I leave him and enter a doorway next to the stairs, which opens out into the dining room. I see the biggest dinner table I've ever seen. It's surrounded by more chairs than I can count as I rush through. There are paintings on the walls and a large glass-fronted cabinet full of ornaments. One of the objects catches my eye and I stop for a moment. It's a bronze statue of death standing with a scythe in his hand. It's on the third shelf up and I crane my neck to examine it. I've seen the same statue elsewhere – in Horse's hut in the Jungle. I can see a gap where the other one must have stood – were they a pair? Horse must have been here. I don't have much time to dwell on it, so I carry on into the next room – the waiting room if I remember rightly – a smaller space where the walls are covered in wooden panels and four fancy sofas are pressed against them. From there, I enter a dark corridor and stride through until I find myself in a massive kitchen. I stop by the door and peer in, but there is no one around. Looking across the room I see a small door that must be the entrance to the cellar. I dash past a table and crouch next to one of those islands where chefs do all their chopping on cooking programmes. I turn my head and look across the whole of the kitchen. It's still clear so I spring to the cellar door and upon grabbing the handle I shudder as a wave of misery comes over me, and I drop to my knees like the handle is connected to electricity wires and designed to electrocute. But it's not that kind of shock – it's more like someone is walking over my grave. I let go and wrap the bottom of my T-shirt over my hands and try again. This time I can turn the handle – and I both push and pull hard on it. No surprises, it's locked, and I crouch down and try to look through the keyhole. There is some light, but I cannot see anything. I put my ear to the door and listen. It sounds like there is music playing but I cannot be certain. My gut tells me that the cellar is very important to our investigation. Things happen there – have happened there – that the outside world is unaware of; we need to get in. I turn around and scan the room to see if there is a key nearby. I check the drawers and the nearby cupboards. As I step towards the large window, what I see takes my breath away. Mrs Astley is talking to Sergeant Gatsby. She has her arms crossed and he holds on to a plastic bag. I cannot hear them but they both look very serious. She turns her head and glances back at the house, so I duck down. Slowly, I lift my head again and I see the policeman handing her the bag. She opens it and pulls out Terry's dripping HEAD holdall. Holy fuck, this is it, I think – the smoking gun.

I cover my mouth to mask the noises of excitement. We were right – I was right – there is a bloody conspiracy; there is a secret group; they do have Terry. We can save him. Fuck, fuck, fuck. I take a deep breath and watch as she drops the soaking holdall back into the plastic bag before rubbing her fingers and wiping them on her coat sleeve. They fished it from the river or the lake and the bag is not yet dry.

Her expression changes. She frowns and tenses her jaw and jabs her finger in the policeman's face. I can just about hear her voice – she must be shouting – but I can't make out what she says. He looks scared and shakes his head. She steps closer to him, and her finger is almost up his nose. I can see his lower lip is quivering. What the hell is she saying to him? I need to find out. I reach over and gently open the window by releasing the catch. I'm in luck – the frame releases and I push it open slightly to hear her voice.

"… that's why we need this," she says. "Let's hope it works so we can calm him down. We can't have him losing his mind right now. He's not ready. When he is, that's when we tell people the festival is back on. Only when we know he's ready. Too soon and it won't work. We have clear instructions on this."

The time of the festival. Like the evacuee that went missing in the forties. That is when they'll do it.

Gatsby nods, looking like a child who's been told off.

"Alright, ma'am," Gatsby says. "I'd better go. They're expecting me at the station."

She grabs his arm, and her expression softens. "We're close now, Len. Don't lose your nerve. Getting these next – final – steps right is critical."

He gives her an awkward smile before dropping his head and turning on his heels to leave. She stands there staring with a blank look on her face. There's no way of telling whether she's happy, sad or angry. It makes the hairs on the back of my neck stand on end. Once Gatsby is out of sight, she turns and strides towards the house. God, she's coming in. I glance over at the back door and lunge across the room towards the corridor, slipping on the smooth floor and fall on my face. I can hear the door being unlocked and I crawl out of the room. I make it around the corner and stop with my back against the wall, panting.

"I thought I heard someone. What on earth are you doing down there on the floor, dear?" I look up and see Mrs Astley grinning at me. I open my mouth, but I cannot speak. There is something about this woman…

She reaches out her hand. "Did you get lost? It's a big old house, isn't it?"

Her voice is surprisingly gentle and – dare I say it – she sounds kind. I try and smile and pull myself back up by running my fingers against the wall.

I hear dripping and see drops of water falling from the plastic bag she carries. She sees me gazing at the bag and cocks her head. The friendly smile drops on one side and there's something about the way she looks at me that I don't like at all. She doesn't blink. She just stares.

I get to my feet slowly, finally, and nod to her, nervously. "Yes, s-s-s-sorry, got l-l-l-lost. Too m-m-many rooms. Felt dizzy. S-s-sat down here."

"Of course. Now to get back to reception, just follow this corridor and then go straight through the waiting room and the dining room and you'll find yourself in the main hall. The reception area is just beyond there. It's not that difficult to find your way back. Surprised you found yourself lost, really." Both ends of her mouth turn upward, and I look away as her stare makes me feel uncomfortable. I begin to back away and nod to her. I do an about turn and pick up the pace. As I enter the waiting room, I look back and see that she still stands there staring – she hasn't moved an inch.

In the main hall, I find Gwyn waiting by the bottom of the stairs.

"Anything?" he says, whispering.

"Yes," I say. "Something big. But we need to get out of here right now."

Gwyn's face changes telling me he hears the urgency in my voice, and we head out without any further questions. We walk through the library and past Rhys and Rebecca. He is still chatting away to the attendant, but she sees us going past. From there, the plan is to leave separately as we arrived and then regroup back at the shop.

"What is it?" Gwyn asks.

I speak fast in a hushed tone as my heart races and my mouth has become dry. "It's all true, Gwyn. Bloody all of it." I grab his arm as I try and guide him out of the place quicker. "And we're the only ones who can stop them."

I've been on this mission to defeat the monsters of this town to keep everyone safe. In missions, we've come against spirits and supernatural things that've tried to hurt us. But we fought back, and we've survived. But now I've come to realise the real danger doesn't come from the afterlife. The real threat – maybe the real monsters – are people. The secret group called the Custodians are the ones planning to kill a child. They're the ones we must fight. And that is a battle that worries me more than all the paranormal forces can throw at us. But it is a fight that we must take on. Terry's life depends on it. Winning is the only way we'll keep him safe.

CHAPTER 42

When we're all back together at HQ, we get a chance to share our experiences. Rebecca is perched on Rhys's desk while he sits in his chair and rests his elbows next to her. Gwyn is cross-legged on the floor with his hands on his knees and I pace around them as I tell them about my strange experience with Mrs Astley and what I saw from the kitchen window.

"Uncle Len is definitely involved then." Rhys now has his hands clasped.

"Yeah, but I'm not sure how willing he is," I say.

"There's no way he'd be happy to help the Custodians," Gwyn says. "I bet they're blackmailing him."

"I don't know," I say, rubbing my chin.

"Why do you think they wanted the bag?" Rebecca asks.

"Not sure," I say. "They said something about *calming him down*. Maybe there's something in it."

"Why did you send us to find it?" Gwyn asks.

"I'm not certain," Rebecca says. "I really don't remember that."

"You told us that Terry was alive then you said *under the bridge* over and over again," I say. "Maybe you didn't know it was the bag that we needed. We – I – assumed whatever was there would help us. Maybe give us proof he was alive."

Gwyn tells us about his unsuccessful trip upstairs. He explains that all but one of the fifteen doors he counted were locked. The one open room was a small toilet with nothing interesting to report about. He looked through keyholes and took photos but didn't see anything that connected the place to Terry.

Rebecca and Rhys had done their job to distract the attendant. But they also learned more about the secret rooms and passages.

"She told us there are rumours of a tunnel that runs deep underneath the house and connects to a huge ancient dungeon," Rhys says. "Really old. Like medieval."

"Dungeon?" Gwyn repeats and looks at us all.

Rhys shrugs. "Not sure how much truth there is to it. It may be a red herring that they tell people to distract them."

"I bet they have plenty of cover stories," Rebecca says.

"What about the secret passages in the walls?" Gwyn asks.

"There was one, but it's been sealed up," Rebecca says. "Apparently."

Everyone is silent. Rebecca sighs.

Gwyn rubs his hands together. "Where does this leave us then?"

"Well," I say, counting in the air with my fingers, "one, we know the Custodians are real, two, that the Robham family are involved, and three, they must have Terry."

Gwyn gives out an impatient snort. "But we're no closer to finding out where he is, are we?"

"If they plan to kill him on the day of the festival, then we have more time," Rhys says.

"Maybe but not long," I say.

"They haven't announced when it'll go ahead yet," Rhys says.

"They haven't said if it will go ahead yet," Gwyn says.

"But assuming it does," Rhys says, "when they do announce it then we know what it means."

Gwyn purses his lips and blows.

"I still think he's being kept at that house," I say.

"What we need is more time there," Rhys says. "Have a proper explore when they aren't expecting tourists."

"We'd have to go there at night," I say.

"Very risky." Rhys taps his fingers on the desk as he thinks. "If we got caught, who knows what they'd do to us. I'm not even sure how we'd get in or out of the place – did you see the locks on the doors and the windows?"

Something comes to me. "I think I know someone who could help us with that. But it won't be easy…"

Gwyn raises his eyebrows.

"In a glass cabinet in the dining room," I say, "I saw a bronze statue of death. It's one of a pair and there was a gap where the second one should've been. I've seen the second one and I know who has it."

"Oh no," Gwyn says. "Horse?"

"Yeah," I say. "It was in the Eagle's Nest."

"Jungle." Rhys says, and he blows through his lips.

"Right," I say. "There's no way he could've taken that during visitors' hours. I bet you anything, he found another way in."

"It's his MO," Rhys says.

"Are you saying what I think you're saying?" Rebecca says.

I nod silently in response and cross my arms.

"Fricking great," Gwyn says, holding his head with his hands. "Not only do we have the fricking Custodians and violent fricking spirits or whatever they are to deal with, we now need that fricking psycho to join our squad as well. Seriously, there must be another way?"

I shake my head slowly from side to side. "There isn't. And I know it won't be easy, but we can do it. I promise you. Each step we've taken so far has been harder than the last. Yet here we are – still going – still battling on. Horse is a nutter, but we need his help to get into that place."

"If we can get in, we can explore the place properly, and we can find a way into the cellar to see what's really going on in there," Rhys says.

"I'll bring *Taid* this time," Rebeca says. "There may be a helping hand on the other side we can reach out to."

"You really think we can get that psycho to help us?" Gwyn asks, his teeth clasped. "We're still in his bad books after the last Jungle operation. Do I need remind you of what happened?"

"No, I remember," I say and clear my throat. "I'm thinking – hoping – that we can use that in our favour," I say. "I have an idea…"

"I hope you're right," Gwyn says. "If we're murdered, we won't be helping Terry. We won't be helping anyone."

"If we can, we should try and go back to Robham House later," I say. "Tonight."

"Agreed," Rhys says.

"Yes," Rebecca says.

"But first…" I say.

"Oh God." Gwyn looks down at the ground, sighs and nods. He knows what's coming.

CHAPTER 43

Gwyn, Rebecca and I head straight to the Jungle to find Horse and his Goons.

"This is a bad idea," Gwyn says grudgingly, as we walk up the farmer's path. "And funnily enough, it's not the first bad idea we've had. Our summer has become a series of bad ideas."

"We've been through this," I say. "It's the only way."

Rebecca sighs. "What's your plan?"

"Erm – just follow my lead," I say.

"That does not sound reassuring," Gwyn says.

I stop walking and glance between both of them. "It's going to be a combination of a carrot and a stick."

"Carrot and a stick?" Rebecca says, touching her throat.

"Yeah, for the carrot, I'll try and pique his interest by telling him what we know about Terry's disappearance. I think he's interested in all the grim, spooky stuff. He was there for the press conference the other day. He was entranced by the whole thing."

"He certainly likes his morbid memorabilia," Gwyn says turning to Rebecca. "No disrespect to your *taid*, of course."

Rebecca shrugs and half smiles. "And what about the stick?"

"I'm going to tell him we had Gwyn's camera with us the

other night and we took photos of the three of them half naked on that mattress in the hut."

"Half naked?" Rebecca says with raised eyebrows.

"Are you fricking crazy?" Gwyn says. "He'll kill us."

"Not if we do it properly," I say. "Make sure he knows the photos are safe and if anything happens to us then photocopies go up around town on lamp posts underneath Terry's posters."

"Oh shit," Gwyn says. "You are playing with fire and the both of us are sat on a big box of dynamite."

"What do you think?" I ask Rebecca.

"It's risky but it could work. Just don't let him into your head," Rebecca says. "He has a reputation as a thug but he's a lot smarter than that and he knows how to mess with people."

"Agreed," I say, and I point down the path. "Come on, we're almost there."

Gwyn shuts his eyes, shakes his head and follows us. "We're about to be murdered. I hope you know that."

I just put the blinkers back up and carry on.

We arrive at the hut and find Horse stood with a hatchet in his hand. He aims it at a tree while his Goons look on. I glance at Rebecca, with her arms crossed and at Gwyn who takes two puffs on his inhaler and wipes the sweat from his forehead, before clearing my throat loudly. I try to act cool, but I have to keep reminding myself to breathe and I suddenly feel a massive urge to piss.

Shag spots us first. "Boss," he says. "We've got company."

Horse tosses the small axe, and it spins through the air and lands in the trunk of the tree opposite. He then turns to face us with a wide smile on his face.

"Now this is a fucking treat," he says. "Is it Christmas Eve? Has Santa come to empty his big bulging sack all over the bedrooms of the good boys and girls?" Horse grins and the two Goons cackle away like Statler and Waldorf.

He gestures for them to quieten down. "Seriously," he says. "Are the thieves finally here to return my stolen property? It's about bloody time. Take it you brought me the Gypsy bitch as a bonus prize?"

We edge a little closer and stop. "We're not returning anything," I say. "We're here because we need your help."

His smile drops and his brow becomes furrowed. "My help? What the…? Oh, this will be interesting. And what if I don't want to help you? What if – instead – I tie the three of you to that tree and use you for target practice?"

My mouth is dry, and I lick my lips. "You wouldn't do that. No one comes to you for help. They all think you're an insane bully, but I know there's more to you. I know you're interested in the same things as we are." I rub my moist palms on my trousers and glance over at Rebecca and Gwyn who look terrified.

"Besides," I say, "I also have photos."

Horse cocks his head and I realise there's no turning back.

"Ahem. See, when we were here the other night, Gwyn brought his camera, and we took photos of the three of you *together*. Now whatever you were up to is your business, but we do have some photos of the three of you asleep in the hut and – honestly – they don't paint a great picture."

Horse glares at me like a lion staring down a gazelle he's about to pounce on and devour. I'm not sure what he'll do next but right now I can see he's thinking. I'm about ready to leg it but all of a sudden, I see an unexpected movement on his face – the corners of his mouth turn upwards, and he smiles; no, stranger still, he starts laughing. The Goons look confused, and Rebecca and Gwyn remain frozen and quiet.

"Ha. Oh well played, boys," he says. "A bloody camera. That took some fucking nerve. And photos of us asleep – I bet you fucking loved that, didn't you? Cocks and arses out and half naked. I bet you've made good use of the pictures already, haven't you, you filthy little bastards. And no doubt you'll tell me the photos are safe and if anything happens to any of you right now then the pictures go up all around town. You'll probably be wanting amnesty for taking my skull as well. Cheeky bastards. Well played, indeed."

I just shrug and nod quietly. Maybe this might work.

"I get it," Horse says. "You've got my attention."

He points to tree stumps near the hut, which I think means he wants us to sit down. He steps over to the tree and pulls out the hatchet before joining us in his seating area.

Perched on the stumps, Gwyn and Rebecca look to me to explain the situation. I tell him what we've learned so far, and after I've spoken, he closes his eyes and starts to stroke his face. I look across at the rest of the group. Gwyn rubs his hands together. Rebecca taps her fingers on the log on which she sits. Shag smirks and shakes his head; he glances over at Pablo, who lights a cigarette and watches Horse.

Horse leans forward. "You're telling me, a secret group that's existed for hundreds of years, runs this town, and sacrifices a boy every forty years to stop a witch's curse. That about the gist of it?"

"More or less," I say.

"You believe us?" Gwyn says.

"Dead kids, curses, witches," Horse says. "Fuck me. Sounds more like the hobbies of the Gypsy girl here." He stands up and starts slapping the hatchet against the palm of his hand, and Gwyn starts biting his nails.

"You're right that no one would come to me for help. But do I believe you?"

It's odd the way he says it. We're used to his nasty, mocking tone but now he sounds uncertain. He might even sound interested.

He glances behind – each way at his Goons. "What do you reckon, boys? Any truth to this nonsense, you think?"

"Ha, good one, boss," Shag says.

Pablo sucks hard on his cigarette. "What part of it isn't bullshit do you think?"

"Ha. The boys here are sceptical," Horse says, his eyes moving across the three of us.

"What about you?" I ask.

"It's a tough pill to swallow. But here's the thing: something isn't right about this town. There's always been a fricking strangeness here. A certain mad grandeur to the place considering it's just a shitty little backwater in the Welsh mountains. The pigs, the council, the hospital, even the bloody library – they all act like they're hiding something. I've always suspected that something wasn't right. It's not a story I would've expected but I knew there was something."

Horse glares at us all – as if to see how we are reacting to what he says. His face doesn't have the usual swagger. There's a vulnerability there that I haven't seen before.

"A lot of people here think it," he says. "It's just no one wants to say it out loud."

I lean forward. "And what about you – what do you think?"

Horse purses his lips and exhales. "Honestly, why should I care? We could carry on as normal – the three of us could beat you all senseless now, take back that skull and forget about any of this bullshit. And if you share the damn photos – so what? It's just another story about me. I don't give a shit what the town arseholes think. They're all backward idiots anyway. And if this secret gang is real and wants to kill the boy, why would I want to get in their way? Why would I want to get on their radar? They've done me no harm. You're the only ones who've threatened me."

"We don't think it's right," Rebecca says. "We're not going to let them get away with it any longer."

Horse scoffs. "Get the little Gypo here, out to save the world."

I see Rebecca frown, but I give her a look and shake my head; we can't do anything to piss him off any more – that wouldn't help.

Horse launches the hatchet at the tree, and he makes a direct hit. "I have no intention of getting involved unless there is something in it for me."

Something comes to me, and I think I may have a way of getting him onside. "But what if you did? And what if we're successful in stopping them and then the town faces the wrath of the witch's curse. Wouldn't you love to see it burn?"

Horse sits back and strokes his chin. "That would be… diabolical. Now that, that is an interesting prospect."

"If the curse is real, wouldn't you like to see what happens next?"

Shag and Pablo look horrified. They glance at each other before Horse turns around and gives them both a wink.

"What kind of help are you looking for from me, exactly?"

"We need to get into Robham House," I say. "Tonight. I know you've made it in there before – can you help us?"

"Yes, that's child's play," Horse says. "But why do you want to go inside that old nonce's palace?"

"We're after something but we're not sure what, yet," I say. "I think we'll know when we see it."

"We think it's where they're keeping Terry," Rebecca says.

"We can't go to the police," Gwyn says.

"Ha. Of course not," Horse says. "If these fuckers are real then they probably own the pigs."

Rebecca and I look over at Gwyn. His head drops.

"One thing though," Horse says. "I will need to come with you."

"Can't you just tell us how to get in there?" I ask.

"I could," he says. "But I wanna see what happens next. That's how you sold this to me so I'm there for the full spectator experience. Oh, and if we pick up any souvenirs on the way, then I get to keep them for my collection."

I look to Gwyn and see the tendons in his neck standing out. Rebecca stares back at me with wide eyes and shrugs.

"Okay," I say. "It's a deal. We'll go tonight." Inside, my stomach is turning.

Horse sits back down on the stump next to us. "Oh and let me be crystal fucking clear on one thing. If your photos are real and they do see the light of day, I'll come after each of you. You two, I'll cut your cocks off and swallow them raw before watching you bleed to death, and you, madam, I'll take that head off and peel away the flesh, so I have a pair of soddin' Gypo skulls in my collection. That means no fucking games. And this witch-baiting group of child killers had better be real, otherwise I'll be holding you to account."

CHAPTER 44

The five of us meet at the entrance to the Robham House driveway. It's just turned midnight and we're all set for the mission ahead. It's another warm night and the sky is clouded over – meaning visibility is minimal. Gwyn and I are dressed in black. Each of us is holding a torch. This isn't the first mission of its kind that we've attempted but tonight the operations team is a bit bigger than usual. Rhys joins us again – more out of necessity than want; knowing it's too important not to come with us. Also, we have a new – unexpected – member joining our ranks.

"Fuck me, I didn't realise the gay SAS were coming." Horse stares at us both. "No shoe polish this time?"

Gwyn drops his torch nervously, and swiftly picks it up.

"We'll do without it tonight," I say.

"Let's go through the plan again," Rhys says.

"Horse shows us into the house and then we split into two groups," I say. "Rebecca and Rhys will stay in the living room and see what information *Taid* can help us with. Gwyn and I will explore. We'll try and get into the cellar first. If we don't succeed there, we'll take it upstairs. Horse…"

"… I'll go wherever the hell I want."

"Just don't take any risks, will you?" I ask.

"I wouldn't dare." Horse gives me a wink and I rub the back of my neck.

We keep the torches low as we walk down the lane. Gwyn keeps glancing over at Horse. I can sense his nervousness. I am the same and know that our mission is dependent on the cooperation of this unpredictable nutjob.

I turn my attention to Horse. "How are we getting in there?"

"We need to go around the back of the building," Horse says. "We climb up a drainpipe and get onto the roof of the extension. There, we can enter through a window in the hallway, which has a dodgy latch."

"That easy, eh?" Gwyn says.

"Actually, yes," Horse says. "Unless, that is, they've fixed it, but I doubt that."

"Are there any alarms or cameras we need to watch out for?" Rebecca asks.

"There's one security camera by the entrance," Rhys says.

"That's for the daytime," Horse says. "No one will be watching it at this time. What you need to watch out for is the old groundskeeper who patrols the place at night. Looks like a right old perv. If he catches you, expect to be chocking on his old cock within the hour. You lads will probably like that." Horse nods in Gwyn's and my direction.

"There are no alarms," Rhys adds. "Rigging up a full security system for a big old house like this would cost a fortune and Lord Robham with his recent divorce is not so flush right now."

"Plus, I expect they have a direct line to the local police so don't have much need for a security system," I say.

"The odd burglary doesn't seem to worry them." Horse looks proud.

We reach the house and turn the torches off. We give the entrance a wide berth and make our way around the edge of the grounds to the back of the house. Whether or not someone is watching, we don't want to take any chances. We pass the spot outside the kitchen where I saw Mrs Astley and Gatsby talking and my heart starts racing. At the back of the house, we see the extension, which looks much newer than the rest of the place.

Horse points to the drainpipe on the side of the wall and begins to climb up. The brackets stick out and make good rungs, so it doesn't look like a difficult climb. When he reaches the top, he looks back down at us and gestures for us to follow him. I go first and when I reach the roof, I see Horse is working on the window. He takes out a penknife and sticks it between the panes to release the catch. He slowly lifts the outer frame, and the window is open. He waggles the knife at me and gives me a thumbs up before folding it and placing it back in his pocket. The rest of the squad have now followed me up onto the roof as well. I make an okay sign with my hand and the three of them nod.

I climb through the window first. The dark hallway is silent and gloomy, apart from the ticking of a clock – the grandfather clock at the bottom of the stairwell. I can smell polish. With all the wooden surfaces, they must get through a ton of the stuff. As the others join me inside, I survey the space and think about all the ghosts that probably haunt it; how interesting it would have been to carry out an investigation here had we been able to. That is, before the stakes of the mission got as high as they are now. But it's odd – I don't sense the same things I did at the farmhouse or at the asylum. The mood here is calmer, quieter, more controlled. I might be wrong – hey, I'm not even sure I have the *klewmeirw* abilities yet – but I don't think the kids have ever been kept in the house – maybe the house is just the way in to where they are held.

When everyone is inside, I put my finger to my mouth and point to the stairs. We're not entirely sure how many people will be in the house. Rhys reckoned the lord and three or so of his remaining staff, which included the butler. Mrs Astley lives in town and leaves at the end of each day. Her presence is not something I'd be missing. His wife left him a couple of years ago, and she'd taken their son with her as well. The ongoing divorce was the talk of the town.

We all tiptoe down the grand stairs and then through the drawing room and around into the music room. This is where Rebeca will set up and try and connect to the other side. She is far enough away from the main stairs to not be heard from the upper level but still close enough to the exit point should we need to leave in a rush. Also, it happens to be the most haunted room in the house according to the guide Rhys and Rebecca spoke to earlier.

Rhys wanders around examining the room. Rebecca takes out *Taid* from her bag and places him on the grand piano. Horse's eyes light up when he sees the skull. After the last couple of encounters, we've warned Rebecca not to take any risks. She may be used to harmless interactions with the other side but there is something in the air right now that makes her a target for the nasty spirits.

"Remember – no picking fights with angry ghosts," I say.

"*Taid* won't be letting them near me," she says.

"Didn't you say that last time?" Gwyn says, and I see him fidgeting with his hands.

I put my hand on his shoulder. "Right," I say. "Gwyn and I will head to the kitchen."

We leave them in the music room and make our way across the main hall, through the dining and waiting rooms and down the lightless and shadow-filled corridor to the kitchen. Remembering my reaction last time, I touch the cellar door carefully but again it pulls me in. I feel my spirits and energy levels drop and I freeze with my palm against it. The door feels cold to the touch but what's behind it is worse. Behind it, there is sadness and loss and doubt and fear. All the quiet calm and control of the house ends at this door.

"What is it?" Gwyn says.

"Nothing," I say, realising it's not something I can easily explain. I take my hand away and Gwyn grabs the handle and pushes and pulls on it.

"Still locked."

"Where did you search for the key?" Gwyn asks.

"All these drawers and cupboards, but I stopped as I got to the end of that counter when I saw your uncle and that woman."

"Let's search the rest then." Gwyn rushes over to the next section and starts opening drawers. Before I join him, the kitchen is filled by the broad beam of a spot lamp.

"Down!" I grab Gwyn's hand and we both duck behind the kitchen counter. The light becomes brighter; someone outside is shining their torch through the window. I can feel beads of sweat running down the side of my forehead. We both have our hands over our mouths and dare not speak or say a word. The light moves across the room as whoever is shining it tries to survey the whole of the space. Then, it drops and moves along to the next window, which is around the corner. If they shine it on the ground, they will see us. We drop down and slither along the floor like snakes and crouch against the next counter. The light beams through the glass and moves along each corner and crevice as it tracks the gaze of whoever is outside. Then it drops again, and we both breathe out. That is, until we hear the handle of the back door being turned. Gwyn's face is pale, and I see his bright eyes shine in the dark like cartoon eyes. The handle is wiggled a little and the door is pushed but it remains closed.

I put my hand on his leg to calm him. "It's locked," I say. "They're checking it."

The light drops and the person leaves us, but we remain fixed in our positions on the floor for a minute or so, until we are sure.

"We need to warn the others," Gwyn says.

"Yes, you go. I'll keep searching."

Gwyn dashes off back in the direction from where we came. I continue to search every corner and space of the kitchen but there is no sign of the key. I keep looking around – for a pot or an unopened drawer or anywhere where the damned thing might be kept. I reach the last drawer and then lean on the counter above and bang my fists on the surface. It's hopeless, I think.

Suddenly, I hear footsteps and I turn my head to see Gwyn return. He looks excited.

"It's not here, Ned," he says.

"What's not here?" I ask.

"The key," he says. "It's not here."

"What? How do you know?"

"Rebecca made a connection. Not a crazy one this time. Someone who used to live and work here. A maid."

I turn around. "A ghost maid?" My jaw drops. "Where is it then?"

"On a chain around Robham's neck," Gwyn says. "How it's always been."

I look to the cellar door and then back at Gwyn, and we both dash back to the music room.

There, Rebecca is sat on the piano stool with the skull in her hands. She is hunched over and looks tired. Rhys is next to her. Horse sits in an armchair in the corner of the room with his feet up on a coffee table.

"Robham has the key?" I ask.

"Yeah," Rhys says. "It's a tradition. The lord holds the key from the day they receive the title until their own death. The cellar is the way in."

"The way in to where?"

"A secret place underneath the house," Rebecca says. "There are two ways in, actually. One is through the cellar and the other is a hidden entrance somewhere outside in the grounds."

I nod and glance across at each of them. "Too dangerous for us to go outside with that guy patrolling. We need to get in through the cellar. We need that key."

"It's really risky," Gwyn says.

"It's the only way," I say.

"And how exactly?" Gwyn says. "We take the key off him while he sleeps?"

"Yes, somehow."

"Can you do that without waking him up?" Rhys asks.

"We have to try," I say.

Horse stands up. "Fucking amateurs. What you need is someone with the stealth and skill of a master thief." He bows in front of us before laying his hand on his chest. "I do of course mean me."

"You'd do this?" Gwyn says.

"Call me a sucker for a challenge." His grin gives me the chills.

"Right," I say. I look to Gwyn who crosses his arms, and then back to Horse. "Let's do it."

As we ready to leave, Gwyn steps up close. "You trust him?" he says.

"No but he's got us this far," I say.

Horse, Gwyn and I leave Rebecca and Rhys in the music room and head upstairs. We walk along the hallway on the upper level, counting the doors. The sixth from the window where we entered is where the lord's quarters are meant to be. We find the entrance and it's big and grand and covered in carved shapes.

Horse turns the doorknob carefully – with a subtlety we've not seen from him before – and opens the door and peers into the bedroom. He pushes it further open and tiptoes inside. This is Horse in his element. We see his full skillset in action and it's difficult not to be impressed. His burglary and stealth skills may be a nine or – dare I say it – a ten. I glance over at Gwyn, and he wrinkles his forehead.

We follow Horse inside and watch as he sneaks over to the bed in the middle of the room. We cannot see the lord but there is someone breathing under the blankets. Gwyn touches my arm and points to the bedside table. An empty bottle of whisky lays on its side next to a glass.

Horse approaches Robham, reaches over, and lifts the corner of the blanket. His face is pink and thin, and we can see his lips move in time with the rumbles of his snoring. Horse reaches over and gently lifts part of the chain that hangs around the sleeping man's neck. He examines it and rubs his chin as he tries to work out how to remove the key. As he does, I notice a strange glowing light coming from the corner of the room. I turn my head and try and see where the source is. I gently tread across the floorboards in its direction and realise that the glowing is coming from the wardrobe next to the window. The door is slightly ajar, allowing the light to escape. Curiously, there is a chair placed in front of the wardrobe. Like someone has been sat there watching it. I look to the bed and see Horse continuing to examine and finger the chain. I step closer to the wardrobe and prise it open with my fingertips. At first, the light makes me blink, and I turn away but then my eyes adapt, and I realise that what I'm looking at is a small television; a security screen that shows a live view of another place. The picture is black and white and only shows one thing – a boy strapped to a bed in an otherwise empty room. He is dressed in robes and looks to be tied to the bed. I get closer to the screen and my mouth opens wide as I realise the boy is Terry Rowlands.

As I gasp, I hear the bedroom door open, and I instinctively shut the wardrobe. I turn to see Mrs Astley and a man we've not seen before, stood in the doorway – they are both holding rifles and have them trained at the three of us. Lord Robham's eyes have opened, and they dart across the room, as he pulls away from Horse, who still has his hands raised like he was intending to choke the sleeping man.

Gwyn looks petrified. Horse smirks – he seems amused that he's been caught.

"Oh, my goodness," Mrs Astley says, wearing a fake expression of worry. "The thief returns." She turns in my direction. "And the lost tourist with you."

"What...?" says Robham in a slurred voice like he's speaking in slow motion.

"This is rather serious, isn't it?" Astley says. "Now, what are we going to do with you lot?"

I glance over at Gwyn and Horse – who both stare at the pair in the doorway – and then look around the room; there is no way out. They have us boxed in. I start to take short, quick breaths as I try to think of a plan. But I am stuck. There's nothing we can do. They have complete control.

"What the…? What the hell is all this?" Robham says again. "Mrs Astley… what… why are you here? Who is… who are they?" He sounds like one of the red-faced men we always see outside the Black Cat pub.

"I'm so sorry, Your Lordship," the man accompanying the housekeeper says. He wears black trousers and a white shirt. Must be the butler, I think. "Seems they slipped past our defences."

"My apologies, Your Lordship," Mrs Astley says. "We'll take them downstairs and deal with them there." She gestures for us to follow her using her gun. "Go on."

"You heard the lady," the butler says. "Come with us right now."

CHAPTER 45

They take us downstairs to the waiting room where we find Rhys and Rebecca sat on one of the sofas. Both their heads hang low; Rhys looks worried, and Rebecca holds her bag tightly to her chest. The groundskeeper who we saw outside with the lamp is stood next to them. He also holds a rifle.

"Sit down," Mrs Astley says. Rhys and Rebecca move up slightly to allow the five of us to fit on the same chair.

"Go check the rest of the house and the grounds," she says. "Let's make sure we have all of them."

The two men leave us and it's only us and the housekeeper. She hovers over us like a schoolteacher about to tell off her pupils, and right now, I'd settle for lines or detention. What happens next is anyone's guess.

"Which of you is going to tell me what you're doing here tonight?" she asks.

The five of us glance at each other. I try and think of a response, but Horse gets there before me.

"Doing a bit of sightseeing," he says. "Fucking lovely place you have here." He looks over at me and winks.

"It's one in the morning," Mrs Astley scoffs. "Breaking and entering is a very serious matter. As is burglary. And who knows what you might have done to His Lordship had we not caught you in time."

"We meant no harm," I say. "We needed to know whether you were keeping Terry here."

"The missing boy?" Mrs Astley says, and her head pushes back like I've just slapped her. "Why would he be here?"

I take a deep breath. "Because you've kidnapped him. Before you sacrifice him to the witch."

"Sacrifice him to the witch?" A horrible fake smile appears on her face. "What an imagination you have."

I lick my dry lips and glance across at the others.

"Oh, you're serious?" she says. "You really believe Lord Robham and his household are behind the disappearance of the missing boy?"

"The Custodians," I say. "The secret group the lord leads and which I bet all of you are part of as well."

I can feel the others staring at me. They're probably wondering why I've gone for the throat. Truth is, I don't know. Maybe I'm tired of all the BS – maybe I want to draw these bastards out into the open.

"You think the lord and a secret group are sacrificing children to a witch?" she says, her eyebrows raised. This is a great performance but I'm buying none of it.

"You know," she continues, "people who believed things like that used to end up in the asylum down the road. You know why? Because it's madness, boy. The lord is a kind and giving gentleman who does a great deal for this town. Especially the children."

"Bullshit," I say, and she steps back like she's surprised by my language. "I saw Terry."

"What?" Gwyn says, grabbing my leg. "Where?"

"Did you now, and where was that?" Astley says.

"On the screen in Robham's bedroom." I turn to Gwyn. "I would've shown you had they not barged in on us."

"Barged in?" Mrs Astley says. "You were in the private sleeping quarters of His Lordship. You had absolutely no right being there."

"Maybe, but I definitely saw him. He was tied up and asleep on a bed. Probably being kept in the cellar of this house."

"This story keeps getting more ludicrous by the sentence," Mrs Astley says. "Have you listened to yourself? A television screen in a wardrobe? Why would someone keep a television in the wardrobe? And that's the least crazy of your assertions. How on earth did you come up with this idea of a secret group that abducts children?"

"The author told us," Gwyn says. "The one who wrote about Henry Blythe."

I kick Gwyn but it's too late.

"We also have Henry Blythe's account of the secret group," I say. "His notes guided us to Lord Robham."

"Henry Blythe?" Mrs Astley says looking across all of us. "The Victorian madman who chased ghosts and insane theories? I suppose you know where he ended his days, don't you? And where is this reliable account?"

"He wrote them in an old bible," I say. "It's somewhere safe."

Mrs Astley drops the smile, and her gaze is piercing, and I notice that I'm gripping my knees so tightly it's making my knuckles white. At that moment, the butler and the lord – now dressed – enter the room. The butler lifts his rifle when he sees us and then steps over to Mrs Astley, whispering something in her ear. She nods and narrows her eyes.

"Who else knows about these wild theories? Are there others in your little club or is this it?"

"Who else knows you're here tonight?" the man asks.

"There are others," Horse says quickly. "We won't say who, but don't you be thinking you can make us disappear."

Mrs Astley smirks. "Disappear? Oh, we'll be letting the law handle this. Mr Perkins, can you please show in the sergeant?"

"Oh no," Gwyn says.

Perkins disappears through the doorway, and I hear Gwyn and Rhys whispering to each other. Lord Robham stays quiet. He has dark circles around his eyes and sways gently like a blade of grass blowing in the wind. What's going on in that head? Why was he watching Terry?

Perkins returns with Sergeant Gatsby and as soon as he sees us he starts shaking his head.

"Sergeant," Mrs Astley says, "I believe Mr Perkins has told you what happened?"

"Yes, he has."

"And you're familiar with all these children?"

"Yes, some of them I know very well."

"Then I'll leave you to deal with them." She says these words in a way that makes me feel uncomfortable.

"Thank you, Mrs Astley." He points to the door with his thumb. "You lot, with me, now."

We follow the sarge out to his police car.

"I only have one car with me, so four of you will need to squeeze in the back."

"I call shotgun," Horse says.

He guides us to the car and makes sure we get in. After locking the door, Gatsby leaves us and returns to speak with Mrs Astley and Lord Robham in the doorway of the house. Horse sits alone in the front while the rest of us balance together in the back like building blocks. After some shifting, Gwyn ends up sat on his big brother's lap and Rebecca leans into me.

"So, now what?" Rebecca asks with a shaky voice.

"Depends…" Horse stares in the direction of the house.

"On what?" she says.

"How much of that bullshit is true."

"This isn't over," I say.

"You really saw him?" Gwyn asks.

"Yes, they do really have him."

"In that case," Horse says, "we won't be dealt with through

the usual channels back at the station. They'll take things into their own hands. Use alternative methods."

"What does that mean?" Rebecca asks.

Horse purses his lips and blows. "Who knows. But I'll take most things over juvie."

"Should we be worried?" Gwyn asks but no one answers and in the back of the car, each of us in turn look at each other.

Out of the dark, Gatsby appears and shocks us as he opens the door. He sits down in the car and sighs.

"Right, you're all in luck," he says. "His Lordship doesn't want to make a big fuss and he's happy for you all to be let off with a warning."

He places his arm on the back of the chair and turns to face us. "But this nonsense about Terry and this secret group needs to end, right? Tonight, you crossed a line. Maybe I should've been clearer with you yesterday. His disappearance is a grave matter for the police and the community. We can't be wasting our valuable resources with distractions like this."

"But Uncle Len," Gwyn says, "Ned saw..."

I poke Gwyn's leg and shake my head.

If the enemy is taking this battle to alternative methods, then we will have to do the same. We cannot trust the police or the local people in power. We're going to have to find our own way to help Terry and defeat the Custodians. This nastiness is at the heart of the town and until we know who's involved, we cannot trust anyone.

"I'll drop each of you off at home, but I won't disturb your poor parents at this time." The sarge glares at each of us. "I will, however, be talking to all of them tomorrow to make sure they understand what happened and realise how serious this situation is." Horse scoffs but the rest of us remain silent.

I am the last to be dropped off, and Gatsby pulls up outside my house and turns the engine off. I reach for the door handle but before I can pull it open, the sergeant starts to speak.

"Wait a second, Ned." He looks up into the rear-view mirror

and I see his eyes. They're red – he's tired. "I know you and your family have had a tough year. But this search for distraction has gone too far. You understand?"

I nod but he cannot see that my hands have knotted into tight fists.

"Your dad still hasn't gone back to work, has he?"

I shake my head and suck my lower lip into my mouth.

"What he went through, I wouldn't wish on anyone but it's time he pulled himself together. He needs to start being a father again for you and your sister."

I shrug my shoulders.

"I'll talk to him when I call him tomorrow." He turns his head and looks at the house.

"It won't help," I say under my breath.

"What was that?"

"It won't help," I say louder.

"It has to," he says. "Can't have you out and about at all hours, breaking into other people's homes. Besides being criminal, it's dangerous as well."

"Why?" I ask bluntly.

He looks up in the mirror directly into my eyes. "In cases like Terry's, when a child's been missing this long, it's unlikely we find them alive. We think he's been taken and there's probably a seriously disturbed individual out there."

"I bet." I sigh and look out of the window. I don't have the energy to argue with him any more.

"Can I go now?" I ask. "I'm knackered."

"Alright." He turns around and places his arm on the back of his seat. "Just promise me, no more investigations. And stay away from Robham House. Next time you may not be so lucky."

"Right." I grab the door handle again and exit the car. Walking towards the house, I can feel him watching me. My eyes are bulging and my teeth are grinding but I've had enough – I'm bloody tired and it's time for bed.

CHAPTER 46

I wake to the sound of my sister yelling my name. I frantically scan the room and see that I'm still fully clothed and sleeping on top of my bed covers. I look to the clock – it's nearly eleven.

"Ned, get down here," she yells again. I see flashes from the night before and realise the call from the sarge must've come through. Great, I think – time to face the music. I go into the living room and find Hannah stood against the fireplace with her arms crossed. Dad sits on the edge of the armchair; his hands are clasped, and he stares at the ground.

"This'll be interesting," I say, before sitting down on the sofa.

"Robham House?" Hannah says. "Seriously?"

"There's a nice mural," I say, half smiling.

"Now is not the time for jokes," Hannah says. "What were you thinking?"

There's no answer I can give that will please her, so I hold my hands up.

"Sergeant Gatsby says they found you with Gwyn and Horse. Horse – of all people – in the lord's bedroom. What were you doing there?"

"You wouldn't believe me if I told you."

"Try us," she says, and Dad looks up.

I take a deep breath. "Lord Robham is part of a secret group that abducts children and sacrifices them to Mari Evans in order to keep her happy and stop her curse on this town from coming true."

Dad puts his hand to his mouth while Rebecca shakes her head. "Oh no," she says. "You're not still on about this? Oh my god, breaking into somebody's house is a new level for you."

"There's more," I say. "I saw Terry. They do have him."

"You saw Terry?" Hannah's eyes narrow. "Did you tell the sarge?"

"I did but he's in on it," I say. "He won't believe us."

"It's a bonkers story." Her head drops. "Where do you think you saw him?"

"He was on a television screen in the lord's wardrobe." Given, these words do sound nuts as they fall from my own mouth.

"In the wardrobe?" she says. "I can see why the sarge might be sceptical."

"Gatsby won't even consider the idea." I sit back and cross my arms. "He's definitely with them."

She purses her lips briefly. "Did any of the others see Terry?"

"No, just me," I say, shrugging.

She rubs her hand over her mouth. "And why on earth was Horse with you? I thought you hated him?"

"He helped us get in there," I say. "He knew of a special way in."

Hannah turns away from me and grabs the fireplace with both hands. She looks over at Dad. "Aren't you going to say anything?"

Dad sits back in the chair and starts shaking his head. "My dear children, what can I say other than I've let you down."

Hannah glares at him and her head rattles uncomfortably like that guy in *Scanners* before his brain explodes.

"I work so hard on the writing but still haven't finished this damned book," Dad says. "I work all the hours God allows me, but my progress is slow, and I struggle to meet my milestones."

"Dad, that is not what we want," Hannah says. "What we need is you. We need you to be our father."

"I understand you're frustrated, Hannah *bach*," he says. "You're also angry at me for not finishing this thing in a prompt fashion. You know that once I finish the book then I will be able to support you properly. The sales will sort out our financial trouble and then of course I will have more time to help around the house – do the cooking and the cleaning."

Hannah turns to face Dad – her nostrils are flaring. "Dad, your son was caught in an older man's bedroom last night. He was held at gunpoint until the police came and picked him up. He's saying he saw the abducted boy, as well. None of this is usual behaviour."

Dad stands up. "You're right, Hannah – it's time I took real responsibility for my family." He bends down and looks at her in the face with a serious smile. "Let me take this as my warning shot. Let me turn these concerns into action. This experience will be seared into my mind. Not a moment will pass without my remembering this very moment." He raises his hand and points to the door. "I will go now back into that shed and not rest until I have finished my draft."

"That isn't what I meant by…" Hannah speaks but is cut off as Dad continues.

"I will do my duty to my family to get the job done so that I may care for my two children – the centre of my universe." He holds his hands over his heart. "I will do that and then be the father you need and more."

And with that, he walks out of the room, leaving his kids alone and – not for the first time – speechless.

Hannah collapses onto the armchair and holds her head in her hands. She starts sobbing gently. I sit there for a second before standing up and going over to her. I sit on the arm of the chair and put my arm around her.

"Don't worry about me," I say. "Don't worry about any of it – we'll be alright."

I leave her like that and go into the kitchen, readying myself to leave. At the door I stop and look at her. I want to be there for her, but she doesn't know that we are now at war. Tears are to be expected but they can't get in the way of the mission and its completion. I'm certain I'm on the right path now.

CHAPTER 47

We didn't arrange to meet back at the shop but regrouping at HQ was always our fail-safe in case anything went wrong. The time is around twelve. Mr B sits behind the counter holding his newspaper. As I enter, he looks up and wears a pinched expression.

"Didn't know if we'd see you in here today," he says.

I scratch my chin and struggle to find the words to respond. He sits forward and drops the newspaper onto the counter.

"What did your dad say about what happened?" he asks.

I clear my throat and shrug.

"It's not good, you know. Going off exploring places like that at night." He cocks his head to the side. "That's someone's house, you know. Bloody stately home and everything."

My head drops.

"I'm sure you've heard it all before at home, but don't you let these boys distract you with their adventures. You can explore most of this town but there are places that are off limits, right?"

Their adventures? I nod.

"Go on then," he says. "They're waiting for you in there. That Gypsy girl is with them as well."

I should have expected a response from Mr B and in fairness to him that wasn't so bad, but it did feel weird. I leave him at the front of the shop and make my way to the back where I find the three of them. Rhys has his feet up and is reading a book. Gwyn is sipping tea from a mug, and Rebecca has her back to me. She leans against the table and appears to be scanning the spines of books in the divination section on the far side of the room.

Gwyn looks up. "Well?"

"As I expected," I say. "You?"

"Same."

"What did they say?" I ask.

"A lot," he says. "First Mum then Dad. Then they argued and Mum blamed Dad for keeping us here."

I nod and Rebecca turns around.

"Didn't think we'd see you this morning," I say.

"Father and the rest were out early," she says. "Police haven't spoken to him yet. After that you probably won't see me. Thought I'd come down here one last time."

I survey the room and assess each of them. They all appear defeated. They think it's over, but I can't have that.

"God, look at you all," I say. "It's like you've given up."

"Given up?" Gwyn says. "How do you expect us to be? There's nothing else we can do. Those bastards hold all the cards."

"Seriously?" I say. "A boy's life is at stake. That boy could be any one of us. I saw him."

"Even if you did," Rebecca says, "they won't believe us. They own the police. They run things here."

"Who knows who else is part of their gang?" Gwyn says.

"Well, we're not," I say. I look to Rhys. "Rhys, not you as well? We can't give up now – surely? We're so close."

Rhys closes his book and looks up. "I don't know, Ned. They're just so powerful. I'm not sure what else we can do."

"Guys, they're going to murder Terry as a gift for that witch. There's no way we can allow that. Doesn't matter how powerful they are, what they're doing is wrong and they can't be allowed to get away with that."

Gwyn lifts the mug to his mouth with both hands while his brother scratches his head.

"How did he look?" Rebecca says with a sad expression on her face.

"I just saw him briefly and the picture wasn't great, but I could see he was tied up and he appeared to be asleep. He was lying on a hospital bed, and he had one of those bags that patients have stuck to their arm."

"Like an IV bag?" Rhys says with a curious look on his face.

"Yeah, think so," I say. "It was hanging on a pole."

"That's odd," he says.

"What would that be for?" Gwyn asks.

"In hospital they give patients fluids with medicines or nutrients if they can't eat," Rhys says.

"Can't eat?" Rebecca says.

"He did look thin, but Terry was always pretty skinny," I say.

"Jesus, they're starving him?" Gwyn stares down at his drink.

"Maybe. But they're keeping him alive," I say. "For now."

Rebecca puts her hands over her face. Gwyn shuts his eyes and shakes his head, while Rhys groans. They're with me, I feel, although they don't want to be.

"See?" I say. "We can't give up on him. Two weeks locked up and having who-knows-what done to him. And even worse – what comes next? What are they saving him for?"

Rebecca bangs her fists on a pile of books on the desk. "There must be someone we can trust to help us?"

"Maybe we should tell his family?" I say. "They'd be willing to consider any possible option."

Gwyn and Rhys glance at each other. "We discussed that before," Gwyn says. "We went past their house on the way here. There was a police car outside. Doubt we'd get close to the place without local bobbies intervening."

"That's assuming all of them are in cahoots with the Custodians," Rebecca says.

"I'm sure they'd be expecting us to approach them," I say. "I would. Reckon if not through the police we must assume they'll have their eyes out for us."

"Evidently they're well connected and right now we don't know who we can trust," Gwyn says.

"Well, there is one person," Rhys says, and we all look over. "Gerald Edwards."

"Yes," I say, clapping my hands.

"He wasn't so keen on us exploring this story any further when we met with him – was he?" Rebecca says.

"He seemed scared," I say. "But he told us enough. If we explained what we know now, he'd have to help us."

Rhys strokes his chin. "You know he started off as a newspaper reporter in one of the big cities in England. Chances are, he'll still have contacts there."

"That's how we save Terry," I say. "We expose this group and blow the lid off the whole damn conspiracy."

Gwyn looks concerned, while Rebecca lays her hand on a pile of books, like she's hoping they'll give her some comfort.

"Guys, we have to try," I say.

"What about telling your families?" Rebecca asks. "Surely they'd believe you so we wouldn't need to take our chances with this writer man."

"I've tried," I say. "No joy."

Gwyn turns his head to look towards the other end of the shop then glances back. "Dad thinks it's all tosh."

"For a man who makes his livelihood from selling books on the subject matter he does," Rhys says, "he's hugely sceptical on anything even slightly out of the ordinary."

"What about your mum?" I ask.

"She won't listen," Gwyn says.

"We told her everything," Rhys says. "She kind of glazed over when we talked about the Custodians and Terry."

"It was weird," Gwyn says.

"That's probably not uncommon," I say. "She's a native of the place. Maybe that's how the Custodians have survived for so long. By being part of the scenery."

"What about Abe?" Gwyn asks. "What'll he do when he finds out? Can you not tell him the truth?"

"Honestly, I don't know," Rebecca says. "He'll believe me, I think, but will likely want us to get away."

The room is silent. Rebecca sighs, Gwyn swirls the remaining tea in his mug, and Rhys taps his knuckles on his chair. I rub my forehead, trying hard to think of ideas. But there is only one.

"We're on our own," Gwyn says.

"Maybe not," I say. "Let's try and convince the author to help us."

I glance at each of them and they in turn look back at me and gently nod their agreement. There is no cheering or pep talk. The room is sober as we realise a child's life rests in the balance and depends on us finding a way to save him and beat the real evil power that has haunted this town for centuries. We return to see the author.

CHAPTER 48

We arrive at the author's house to see things are happening. There's a car in the driveway and the boot and the back doors are open. Inside the vehicle is a bunch of boxes, full of household stuff. As always, Rebecca rides on the back of my Chopper and Gwyn is on his BMX. I look over at Gwyn.

"Has he been shopping?" Gwyn asks.

"I don't think he's coming," Rebecca says from behind.

Someone appears from the house with a big box in their arms. We can't see their face and they are unable to see us. They stride over to the car and place what they're carrying onto the back seat. It is then we see him, Gerald Edwards, huffing and puffing as he shuffles back a couple of steps. He stares at us.

"Moving, are you?" I yell over at him.

"You shouldn't be here," he says.

"Why not?" I reply.

"You told them I helped you, didn't you?" He looks like he's about to cry.

"Oh," I say.

"Why would you do that?" He holds his hands up like he's expecting an answer. "For goodness' sake, why?"

I glance across at Gwyn who rests his chin on his handlebar.

"We were desperate…" I say.

"Well, now they know." His eyes glare at the ground between us, and his chest moves to tell us he's taking some big, deep breaths. "It's my fault, I suppose. Stupid of me to share something like that with a group of children."

"But we've seen him," I shout. "They have Terry. I've seen him. They have him tied up somewhere at Robham House."

"Oh, dear God." Edwards puts his hands over his eyes.

"They're going to kill him, aren't they?" Gwyn says.

He looks up and his eyes are red. "You must forget about him. There's no hope for the boy now."

"What?" I say starkly, like he's insulted me. "So long as he's alive, there's always hope."

Edwards dashes back into his house. I look over at the other two and shrug before dropping my bike and following him inside. In the hallway I find him coming out of his downstairs toilet. He's dabbing his eyes with tissue paper.

"We can't give up on him," I say. "Imagine how alone and scared he must feel."

"You really don't realise how powerful they are, do you?" Edwards's voice is trembling.

"You can help us though," Rebecca says. "You used to be a reporter? You must still have connections?"

Edwards makes a strange noise that's a mixture of a laugh and a sneeze. "Oh God, that was a long time ago now."

"But it's worth trying," Gwyn says.

He starts shaking his head. "You don't realise, do you?"

"What?" I say.

"Whatever I do, they'll know."

"And why is that such a problem?" I ask. "Why are you so afraid of them?"

"My dear boy, you have no idea what you're up against here."

I grit my teeth before I respond. "An elderly lady, an alcoholic lord, and a few old men with shotguns? How dangerous can they be exactly?"

"Boy, that barely scratches the surface. That town is run, administered and policed by the Custodians. They're everywhere and they're ruthless."

"Ruthless?" Gwyn's voice cracks.

"They leave nothing to chance," he says. "If you've crossed them, they'll deal with you and make sure you're no longer a threat."

"They didn't kill us when they got the chance," I say.

"Killing? Killing isn't practical. They'll find leverage. They'll find other ways of controlling you, of destroying you. If they had to kill every person that had been a threat to them, that town would have ceased to exist a long time ago!"

"But what could they do...?" I say and glance over at Rebecca and Gwyn.

"Wait," he says, interrupting me. "What did you mean by *when they got the chance*?"

"Well..." I lick my dry lips. "They caught us at Robham House last night."

Edwards's face becomes white like the snow that covers the *Cewri* each winter, and he falls into the chair behind him in the hallway. "What were you doing there?"

"Went looking for Terry," I say. "Found him as well, but we couldn't help him."

"And they caught you how?" He holds his hands up to his mouth.

"Mrs Astley and that Perkins guy caught us. The lord was there as well. Gatsby took us home."

"Oh, they know who you are, and they know you're on to them." The colour of the man's face has shifted from white to green.

Gwyn pushes me aside. "What will they do?"

"Whatever they need to, to keep you quiet," Edwards says.

"But we're fine. They let us go," I say.

"Son, I'm sorry but it's not over. If it's not you, then it's your families."

"What do you mean?" Rebecca says. "You're saying our families may be in danger?"

"I'm saying don't rule anything out. They'll come after you in whatever way they can to make sure they have complete control over you. To make sure you tell no one."

I look into the hallway mirror and make eye contact with Gwyn and Rebecca who are stood behind me. Rebecca frowns and Gwyn's jaw drops, each in their own way appearing scared.

I bite my lip and turn to face Edwards again. "Right, and what about you? What've they got over you?"

Edwards looks up and gives me a knowing smile. "Let's just say, I fell in love with someone I shouldn't have. We were both young, but he was younger than I expected."

I hear Gwyn gasp. It's not what I thought but I'm beyond surprises right now.

"So, what – they threatened you with the law?"

"It happened years ago when I was still in Manchester. The man I…"

"Loved?" Rebecca gave him a gentle smile.

"The man I loved. His mother made a complaint to the police. It didn't go anywhere but it was enough for me to lose my job. It was the late fifties. There were certain brushes you didn't want to be tarnished with."

"Then you came here?" Rebecca asks.

"Yes, had some success with my first couple of books. Enough to set me up comfortably. I found out about Henry Blythe and decided it was a story that had to be told. But when I uncovered a trail that took me towards the Custodians and I started asking questions in the town, I got their attention. They dug up my history in Manchester and made sure they knew everything they needed about me. They told me to drop my interest or else the investigation would start again and this time it wouldn't go away."

"But you wrote the book anyway?" Gwyn says.

"I wrote the book and detailed Henry's life but made barely any mention of the Custodians. Maybe I was trying to create a road map that would lead others to find more out about them."

"It worked," Rebecca says.

"I felt ashamed for not writing the whole story and that was my last book."

"Who came here?" I ask.

"That policeman, Gatsby, and the Astley woman. They came this morning."

"They're efficient – I'll give them that," I say. "What did they tell you?"

"He stayed in the car. She came to the door and reminded me of the promise I was forced into making twenty years ago. She said I had broken my word so would now face the consequences."

"Consequences?" I say.

"She was telling me to disappear while I still could," he says.

"But this is your home," Rebecca says. "You've lived here for years. You can't just abandon everything like that."

"Stay," I say. "Help us."

Edwards starts shaking his head. "I'm too old to be starting fights. Besides, it's hopeless. They're too powerful."

"You're our last hope," Gwyn says.

Edwards rubs his face and stands up. "Children, you need to leave."

"Don't abandon us," I say.

He glares at each of us in turn. "Listen to me. You need to leave here. More importantly, you need to get home. I'm acting on my warning and doing as they asked to avoid further pain. But your judgement is still awaiting you. Get home and check on your families. I'm not doing this to scare you. I want you to be prepared. These people have been getting away with murder for hundreds of years. You know how? Sheer cold ruthlessness. Cutting down enemies and leaving no stone unturned. You may think you're clear of them but take it from me, you're not. Get back to your families and be prepared for what's coming because it's not going to be pleasant."

The three of us stand silently in the hallway uncertain of what to do as Edwards leaves us. He returns from his dining area with another full box.

"Did you not hear me? Out – go!"

We mope our way back to the bikes. I lift mine and take one more look at the old man rushing around like he's on fire, and desperate to leave the home he's lived in for nearly three decades.

"It's crazy," I say.

"Ned," Gwyn says, "what if he's right? What if our families are at risk?"

"We should get going," Rebecca says.

I shake my head and punch the handlebars. "Okay, let's go."

CHAPTER 49

We drop off Rebecca first. As we near the Travellers' site, Gwyn – who's cycling alongside me – calls out to her on the back of my bike. "What'll your people do if the Custodians threaten them?"

"I don't know," she replies, yelling into my ear.

"I can't imagine they'd scare easily," I say.

"No, but it depends on how they threaten us."

"Maybe Uncle Len won't do it. Maybe he'll just tell them you got into trouble."

"Doubt it," I say, "but perhaps you should have a story ready, in case."

"Story?" she repeats.

"Yeah, you know, for your dad. To explain why you were caught inside Robham House last night."

"I'll tell him we were looking for ghosts."

"Will that work?" Gwyn says.

"He won't be happy, but it should do the trick. He likes that I have friends here."

I see Gwyn smile briefly and for half a millisecond or so we forget about the dire situation we're in. Friends on a ghost hunt, I think. If it were only that simple.

We arrive at the Travellers' site to find that it's a hive of activity. There are people rushing around between vehicles and caravans, carrying objects, taking down clothes from washing lines and clearing up.

"Oh no," I say.

"They've been here," Gwyn says.

"I need to find Father." Rebecca leaps off the back of the bike in the direction of her caravan. Gwyn and I watch as she opens the door, pops her head inside and then turns to survey the rest of the site. She yells something at an older woman who is folding up clothes on a table. The lady points in our direction and Gwyn and I glance at each other.

"You've brought a shitstorm on us here, boys." Abraham strides between us.

"What happened?" I say and Rebecca's father turns around.

"You've unleashed the Custodians on us."

"You… know about them?" I ask hesitantly. I can see Rebecca watching. Cautiously, she approaches.

"Of course I do. That group and our people have been at peace for the last two centuries but your incursion into the lord's house last night has broken our truce."

"Father?"

Abraham turns to face his daughter.

"Father, I'm sorry. They have the boy. We were trying to help."

Abraham shakes both his fists and Rebecca winces.

"I know, my love. There's no use crying about it now."

"What's happening?" she asks.

"We have to leave here now," he says.

"Who was it?" I ask.

"The policeman and that woman. She did all the talking while he stayed in the car, watching."

"And what did she say?"

Abraham stops pacing momentarily. "Told us we'd interfered

in their business. That we had breached the agreement and broken the truce. Then she returned to the car and the policeman came out. He said that a witness was about to come forwards to say they'd seen the missing boy being taken away by members of our community here; that the investigation would soon turn to us and that riot police would be brought in to arrest the whole community."

"That's bollocks," Gwyn says.

"They can't do that," I say. "It's completely made up. There are no witnesses. They have Terry. They're blagging to scare you."

"You don't know these people," Abraham says looking between Gwyn and me. "They've controlled this place for so long… They're capable of anything."

His words remind me of the author, and my stomach is in knots.

"Dad, we can't run and hide," Rebecca says. "They'll kill the boy."

"I'm sorry, my love. We must. I know how this will play out. They'll bring the riot police in, and you know our people won't go down without a fight. It'll be a bloodbath."

He reached over and grabbed Rebecca's hand.

"I can't put our people in harm's way. I can't put you in danger. I can't put you at risk in any way. Never." He shakes his head emphatically.

"Dad, I can't leave my friends to battle these people alone. Terry will die and the Custodians will get away with murder… again."

"Oh daughter, you have no idea how big this thing is, do you? You have no idea of the powers at work here. They're doing something they must, and we cannot interfere in their business no matter how dark their methods are."

"Then I won't go." Rebecca crosses her arms. "I will stay and help fight the Custodians."

Abraham stares at his daughter then calls out to someone stood between two buses. A huge, hulking man appears and rushes over. He grabs Rebecca and carries her in the direction of the caravan.

"You can't do that," I say.

"I can and just have. Now, you two, listen to me. I know your intentions are good but you're in over your head. You're not searching for ghosts. You're up against a group of dedicated people who are very organised and capable of doing terribly bad things for their cause. You should go home right now to your families and see what damage they've inflicted there. You make whatever amends you need to and then you give up. Leave the Custodians to their business. There's no way you can win against them."

I look over at Gwyn. His face is pale. He nods his agreement, but I shake my head.

"We need to go, Ned," he says.

"What about Rebecca?" I say. "What about Terry?"

"It's time to go," Gwyn says again. He starts turning his bike around.

"I can't leave it like this," I say. "We're so close."

"Listen to your friend," Abraham says. "There's no way you come out of this on top."

I take a deep breath, bite my lower lip and gently nod. I'm not ready to give up yet but I do need to get home to make sure Hannah and Dad are safe.

I look over at Rebecca's caravan and can see her watching us through the window. She is crying. I raise my hand and wave slowly.

As I turn my bike, and we ready ourselves to cycle away, Abraham places his hand on my shoulder.

"I'm sorry," he says.

"What will you do?" I ask.

"We'll find somewhere safe."

"Will you come back here?"

"I don't know if we can."

With that, Gwyn pedals away and I follow him to see the state of things at home.

CHAPTER 50

Gwyn and I reach the shop. Nothing seems out of the ordinary from outside. He turns to face me and shrugs his shoulders.

"Go," I say. I lift my hand and wave then turn my handlebars in the direction of home. My feet push the pedals like I'm a crazed machine until I reach my road. There, I stop and glance down at my tired legs – almost expecting to see smoke rising from the frame.

I'm not quite sure what to expect at my house. Do I need to prepare for battle? No, they wouldn't hurt us directly, or so we've been told. It's not how they do things. They'd come in the shadows at night if that was the case. This'll be something else. This'll be…

I notice a white transit van parked outside the house. Odd, I think. I get nearer and can hear banging. Three large men are stood by our door. The one at the front has a skinhead and wears a vest like Rambo. He is knocking hard and yelling something. Down the street I see Auntie Val striding. Before she gets near our place, I drop my bike and cross over to catch her.

"Ned *bach*, where have you been?" she says.

"I was out," I say.

"You weren't here when they arrived?"

"They? Who are they?" My levels of worry are growing.

"Debt collectors. Come looking for payments. One of those bills, I reckon. Although sooner than I expected. Hannah phoned me. She's stuck inside. I've told her not to let them in."

I find myself gaping at the skinheads. "What'll they do?"

She turns and glares in the same direction. "They'll take anything valuable they can lay their hands on."

"We haven't got much," I say.

Auntie Val closes her mouth tight and gives my shoulder a squeeze. She stares at the house, and I can see her thinking.

"I don't think your dad is around," she says.

"He's probably in the shed," I say.

She sighs. "That brother of mine…"

We hear yelling and see Hannah at the window shouting at the three men. One of them taps another on the shoulder and then leaves, heading around the side of the house.

"That poor girl," Auntie Val says.

"What if they break down the door?" I ask.

"They shouldn't," she says, "but you never know with these types."

Auntie Val heads over to the debt collectors and I follow behind. She's smaller than the two meatheads, but she's fearless, nonetheless. I am in shock. I expected an attack from the Custodians, but nothing like this – this seems a cowardly and low blow. Thinking about it makes my teeth grind and my hands contract into fists. In my mind's eye I can see myself leaping forwards with a kung fu kick into the one in the vest before grabbing the other in a headlock and banging his head down onto the doorstep. Sadly, the daydream breaks down when I hear Auntie Val's quivering voice as she tries to get their attention.

"Excuse me," she says.

"What?" says the shortest of the two, who appears to be wearing an Aston Villa top.

"Can I help you?"

"You live here?" he says, frowning.

"No, I'm a relative."

Both turn to face her. "The proprietor of the house hasn't paid the water bill in over six months," says the one in the football shirt. "They sent him the final notice last month."

She glances over at me. "You do know what this family has been through this year, don't you?"

"That's none of our concern, I'm afraid," he says. "We've acquired the debt from the water board and now it's ours to collect."

"You have the notice of enforcement?" she asks.

"Right here, love." He pulls out a piece of paper from his back pocket and hands it to her. She unfolds the paper and examines it.

"Why today?" I yell out.

"What?" The meathead in a vest glares down at me with a puzzled expression.

"Why are you here today?" I say again.

"Dunno, gaffer sent us. We just do the collecting, mate."

Auntie Val looks up. "Right. This is dated today. That means you need to give them seven days' notice."

The two meatheads glance at each other with an expression that suggests they did not expect her to know that. The look on Auntie Val's face turns to shock as she glances past them in the direction of a high-pressure jet of cold water that appears from nowhere. It's aimed at the two debt collectors and they both yelp as the stream sprays each of them in turn. At the corner of our house, I see Dad holding a hosepipe with a crazed look in his eyes. Speaking of Rambo, this is proper *First Blood* stuff, but this time Dad is the lone wolf hero taking on a bigger, more powerful force.

Auntie Val shakes her head. "No, Gethin." She tries to get Dad to stop. He continues to spray the two men and they yell and curse at him. They step away – back in the direction of the van – and I can see Dad cackling. They both leap inside wiping their wet faces. Dad returns to the side of the house and turns the tap off.

"That'll show them," Dad says defiantly. He speaks with more confidence than I've heard in a long time.

"Oh, you idiot," Auntie Val says. "They were about to leave anyway. I checked their paperwork. They need to give you seven days' notice before they start harassing properly."

Something occurs to me as we stand at the front of the house, staring at the van. "Auntie Val…"

"Seven days?" Dad says, the smile dropping from his face.

"Auntie Val…" I say again.

"Yes, seven days. Now you've gone and angered them for no reason."

"Oh," Dad says. The two meatheads in the van are scathing and I see their upset faces as they discuss what comes next.

"Auntie Val…"

Finally, she turns to face me. "What is it, Ned?"

"What happened to the third man?"

She and Dad look at each other and their eyes widen.

"Oh dear," Dad says.

"It's okay," she says. "They can't break into your house. So long as the door is closed, you're okay."

"Bugger," Dad says, and he turns to see the third meathead appearing from around the corner. In his arms, he carries a hedge trimmer from the shed and Dad's typewriter.

"No, you can't take that." Dad scrambles over to the big muscular man but he swipes him out of the way like a wiper swats a fly off a windscreen.

"You can't take anything right now," Auntie Val says. "You need to allow seven days before you do anything."

"Go ahead and stop me, then."

I try and block his path, but he uses his forearm to knock me down and turns his back to Auntie Val who can only reach and grab at the items he carries. Dad follows him and pleads to the man not to take his typewriter. The Villa meathead is now out and opening the back of the van and helping his friend inside. I stay on the floor and watch it all unfold. I am shaking with rage and pick up a rock and throw it at the van. The Villa meathead storms over and lifts his hand up like he's about to strike me.

"Little shit," he says.

"No, Gary. Leave it," says the one in the vest through the van window.

They close the back of the vehicle and make their way to the front. Auntie Val now stands silently at the side. Dad follows the two men and begs them. He has tears in his eyes. I'm uncertain of what to make of this. He's more upset than I've seen him since Mum died. Rambo has certainly left us. He cares more for that bloody typewriter than anything else. One of the meatheads pushes him away again and Dad drops to his knees. The van door slams shut, and the engine starts up and they drive away leaving Dad on the ground sobbing. Auntie Val stares at him. I look up to the bedroom window and see Hannah. Her face is empty as she peers out.

CHAPTER 51

Not long after, Dad, Hannah and I sit at the kitchen table while Auntie Val makes us all tea and insists on filling each cup with teaspoons of sugar to help us with the shock.

"Bastards," she says, over and over again. "I was expecting it but bastards nonetheless."

"We need to get that money before they come back," Hannah says.

"I can help with that in the short term, but Gethin, you have to start earning."

Dad hasn't said a thing since the meatheads left.

"What happens if you don't pay them?" I ask.

"Things'll just get worse. They'll increase the debt. Try and take more things. Get more aggressive."

"More aggressive?" Hannah blows through her lips.

Auntie Val takes a deep breath and nods.

"Why do you think they came today?" I ask.

"Does it matter?" Hannah sips on her very sweet tea and makes a face.

"Who knows?" Auntie Val picks up her cup with one hand and puts the other on her hip. "It's been on the cards for weeks. How many reminders did they send?"

"Five, I think," Hannah says.

"Right," Auntie Val says. "You can't be ignoring bills like that."

"I wasn't ignoring them." Hannah darts her eyes at Dad, but he doesn't respond.

"We'll get this one paid, but you need some income sooner or later."

"Auntie Val, you shouldn't have to help out like this all the time," Hannah says.

"It's okay, Hannah *bach*. You're my family and I can afford to help a little, here and there." She steps away from the fridge and leans her head towards Dad. "But, Gethin, I can't keep doing this. You need to be stepping up to take care of your family."

Dad faces the table and whispers something under his breath.

"What did you say, Dad?" Hannah asks.

"I said, Mair gave me that typewriter. She bought it for me from that charity shop on the High Street, not long after we were first married."

Hannah glances at me and then at Auntie Val. "Dad, you never said."

"Didn't I?" He lifts his head and wears a slight smile. "I first met your mother at a youth club social in town. She was younger than me at school, so I'd never really noticed her before. She was beautiful and caught my attention straight away, but she looked sad, so I went up to her and started telling her a story."

"What about, Dad?"

"To be honest, I can't remember. Something about a princess trapped in a tower, I think. I managed to make her smile and she asked me whether I was her Prince Charming. I said I could be. And that was it, the start of our life together."

He glances across at the three of us.

"After that, she always asked for my stories. Whenever she felt sad or down, I would cheer her up with a story. She said I had a gift for making them up. I wasn't convinced. But a year or so after we were married, she was on her way home from the hospital and saw the typewriter in the charity shop window. She bought it for me and brought it home. This would be how I would write my stories down, she said. She made me promise that I would use it to write."

"What happened?" I ask. "Did you use the typewriter?"

"Well, I – we – both got a little distracted in the days that followed. That very week we found out that your sister was on the way. In the following months I put the typewriter away in the attic and started to focus on working. Earning money to prepare for the new baby."

"You gave up your writing for me?" Hannah asks.

"It just wasn't as important, and I forgot about it. I didn't think about it for years until your mother passed, then one day I was at her grave, and I remembered the promise I made. I felt so sad and useless. I thought that perhaps the typewriter and a story might help. If I wrote the story, then everything would be better. No one would be sad."

Hannah reaches over and places her hand on his.

"Why didn't you tell us all this, Dad?" I ask.

Dad shrugs. "I've been distracted. Had things on my mind."

"If we pay the debt then we might be able to get it back," Auntie Val says.

"Pay the debt." Dad repeats her words and nods his head.

"Pay all the debts, Gethin," she says. "Pay all the bills. That's how we make things better. It's what Mair would've wanted."

Dad bites his lip and starts to cry. Hannah looks to Auntie Val and back at Dad. She reaches her arm around him and strokes his greying hair. Val steps closer and puts her hand on Hannah's shoulder. The mood in the room feels lighter as we finally connect with Dad, but I feel no relief. I look outside through the window and flex my fingers as my hands rest on the table. This was the doing of the bloody Custodians. They brought the battle to my home and my family – they'd made it personal. But it certainly didn't mean the war was over. I'd find a way of getting my revenge and help Terry before it was too late. What of Gwyn and Rhys, though? Rebecca, Edwards and I had each faced their wrath. What would happen to the two brothers, and would their family be brought into it or would their uncle – the filthy, bastard copper – protect them?

After the drama with the meatheads, Auntie Val buys us fish and chips and we settle down in front of the television for the rest of the evening. Hannah and Dad laugh as we watch *Porridge*, but I end up in bed early, knackered after barely sleeping the night before. The last thing I see before I sleep is the black and white picture of Terry that I saw in the wardrobe; tied up and asleep.

"It's not over," I say aloud before dozing off, still sleeping on top of the covers in the hot summer air.

CHAPTER 52

I am up first in the house. As I scramble around in the kitchen making myself some breakfast and a drink, the phone rings and I answer it.

"Hello?"

"Ned." Gwyn yelps my name. "They've got us, Ned. They've got us bad."

"What?" I say. "What is it, Gwyn? What've they done?"

"Can't talk. Must go. Come to the shop now. Come right now."

He hangs up and I hear the dial tone.

"Shit." I drop the handset of the phone and dash out of the house.

As I get closer to the High Street, the sky darkens and there's a smell of burning in the air. A thick black blanket grows over the town, like the ancient evil is finally making itself known. Oh no, I think, and ease off the pedalling for fear of what I might find when I get there.

A crowd has gathered near the shop. Policemen stand between them and the building. I hear yelling and the hum of machinery. A fire engine has its ladder raised and a fireman with a yellow helmet stands at the end. He holds a long hosepipe and directs a thick jet of water at the inferno. The smell is strong now and I know exactly what it is – burning paper. I take a deep breath when I see the fire and it makes me cough. A huge red blaze bursts from the building like the doors of hell have opened and it reaches up into the sky, feeding the darkness that sits overhead. At the front of the crowd, I see Gwyn, Rhys and their dad. Mr B's arms are crossed, and he holds his hand up over his mouth.

Gwyn takes a few puffs on his inhaler before turning his head and rushing over when he sees me.

"What happened?" I ask.

"What do you think?" Gwyn bats back.

"I didn't think they'd be capable of doing something like this."

"They murder children and who knows what else," Gwyn says. "I'd say a pile of second-hand books didn't stand much of a chance."

"When did it start?" I ask.

"Early this morning. Dad got a call from Mrs Jones at dawn."

"She called the fire engine as well?"

"Yeah, but it took them ages," he says. "We got here first."

"Figures." I turn to face the burning building. "How bad is the damage?"

"Really bad. One of the firemen said there's little chance of saving the place. All the books make it into one big bonfire."

"Right," I say, and I scan across the street again. "Your dad, okay?"

Gwyn shakes his head. "That was his life. There were a lot of rare books in there. Probably shouldn't have kept them all together like that. Doubtful insurance will cover it all."

Gwyn glances past me and a pained expression comes to his face. "Mum's here."

He strides over and takes her hand. They both approach Mr B and his wife gently taps his shoulder before putting her arm around him. He turns around and hugs her. Gwyn says something to Rhys, and he looks over at me. I nod to him, and he comes over.

"You alright?" I ask.

"Been better." Rhys's eyes are red, and his skin is black, like he's been closer to the fire than the rest of the family.

I rub my chin, unsure of what to say. "This is crazy."

"Should've expected it, really. Did they get to you as well?"

"Yeah," I say. "Set debt collectors on us."

"Debt collectors? Jesus." He shakes his head and pushes his fingers through his long hair.

"Yeah. A distraction or an attempt to disarm us, I guess." I take a deep breath not knowing what else to say. I nod to the fire. "This though, this is a different level, man. I don't understand. Why target the shop? Can't be because we meet here?"

"It gets rid of the bible with Henry Blythe's notes. Plus, it takes Gwyn and I out of the equation."

I feel like I've been punched in the gut. "Will you have to leave?"

"Mum's been wanting to take us back to Bangor for years," he says. "You know she hates this town. It was only the bookshop that kept us here."

I can feel my head drop. "How would they know...?"

"Her brother would know," he says.

Shit, of course. "Do you think he has anything to do with this?"

"I hope not – for his sake. If he can do something like this to his own family, who knows what else he's capable of?"

I try and see through the crowd. I spy Gatsby's blackened, serious face briefly. He stands between the people and the fire. I exhale hard. "When will you go?"

"As soon as she can get us away," Rhys says. "We'll probably have to move into *Nain*'s house. Dad put all our money into this place so I've no idea how we'll get by without help." He places both his hands over his face and rubs his eyes. "It's a fucking disaster."

A fireman approaches Mr B and his wife and speaks to them while pointing to the blaze. He's explaining something. From where I stand it looks like the flames have eased and the fire is under control. But it's also clear the shop is destroyed. The building is an empty, smoking shell.

Gwyn approaches.

"What did the fireman say?" I ask.

"He says it's all gone," Gwyn says. "Everything is fricking destroyed."

"Those bastards," I say. "I won't let them get away with this."

Gwyn bites his lip and starts shaking his head. "Ned, it's over. We've lost."

"No, we haven't," I say defiantly. "They've split us up, sure. But so long as I'm here, I won't let them get away with this and Terry's murder."

"Jesus, Ned. Wake up, will you?" Gwyn raises his voice and I step back in surprise. "They own this place. What exactly can one boy do against it all? Nothing is beyond them, Ned. Don't you see how dangerous they are? We're lucky no one was hurt in that fire. Next time we – you – won't be. Next time, you'll just disappear like Terry. They'll kill you. You'll be done for, and that'll be the end of it. Just another missing child. In a couple of years, you'll be forgotten, and then a few decades later the same thing will happen again."

"Gwyn," I say. "I can't let it go. Don't you see? I can't."

"Ned, you have to – otherwise they'll do so much more."

I look down. "But I'm not sure if I can. I'm not sure I know how to stop."

"Ned, you're my best friend but you must stop this."

I shake my head. I start to sniff. I wipe away the tears from my eyes with my forearm.

"I know why you wanted these missions. It's because of your mother. The way she died like that, with no reason or cause. You thought you saw a ghost or a fricking demon following her in that night – and who knows, maybe you did – but since then, you've been searching for something. Maybe someone to blame. An enemy that you can take on and fight like they do in the movies.

At first it was a bit of fun but right now you're in danger. You've put us all in danger."

"What the hell?" I wipe tears from my cheek and bare my teeth as a burst of fury leaps up inside me. "Something evil did kill my mother and I had to find it and destroy it before someone else was hurt. Each investigation we did was part of that mission. It was something I had to do."

"Hanging around derelict buildings was one thing, Ned. But this war with the Custodians is real."

"Real?" I say. "What about all the other stuff we've seen? The things you've seen? The things you've felt? What about Terry turning up in that photo of Henry Blythe's grave?"

He rubs his forehead and shakes his head. "Maybe it was double exposure."

"You know that's impossible," I say. "You've experienced enough now to know it's real. There's a whole load of weird shit out there we just can't explain."

"Yeah, well…" Gwyn coughs and takes another puff on his inhaler.

"But honestly," I say, "whatever you believe, it was still the thread that led us to where we are now."

"Where we are now is a shitstorm, Ned." He points to the shop. "Look at what they did. They've ruined my family. They've made Rebecca and her people leave their home and run away. That author as well. It's a surprise they haven't got to your family yet."

I cross my arms. "They did. We had to fight off debt collector meatheads last night."

"Debt collectors?" Gwyn cocks his head to the side. "Did they take anything?"

"Not much." I shrug my shoulders. "Dad's typewriter."

Gwyn's jaw drops. "A typewriter? A fricking typewriter? We've lost everything and you lose a typewriter?"

"It's just the start," I say. "They'll be back unless we can pay off the debt."

"Ned, our family business is ruined. Dad put our life savings into this shop and now look at it. Honestly, if you were standing where I'm standing now, you wouldn't be so keen to keep the battle alive. You'd realise they've won. You'd understand that fighting them is futile."

"Gwyn…" I start to speak but he walks away and goes back to his parents.

I turn to Rhys. "What do you think? You agree? That it's time to give up?"

He starts to shake his head. "I've got nothing left to offer you."

"We – I – need you, Rhys. You're my Q. You're more than those books. You always have been."

His head drops then he looks up at me, straight in the eye. "Sorry, Ned. I can't." He turns to walk away but glances back. "But whatever you do, Ned, don't do it alone."

Rhys joins the rest of his family and the four of them embrace. I watch and realise there's nothing more to be done here. I blink back tears and take some deep breaths to regain some calm before wheeling my bike down the High Street. I keep walking, with my head down, without much consideration of where I'm going. My mind is a cauldron bubbling over from all the crazy thoughts and feelings. I feel so powerless and angry. Have I taken this thing too far? Setting fire to the shop wasn't my doing. I may have caught their attention, but it is the Custodians who are doing all these horrible things. They're trying to protect themselves so they can get away with murder. Actual, bloody murder. Maybe I was looking for a monster under the bed at the start of this mission. But I've found it and now what do I do? Do I give up? I can't. Maybe this was down to Mum at the start, but it certainly isn't any more. Right now, a boy's life hangs in the balance, and I'm the only person standing in their way; the last man standing. I've tried so hard to keep everyone safe, but I failed. I failed my friends and my family. But I don't intend to give up. I will keep going until I have nothing more to give.

CHAPTER 53

I lift my head and realise I've walked to the church. I put my bike down and take a seat on the churchyard wall. I need time to think but time is something I don't have much of right now. I need ideas. I need a plan.

I hear pained moaning coming from behind me and I look across the graveyard. Next to a large headstone I see a pair of shoes sticking out and they appear familiar. I leap over the wall and approach the feet, slowly, uncertain of what I might find. Lying on the ground with an empty bottle in his hand is Horse. His eyes are open, and he stares at me.

He coughs. "Alright, gay boy. Bet you think this is hilarious, don't you?" His voice is slurred and lacks the usual cocky swagger.

"What are you doing here?" I ask.

He looks around and touches the grave. "To be honest, I'm not fucking sure. The last thing I remember was being at the Eagle's Nest. It was dark. I told the Goons I was going for a walk alone and then somehow ended up here."

"What were you drinking?"

"Vodka." He rubs his face and makes a noise with his throat. "Haven't got any water, have you?" He sticks out his tongue like a snake that's searching for something. "Throat's as dry as a nun's fanny."

I shake my head. He starts to sniff the air. "You smell burning or have I had a stroke?"

"Yeah, there's been a fire on the High Street. The bookshop is gone. Bastard Custodians."

"Custodians? Fuck. Good effort. Did they... so they got to everyone?"

"Looks like it," I say. "You?"

He turns away like he's thinking about something. "I didn't give them enough credit. They're more organised than I thought." He turns his head back to face me. "The old man was caught by the bastard pigs yesterday. Did a random search of him and found a block of resin. He swears he had nothing on him. He was on parole so getting caught with it means an instant return to Strangeways. Those shits planted it on him. He was on his way to work. Been trying to keep it clean for the family." Horse rubs his face and shakes his head. Dare I say it, he looks hurt and weak. This is not something I've seen before.

"He's done a lot of stuff in his past, but this time he didn't deserve it. Won't see the light of day now for another ten years. Because of those fuckers."

"I'm not giving up," I say. "Will you help me?"

Horse groans and gets to his feet. "I'm not sure you have the stomach for what I'm planning."

"What are you going to do? Go after Robham?"

"That lord is a pussy. It's the Astley woman that needs to be dealt with. She's the brains and the cock and balls of the operation. I'm gonna make her pay."

"That's not going to help Terry though, is it?" I say.

"Lad's a lost cause," he says. "What I'm after right now is cold, sweet vengeance. The old man may be locked up, but I'll give him something to smile about."

I can't help but throw my hands up in the air. "Bloody hell, Horse. He's not a lost cause. There's still plenty we can do."

"If you want to do anything, get help from the pigs," he says, running his fingers through his hair. "The proper pigs I mean. Not the corrupt fucks we have here. Find some proof of what the bastards are doing. Maybe talk to that detective who's always on telly. She's from the city and at odds with the rest of them. Very unlikely to be in the pockets of these fucks."

"Proof," I say. "What proof is there?"

"That's for you to figure out. I've got my own mission, now."

"What will you do…?"

He stops and appears to be thinking. The emotion falls from his face and leaves that psychopathic look that scares the inhabitants of the town shitless. "Something… fucking dramatic, I think."

Horse ambles off, out of the churchyard, leaving his empty vodka bottle on the ground between the graves. I'm not sure if I'm reassured that we are both on the same side. He's looking for blood whereas I'm looking to help Terry. Some revenge and justice would be good as well but I'm not sure if that's possible. Especially, since now, I'll be on this mission alone. I wish my friends were with me, but they've been taken away. I failed them. And my family as well. I thought defeating the monsters would keep them safe. But I was wrong. And I was wrong about who the real monsters were as well. Is everyone still in danger? I don't know and I can't dwell on that right now. Right at this moment in time, I need to find something I can show the detective. This may be my last chance. Terry's last chance.

CHAPTER 54

First things first, I need to know more about this detective. Despite what Horse says, I don't know for certain that she is to be trusted. She might be from the city, but I don't know the reach or how much influence the Custodians have across the country. The only way I can better understand this woman is to do some research: spy on her, get back to doing some basic recon. They say she drives down here from Bangor each day. And when we see her on the news, she's usually at the police station, so that is where I must start my mission.

I cycle over to the standalone red-brick building that's been here since the Second World War; since the original building burned down – for whatever reason that was. It all seems so normal today. The birds are singing, and tree branches cast scattered shadows across the pavement. I think about the press conference they held outside the place. So much of that weird event makes more sense, knowing what we know now.

Outside the station, three cars are parked: a panda, a red Ford Escort, and a white Mercedes-Benz. There are normally two police cars, but one is likely attending to the fire on the High Street. There were police officers there, but now the fire is under control – and by this point the building is no more than a soaked, smoking shell – there won't be much for them to do. If Gatsby is here, I need to stay out of view. When the detective is not around, he is usually the most senior officer here. I can't say for certain whether the other bobbies are with the Custodians, but I can't take any chances. If they found me again, it would mean more trouble. I survey the street and decide to hide behind the sycamore opposite the station for now.

I lean my bike against the wall and step close to the tree to start my watch. After a minute or two, I realise this wasn't a very good plan. How long would I have to wait? I should've brought supplies. This is why I needed a Q – to make sure I was prepared for missions. Thankfully, the sun is warm, so I am okay in my jeans and T-shirt. But I would be needing something to snack on and drink soon. I left the house at speed after Gwyn's call and didn't have time for breakfast.

In the distance I hear a car and I hug the tree. It's okay – it's just the postman's van passing. I wonder what I'll do when I see her. I can't just go up to her right now with the information I have – can I? I still need some proof to show her. Plus, she might just dob me into the Custodians. And if I wanted to speak to her, I'd be better off doing it somewhere where Gatsby wouldn't see – away from here.

I hear another engine and peer around the tree to see a panda car approaching. This time I stay completely out of view. When it stops, I look and see Gatsby getting out of the car with another policeman. Gatsby is grinning and laughs at something the other one says. He's just come from the fire that destroyed his sister's family business. If it wasn't for the black marks on his face, he could easily be returning from lunch.

I drag my nails down the bark of the tree and feel my face tensing. How I would love to wipe that stupid smile from his face and smash the windows of his car. The two policemen approach the doorway to the building and Gatsby stops and turns in my direction. Instinctively, I dip behind the tree, but I think I've been spotted, and I expect him to appear next to me. I wait steadily and bite my lower lip. The moment lasts a lifetime, but no one comes, and I hear the door of the station close. I can feel my heart beating like a Phil Collins drum solo. I peek around the tree to check if they're still there, but they've gone inside.

Does that mean all the bobbies from the fire are back here? There's been a few more in town recently helping with Terry's investigation, so maybe not. I wonder what is left of the shop. Wouldn't it be great if the books had been undamaged, and they were still able to sell them? The Bowens wouldn't need to go back to Bangor, and I wouldn't lose Gwyn and Rhys. Without them, I'm alone. No support or backup. No Q or HQ. No friends. My stomach drops when I think I might not see them again.

I clear my throat. "Man up, boy," I say aloud. "You can still save Terry." My voice starts cracking. I'm not sure if I believe this any more, but something keeps me going. I lower my head and start to laugh. Not because the situation is funny but because it is futile, lost, desperate. One kid against a secret evil army. In *Star Wars*, the rebels were up against a much bigger and more powerful force with the Empire. Did they win in the end? I don't know – I haven't seen the last film yet. I had the chance, but I didn't go and see it. I wanted to focus my efforts on my mission – not waste time watching movies. Maybe that was a mistake… No, it wasn't, I say to myself and I slap my face. Stop doubting yourself. The danger and the evil threat are still very real and you're the only one who can stop it.

The groaning front doors of the building pull me out of my moment of despair. I look to see the detective walking down the steps with our local MP, Pierce Bastard Chelmsley. They both chat and seem more friendly than when I saw them together at the press conference. What the hell might he be doing here, I wonder? Is he so worried about the case that he's here to give a hand? It's a long way from his house in Surrey. I'd bet anything that he's in with the Custodians. And if he is, does that mean they have a direct line to the prime minister? Does that mean the Government are involved? Oh Jesus.

The doors open again, and the snake Gatsby comes out. He calls after the other two and they turn around and the MP returns and Gatsby hands him a file. They speak briefly as the detective looks on. She glances at her watch and appears keen to get away, but the two men are joking and laughing. Gatsby points to the file, and the MP nods. I wish I knew what they were talking about. Detective Thomas turns away and opens the door of the red Ford Escort. Meanwhile, Gatsby raises his hand to say goodbye and he heads back inside while Chelmsley goes over to the other vehicle. No surprises, the white Mercedes-Benz is his.

The MP is first to pull away and after reversing out of the parking spot he puts his foot down and disappears down the road. The detective takes her time – perhaps she was waiting for him to leave. As she starts her engine, I realise I need to get my Chopper ready, so I scramble to the wall and jump on the seat. The Ford Escort leaves the station and heads down the street. I cycle after it, having to push hard on the pedals to keep up. I'm not sure what the plan is here but I intend to follow her wherever she goes. Maybe a plan will come to me when we get there. She reaches the end of the road and turns left onto the High Street. We pass the smoking shop, and she slows to speak with a policeman who is guiding traffic around the parked fire engine. They're not all at the station it seems. I quickly scan across at the scenery and see that the crowds have gone. I can see no sign of the Bowens either. The shop is done for. There's no way any of those poor bloody books have survived.

The detective pulls away and speeds up. My legs burn as I try hard to avoid losing sight of the car. She passes all the shops, and heads in the direction of the A52. If she gets to the main road, I'll have to give up as there's no way I can keep up with her.

We reach the town limits, and it starts to look like she's on her way back to the city, on the road north. Away from the thirty limits, she picks up the pace on the twisty road. Ahead and to my left I see Ogyn Lake and, in the distance – on the other side of the road – looms Plum Mountain. Out of nowhere, a thought comes to me – I start to wonder what kind of secrets that mine might be hiding? I focus so much on the scenery that I fail to notice her car has slowed down and is indicating that it's about to turn left. Oh God, I think. That can mean only one thing – she's going to Robham House.

I stop at the end of the lane and watch as the red car bobs its way down the track. Why would she be going there? Is she in cahoots with the Custodians or is this part of the investigation? Damn it, I think. I can't follow her. There's no way I can be caught there again. I look around at the road. Next to the entrance, the ditch is deep and dry. There's enough space for me and my bike to hide while I wait for her. I drop my Chopper into it and then leap in myself. The ditch is full of thick, soft grass. I lay back and find my breathing becoming steadier and heavier. It really is comfortable and after all the rushing around and the drama of the morning, I am knackered. I don't want to think of anything or anyone. I am happy shutting off the world and before long I find my eyes closing and everything goes quiet.

I wake up to the sound of a car passing. I sit up instantly and crane my neck to see the vehicle, but it has turned and driven away. Bollocks. I've lost her again.

"Idiot," I say. How could I have fallen asleep at such a crucial moment? Snipers in the army would be court-martialled for such behaviour. I get up and pull my bike out of the hole. I scan across the lane and search the view of Robham House that I have from this position but can see no sign of her car. Back to the drawing board. I would have to return to town and start the stakeout at the police station again. This time I would make sure I was better prepared.

I jump on the bike and begin cycling back towards town. After a few minutes, I come to realise that the tyre of my front wheel is going down. Damn it, the wheel must have picked up a thorn from the hedge. I stop at the side of the road and examine the tyre. I'll have to wheel it home.

While I am on my knees, I hear a vehicle coming towards me fast down the road. I look up and see a red Ford Escort, but the car fails to see me and the last thought I have before blacking out is how hard the frame of the bike is as it hits my head and knocks me into the side of the road.

CHAPTER 55

Darkness cradles me but not because I am in a hole but because it is night. It's the early hours and I am in bed. The winter air is cold, and I hold the covers tight around me. I often wake up around this time. It's when Mum comes home from her nightshift. It's like I can feel she is near. I hear the front door open. Then footsteps on the landing. Always the first thing she does when she returns is to check on Hannah and me. I am usually half awake. Conscious enough to know she's there but not enough to sit up and speak to her. She treads lightly across the landing and then I hear the door open gently and dim light from the hallway comes in. Mum tiptoes in, and her routine is the same. She checks the curtains are fully drawn then she crouches down next to me. She pulls the covers of the bed up and tucks me in. She leans in, moves a strand of hair away from my forehead and then gently kisses it.

"My little hero," she whispers.

For some reason on this occasion something makes me open my eyes and I look up at her. My mouth falls open and my arms and legs flinch under the covers as I see her face. A dark, hideous shape surrounds her head. I can sense it as well – something evil and hateful is attached to her. The shock makes me yell and she is startled. I scramble for the lamp on my bedside table and turn it on. As the light comes on, the dark shape slinks away from her into the shadows. After overcoming the brief shock, she leans in and hugs me.

"It's okay, Ned. You just had a nightmare – that's all."

She holds me tight and strokes my hair.

"No," I say. "I saw something – a darkness around you. Something bad is going to happen."

"Can you see it now?" she asks.

I look all around her and shake my head. I scan the room and grab the lamp and shine it into the dark corners.

"See? Just a bad dream. That's all. No harm."

"Mum, please. I think something bad is going to happen to you."

She smiles at me in that way that makes the worse days better. "Oh, my little hero. Always watching out for me. Always so protective."

"Please listen to me, Mum. Don't go to bed. Something bad will happen to you in the night if you do."

"Oh, come on now," she says, groaning gently. "I've worked a ten-hour shift. I am dead on my feet. If I don't get to bed soon, then bad things will happen. Bad things to your father most likely because I will be in a very bad mood in the morning." That smile returns to her face.

"Please don't go…" I'm desperate to keep her with me.

"Listen, *cariad*. Sometimes life can seem scary, but your mind will always make things appear worse than they really are. Bad dreams are nothing more than horror films you watch on telly. Afterwards, you turn the telly off and forget about them. Do me a favour now and forget about that bad dream." She turns the lamp off and kisses me again on the forehead.

"Just a bad dream, my little hero." She gets to her feet. "You be brave now and get back to sleep. I will see you tomorrow, after school. Love you more than the moon and the stars."

She leaves the room and I lie awake in my bed hoping she

is right but inside I know she is not. I know something bad is coming.

Dad finds her in bed when he returns at lunchtime. Her face is pale, and her chest is still. She didn't wake from her sleep and died in the night. The doctors couldn't find a cause. She was young and healthy in their book. There was no reason for it. Sometimes it happens – that's what they told us – and it's the lack of a cause that families struggle with the most. It's what they said.

No one saw it coming, apparently. But I did, and what did I see? What was it that followed her in from the night? Inside, I knew it was something evil and ancient that preys on the innocent. That is what killed her – the nasty, horrid, soulless filth. I could feel its intent. I knew exactly what it planned to do. And it was knowing that made me angry. More than angry. Anger is what happens when someone calls you a name you don't like, or they trip you up at assembly and you fall on your face in front of the school. I'm not sure what word best describes how I felt. My every thought and my every moment were controlled – dominated – by rage. It's okay to be sad, is what everyone told me. But they didn't understand. It wasn't sadness that haunted me, it was teeth-grinding, wall-punching, loud-swearing, and mouth-spitting fury. I couldn't eat or sleep. I couldn't talk to anyone about it or tell them what happened. Not Hannah, not Gwyn, not Dad – no one. There was a fire inside that would not let me rest. It filled my whole body – from my head and my heart to my knuckles and fists. From the second I woke up to the moment I fell asleep. Everything else came second place after the rage. I thought I would never be normal again. That was, until one day, as I painted my model soldiers, a thought popped into my head, and the fires burned a little less and the guns stopped firing. What happened to Mum was a declaration of war. It wasn't a sucker punch that the thing had got away with and then slunk back into the night. This was the start of it, the beginning of battle. The invasion of Poland or bombing of Pearl Harbour. What happened next was down to me. And my response would be to fight back with everything I had. I couldn't turn back time to stop what happened, but I would find out what the evil that killed my mother was, and I would destroy it. Bring it out of the shadows and into the light so I could obliterate it for revenge and stop it before someone else was hurt. That was my mission and until my mission was complete, nothing else mattered. I would give the mission everything I had. Everything.

CHAPTER 56

My head hurts like a ton of bricks has been dropped on it. I open my eyes and I'm lying on a bed. The room is bright, and it takes a moment for me to be able to see properly. There's someone standing in front of me. I see a dark figure surrounded by bright white light.

"Did I die?" I mumble.

They step closer and I see her face.

"Not today but you were lucky," Hannah says. "How are you feeling?"

I think about the question for a second. "Weird."

"Do you remember what happened?" she asks.

"My bike," I say. "There's a problem with my bike."

"You were by the side of the road when it happened," she says.

"When what happened?" I ask.

"When I knocked you down with my car." Someone else has spoken – not Hannah. She steps closer – I know her. It's the detective.

"You're not supposed to see me," I say.

"Well, I didn't," she says. "And you're lucky to be alive."

I stare at Hannah – her arms are crossed but there's a grin on her face.

"You were crouched at the side of the road with your bike and my car hit the bike, which in turn hit you." The detective takes a deep breath. "I'm so glad you're okay. The bike hit you very hard. You went flying into the ditch."

I remember it now. The car hit the bike and the bike hit my head. I was knocked out by my Chopper.

"The detective called the ambulance," Hannah says. "They brought you here."

"You came with them?" I ask.

"I followed," she says. "I needed to know you were okay."

"Is this… is this Mum's hospital?" I ask.

The smile on Hannah's face fades away, and she nods.

"They knew you," the detective says. "Some of the nurses recognised you when you arrived. They said you were Mair's boy."

"Dad and I came as soon as they called," Hannah says.

"Dad's here?"

"He went to get some coffee," Hannah says.

"I… how bad is it?"

"Not bad," Hannah says. "Just a bit of concussion. They want to keep you in overnight, but you should be home tomorrow."

My toes curl as I remember why I was at the side of the road. "But I have things to do… I can't stay here."

"You're going nowhere," Hannah says. "Everything can wait until tomorrow."

The detective looks at her watch. "I'd better be going. Glad you're okay, Ned."

I hear myself gasp as she says my name.

"If it's okay I might call on you again?" she says.

"You don't need to worry about him," Hannah says.

"No, I really would like to."

"It's okay," I say. I can feel my eyes narrowing as I stare at her. Does she work for the Custodians? She seems nice but why else would she have been at Robham House? If she visits again then maybe I can find out more about her. Something is fishy about the way she stuck around and now wants to see me again. Like she wants to keep an eye on me. I don't know whether I should trust her or not.

The detective leaves and Hannah sits down in the chair next to my bed. I scan the room – there are five other beds – all empty.

"It's weird," she says. "You're the only one here, but a lot of the private rooms down the corridor are full. You can hear coughing everywhere. The place is full of kids with that bug that's been going around."

"The one Jenny's brother had? That's still happening?" I ask.

"Yeah. Quite a few more cases now as well."

"And they're keeping them isolated?" I ask.

"Yep," she says. "One of the nurses told me they don't know what it is. Seems to only affect children and it won't go away easily."

"Anyone I know?" I ask.

"I was only able to see one of them. The chippy's daughter. She's in form one at my school."

"Christine?" I ask. I remember her. "Is she alright?"

"Don't know much about it at the moment."

God, it's the witch! Is this why the tribute is needed? To stop all the town kids from getting ill? If I stop them from killing Terry, will that mean the whole town will be overrun by this bug? There must be something I can do to help. But even if I can't, I won't stop. Terry has nothing to do with this whole thing. He doesn't deserve to be the tribute.

"What's wrong?" Hannah sees that I'm thinking.

"*Pestilence*," I mumble under my breath.

"What did you say?"

I look up. "Oh nothing. I just remembered what happened earlier on the High Street."

"Right," she says. "Detective Thomas told me. We thought you might've been there. I heard the phone ring this morning. How bad was it?"

"Very bad."

"No one hurt though?"

"No."

"How were the Bowens?" she asks.

I shake my head. "Devastated. I expect they'll have packed up and gone back to Bangor by now."

"Mrs B always wanted that, didn't she?"

"Yeah." I do a swallowing action, like I'm trying to bury the sadness away somewhere where it won't affect my thinking.

"What does that mean for your investigations?" Hannah raises her eyebrows.

"I don't know yet."

"And the whole Robham-witch conspiracy thing? Do you still believe they have Terry?" Her voice is surprisingly calm.

"I don't know." I can't tell her the truth of it. She'll just worry.

"No new news about it – him – is there?" I ask.

"No. Maybe should've asked the detective while she was still here. She'd be the one to know."

"I'm tired of the whole thing to be honest." I exhale loudly, perhaps overdoing it; acting was never a great skill of mine. I'd rate myself as three or four at most for this skill.

Hannah leans forward in her chair. "One thing I did wonder. Why were you out on that road where she hit you?"

"I – erm – wanted to get away from town. Things didn't end well with Gwyn, and I needed a break from everyone."

"But why that direction? There's nothing that way other than the main road. And Robham House."

She suspects something.

"I wasn't really thinking clearly…" I start but get interrupted by a loud bang. Dad has used his boot to push the door open and it's smashed against the wall. He walks in with a hot drink in one hand, a bottle of coke in the other, and a bag of crisps held in his teeth. He hands the bottle to Hannah and gives her the crisps. She looks at the packet. "Nice healthy breakfast. Thanks, Dad."

"Sorry, all I could get. Cafe's closed and I didn't have change for the vending machine." He turns to face me. "Ned, my boy. You're awake. You had us quite worried there. How are you feeling?"

"I'm alright," I say. "Bit of a headache."

Hannah looks concerned, and she leans in. "How bad is it? Doctor should have been in here by now to check on you. He said he'd return when you woke up."

"Don't stress, Hannah," I say. "I'm fine."

"I saw some doctors and a couple of nurses down the corridor," Dad says. "Those sick kids are in need of a lot of attention."

"That's not good enough." Hannah puts her tea on the side and drops her crisps on the chair before striding out of the room.

"You steer clear of those kids," Dad yells after her. "Don't want you catching that bloody thing." He turns to face me. "The sooner we have you out of here the better."

"I have to stay the night," I say.

"Don't you worry, I'll make sure you have company." Dad smiles and sips his tea.

"Did you get your typewriter back?" I ask.

"Working on it," he says.

"What about your book?" I ask.

"I'll get back to it when I can," he says. I stare at him. He seems different than the last time I saw him. Like he's woken up from a spell that had control over him. Was this it, I wonder? Was Dad back?

He looks around at the room. "It's odd being back here. I haven't been here since your mother…" He trails off.

"Since she died?" I finish the sentence for him.

"Since she died," he says.

"Do you think about her a lot?" I ask him.

He nods. "Most of the time, I feel like she's nearby."

"Maybe she is."

He doesn't respond. He just smiles and closes his eyes tight like he's imagining it.

"How are you finding it all?" he asks and I'm overcome with feelings. I can't remember him asking me that before. I try to hold back the tears, but I cannot help it and start to sob. I feel everything suddenly explode and overwhelm me – Mum, Terry, Gwyn, the bookshop, the Custodians, Henry bloody Blythe – it's all too much for my shoulders to keep carrying this stuff. My face is down on the covers of the bed. I hold the cloth tight and pull it up as close to my face as I can. I can't look up at Dad, I don't want him seeing me like this. This is not how a hero acts. A hero doesn't cry like a little baby. A hero sucks it all up and carries on. John Rambo fought an army of police officers single-handedly in the forest without shedding a single tear. What kind of hero am I? I hope Mum isn't around to see this. I feel Dad's hands on my back. He strokes my shoulders.

"There, there, my boy. It's okay. Let it out. I'm here with you."

The sobbing eases off and I begin to feel better. My brain is less foggy. I sniff and use my bed covers to wipe my nose and dry my eyes. I can't stop gasping so I take a few deep breaths. I feel bad that I've broken down like that, but the feelings seem to wash over me more so now – like I'm a fish in a wild, fast river. I cannot control any of it, I just need to let it all wash over me and not let it sweep me away with it.

Hannah enters the room and stops near the end of my bed. She looks across from me to Dad and nods. "Everything okay?"

"Yep," we both say at the same time.

"Jinx," Dad says smiling. He grabs my hand and squeezes it.

"Good," she says. "Doctor should be with us shortly, but you know it's crazy out there. They're all panicking. I think this bug might be serious."

I sigh. This makes things far trickier. Now the witch and her bloody curse is threatening us. If I do save Terry, does that mean the rest of the kids in town will suffer? There must be something I can do. As I start thinking, Hannah raises her glass bottle of coke to her mouth and takes a long sip. I'm reminded of something Rhys said about the new town museum and realise there's one thing I can try.

CHAPTER 57

Dad stays with me for the rest of the day and the night, and the next morning he takes me home. Everything seems fine with my head, but I can't help feeling that the early checkout has been enabled by the developing bug situation at the hospital. Nonetheless, I'm glad to be home.

Not long after I arrive, Hannah comes into the living room to say there's someone on the phone for me. She looks pale and I wonder whether she's been having trouble sleeping again.

"Phone? Who?" I say abruptly.

"Gwyn," she says.

I go into the hall and pick up the handset. "Hello?"

There's brief silence on the other end.

"Hi, Ned," the voice says sheepishly.

"Missing me already?" I say.

"I – erm – heard about your accident," he says. "You okay?"

"Bit sore, but I'll be alright. How did you hear about it?"

"Our neighbours saw you being taken away by the ambulance. I tried phoning yesterday but there was no answer. So, you were knocked down by the detective's car?"

"Kind of," I say.

"You were following her?" he asks.

"Yeah, all the way to Robham House."

"She went to Robham House? Jeez," he says. "You think she's with them?"

"I don't know," I say. "Trying to work that out."

He pauses and clicks his tongue. "What are you going to do?"

"Dunno yet. Haven't decided." I sigh. "Why do you care, Gwyn? Thought you were done with all this?"

"I... I was very upset yesterday – so angry about what those bastards did to us. But today... I realised I can't just walk away from it all."

"Where are you?" I ask.

"*Nain*'s house in Bangor," he says.

"Are you staying there?"

"For now, yes. Does your head hurt?"

"A bit," I say. "How's your dad?"

"Gutted still. Bought most of the papers in the corner shop this morning and did all the crosswords."

"And Rhys?"

"Rhys doesn't say much. He sits in the corner reading."

There's a gap before I speak again. "I need to know if I can trust the detective. Any ideas?"

"Can you talk to her?"

"Yeah, I think so. She came to visit me in hospital. I think she felt guilty."

"Or she's checking on you for the Custodians."

My ear gets too warm, so I switch hands and place the handset against the other ear. "That did cross my mind. But she did get me to the hospital. Could easily have left me for dead at the side of the road."

"Think about it, though. If she had, then another missing child would've attracted more attention. If she's with the Custodians, then it makes more sense to get you help and then keep an eye on you. And, actually, are you sure it was an accident?"

I purse my lips and blow. "I don't know. Assumed it was. My bike was sticking out into the road, and she does drive fast. If I can talk to her, what do you think I should ask her?"

"Ask her about the investigation. If she's with them, she's more likely to make up an excuse or blame someone. If she genuinely seems stumped, then she's more likely to be clean."

I think about this for a moment. It's not bad. At least it's better than the other ideas I've had. Damn it, I think, that is why I needed Gwyn. His analytical skills. And Rhys for that matter. John Rambo was caught at the end because he was alone. Indiana Jones, however, defeated the Nazis because he had Marcus and Salah behind him. Heroes needed their sidekicks and teams if they were to succeed. My first mission alone and I end up out cold at the side of the road.

"Good, I'll try that," I say. "There was another thing – the hospital's full of sick kids with this bug."

"You think it's the curse?" he asks.

"Has to be," I say.

"Fricking pestilence. That means Terry won't have long. No word of *Gŵyl Awst* going ahead yet?"

"No," I say. "But I've been thinking it through. What happens if we do manage to save Terry and stop them? If there's no tribute, how bad could this illness get?"

"Those children's graves..." Gwyn trails off.

"Yeah."

"We can't let them sacrifice him though, can we?" he says.

"No, we can't. First, we deal with them. Then we deal with the witch."

"Is there any way of stopping the curse?" he asks.

I purse my lips and blow. "I have one idea – use witch bottles to trap it. Maybe minimise the impact of the curse?"

"From that stash in the library or new museum or whatever it is?"

"Yeah. I don't really know how to use them, though. Do you think Rhys would know? He's the one who told me about them."

"Probably not without his books," Gwyn says.

"Arse." I rub my eyes with my fingers. "I'll figure something out."

"Mmm." Gwyn exhales heavily. "I need to go. Let me know how it goes with the detective?"

"Okay," I say. "Will I see you soon?"

"Not sure," he says. "Don't know when we'll be back there."

"Was there anything left of the shop?" I ask.

"Not much. Seems the firemen did well to stop the blaze from burning down the whole of the High Street."

I lean my head against the wall and shift it when it touches my bump. "Those bastards…"

"Mmm. Anyway… Hannah took my number. Call me if there's any developments or you want to discuss anything."

"Will do."

We say our goodbyes and I hang up the phone. I stand in the hallway rubbing my chin. Now we must stop the Custodians and the bloody witch. We struggle enough with the living. How the hell do we stop a supernatural curse?

My brain won't shut up. I keep going through the details. Hannah goes out to the shops while I lie on the sofa in my pyjamas watching the news. I didn't used to watch the news but now it seems important that I do; since Terry went missing, that is. It's almost two weeks since he was last seen. The way they talk about it has changed quite a bit over this time. It's clear they're not expecting to find him alive again. Why would they after so long? They probably think some nonce has done him in and hidden the body somewhere. I doubt anyone's thinking he's being kept alive. I mean, how could he be? A little twelve-year-old kid? The whole thing is madness. Jesus, he must be terrified.

It begs the question – why wait so long? Especially now it seems the witch's curse is starting to happen. Why would they be keeping him tied up to the bed for all this time? There's been no mention of the festival either. What could they be waiting for? There's still time to stop them, for now. But if I do manage it, and save Terry, what happens to the sick kids? It makes me think of Dad's story about the King who sacrificed his son to stop a war. Is it okay to do one terrible thing to stop many other bad things from happening? That's the problem the Custodians have been facing for hundreds of years. But what if I can stop the sacrifice and still save everyone? Still keep everyone safe. What if I can't...? There's a knock at the front door. I get up, turn the sound down on the telly and peer past the curtains to make sure it's not the meatheads again. I see Detective Thomas stood with her arms crossed. She spots me and narrows her eyes. Can't ignore her now. Right, I think, let's see whose side you're on.

I open the door and see her wide smile facing me. "Hello, Ned. The hospital told me you were home."

"Got back this morning," I say. "Come in."

She follows me into the living room and sits down on the sofa. She opens her bag and hands me a bottle of Lucozade and a punnet of green grapes. "For you."

"Thanks," I say.

"How are you feeling?" she asks.

"Head's a bit sore," I say, stroking my temple. "Fine otherwise."

"Very glad to hear it." She turns her head each way. "No one else home?"

"No. Dad's out getting some stuff for work and Hannah's gone to the shops."

I see her eyes turning to the news coverage on the telly. Here's my chance.

"Having any luck with that?" I ask.

"Sorry?" she says, distracted.

"Any luck with the investigation? It's why you're here, isn't it? In town, that is."

"No, no luck." Her voice becomes deeper. "Did you know Terry?"

"He was in the year below. I knew him but not that well. Do you know what happened to him?"

"We're still exploring all avenues."

That's what Columbo would say to someone when he doesn't want to talk about an investigation. What does that mean? I clasp my hands on my lap. "You're not going to tell me, are you?"

She gives me a gentle smile and shakes her head. Something catches her eye, and she looks up to the sideboard behind the sofa.

"Is that your mother?"

I glance over to see what she's looking at then nod. "Yeah, that *was* her."

Her face drops. "Was? Oh, I'm sorry. I shouldn't have… She was very young."

"It happened earlier this year." I clear my throat.

"Was she sick?" she asks.

"No. She was fine but then one day after work she went to sleep and never woke up."

"She wasn't ill?" she asks again.

"No, until that day, she was fit as a fiddle. They think it was her heart, but they could never say for certain."

"Oh God. I can't imagine. Well, I…"

I can hear her breathing loudly through her nose.

"… I lost a baby boy to cot death. One moment he was fine and the next he'd left us. Just went to sleep…"

"Right. Sorry," I say, slightly taken aback.

"Oh, it's fine now. I'm saying I understand. The shock of it. That's the thing I struggled with the most. Not understanding why. At least when someone is ill or gets hurt then you know something's not right. That something is coming. But when it happens out of the blue then the why never really goes away. Does it?" She looks up at me. "Anyway, sorry, that was years ago now. It's just, he would've been your age had he lived."

I know I'm meant to be testing her to see if she's working with the Custodians, but right now I'm lost for words. My gut says there's no way she can be with them.

"Is that why you came to check on me?" I ask.

"Maybe, yes… no… I don't know. I just wanted to make sure you were alright. Seeing you on the side of that road was such a shock. And this case has been so…" She trails off and her head drops.

"I thought you lot would be used to grim cases. Murders and kidnappings and such."

"You never really get used to them," she says. "And if you do then maybe it's time to change your job."

"You really don't know what happened to him, do you?" I ask.

She looks away and shakes her head. "Honestly? No, we don't."

Maybe I should say something now. Tell her that I know where he is. She can't be with the Custodians. Why would she share that stuff with me? Unless she's playing me. Maybe she's testing me. Maybe she's even smarter than I think. Damn it, I wish Gwyn was here. This was the type of thing he was good at. I need to buy time and think about it more before I tell her. What else can I find out?

"Can I get you a tea or anything?"

She smiles and sits up. "No, I'd better be off. I'm glad to see that you're back home and feeling better."

"Thanks for the visit."

"Would you mind if I dropped by again tomorrow?" she asks.

"Please do. Around the same time is perfect."

A thought comes to me as I walk her to the door. "I guess you're based here most of the time now."

"Yeah, I'm down here every day, almost. I only go back to my office in Bangor when I need to check the files or talk to the gaffer."

"So when you ran into me yesterday, were you on your way back from the city?"

She stops by the door. Her mouth becomes small, and she shakes her head. "No. I was on my way back from Robham House. That bloody Lord Arseface wanted a private chat. I swear that man cares more about his social life than he does about the people of this town. You know he wants the *Gŵyl Awst* festival to go ahead – even though we still have an investigation underway. And that poor boy's family and the community are still missing a child."

She steps through the door and turns her head before leaving. "Worst thing is, he's got his way. Friends with my boss – he is – and the local MP. They all reckon it's good for the town, despite what I advised."

"*Gŵyl Awst* is happening?"

"This Saturday," she says, striding towards her car. "No doubt they'll be making a fuss about it in the coming days. Anyway, I'll see you tomorrow."

"See ya," I say back but my words fall to the ground as I quickly digest this new information.

That's it, I think. Terry's date with destiny has been set. The clock has officially started to run out. Only I can save him now. If I do – and that's a big if – I must also save the town kids. I can't allow her curse to run wild. I need to stop it – I need the witch bottles. No doubt someone will have tried using them before but I have no other options so I can only hope I'll be lucky. I need to break into the back of the library or heritage centre or whatever it is they're going to call it and get hold of the stash. Then, I'll have to figure out how to use the damn things. I slam the front door shut, sigh and rub my head.

CHAPTER 58

I run upstairs to get changed. I think about my conversation with the detective. There's no way she's in cahoots with the Custodians based on what she said. I must trust her and tell her what I know. I would've told her just then but the news about the festival caught me by surprise. I don't have any proof but if she's as good a person as my gut tells me she is – or police officer for that matter – then she will take me seriously. At least enough to start investigating the Custodians and find proof herself. I'll call Gwyn later and talk him through it as well to make sure it all makes sense.

I hear the front door open, and someone comes in.

"Hannah, is that you?" I yell at the top of the stairs.

There's no response but I hear a noise that I am familiar with after my night at the hospital – a dry, persistent cough. I head down the stairs, slowly. I don't want to reach the living room where I know what I will face.

Collapsed on the sofa, with her shopping around her, is Hannah. She coughs so loudly that she is unable to hear me enter the room. It's like she's choking. Oh God, I think, the curse has finally arrived at our house. I head to the kitchen to get Hannah a glass of water then I hand it to her, and she sips.

It seems to help and after a few deep breaths, the coughing eases off.

"You okay?" I ask.

"I should be asking you that," she says.

"You've got the bug," I say.

"You don't know that."

"You got too close to those kids yesterday," I say. "We should get you to the doctor."

"No, I just need some rest," she says defiantly. "It's a cold – that's all."

I place my hand on her head. "Hannah, you're burning up."

"Stop fussing, Ned, I'm fine," she says. "I took some tablets before. I'll be alright once they kick in. Jesus, you should be the one resting. You're still recovering from concussion."

"I'm okay," I say. "In fact, I was going to head out for some fresh air. Staying in here is doing my head in."

Before she objects, I leave her and take the shopping bags into the kitchen and unpack everything. Back in the living room, I find Hannah curled up asleep on the sofa. Resting is probably the best thing for her right now, I guess, so I grab a blanket and tuck her in before heading out. I've no idea how long Dad will be, so I check the time and make a mental note to return within a couple of hours to check on her.

Damn it. Outside the house I see my bike, which is still bent from being smacked by the detective's car. Dad must've brought it back with his van. I'll have to head to the library on foot.

Along the High Street, I see notices have been put up underneath the missing child posters.

Brothers and Sisters of Nant-y-Wrach.

In light of recent sad events, we considered cancelling the Gŵyl Awst festival this year, but due to popular demand, and with the support of the Rowlands family, our annual harvest celebration will go ahead. The festivities will be moderate and considerate given the ongoing situation. We look forward to sharing this important milestone with you as we do each year – this Saturday, 2nd August 1983.

Sincerely,

Nant-y-Wrach Town Council and Lord Edward Robham

Reading the notice makes me sick to my stomach so I carry on with my head down. I glance over at the bookshop – now barricaded by plywood and pasted in *Danger – Restricted Access* signs. That does nothing to raise the spirits either, so I pick up my pace and head over to the library.

I stand outside, staring at the old grey building. The place has a long history. It was once the town courthouse where lots of acts of justice (and apparently injustice) took place. There is scaffolding around the back of the building where they've been refurbishing. The front – where the main library is – looks like business as usual. I move a little closer and nod to a girl coming out who I think may be in Hannah's class at school. I stand at the corner of the building craning my neck and trying to see what is going on at the back. Oddly, it seems quiet. It's late morning so I'd expect there to be someone at work. But I knew from Dad that builders and contractors were often a law unto themselves when it came to projects. Maybe I was in luck. I scan around me and when I see there is no one around, I proceed along the wall. How I wished I'd had one of Rhys's briefings before this operation, or even that I had Gwyn with me whingeing away.

I reach the scaffold and look up between the metal poles of the frame. There is plastic sheeting billowing above me, and I move my head to the side to get a clear view overhead; there is definitely no one there. Surveying the back of the building, it looks like most of the work has been done. The heritage centre is a concrete add-on to the main grey stone of the library. It doesn't really match from the outside, but the back of the building is away from the main road so doesn't really matter in some ways. I reach a new door – the type you might see on an extension to a house and stop to check the area around me once again. I keep expecting some fat builder to start yelling at me, but I am alone.

I turn the handle, expecting my luck to end and for the door to be locked and there to be no way in but it turns; it's open. "Shit."

Inside is dark. I can see the walls have been plastered and are still clean and white. I've spent so much time in old, abandoned houses recently that being in a new building is a strange feeling. The smell of paint is strong, and the floor is bright and shiny. As my eyes get used to the low light, it becomes clear the room is full of dividers, set out to form a path from a door at the opposite end towards the rear of the building. These are the same types of dividers that they use in classrooms at school to separate groups and hang posters on. I reach into my bag and take out a torch. I shine the light on the partition and see the nearest has 'Seventies and Eighties' written on the top and it shows photos from around the town and the area. There are photos of Gatsby, my school, and the High Street. There are mentions of Robham. Lots of Robham, in fact. Up on the wall are the words, 'Robham *Nant-y-Wrach* Library and Heritage Centre'. It really is a mouthful. I follow the path between the room dividers and see that they tell the story of the town. Every few steps, the years go back further. Photos become black and white and the town changes slightly as I go back in time. One thing that remains the same is the mention of Lord Robham. Not the same man of course but a title handed down from father to son over hundreds of years. There's no doubting the message here – the histories of the Robham family and this town are tightly wound together.

There are pictures of paintings and documents from the time of the witch trial. I stare and read through the details but there is nothing there I don't know. The main thing that stands out is the name of the trial judge – Lord Oliver Robham. They were here then, and they played their part. They took the side of the

Royalists during the English Civil War. They were involved in the reformation of the church in Wales. They began mining Plum Mountain for lead in the 1790s. A Lord Robham commanded armies at Waterloo. The family paid for the asylum. One of the Robhams served in the Battle of the Somme. The name is everywhere, and it gets my hackles up, and I can't help but reach out and hit the partition wall, pushing the thing over. It clatters as it falls to the ground, and I freeze and watch the library door expecting someone to come in. Nothing happens but I do notice two boxes on the other side – and as I shine the torch in their direction, green light reflects back. I quickly spy through the window at the top of the door and see the main hall of the library. The librarian is busy talking to someone and does not appear to have heard me. With eyes still focused on the door, I make my way over to the boxes.

I look down into the container to see it's full of green glass bottles. There are other items as well – horseshoes, pieces of wood covered in witch marks and various rusty tools and kitchen wear. Nothing of value it seems; no wonder security was so lacking.

I lift one of the glass bottles and, peering closely, can see it's full of something – a liquid and small metal objects. Nails or wires perhaps. There's something that looks like fur or hair as well. I put it back and grab one of the other bottles. It looks the same. The bottle is sealed shut with an old cork. I pick up another, and then another, and see that all of them are set up like this. These were the witch bottles. How many would I need to take? I'm guessing the more I have then the stronger the effect – the more curse I can trap inside. I count eight in the box and take them all. I open my rucksack and pile them in carefully but quickly, with eyes both on the doors into the library and out to the back. I zip up my bag and – not wanting to push my luck any more – dash out of the back door with the clanking objects.

I get to the street and stop. I take out one of the bottles and stare at the little glass object in my hand; will it really help me to stop the witch? I honestly don't know, but it's the only option I have. A more pressing question might be, how do I use it? I wish I had the resources of the bookshop to hand, but that is all gone now. I could try the library again, but I doubt they'd have any of the more interesting books I needed for this. Would there be anyone other than Rhys I could ask that might have that type of knowledge? Rebecca is the only one I can think of, but she is no longer around. I don't even have a phone number. I review my options and realise what I must do. I put the bottle back in the rucksack and head down the street in the direction of the Travellers' site. I must find Rebecca.

CHAPTER 59

It's around the middle of the day and the hot sun is bearing down on me. My lips are dry and I'm desperate for a drink. I imagine myself to be like Clint Eastwood in *The Good, The Bad and The Ugly*, stumbling through the scorching heat of the desert, face cracking and skin red from sunburn. I keep thinking about Hannah and that I need to get back to her. I've no idea how long Dad will be, and if she really has the bug, then someone needs to keep an eye on her. But I do need to get help now. With only three days until the festival, I haven't got much time left and there's still a lot of thinking and planning to do. I'm used to working in a team but now it's all on me to make things happen. It feels like I'm making things up as I go along and the whole thing is terrifying.

It's a good mile from town to the Travellers' site. I'm not sure what exactly I'm looking for when I get there. What I need is something that tells me where their other home is – the place they usually go to in the winter – where I can find Rebecca right now.

I arrive to see that most of the vehicles and caravans are gone. They've left a lot of their stuff behind. Is this because they left in a rush or is this how they normally leave it? It certainly makes sure no one else will take over their site. Near the hedge, they've left one of the older caravans. I step closer and stare through the window. It's full of old newspapers and rubbish. That's as good a place as any to start searching. I pull on the handle and the door creaks open. I step inside and there's a stench of damp. The small bed near the window is covered in mould. I scan over a pile of papers next to the sink; bills, receipts, tabloids and local rags – but nothing with any addresses or place names on.

I turn my head as I hear the roar of an engine approaching – it reminds me of something. Someone is coming. Without much thought I drop beneath the window and peer through the ragged net curtain. A motorcycle pulls into the site and slowly drives past the caravan, then stops somewhere out of view. The engine is turned off. I dart over to the other window and peek out. A tall man gets off the bike and removes his helmet. I see Abraham's face and gasp a breath of relief.

I leap out of the caravan and Abraham steps back, startled.

"Jesus, Mary and Joseph, boy. You scared the piss out of me."

"Sorry," I say.

"What the hell are you doing here?" he asks.

"Searching."

His forehead wrinkles. "Searching for what?"

"Something that tells me where you lot went to," I say. "I need to see Rebecca."

"Why do you need to see her?"

"I need her help. We're on the last lap here and I've one last chance to stop things."

He crosses his arms. "She can't be helping you with those Custodians. And you, lad, shouldn't be fighting them alone either."

"All I need is information," I say desperately.

"What do you need to know? Maybe I can help."

I take out one of the witch bottles and show it to him. "Any idea how to stop a curse using one of these?"

He shakes his head. "Shit, no, lad. Rebecca's the one you need for that."

"Can you tell me how to get to the other site?"

"No point. We didn't go there. Too risky. Easy for the Custodians to find us if they wanted to."

"So where did you go?" I ask.

He takes a deep breath and blows out through his lips. "You know I can't have her getting involved again. The Custodians are capable of dark acts. Very dark acts indeed."

"I promise I won't involve her any more. All I need is information on how to use this thing." The bottle clinks as I tap it with my finger. "Kids all over town are getting ill because of the curse. I think my sister has it as well. Please, Abe, I'm desperate. Just let me see Rebecca for a few minutes. Tell me where she is."

He looks around at the site and starts nodding. "Alright, you can speak to her, but that's all. We're staying at a farm on the north side of the *Cewri*."

"Right," I say, sighing. "Is there a bus I can take to get there?"

"Let me take you there myself." He points to the bike with his thumb. "You remember how to ride on the back of this thing, don't you?"

"I do," I say.

"Right then, see if you can help me first. I came back here to find my adjustable spanner. We left this place in such a rush that we ended up leaving lots of things. I've been back here already three times this week."

We search in the long grass near where Abraham usually parks his motorbikes, and I spot the missing tool in no time. The shining silver metal sparkles in the bright sunlight. I hand it over to Abraham.

"Good lad," he says.

"Must be important to you?" I say.

"Best tool in any mechanic's toolbox."

Feeling the urge to get going, I look over at the bike and then back at Abraham. "We can go now?" I bite my lower lip.

"You're keen. You think it's life or death."

"I do."

"Right. Get on."

He hands me his helmet and rides without one himself. Were it not for the circumstances, riding on the back of a motorbike through the mountains would've been a highlight of my summer, but as things stand, with my mind full of worries and strange thoughts, the journey passes me by without making much of an impact. Before long, I notice that we've turned down a rough farm lane that goes down the middle of a field full of sheep. Beyond a small, wooded area, I see the bus and caravans and other vehicles parked up. They're hidden away from the main road, so I see why this site is a good place for them to lay low.

Abraham turns left across the field and then pulls up at the camp between two caravans.

"Over there," he says, and I leap off the bike and dash across the site. Rebecca is sat on a box holding *Taid*. She's listening to an older lady who sits facing her. Must be a consultation. I get nearer and Rebecca's eyes brighten when she sees me. She says something to the lady and strides over and pokes me in the shoulder.

"You're alive," she says.

"Er, yes," I say. "Should I not be?"

"I heard you were in a car accident."

"Yeah, well… too busy to die."

Her smile becomes a frown. "I didn't expect to see you so soon."

"I need your help," I say.

"Okay, let me finish up here. You can wait inside." She points to her caravan, and I go and sit in the mobile house. Still looks the same. It's only been three days since I've seen her, but it feels like a lot has happened. I plonk myself down next to the table and take out one of the witch bottles and examine it. Will this little thing do the trick, I wonder? The door creaks open and – instinctively – I put the bottle back in my pocket. Abraham enters and grabs something from a cupboard.

"You want a drink or anything?" he says.

"Oh yes, some water would be great, thanks."

Abraham fills a glass from the tap and hands it to me.

"I need to head into town shortly," he says. "I can give you a lift back there once you're done here. Shouldn't take long, should it?" I take his glare as a warning.

"No, it won't," I say, catching my breath after downing the drink. "A lift would be good, thanks." I realise I have no money in my pocket anyway to get the bus, so this is a welcome offer.

"Just come and get me, will you?" He strides out of the caravan, and I continue to nod. The door creaks open again, and Rebecca steps inside.

She goes over to the sink and fills a glass of water. "Do you want any?"

I show her the empty glass and shake my head; she sits down facing me. She purses her lips and exhales. "Fourth consultation this morning. Takes it out of you."

"How do they know where to find you?" I ask. "I thought this place was meant to be a secret?"

"All friends of the farmer so far," she says. "It's part of the deal for allowing us to camp here."

"He lets you stay here for that?" I ask.

"And some labouring. He and Father go way back."

"Did the lady get what she wanted?" I ask.

"Some of it," she says taking another sip of the water. "The energy and noise on the other side is still crazy."

"Because of the witch?"

"Probably," she says. "I hear the festival's finally going ahead so I guess the end is in sight?"

I nod, silently.

"And you finally know when the tribute will take place," she says.

"Yeah," I say.

"That poor boy." She closes her eyes tight. "Are you still trying to stop it?"

I cross my arms and look out of the window. "I am going to stop it."

"And what about the curse?" she asks.

"It's started already. It's why I wanted to speak with you." I take out the eight glass bottles in my bag and place them each, side by side, on the table like they're soldiers lining up for roll call. Rebecca lowers her head and stares closely at each of them.

"I really hope you know what these are," I say, "and more importantly, how to use them."

*

Rebecca holds one of the witch bottles in her hands and examines it. I've told her about the burning down of the bookshop, my meetings with the detective, and the sick children at the hospital, and now she quietly stares at the small green glass container.

"I remember Rhys telling me there was a bunch of these things being kept at the new town museum. He said they were meant to protect people from witchcraft by trapping evil spirits and nasty spells inside. It's all I could think of to stop the curse. Do you know what I need to do to get them ready?"

"These are incredible," she says. "I've read about them before but never saw one."

"Can you help?" I ask again, feeling out of my depth.

"Yes, I think I can," she says and gives me a hopeful smile. "You'll need to open them up first and release what's inside."

"Release?" I say. "You mean these have already caught something?"

"Not a full entity. Perhaps pieces of a spell or a curse."

"Anything I should be worried about?" I ask.

"Whatever is in them is not friendly," she says and shakes one of the bottles.

"Can I still use it?" I ask.

"Yes, once you've released what's trapped inside. Also, you'll need to replace the various components."

"And – erm – what are they?"

"Right. Let me check something first." She reaches over to the counter to grab a familiar object that is wrapped in purple velvet. "Do you have anything to write with?"

"Yes," I say and reach into my rucksack to grab a notepad and a pencil. Despite everything going on, I still come prepared.

"Okay, write this stuff down." She places her hand on the skull, closes her eyes and starts to nod. "You'll need a handful of sharp metallic items like nails, razor blades and pins. Take these and fill each bottle with as much as you can fit in."

"What do they do?" I ask.

"This is the stuff that helps trap the entity's energy or curse," she says. "On top of this, load each bottle with salt. This will help with purification. Then cut a piece of red string or ribbon and place that in the bottle. This'll help protect those around from the negative effects of the evil trapped inside."

"Okay," I say, writing furiously like I'm jotting down details of a recipe. "What about the liquid?"

"Oh, right." She furrows her brow. "For that you need urine. Urine or wine. Maybe a mixture. Consecrated wine would be great if you can get hold of it. If not, you could mix in some consecrated soil. Maybe from the church."

"Piss?" I say. "Is that what the liquid is?"

"Probably," she says. "It marks the bottle as belonging to you. In the same way dogs mark their territory by peeing everywhere they go."

I sigh. "Right. Is that it?"

"Then you stick the cap back on and seal it with candle wax. Black, ideally, but white if you don't have that colour."

"Okay."

"There are some words to say as well: *Earth protected from hallowed ground; needles, nails rusting fast. Keep all harm inside and locked, within this dungeon made of glass.*"

I write the whole thing down and read the sentence out silently in my head. "*Taid* told you all this?"

"More or less," she says. "Speak those words once you've filled the bottle. Keep repeating them – as many times as you can."

"Then it's done?" I ask.

"That's it." She opens her eyes and takes her hands off the skull. "You just need to hide these bottles somewhere near the target of the curse. If they do their jobs, they will attract any negative spells heading in that direction and trap them inside."

"I guess the hospital would be the best place for them then?"

She shrugs and I close the notepad and drop it back in the rucksack.

"Do you think this'll work?" I ask.

"I don't know," she says in a flat tone. "You're right that it's the only option you have, but someone must've tried this before in the past."

"Maybe they weren't doing it right?" I say hopefully.

"Maybe." She looks out of the window like her mind is taking her somewhere else. "Have you considered that his sacrifice may be the only way to stop her curse?"

I lay my hands out on the table and stare at them. "No way," I say. "Whatever happens I can't let Terry be killed like his life means nothing."

She looks back at me with a gentle smile and nods her head. "What about the detective? Do you think she'll help you?"

"My gut tells me she is not with them. Getting her help will be part A of the plan."

"And part B?"

I point to the witch bottles. "Part B."

"Right." She picks up the end bottle. "One thing – when you open it, turn it away and be aware that it may have some strange effects."

"What kind of strange effects?"

"Depends on what the spell or curse was intended for."

"But not serious, right?"

"Hopefully not."

Hopefully? I close my notebook and start gathering everything back in my rucksack, but something occurs to me. "If I set up the bottles now – will they work straight away? Seeing as the curse is starting to take effect and kids in town are already getting ill."

"I've been thinking about that," she says. "Timing seems to be everything here. The energy has been increasing rapidly over these last few days and I think the Custodians plan for the tribute to happen at a specific point. That's why the sacrifice doesn't happen straight away. They wait until the right time. Maybe until after the curse has started but before it peaks. That might be why they hold off the festival."

She hands me the glass bottle reluctantly like she doesn't want me to have it. Her shoulders have slumped, and she bites the inside of her mouth.

"I wish I could help you," she says. "But Abe won't let me leave this place. He's terrified of what the Custodians might do."

She reaches over and grabs my hand. "You shouldn't be doing this alone."

"It's okay," I say. "I'm ready."

"No," she says. "You shouldn't even be on this path."

"What do you mean?" I ask.

She swallows like she's about to tell me something important. "Look, I know you think it's your job to keep everyone safe; to take on this fight because of your mother."

"Oh, right," I say. "What's Gwyn been telling you?"

She shakes her head. "Not just Gwyn – *Taid*. He tells me the last time you saw your mother alive, something from the darkness clung to her and you believe that thing is what caused her death."

I look down at the floor. "I should've stopped it. But I didn't. Too shocked or scared or something but I didn't…"

"*Taid* didn't want me telling you this – he says you need to work it out for yourself otherwise the meaning is lost – but I'm sorry, I must. What you saw was not some evil entity come to kill your mother. It was a portent the *klewmeirw* call *Cysgod Annwn*

– a dark halo that comes to and follows those close to death. You do have some *klewmeirw* in you; I know you do because you've been sensing entities from the other side in the places we've investigated. But what you saw with your mother that night was not an entity – it was a sign of her imminent death – not a demon or *cythraul* come to murder her. I'm telling you this because you need to know it was not your path – you've been on this mission to defeat the monsters to keep everyone safe, but you never needed to. Going after the Custodians is dangerous. And I think you may end up sacrificing yourself to save Terry. So please stop – let things play out. This is not your path. Walk away and live or keep fighting and..."

She licks her lips, and her eyes are welling up. I am at a loss of what to say. I pull my hand away from hers and grab my bag. "No, that can't be right. What I saw is what killed her. I could feel its intent. I knew what it was going to do."

Rebecca shakes her head. "*Cysgod Annwn* can feel like that, but it isn't a spirit or evil entity – it's a dark mark that tells us who will soon cross over into the otherworld. Your mother wasn't killed. This was never your battle. Please turn back – stop before you end up being marked by the *Cysgod* yourself."

I put my hands over my face. "Whatever it was, I can't stop. Terry will die. I must try. I must."

Glancing out the window, I see Abe loitering by the door – he's waiting for me. I get up and lift my rucksack onto my shoulders. "I – erm – I'd better be going."

"Wait," she calls after me. "*Taid* says you don't need to act the hero. It's not your job to keep everyone safe. In her eyes you'll always be her little hero, regardless of your actions."

I leap out of the caravan and let the door slam closed behind me. Rebecca remains inside but I know she's watching through the window. My eyes are filling with tears, and I take deep breaths to keep the sobs at bay.

"Ready to go, are we?" Abe says and I nod, wiping my cheek.

I stride away in the direction of the motorcycle, and before he can see my face, I grab his helmet and put it on, hoping it hides the streams of salty tears.

CHAPTER 60

I hold on tight to Abraham as we ride back. I tense my hands to stop them from trembling. I wish Rebecca hadn't told me what she did. It's thrown me completely. Whether or not the dark halo killed Mum, my current situation is unchanged, and the mission must still go on. I knew Rebecca had access to the other side, but there were things I didn't want to ask or know about. It was too much, and I've had other priorities on my mind. I miss Mum so much. I try to be strong but inside I want nothing more than to hear her come home and reach over and pull me close and tell me that everything is going to be okay.

Focus, I think. I need to get the witch bottles ready. I need to prepare myself to speak with the detective. Rebecca shouldn't have distracted me like that. I was about to go into battle alone and she should've known better. How dare she. She is meant to be my friend, but she's let me down.

"You okay back there?" Abraham yells.

"Yeah," I say.

Focus. Get your head together, lad. Battle is coming and this is the eve of war. You must do this alone. Terry's life depends on you. The children of this town depend on you.

Abraham slows down and drops me off on the High Street.

"Don't do anything stupid," he says.

I can't help but scoff. "I won't."

He takes the helmet, hangs it on the back of the bike then gives me a nod. He squeezes my shoulder when he sees my face, before disappearing down the street. I see another of the notices about the festival and feel my stomach doing a somersault. I'll go to the churchyard now, I think.

In the shadow of the church, I tread between the headstones and see one of the older graves has recently been dug up. Probably to allow family members to be buried together. It helps me because it means I have a big pile of soil to take. I can't put the soil in the bottles yet, so I grab an old piece of newspaper near the hedge and fill it with soil. I stick it in my pocket and decide to head for home to check on Hannah.

When I reach the end of my street, I gasp at what I see; outside my house is an ambulance. The front door is open. I leg it over to the house but slow down near the big white emergency vehicle. Part of me is terrified at what I will find. Oh God, I shouldn't have left her. It's my fault if anything bad has happened. My heart is racing as I reach the door and look in. Right at that moment, paramedics barge out pulling a stretcher along. Hannah is lying on it. Her face is soaked in sweat, she looks lifeless like a zombie, and she has a large oxygen mask over her mouth and nose.

"Is she okay?" I yell but the paramedics push me aside and wheel the trolley quickly to the ambulance. Dad emerges from the house after them.

"What is it, Dad? Is she okay?"

"She was like that when I got home," he says. "I couldn't wake her. Her breathing wasn't right, and she was burning up."

I can feel myself starting to become tearful. "Dad, will she be okay?"

"I don't know, Ned. I'm going with her. You stay here with Val."

Auntie Val comes out of the house and hands Dad a bag.

"I want to come with you," I say.

"You can't. She probably has the bug. I can't risk you getting it as well."

"You can't – sniff – leave me." I'm fighting off the sobs. "Dad, don't go." Everything is falling to pieces and it's all my fault.

Dad turns to face me. He leans in and puts his head next to mine. "Stay here. I'll call as soon as I know anything."

He looks over at Auntie Val and she steps closer and puts her arm around me. I'm sobbing now like a little child. I want to stop but I can't help it. It's all too much. Dad steps up into the back of the ambulance, waves one last time and the paramedic closes the door. The ambulance lights start to flash, and the siren begins to sound before the vehicle speeds off down the street. I continue to cry my heart out, my hands covering my face.

"Come on, Ned *bach*," Auntie Val says. "Let's go inside."

CHAPTER 61

The night is grey and depressing in the house, but despite circumstances, I feel strangely calm. Probably because of the bucketload of tears that fell from my eyes earlier. I get tired of waiting for news from the hospital so after dinner I leave Auntie Val sat on the sofa watching *Tomorrow's World* and I head out to Dad's shed to look for something to help me open the witch bottles.

It's odd not to find Dad typing away with a grumpy look on his face when I open the door. The shed is dusty and muggy, and I'm not sure how he managed to spend so much time in here. There are notes stuck to the wall – names of characters and how they connect, scenes in his book and settings. In the corner is a pile of typed pages. I examine the first page, which has the title of the book on it: *The Greatest Sacrifice* by Gethin Evans. Scanning across the pages, I see he had reached page 194 before he had to stop. I feel bad in some ways. I was the one that brought the wrath of the Custodians to our house. He didn't deserve that.

I place the eight bottles on the table and scan the area. In the corner, I see a pair of pliers. I grab them and try and pull the cork out of the first witch bottle. Remembering Rebecca's warning, I hold the end away from my face. But no matter how hard I try,

I am unable to get the stopper out. I grab a screwdriver from a drawer underneath the desk and try to wedge the cork from the bottle. It splits as I push on the screwdriver and the air almost knocks me to the ground when it hits my face. The smell reminds me of the sewers at the edge of town on Boxing Day when the Christmas Day shit and piss stink the place up to high heaven.

I hold the bottle at arm's length and cover my face, but as I do I notice a sound emerge from below; quiet to start with but it gets louder and louder – a mixture of scissors snipping and breathy whispers and I sense things on the floor edging towards me, getting closer, until they start moving over my feet and up my legs and I start kicking at them but I cannot see the creatures – I can only hear them and feel them – so I try and swipe them away, but I cannot touch them with my hands either – I only sense them moving over my body – countless tiny creatures climbing up my body and crawling over my thighs, onto my stomach and over my bum, up my back, and up to my shoulders and then across my face and over my head. The invisible creepy crawlies make my skin tingle, and they cover me all over, and they are loud, and I panic and drop onto the floor and slap my skin and roll around like I'm on fire, trying to swipe them off but there is no sign of them at all when I try to grab them or swat them. I yelp and start flailing, losing control of my arms and legs as I expect them to start eating me at any moment – burrowing in through my skin and working their way into my flesh and bursting my blood vessels open and stripping me of meat until I'm a pile of bones on the floor of the shed. Then, almost at once, the crawling and tingling and sounds stop, and I lie on my back stroking and touching my body all over searching for proof that I was covered in something – ants or beetles or bloody scorpions, but there is nothing. I sit up, slowly, and start to sense that I am not alone – there is a presence nearby and I turn my head and wrinkle my nose expecting to see something horrible and rotten lurking in the corner. I don't see anything or anyone but somewhere, far away,

I hear a raspy voice whisper the words, *red eyes*. It's followed by a rough and long throaty cackle. It's a female voice but it doesn't sound like a woman. The voice is grizzly and soured by bitterness and hatred. I can feel it; I can feel her. I become dizzy and run outside and throw up my dinner into the drains. I collapse on the ground next to the hole and take a few deep breaths. After a few minutes, whatever weirdness I experienced passes. I sit silently on the ground staring into the darkness of the garden. If that was a taster for her powers, then it doesn't bode well. It makes me despair. I'm trying to beat an ancient evil with a few old bottles. I should throw them in the bin and give up. Chances of success are zero to stupidly low. Apparently, I shouldn't even be on this path. But I am.

"Red eyes," I say. What does that mean?

Fear and doubt swell inside, and I feel the need to focus on something else. The night air is warm. I get up and walk over to the wild honeysuckles growing in the hedge and breathe in their smell to try and forget about the stink of whatever horror was in the bottle. I look over at the window and peek inside. I can see the glow of the television against the open door between the kitchen and the lounge. No word from the hospital yet, I guess.

I take a deep breath and think about the situation. The force I experienced when I opened the bottle was a light breeze compared to the hurricane of evil that Terry will face if I don't do something. I am scared, yes, but I must continue. That is what soldiers are trained to do. They see their fears and they face up to them and they do whatever is asked of them anyway. That is what it is to be brave; to be a hero. They don't cower and run away like little kids. I must keep fighting. It's the only way I'll rescue him. I take a deep breath and return to the shed.

The smell seems to have cleared but I leave the door open. I pick up the bottle and examine it. If I can't pull out the whole cork, then maybe I can remove it piece by piece. The first layer brakes off and I can see that about a third of the stopper has been removed. I stick the screwdriver in again and another large chunk comes loose. Careful not to push the final layer of cork into the bottle, I force the screwdriver in again, right at the edge and this enables me to slowly edge it out. I take the open bottle outside and rinse it under the tap. I wash it until all the gunk and liquid that was in it before is gone. Inside are the remains of a few rusty nails, which I cannot seem to pull out. That's fine, I think. I'll put in a few more and then add the other ingredients as well.

After my experience with the first bottle, I open the other seven outside, with my face wrapped up in a towel like I'm a ninja. I rinse them under the tap as soon as they're opened, which seems to help clear away the smell – although God knows what I'm washing away down the drains. The weird presence doesn't come to me again – maybe it was just the first bottle that had the nasty thing trapped inside. Whatever the case, I now have eight open bottles, ready to fill and seal. There are nails in Dad's shed that I can use. I divide a handful between all bottles before adding the salt and a red ribbon I took from one of Hannah's drawers. I then use a funnel to pour in the graveyard soil. On the side I have the piece of paper with the lines I must recite, and I begin to speak the words as I fill the first bottle.

"Earth protected from hallowed ground. Needles, nails rusting fast. Keep all harm inside and locked, within this dungeon made of glass."

Once the bottle is half full, I move on to the next and carry on saying these words repeatedly. After reaching the end, I sigh, and realise it's time to take a whiz. Peeing into each bottle is tricky, even with the funnel. Some gets on my hands, and I dry them on my ninja face towel. To seal the bottles, I use corks I found in the kitchen that mum used to keep from her bottles of wine. No idea why she kept them – maybe she thought they would be useful. Well, they were but perhaps not for the intended reason. Random objects of hers are still everywhere around the house. What would she think of this now, I wonder? Using a cork from one of her bottles of wine to try and craft an object that I hope will save the town's kids from an evil curse. None of these words makes any sense but they are the state of things. Crazy, I know.

After pushing in the cork stoppers, I melt candle wax and drip it over the ends of the bottles to make sure the corks are fully sealed. I pick up each bottle in turn and repeat the words Rebeca gave me a few more times.

I sit and stare at them until I hear the back door open. I move the ninja face towel to hide the bottles. Auntie Val approaches and I dare not turn around. I'm not sure what news she has to share with me, and I hold my breath.

"Hannah's okay."

I breathe out and turn to face her.

"She's stable, anyway. They've got her on oxygen and they're giving her medicine to get the fever down."

"Is it the…?" I don't need to finish the sentence before Auntie Val responds.

"They think so."

"What does that mean?" I ask.

"They don't know yet." She steps closer and strokes my arm. "But you know she's in the best place for her right now. They'll take good care of her."

"It's my fault," I say. "For getting knocked down. If Hannah hadn't been at the hospital, she wouldn't have got this thing."

"Oh, Ned *bach*, you don't know that. This thing is everywhere right now. Kids all around town are getting it. We should be grateful that you haven't picked it up."

"I want to see her," I say. "Can we visit her tomorrow?"

"I'm sorry, no. Strict instructions from your dad. And he's right. It's not worth the risk."

I cross my arms and shake my head.

"Come on," she says. "Come inside and watch telly with me. Let's try not to worry too much about anything tonight. Things will look better in the morning, I'm sure."

She turns away towards the door. "God, this shed stinks. Did my brother use this place as a toilet as well?"

I shrug, and as I hear the door close, I remove the towel and examine the witch bottles one last time. Not much more I can do now, I suppose. May as well take it easy for a bit, as tomorrow would likely be a long day. First things first, I would be expecting a visit from the detective in the morning. Who knows what would happen after that?

CHAPTER 62

I spend most of the morning pacing around the house trying to keep busy. I start watching television, but I get bored. I go upstairs and start reading *The Hamley Book of the Paranormal* but that doesn't last long either and I find myself opening a notepad and scribbling *red eyes* repeatedly as I try and think of what it means. I get frustrated and go out to the shed and repeat the witch mantra to the bottles. By now, I don't need the paper any more – I know it all by heart. In the living room I settle back on the sofa as the news comes on. There's a local report from town by a reporter speaking to residents about their views on the town leaders' decision to go ahead with the *Gŵyl Awst* festival. Some say it's inappropriate given the missing child, but others – perhaps unsurprisingly – say it's what the town needs right now. This includes Terry's parents, and it makes me wonder whether the Custodians have got to them somehow as well. Could they persuade parents to give up on their child in the interest of a greater cause? I don't know. His family is poor and has five other kids. Maybe they've paid them off? Surely not, I hope. But this whole experience has been one surprise after another so my expectations of what's possible has changed completely.

Auntie Val has returned to her house to go and address a few things. We don't often go around hers. Whenever she babysits, it's always here. Hadn't really thought about that before but it is peculiar. I wonder why that is? A knock at the front door breaks my trail of thought. It's time.

I open the door and let Detective Thomas into the house. She asks where everyone is, and I tell her about Hannah.

"Oh no, I'm so sorry to hear that," she says, shaking her head. "Oh God, if it wasn't for the accident, she wouldn't have been exposed to the bug."

I shrug. "It's all over town now anyway, apparently."

She puts her hand to her mouth and blinks repeatedly.

I sit forward on the sofa and rub my hands together. "I have something else I need to talk to you about right now, though."

She looks up. "Oh?"

I clear my throat. "I know where Terry is."

All the emotion drops from her face, and she sits upright in the armchair. "What… What do you mean?"

"I know where he is – who has him, that is."

She stops like she's frozen, then almost in slow motion she reaches into her pocket and takes out a notepad and scribbles something in it. "Tell me everything, Ned."

"I didn't know whether I could tell you," I say. "I didn't know whether you were on their side. I still can't be certain, to be honest. But I haven't got any other options right now."

"Who are they, Ned?"

"The Apotropaic Custodians."

"The apo– what?"

"Apotropaic. It means to ward off evil."

Her eyes widen. "Right, so you say these Apo–, these Custodians have taken Terry? Do you know if they've hurt him?"

"He's still alive," I say. "For now, at least. They intend to make a tribute of him. The day after tomorrow; the day of the festival."

"Tribute, meaning kill?"

"They intend to sacrifice him to stave off a witch's curse. They've been around for hundreds of years. Every forty years, they take a boy from the town and sacrifice him to stop the curse. Only this time, the curse is coming true already and all these kids are getting ill."

"Every forty years…?" Her face has become pale. "But who are they?"

"A secret group that runs this town. Lord Robham is one of them. Also, some of the local coppers. Who knows who else?"

"You say a secret group has existed in this town for hundreds of years for the sole purpose of kidnapping and sacrificing children? And right now, they have Terry captive with the intention of killing him on Saturday?"

She blinks repeatedly and rubs her face.

"Do you believe me?"

"It's a lot to take in, if I'm honest, Ned."

"I know."

"How did you come to know about this?" she asks.

"It's a long story," I say. "But I've seen him."

"Terry?"

"Yes. They have him tied to a bed somewhere in Robham House. I saw him on a video screen there."

"Are you sure?"

"Yeah, I'm sure."

"Why haven't you mentioned any of this to me before?"

"I didn't know if I could trust you. The Custodians are everywhere here and they're dangerous. They burned down the bookshop that my friend's family owned. They threaten and hurt anyone who gets in their way. They drive people out of town. They're ruthless and they'll use whatever they can to scare you."

"They were behind the fire?"

"Yes," I say.

"And some of the local police officers are part of this group?"

"Sergeant Gatsby for one."

Her eyes are bulging from their sockets. "Are you sure?"

"Yeah. To be honest, I wasn't sure about you until we spoke."

Her jaw drops and she looks away. "You were following me when I struck you."

I nod and lower my head.

"One big question I have is…"

"Proof? I have none, I'm afraid. You must take my word for it. There are others who know as well. My friends, Gwyn and Rhys Bowen, and Rebecca – funny, I don't know her surname. There was also an author called Gerald Edwards who lived nearby but they scared him away by blackmailing him."

"Blackmail?" she says, her face twisting from one confused look to the next.

"They used some trouble he got into years ago against him."

"Right." She pauses. "This is a lot to investigate without any evidence."

"Get over to Robham House and search the place. You'll find Terry there, somewhere."

"Where was the television monitor you saw him on?" she asks.

"In the wardrobe, in the lord's bedroom."

"Where?"

I purse my lips and blow. "I know. It all sounds crazy. All of it. I wouldn't believe me either. But a boy's life depends on it. If we don't do something now, they'll kill him. On Saturday."

"It's not that. I… I do believe you. At least, I believe you think what you're saying is true."

"So, what will you do?" I ask.

"You're saying we have until Saturday to save him?"

"The day of the festival is when they'll do it."

"Right. I'll need you to come with me to the station to give a full statement."

"No," I say firmly. "We can't do that. They'll know I've told you. After that, we'll be done for."

"Right," she says. "Then – erm – we should go to the station in Bangor."

"What if they have contacts there as well? We don't know how far their reach is."

"They really have put the fear of God into you, haven't they?" She rubs her face.

"They're evil," I say. "Why can't you get some of your city police together and go and raid Robham House. That's the quickest way to save Terry, isn't it?"

"It's not that simple, Ned. We can't just barge our way in. We need a warrant and that is very difficult to get without any evidence."

"I'm your evidence." I realise my voice is getting louder as I become more frustrated.

"It's okay, Ned," she says in a softer voice. "I'm here to help. I just need to figure things out a little. I'll go back to the station and speak to my boss about this. Don't worry – he can be trusted."

"Why don't you call him from here?" I say, trying to help things along.

She shakes her head. "He's off today. I'll need to go and find him. He'll probably be on the golf course."

I rub my hands together, unable to keep them still and I feel her gaze. She leans forward and places her two hands on my knees.

"Ned, we'll get this done and save Terry. You've done a very brave thing telling me all this. Now leave it with me and I'll go and figure out how we best move things forward. I'll be needing a full statement from you at some point but for now you've given me enough information to act on – in the interest of preventing loss of life."

She stands up. "I'd better go. I have lots to do. Don't go too far – we'll be needing to speak to you again soon."

She heads towards the door, and I call after her. "Detective Thomas. Please be careful. Only share this with those you one hundred per cent trust. They're really bloody dangerous."

She raises her hand, gives me a gentle smile and leaves. That's that, I think. I've done all I can for Terry. Now the small matter of tackling the witch and the curse.

CHAPTER 63

Two hours have passed since the detective left. Auntie Val has returned, and she's busy cleaning the house. I'm on the sofa but I struggle to sit still. The television is on, but the volume is turned down. I just stare at the screen. I can't stop thinking about what happens next. If the detective goes to Robham House with a group of police officers, will they be allowed to enter peacefully, or will it erupt into a war between the Custodians and the law? The Custodians do have weapons there – I've seen them with shotguns. It could be a shoot-out. That would be exciting to watch but I shouldn't hope for that; people might get hurt. Although I would love to see Mrs Astley getting her comeuppance. And that tosser, Gatsby, being taken away in handcuffs. Could the police force their way into the building if they needed to? I suppose it depended on the warrant. They would surely have to if a child's life is at risk. It would need to be a surprise attack otherwise the Custodians might have time to take Terry away and hide him someplace else. That gets me thinking; the only real proof we have that he's there is the screen in the lord's bedroom. We never actually found out exactly where he was being kept. What if he was elsewhere? That would scupper plans. Wherever it is, these fuckers have been doing this for so long they must have become pretty good at hiding their tracks.

Anyway, that was part A of my plan. It was underway and there wasn't much I could do now, other than wait. For part B, however, I still have a mission to complete – I need to hide the witch bottles at the hospital.

Auntie Val walks past with a feather duster, and I'm reminded of the other pressing worry.

"Why hasn't Dad phoned yet?" I ask.

She stops and looks over. "I don't know, Ned. But I wouldn't read too much into it. He probably hasn't had a chance to get to the payphone yet."

She glances at the silent television and then back at me. "Why don't you go out for a bit? See a friend or go for a walk?"

"My friends are all gone," I say.

"Ned *bach*, don't be so dramatic. There must be other children round here who you can play with?"

I scoff. "Play? No, there's no one here I want to play with."

Auntie Val makes a face. "Okay, sorry. What about just going outside and getting some fresh air? Weatherman says our heatwave will end this weekend – just in time for the festival. They're predicting huge thunderstorms. You should make the most of the sun while it's still with us. Reckon the rest of the summer will be the usual wet, cold drizzle."

I sigh and cross my arms. "I just need to know Hannah's alright, Auntie Val."

"I know, *cariad*. I'm sure we'll get some news soon."

She sits down next to me on the sofa, places her hand on my knee and gives me that soothing smile that has kept our family afloat this year.

"Tell you what. We need some bread and milk. Why don't you nip to the shops to get some?" She reaches into her pocket and pulls out a five-pound note. "There you go. Use the change to buy yourself a comic or some sweets."

I realise this is my chance. I take the money and nod. Waiting inside isn't going to speed things up. I might as well go to the hospital now and complete my mission. Maybe I can see Hannah as well. Kill two birds with one stone. Whatever the case, I need the bottles to be near the sick children for full effect.

I put my shoes on and place all the glass bottles in my rucksack before heading out in the direction of the High Street, where I'll get the bus. The sky is blue, and the air is muggy. Soon it would be business as usual with the weather. The crazy events of the last two weeks have left me oblivious to the constant warm temperatures, but it would be odd to have it change.

I walk through Bryce Estate, past the churchyard, and into the Hanging Gardens. Beyond the park, I see a bus pulling up at a stop. I dash over and tell the driver, "Return to the hospital, please," before handing him the five-pound note.

I arrive back at *Nant-y-Wrach* District Hospital, having only left the place a couple of days before. I stand outside and stare at the building. I'd need to be careful. Wouldn't want to run into Dad or any of Mum's old colleagues. I'd want to avoid the bug as well. I will likely still be needed later to help the detective so I couldn't afford to get ill. Who knows what the following days would bring? No doubt I'd be talking to the police a lot. There might even be television interviews. They'd probably want to know who was responsible for saving Terry's life. Obviously, that would be the police, but I'd be the one who did the legwork. That was after my own – and my friends' – investigations. We were the ones who faced dangers and went up against the Custodians. We were the ones who found Terry. Maybe Gerald Edwards would want to write a book about our adventures? Wouldn't that be great for him at the end of it? Revenge for his decades of torment at the hands of the Custodians. The book could be called *The Children Who Brought Down the Custodians*. It could lead to a film as well. My character could be played by that lad who makes friends with ET. I shake my head and realise I'm getting distracted, so I go in.

The main entrance is busy with outpatients coming and going as well as the odd emergency in an ambulance. Inside, I scan the whole reception area to make sure Dad isn't around. The children's ward – where I stayed – and where they keep the sick kids is down a long corridor beyond the reception. I enter through double doors and suddenly it's a lot quieter. The air smells the same as it did when I stayed here. I see a nurse pushing a man in a wheelchair away from me. A couple walk towards me and they're carrying flowers. My footsteps echo along the walls and every sound I make seems to emphasise my arrival.

I reach the end of the corridor and stop at the corner. Further along, I see the doors of the children's ward at the end. Beyond that point is where the separate rooms are where they keep the infected kids. The doors open and I bolt back behind the wall. I peer around the corner to see a doctor in a white coat walking towards me. I take a deep breath and jog down to the double doors. There, I stop and push them open so that I can see inside. There's no one about at the minute, which I think is a little strange but perhaps it's lucky for me. There are doors on the right and the left inside. It's very likely that Hannah is in one of these rooms. My heart is beginning to beat harder. I don't know what to expect when I find her. What if she's seriously ill? What'll I do then? I have a mission to complete but I must see her first to make sure she's okay. If she's not, I'm not sure how I'll go on with what I must do.

I go in through the doors and check the first room and see a boy and his family. He has a tube in his mouth and wires running from his chest to a machine. In the second room it's the same, this time a girl and her mother. I dash to the other side and see a boy and the next room is a bit bigger and has three girls in it in side-by-side beds. All of them look dreadful and have the same machines and tubes and wires attached to them. I have no idea what it all means but it can't be good. I cross back to the other side and peer through the glass window in the door but a nurse stands in the way so I can't see what is happening. She wears a facemask. I turn my head one way and then the next and eventually she shifts, and

I see Dad's face. He's talking to the nurse. He's rubbing his chin and his eyes are red and he looks tired and pale. I duck down to avoid being seen and then lift my head again. Now they are on the other side of the bed, and I see Hannah. Oh shit, it's the same as the other kids. She lies there with her eyes closed. She looks like she could be dead. She has the tube and the wires stuck to her. What the hell are they for? Why do they need to treat her like that, like she's some bloody cyborg monster? I feel like I'm about to throw up, so I dash into the toilet next to her room. I retch and dry heave a bit, but nothing comes up. She's okay, I tell myself. She must be. They're taking care of her. The tubes and the wires are all part of it and will help her get better. The doctors will give her all the care she needs, and when I stop that curse, all the kids in the hospital will be fine. I'll be the hero that saves everyone. They'll all know about it. Tears start to stream from my eyes but it's okay. I'll save everyone, I know I will.

Someone comes into the toilet. "You okay in there?" A lady's voice.

I clear my throat. "Yes, fine. Thanks."

"Are you sure? I just thought I could hear you being sick?"

"Honestly, I'm okay. Just leave me, will you?"

"You're not crying, are you?"

"I'm bloody good. Leave me."

"Alright," she says, and I hear the toilet doors open and close.

I take a few deep breaths and look up. The ceiling is made up of small squares of plaster. If I can reach up there and lift one, then I can hide the bottles inside. They'd be safe there, I reckon.

I get up onto the toilet and reach up. I need to climb further so with hands pushing against the sides of the cubicle, I step up onto the tank. This time, I'm able to reach the ceiling. I push the square piece of plaster right above me and lift it over to the side. I stick my head in and shine my torch to see a dark space full of wires and pipes. Perfect, I think. I take out the first bottle from my bag and stare at it like I'm wishing it luck. I lift it up and put it out of the way inside the ceiling space. After repeating this process with the seven others, I shine my torch into the space again. They all seem secret and safe here so hopefully won't be found. Will they do the trick? I don't know. I'm leaving them all together because it's the easiest option, but I don't know whether I should be spreading them out – perhaps even placing them outside the ward to form a defensive line around the patients? Everything is a guess at this stage, so I leave them as they are and pull the square ceiling piece over and put it back over the hole.

I decide it's time I leave the hospital and return home. Dad can't see me here. He'll freak out even more. I stick my head out of the bathroom and check that the coast is clear before legging it over to the double doors. I take another look around before leaving. As I push the doors open, I see the faint line of shapes on the door. I step back to get a better view and can't help but release a low guttural laugh when I realise they're witch marks. The bloody Custodians have been here, and they've marked the doors to try and keep the curse at bay. I shake my head. It's all too much to think about. I push through and stride down the corridor back towards the entrance. I'll get the bus back to the High Street and go to the shop as planned. Auntie Val will be none the wiser. I'll just tell her I ran into some friends along the way.

There is drama at the main entrance of the hospital. An ambulance has just arrived with sirens blazing. Paramedics are running with a stretcher. I stop as they pass in front of me. It's a woman covered in blood with a neck brace on and a mask over her face attached to a small balloon that's being repeatedly squeezed by the paramedic. As she passes, I see dark unnatural shadow around her. I gasp like I've been punched in the gut.

"*Cysgod Annwn,*" I whisper.

She has the dark halo. Rebecca was right. It's not an entity, it's the mark of death. This poor lady doesn't have long left…

But wait, I say to myself, there's more. It can't be, it just can't! But it is – it's the detective. I put my hands to my face as I watch her being taken into casualty. Not far behind is the tall, uniformed figure of Sergeant Len Gatsby. He carries his helmet under his arm. I can't see his face and he can't see me stood behind him. A doctor walks over and they speak. I try to listen in, but I'm not able to hear all their words. All I recognise are *speeding*, *accident* and *serious*. I'm frozen to the spot where I stand. I can't move. All Gatsby needs to do is turn around and he'd easily spot me. But he doesn't turn. The doctor leaves him, and he stands and stares in the direction they took the detective. I want to know what his face looks like – I want to see whether he feels sad or whether he's smiling. The bastard. The absolute bastard. This was his doing. After a few seconds, he turns and strides out of the hospital. I kick a fire extinguisher off the wall and howl from the pain. I get a couple of glances in my direction, but the place is too busy for many people to notice.

I run in the direction of casualty. It's not difficult to see where they've taken her. There is one bed where the curtain is closed, and I can see several feet beneath and hear voices yelling inside. There's commotion as they work hard to save her life. Nurses run to and from the area – one of them gives me a *'you shouldn't be here'* glance but she's too preoccupied to care. The shouting gets louder, and I can just about see through an opening in the curtains and they're giving her a shock like they do in the films. The dark halo is still there but it's bigger like it's getting stronger. I hear a doctor shouting "Clear!" He yells it again and again. Then it stops and the place becomes silent.

Why've they stopped? They can't stop. They must keep going. They must keep her alive. If they stop, she dies. If she dies, then how will I… How will I…?

Distraught nurses and an annoyed-looking doctor walk away. I watch and see the *Cysgod Annwn* fade and disappear. Her life is over. The curtain is still closed, but I step closer and peer in around the side. The detective – her body – is a mess. They've torn open her clothes. Her skin is black and blue and covered in blood. I feel sick and the retching starts again. I put my hand to my mouth and run back the way I came through the reception area and out through the doors. Outside, there's a green space surrounded by trees. I fall to my knees behind a bush and this time manage to throw up everything I'd eaten that day plus a bit of what I hadn't. When it stops, I fall to my side and lie on my back. I stare up at a tree.

They got her. That poor, kind woman. They fucking got her. How the hell did they know? Somebody must have double-crossed her. I close my eyes. I wish I'd never heard about any of it. It's not my path but I'm still on it and it keeps getting worse and worse. Please, could something make it all go away. First, they ruined lives and now they're taking lives. They really will do anything to stop those in their way. I can't believe it. I honestly can't. I feel like I'm in a horror film, but the truth has become stranger than any story I've ever read or watched. My hope is dying. I don't know if I have the strength to carry on with this madness. There's so much suffering and pain. There's only me left now. If I don't stop them then no one will. This is what it comes down to – one thirteen-year-old boy fighting a dangerous conspiracy of bastard murderers. I don't even know how I can stop them from killing Terry. Maybe I should leave him to his fate. There's too much in my way and it's not a path I should be on, anyway. I'm not strong enough. They're too powerful. If they complete it, then the curse goes away for another forty years. Hannah and the other children are saved. Terry is the only sacrifice. Terry dies to stop many more deaths and much more suffering.

I stare at the sky and my mind takes me elsewhere. I'm back in my bedroom one night when Mum worked late at the hospital. I'm lying in bed, but I can't sleep until I know she's home. I hear the front door open, and I wait for her to tiptoe into my room to check on me before she goes to bed. She enters silently and kneels next to the bed to tuck me in, before stroking my hair and kissing my forehead. She leans in and whispers in my ear, *goodnight my little hero*. That is usually when I drift off into the peaceful embrace of sleep. But this time – in my mind's eye – I turn my head and whisper back to her, "I'm your hero. I won't let you down."

Am I talking to her? I don't know but I believe she's watching me, somewhere, and I can't give up. I don't believe I'm the hero she says I am until I've saved Terry, until I've saved everyone. That's the only way I can make it right for not saving her. I open my eyes, make a growling noise from my throat, and breathe out so hard that a spray of saliva and phlegm flies out. I sit up and grind my teeth together and hear loud creaking in my head and push my knuckles down into the ground making my knuckles tender against the pebbles and the twigs lining the soil.

I'm not done yet. I won't let Terry die at the hands of those evil bastards. Maybe this wasn't my path, but it fricking well is now. I know I stand alone but I won't let them win. I started this journey intending to give it my all. And that I will. To the end, whatever that means. I will take the battle to my enemy. Whichever way we go from here, at least I know the end is near.

CHAPTER 64

I get the bus back into town, pick up a loaf and a bottle of milk at the shop then return home.

"You took your time," Auntie Val says. "Did you stop off anywhere else on the way?"

"Saw some friends," I say. My voice is flat. My body feels numb. "They invited me out tomorrow for the day. I'll probably be gone early."

She smiles. "Oh, good for you, Ned. Anyone I know?"

I shake my head.

"By the way, did you see any of the commotion around town?"

"Commotion?" I repeat.

"It was on the radio before," she says. "That detective leading the investigation into the missing child was in a car accident."

I swallow and lick my lips. "What happened?"

"Don't know, but it sounds serious from what they're saying."

I rub my jaw. "Serious. Right. I'm going to phone Gwyn."

"Okay."

I listen patiently to the dial tone. I'm desperate to tell Gwyn – or anyone for that matter – what happened. There's no answer. I'm coming to the realisation that I am really going to be doing this alone. So be it, I think. I hang up the phone and head upstairs.

I sit on my bed and think about what I need for the mission. My objective is to find the other way into the dungeon – the hidden entrance that's out in the grounds somewhere. There's no way I can get in through the cellar door in the house. If I can find a way in without being spotted, I might be able to find Terry. It's a big if but it's the only plan I have. I'll head down there before dawn when it's still dark and find a spot where I can watch the house. The Custodians will no doubt be carefully watching the place to make sure there's no more interference. All I need is to see one person coming or going through the secret entrance and to discover where it is.

I'll need to pack a bag for the mission. Take supplies to keep me going for the day. I don't know how long I'll need to be there for. Dark clothes will be needed – as will the black polish for my face. Best take some tools as well – wire cutters from the shed and scissors in case I need to cut through rope. Do I have any weapons? I think Dad has a penknife somewhere that I can take. Probably a good idea to have it to hand in case it's needed.

As I start to pack my rucksack, I hear someone coming in through the back door. Dad. I go and sit at the top of the stairs and listen.

I hear him telling Auntie Val that Hannah's condition hasn't changed much. He's come back for a change of clothes. He says they think the bug is a type of flu. She says that's odd in the summer and asks him where it could have come from, but he has no idea. She asks about the other children, and he tells her that another one has died. It goes all quiet and the door at the bottom of the stairs opens and he heads up.

"Ned," he says. "What are you doing there?"

I shrug my shoulders.

"Were you listening?" he asks.

I nod.

"So, you heard me say there's not much change?"

"Yeah," I say. "You also said one of the other children died?"

He comes up the stairs. "Yes. Very sad but the boy already had a lot of health problems. You know Hannah's fit as a fiddle. If anyone can get through this thing, she can."

I bite my lip and nod.

"Are you okay here?" he asks.

"Can I see her?" I ask.

"No, it's too risky. Can't have you there around those other sick kids. That's how Hannah got it."

He puts his hand on my knee and looks into my eyes. "I'll be back soon, and so will she, alright? I promise."

"You can't promise me that," I say.

Dad sighs. "Just stay here with Val, okay? I need to get back to the hospital."

He pats me on the shoulder and steps up past me.

"Alright, Dad," I say. "I'll be here."

I get up and head back to my bedroom to finish packing.

CHAPTER 65

Sunrise is at five thirty, so I am up one hour earlier when it's still night. My aim is to get to Robham House before light so I can find a good spot to carry out my recon. I try and leave the house as quietly as I can. The streets nearby are silent. The night is still with me, for now. Funny how they say it's only darkest before dawn. I know it's meant to mean something else but right now the dark still looks the same to me as it did before I fell asleep. Maybe I've become too used to the dark. Unable to distinguish between the subtle shades of night. For me now, it is all black.

I pass the bus shelter at the corner of *Goedwig* Street and see Terry's face on a missing poster. I take it down, fold it up and pop it in my pocket. Not sure why. Maybe so I have a reminder of why I'm on this mission. So, I remember – no matter how hard it gets – a boy's life depends on it.

On the High Street I stop when I see a silhouette of a four-legged creature sniffing the bins outside the newsagents. At first, I think it's a dog but then I realise it's a fox. I knew they lived in the surrounding fields and woods but had never heard of them coming into the town before. For the briefest moment, I forget about the urgent situation I am in, and I watch this wild creature exploring the world of people. The fox is on its own mission. Probably out searching for food for its young. It risks its own safety to keep its loved ones alive. I step closer and accidentally kick an empty can on the ground. It stops what it's doing, looks up and runs off between the buildings.

On the High Street, the street lights above me flicker. Each one in turn as I walk underneath them. I don't sense anything paranormal, but maybe the spirits are with me. The *Hamley Book of the Paranormal* says that hauntings sometimes caused electromagnetic interference – often manifesting as flickering lights or static on radios. Not that long ago, I would've found this exciting, but right now, I feel numb. I may be surrounded by the night, but I don't feel scared. There is only the mission. I cross the street to the opposite side when I reach the shell of the old bookshop; I don't need reminding of what happened there.

Outside the town, the road is darker, but I see sunlight emerging from behind the *Cewri*. I realise I need to get to Robham House before the sun is up in the sky, so I pick up the pace. I can hear sheep or cows moving around in the fields and I feel a little less alone. It occurs to me that I cannot dwell too much on the fact that this was a solo mission. Sometimes, that was how it had to be. When the chips were down and most people had given up, that was the time for heroes; when sacrifices were necessary and sturdy beliefs were as powerful as weapons.

I reach the end of the Robham House lane and stop. This is where I would need to be most careful. If I was caught again then that would be that. There would be no more chances. The Custodians had made it very clear they wouldn't tolerate interferences. They would do whatever necessary to get their job done. This was a deadly solo mission with zero room for error.

As I get close to the house I duck down and try and stay in the shadows. The lights are on, but the curtains are drawn so I cannot see if anyone is up and about at this time. The small woodland on the far side of the house that follows the main road and leads up to Ogyn Lake is where I intend to hide. At the end of the lane, I enter the shadows of a dark hedgerow. There, I stop for a moment and scan the area. I can hear footsteps in the gravel coming from the other end of the house. I move swiftly, treading lightly and keeping low as I move away from the plodding feet. I turn my head to see the lights of torches bobbing about in the dark. They'll see me if they point the light in the right direction. I keep going but trip on a large rock and give my knee a dead leg. It hurts like hell. I want to howl but I bite my finger. I can hear voices. I need to get up and keep going. I crawl a few steps then push myself up and run the last length to the woods, diving behind the first tree I come across. With my back against the trunk, I turn and see two figures carrying torches and examining the dark corners of the grounds. If they come into the woods, it will be very difficult for me to get away from them. I watch as they make their way along the perimeter. They're very careful and I wonder whether they're conducting a routine check or whether I've been spotted. The lights become brighter, so I lower my head and try to keep completely out of sight behind the tree. I can see they are near. In fact, I can hear what they're saying. One of them says, "Area C, clear. On to Area D and the hatch now. Over," and the torchlights move further along the edge of the woodland in the direction of the lake.

I try and calm myself by breathing steadily and my racing heart begins to slow. I've completed the first part of the mission and have arrived at my destination safely. As I get set up and begin my recon, the man's words pop into my head and I think, *what's the hatch?*

CHAPTER 66

The sun is up in the sky by now and the bright new day has not brought me any progress yet. I realised earlier that my position at the edge of the woods was too exposed, so I went in deeper and found a good hiding spot. I am now lying on the ground behind a large tree trunk. There's thicket all around and a few more trees ahead as well, but I have a clear line of vision for most of the grounds and the house from where I am. The only thing that's tricky is that I must remain low and on my front, and the ground is not so comfortable. But hey, I think, if army snipers can do this for days on end, then I should be able to do it for a few hours. I am assuming I will get what I need in a few hours, but I don't know how long this will take. The only thing I do know is that I need to complete my mission by tomorrow. If I don't then I definitely will have failed.

Aside from curtains opening and the coming and going of a postman, not much happens over the next couple of hours. Through my mini-binoculars I see Mrs Astley staring out from a window in the house. Her sight gives me the shivers. I wonder what she is thinking. What does this event mean to her? It happens once every forty years. Is she excited and proud to play her part or does the whole thing fill her with dread? I really can't tell from her face. She looks neither sad nor happy and makes it seem like it could be the start of any other day. Business as usual. Jeez, I think. If I was a Royal Marine sniper, I could easily take her out from here. That would scupper their plans, I reckon.

The groundskeeper – this time alone – comes by again, but he keeps his distance. I've noted he does his rounds every hour. In the light, his route is closer to the house, and I reckon he sees now that no threats are hiding along the hedge line and at the edge of the woods. He is wrong, of course. He speaks into the walkie-talkie again and then heads in the direction of the lake.

The early wake-up is starting to take its toll on me. I take a sip of water and eat a slice of bread. I have a whole loaf with me and plan to ration it. I look at my watch; it's just after nine. I'll give it another hour before I move my position to another vantage point.

As I scan the horizon, a white transit van turns up and stops in front of the house. The driver gets out and opens the back doors. My jaw drops when I see three little men jump out of the back. By little, I mean kid size. I think they're dwarfs like the travelling thieves in *Time Bandits* or the munchkins in *Wizard of Oz*. What the hell is this?

Mrs Astley comes out of the house and greets the three of them. A maid follows her and picks up two boxes from the van and carries them along the side of the house. I expect her to take the boxes to the back, but she continues along this route and across the grounds to the gardens that are surrounded by hedges and shrubbery. The driver then guides the three dwarfs in the same direction. The maid returns with her arms empty. She picks up another couple of boxes and goes the same way again. She passes the driver who returns to the van alone. He takes out another box, leaves it on the side for the maid and drives away.

There is obviously some kind of place in the gardens. Maybe this is the hatch. Maybe it's the secret entrance I am after. I wasn't planning on moving for another hour, but this may be an opportunity I cannot ignore.

I pack away my stuff and crawl into the woods until out of sight. I get to my feet and head between the trees in the direction of the lake. The gardens back up against the wooded area, which means I can sneak in while still undercover. The groundsman is not due on his rounds for another half hour by my guess, but I want to be quick, so I can see the maid coming out of wherever she's been dropping off those boxes. I find a narrow gap in the hedge and go in, pulling the branches back, so I can peer out without being spotted. On the other side, I see the lake behind, I see flower beds, I see rows and rows of plants and I see a long greenhouse with dirty windows. The door opens and out comes the maid. She stops, turns in my direction and I dip back into the hedge. Then she carries on towards the house.

This is my chance, I think. I leap out of the hedge and run over to the greenhouse. I try and peer in, but the windows are smeared with white stuff. I follow the wall around to the door and go in. There are three long benches. Each with piles of overgrown potted plants and rusty gardening tools that look like they haven't been used in years. I scan the long room but can see no sign of a door or secret hatch. I move around the long bench until I reach the far end and there, I see it. On the ground, at the end of the bench, there is an open door in the floor and a stone stairwell that leads into the ground. Well, bloody hell, this is it. This is the secret entrance I've been looking for. This is where Terry must be. From behind, I hear footsteps approaching and I realise there is only one direction I can go – I must go down through the hatch.

CHAPTER 67

Burning lanterns light up the stairwell down into the underground area. I leap down the steps as I hear someone close behind. It smells like stale water mixed with must and what I can only describe as death, and I can hear dripping coming from somewhere. It's like some castle dungeon in one of the old Hammer horror films. At the bottom, there is only one direction to go so I follow the path. A shiver goes up my spine and I'm not sure if it's the cold underground air or the fear that's starting to take hold of me. This is a place where bad things have happened – I'm not clear on what but I know there's been a lot of suffering and pain here. There's no easy way out, and if they find me then it really is game over.

I touch the walls and they're cold and clammy. The stones suggest the place is very old. They pile onto each other and connect in the middle overhead to form a long archway. I feel dread when I touch them. Dread and doom and despair. Is it my *klewmeirw* parts that tell me this? Seeing the *Cysgod Annwn* made me realise I must possess some of their skills and abilities. Nowhere near Rebecca who's a definite ten for the psychic mediumship thing. I'm a one or two but my skills are different. I see when death is coming (which to be honest wouldn't be my first choice for a superpower) but I'm not able to connect to the other side the way she does. It makes me wonder if all the intense, strange feelings about the town and experiences at the haunted sites were really my *klewmeirw* parts sensing the paranormal energy or whatever it was. I got frustrated because I knew something was up but could find no proof. Whatever the case, there is no doubt my current location is a place with a nasty history. I'm not sure what I will find here but I expect the worst.

Ahead, I reach a point where the tunnel meets another. I can now go left or right. Both ways look equally grim and unappealing. I try and listen for sounds or any indication of where Terry may be being kept. Then I think about my position. Based on where the garden is and the direction in which I had walked, the route left should take me towards the house. The other way... I'm not so sure.

I turn left and carry on. The tunnel is lined with empty rooms – cells may be a better word – on either side. I hear someone coming so I leap into one of these rooms and press my back against the wall. I can't tell if it is one of the dwarfs or someone else. I peer around the corner, but they're gone. I get curious about what the cell looks like. I pull out a small torch from my bag and shine it around the space. There's nothing to see, aside from chains hanging from the walls – the ends of which look like they were designed for holding on to arms or legs. Who the hell built this place? What I wouldn't give to have Rhys's knowledge to hand. And Gwyn. And Rebecca for that matter. Thinking about them makes me feel lonely. Doing this by myself is crazy and the chances of survival are really near zero. But I must fight. If I am sacrificed on my mission to save Terry, then so be it. But I will not stop fighting. I will fight until the end. I won't let them win.

I turn my torch off and step out of the room. The footsteps have passed. Further ahead, the damp walls reflect bright light coming from somewhere. It's stronger than what I've seen from the lanterns. The wall begins to curve around to the right; I press my back up against it and edge forwards. I can hear loud voices.

The sounds echo loudly down the tunnel towards me. As I get nearer, I crane my neck and see the tunnel opens to a huge, empty room. The three munchkins are moving about in circles and waving their hands around. What the hell are they doing? There are others with them... Normal-sized adults but I can't see them very well from my current position. There is another cell on the opposite wall; if I can make it inside, then that would give me a better vantage point to spy on the group without being spotted. I just need to cross the tunnel without being noticed. I glance towards the large space a couple of times. It seems the group is distracted by whatever the dwarfs are doing so right now is the time to make the leap. I take a deep breath and spring over as light-footed as I can into the cell. Inside, I slip on a wet patch and land on my front. I hit the ground with a thud and my heart almost stops. They must have heard me. I lie there expecting someone to come for me, but no one does. I turn onto my back and look around. Somehow, I got away with it. I move closer to the door and peer around the side. I can now see the three munchkins more clearly. They are all repeating the same actions according to the wishes of someone who is stood out of sight. It looks like they're acting. Yes, they're bloody actors. They're preparing for a show. They keep turning to look at whoever is stood to the side. That person is directing them on what to say and what to do, but I can't hear these instructions. What could this be, I wonder? One of the dwarfs puts on a black long-haired wig and pretends to ride a broom around the room. Oh God, it comes to me: he's acting the role of the witch. They're preparing to re-enact her story. Why would they do that? And with dwarfs as well? It's nuts. Is it part of the ceremony? Before the sacrifice, they put on a show to celebrate the event? If it happens every forty years, then maybe it's worth the fuss. The Olympics is every four years, and they always go to town with that.

This must be where it will happen then. This secret underground dungeon is where they keep the tribute captive and where they carry out the sacrifice as well. I keep thinking the weirdness has peaked but it just keeps getting stranger and stranger.

The dwarf playing the witch trips on the broom and another one jumps. The person at the side has thrown something at him. She steps into view and yells. This time I can hear and see her clearly – Mrs Astley.

"You need to get this right. You were briefed weeks ago. We were told you could handle these circumstances with no trouble, but you keep messing it up." She paces around them like a schoolteacher dressing down school children.

"Getting this right is imperative. We can accept no errors. There will be very important people here tomorrow night for this. If you fail, it will not be good for you. You knew this from the start."

Tomorrow night, I think. Showtime. Another of the three actors places his hand on the shoulder of the one dressed as a witch. He says something to Mrs Astley and appears to be consoling his friend.

Something occurs to me. The Astley woman didn't come down the same route as I did from the house. This dungeon must be connected to it somehow so there must be a secret tunnel – just as we'd thought – from the cellar. Why were the dwarfs brought in through the hatch, I wonder? Maybe as entertainers they're not allowed to come through the house.

"I need to get back to the house now to attend to some things, so I'll leave you to your rehearsals," she says. "Janet will show you where the changing rooms are. Remember, no mistakes."

The three actors follow the maid and Mrs Astley. They disappear into a dark archway on the opposite side of the space to where I am hiding. I glance in both directions and as soon as it's clear, I come out of the cell. I tiptoe out into the open space where the group stood. The room is peculiar. It's round and there are two ways in and out – an archway on each end. There are also two cells on either side of the room. The four doorways are about the same distance from each other. I look up and see a gallery. It appears to be a place where people can stand and watch the round area below; the stage, if that's what it is.

The whole space reminds me of the insides of one of those Italian churches I've seen in books at school. The ones with huge dome roofs. Only this is underground and from what I remember, the grounds and the gardens above are flat. Inside, the ceiling is covered in stones stacked up to create a curved arch. A lot of effort went into building this place. And that probably happened a long time ago. Maybe hundreds of years ago. It is well lit up. I see shivering shadows from the flickering flames of lanterns burning on the walls around the stage area and above in the gallery.

I stride over to the nearest cell and peer in – it's dark. I shine the torch and see the same type of empty room with chains on the wall as I saw earlier. I go over to the other cell expecting to see another empty space but this time what I see knocks the air out of my lungs. Here, through the barred window, I see a dimly lit room. In the middle of the room is a hospital bed and on that bed is a sleeping boy. He is one year younger than me and plays in goal for the *Nant-y-Wrach* secondary school junior team. He is the missing boy, Terry Rowlands. I pull on the door, but it won't open – there is a lock. I step back and examine the walls around it. The door is the only way in or out. I look in again. Terry could be in a hospital ward based on the set-up. There is a bag on a pole connected to his arm. Another bag that looks like it's full of piss hangs off the side of the bed. There is a machine as well that beeps as his heart beats and tubes going into his nose. He's skinny as hell and pale like he hasn't eaten or seen daylight since he was taken. Why is he in the bed like that? Was he hurt or have they put him to sleep? Shit, I think. Even if I can get into the cell there's no way I can carry him out of here. I'd have to wake him up – what if I can't?

I take a deep breath and try and calm myself. Think, Ned. What do I do? The penknife, I think. I'll try and pick the lock. I take out my Swiss army knife and open it up. The thin blade fits into the door lock. I turn it each way and try and fiddle with it to make it open. I've never done this before, but they always make it look easy in the movies.

I stop when I hear something. Terry is mumbling. Is he dreaming? What's he saying? I can't follow his words. His lips are barely moving. It sounds like, *hey humming*.

"What is it?" I say. "Tell me, Terry."

This time his voice is clearer, and I hear his words but it's too late.

"They're coming."

Something hits me hard on the side of the head and the world disappears.

CHAPTER 68

My head hurts and something hard and metallic pushes down on my tongue. I open my eyes, but I'm still surrounded by the night. I reach my hands up and feel my head. There is a metal frame around it and part of the thing is in my mouth. It pushes tightly down on my tongue and feels horrible. The metal is old, and I can taste the bitter rust. My jaw is sore, and I can't stop the spit from building up under my tongue. I try and wipe my mouth on my arm, but the frame gets in the way. Why did I come here? I couldn't stop myself. I had to do something. I saw him at least. So close. But it's just me alone against these people. What hope did I have? Stop it, I think. There's always hope. I'm here because I couldn't let them kill a child. Tears start to stream down my cheek, and I can't help sobbing. I'm alone in this nightmare place and my hope is fading. I reach up my hand to try and wipe the tears away from my cheek, but the bloody metal frame gets in the way, and I roar with frustration and the anger takes over helping me overcome the stupid little crying boy.

I scan my surroundings. The only light I see comes from a square ahead of me. I get to my feet. Damn it, my bag is gone. They've taken my kit and the only thing I have in my pocket is the folded missing poster. I step over to the square barred window. I see the round stage outside – I am in the cell opposite to Terry's. Someone steps into view and peers through the window. Mrs Astley.

"Awake now, are we?"

Her smug face makes me sneer and hiss, and I grab the bars of the window. I try and speak but the metal in my mouth makes it impossible. All I can do is make grunting noises from my throat that make me sound like an animal.

"Ah, the scold's bridle," she says. "Also called the witch's bridle. Used hundreds of years ago as a punishment. Stops the wearer from speaking, you see. I guess you do. I understand it's rather uncomfortable to wear as well. You should be proud really. That device is about 500 years old. It's been in a lot of mouths."

I want to be sick. She steps closer to the door and glares at me. "Oh, little Ned. I told you not to come back here, didn't I?"

She knows my name, but that's no matter. Everyone knows each other in this town.

"But you did, so what do we do with you now – especially since you've seen everything here? Well, I'll tell you something, you haven't seen it all. But you will, Ned." She smirks and I wish she was the one with the bloody rusty metal forced into her gob.

"We're going to let you watch tomorrow night's show. You're going to have a ringside seat to the main event. Honestly, you should feel very lucky. Very few get to see the inner sanctum let alone view the Ceremony of the Tribute."

I try and scream and start kicking the door. But she looks on like some spectator at the zoo watching a wild animal.

"That's alright. I understand why you'd get excited. It must be quite overwhelming for you. It's a huge event for our town. Something that happens only once every forty years. I was a young woman the last time it happened. I was on the periphery then, while my dear old mother managed the ceremony. This time I'm in charge."

I bang my fists against the door.

"Oh, calm yourself, boy. You'll hurt your hands doing that. You must know this whole process is completely necessary. It's part of a tradition that goes back over 300 years. The hospital is already full of sick children. All afflicted by the terrible pestilence cast down by Mari Evans. The little boy in that other cell is a town hero, you know. He will lay down his life to save countless others."

I bang and kick at the door, grunting as much as I can with my throat. My hands become raw but the anger that fills my body is overwhelming. I must stop as I become breathless and my body aches.

She peers in at me. "I'd give that a rest if I was you. You'll just end up hurting yourself and that won't help anyone. There's no point making such a fuss. No one outside the Sanctum will hear you. And everyone here is part of our group."

She seems to spot something in her side vision and turns. "Oh, look. Our little entertainers have returned. Now rather than hurting yourself, why don't you watch these men rehearse for their show tomorrow night. It's very important they get it right and I think having more of an audience while they practise will help."

She turns around and yells something at the three dwarfs. I look past her and can see they are now wearing costumes. The one playing the witch has a long-haired wig and wears a grey rag dress. I presume he must be the witch. The second wears an old-fashioned suit with coat-tails – is he meant to be Lord Robham? I can't say. The third carries a pitchfork and wears brown rags – perhaps he is one of the poor villagers?

Mrs Astley clears her throat. "Now, my small friends, I do hope the costumes will help with your performance. We also have an additional spectator who has come here specially to see you."

They turn their heads towards my cell, and the whites of their eyes are luminescent in the low light.

What am I doing here, I ask myself again? I should be home with Auntie Val waiting for news about Hannah. What time is it,

I wonder? I've lost track of how long I've been in this blasted hole. I've no idea when I will make it out…

But then it dawns on me: they won't let me out. Not now. I know too much. They'll kill me when they kill Terry. My body will disappear and never see the light of day again; the same way it's happened repeatedly across the centuries. I start blinking as tears fill my eyes. I start to cry again. How pitiful I must sound – barely able to speak and grunting my sobs. My shudders turn to deep breaths and despair becomes rage and I bash the door again – this time with the palms of my hands and my knees. I keep hitting it repeatedly. I can see the three actors in their costumes watching me. Each one trying to hide the horror on his face.

Mrs Astley gestures to the maid to come over. "This won't work. Get the medic."

I find my energy dipping again and I slow down my banging. Mrs Astley steps up to the door. "Now I'm afraid we're going to need some silence to allow these performers to get their routine down. To do this we're going to give you something to help calm you a little. Now, please help us to not hurt you by stepping away from the door when we open the lock."

I scream something at her, but I can't form a single proper word. It sounds more like the braying of a mule.

The butler steps into view and I hear a key being inserted into the lock and turned. I'm ready to jump and attack whoever comes first into the cell but as soon as the door opens, the butler swings at my head with something and connects with the bridle causing a wave of sharp pain across my mouth and jaw. I fall to the ground grabbing my face. Before I know it, a man – who I've not seen before – is kneeling next to me and injecting something into my arm.

'No,' I want to tell him, but my throat gurgles and the words come out as a slurred howl. He puts his hands around my neck and as I feel myself become light and the world around me fades away, he helps lay me down on the floor. The last thought I experience is that I sense my head is on a pillow, but this is not my bed, or is it?

CHAPTER 69

I am lost in the performance that surrounds me. Am I asleep or am I awake? Have I died even? Up is down, left is right, light is dark, day is night. Everything rotates and turns before stopping and I'm away in another place and another time. I'm lying in bed saying goodnight to Mum as the dark halo clings to her and won't let go. Three munchkins from *Wizard of Oz* join us and they skip around her, singing *Mari Evans is Coming* in voices that sound like children. I just want to pull her close and warn her, but they won't let me. They keep dancing around her and getting in the way. Horse pops up at the bottom of my bed holding *Taid*, and the skull now has a jaw and Horse makes him speak by moving it up and down.

"You should have stayed away," *Taid* says in Horse's voice. "Not your sacrifice to make."

Rhys and Rebecca stand by my bookshelf in the bedroom looking at my books. They chat to each other and take no notice of anything else going on.

Then I am in another location. Maybe back in the underground cell beneath the grounds of Robham House. Someone is filling my mouth. I can feel the harsh metal of the bridle pushing down on my tired tongue and my dry mouth welcomes the water being sprayed into it, but my throat struggles and I start choking and coughing.

"Need to drink something," a voice says. It's the same person holding my jaw and filling it with water.

They stop and I'm lost again in the void. I turn my head and see that I am in the cellar of the *Cartref-Y-Gwynt* Farm. I've been looking into the dark space. Above, I see Dad sat at the edge of the hole with his typewriter on his lap.

"Let me finish this chapter and I'll help you," he says. "I need to tell readers why the sacrifice must be made but I'm struggling with the explanation."

Gwyn appears behind him and he's blue. His asthma is killing him. I have the inhaler in my hand. I reach up and try to hand it to him. But Dad won't take it. Gwyn can't breathe and he can't reach down because there is someone holding on to him. Mrs Astley's head appears, and she refuses to take the inhaler. She is holding on to Gwyn and pulling him away from the hole.

"I'm trying to help you," I yell. "That's all I've been trying to do from the start."

"Aw, Mummy's little hero." Horse's voice. His head pops out, and he stares into the hole.

Then others turn up. Hannah, Gwyn, Auntie Val, Rhys, Mr B. Horse's Goons appear and Shag is naked from his waist down but that doesn't matter now.

"They're going to kill him. They're going to give him to the witch," I roar. No one listens and my frustration grows.

Henry Blythe steps forward. His face is sad. "I wanted your attention," he says. "I didn't want you to follow in my footsteps. That is pure lunacy. And lunacy is something I am most familiar with."

"I wanted to fight the monsters that killed Mum," I plead to the crowd above. "I wanted revenge. I wanted something or someone to pay for what happened to her. It's the only way I could live with myself. I have to keep you all safe."

"They are the real monsters," Henry says, pointing at Mrs Astley. "They will kill Terry and they will kill you."

"No," I shout, but murmurs from above drown out my voice and other heads join Astley, and my audience grows. These people wear horse-skull masks over their faces. But the rest of their bodies are dressed well. More than well, in fact. The men are wearing black-tie suits, and the women are wearing ballroom gowns. What is this, I think? Who are these people? They're cheering and clapping like they're watching a show. This isn't a show – it's a murder. I want to jump up there and fight them – knock them all to their senses. The people I know just stare down at me like they don't have any feelings. Like they don't care. They don't appear sad or angry – they just watch.

"I was trying to keep you all safe," I say again but no one can hear me above the laughing and cheering of the crowd. "It's all I wanted but look at me now." I am no longer shouting. I am softly speaking into the dark. "I face the same fate as Terry." I am now whispering the words to myself. No one else can hear.

"Ned." A dark, slurred voice calls to me from the darkness of the cellar and I turn to see the three little men moving rhythmically towards me like they're dancing. I can't see them so well – I only see their shapes – but their eyes are glowing a red colour. *Red eyes*, I think. I forgot about the red eyes. What did it mean?

"Ned." It speaks again. It's not the three little men speaking. Who is it? It sounds familiar. I don't recognise the voice but I'm sure it's someone I know.

The dwarfs dance and I hear music. It sounds like a flute. I close my eyes as I listen to it. I begin to feel sensations on my skin. My mouth is sore. My arms are heavy. I examine my hands and the chains attached to them. I look up and see the stage area is lit differently now. There are spotlights shining down from above.

I am on the floor, so I get up and walk towards the barred window. I can almost touch it with my face but the chains on my wrists don't allow me to raise my hands and grab the bars or the door. All I can do is stand there and gape.

I gasp as I realise this is all real. All the things I felt and heard before were dreams or nightmares but now I am awake and the true horror of the situation dawns on me. They knocked me out with something. How long for? I have no idea. But now I am awake. I look up and see there are crowds of well-dressed people wearing the skull masks. Some parts of it weren't a dream.

Is this it, then? Was I asleep for over a day and this is the night of the festival, the tribute? Shit. Then that's it. Both Terry and I are buggered. No, I mumble aloud. It's not over yet. It's not over until it's over. So long as I can fight, I will continue to battle on. The Custodians won't have an easy ride on this – no matter what they have planned. I will hurt them until the end.

I peer out through the barred window and see a podium has been placed in the middle of the stage. A man in a black-tie suit, wearing a horse-skull mask, steps forward. I recognise him despite his covered face – it's Lord Robham. His hands and the cards he holds are trembling.

CHAPTER 70

"Ladies and gentlemen," he says in a loud, quivering voice. "I hope you all enjoyed dinner. Now we move on to the main event. You join us tonight at this most historic of occasions – the generational tribute from the townsfolk of *Nant-y-Wrach* to the witch, Mari Evans. This is the tenth event of its kind in the last 360 years. We, the Apotropaic Custodians, have maintained this tradition for nearly four centuries, protecting this town – and the people of the world in fact – from the terrible curse of Mari Evans. In secret and with our own resources we have kept the evil powers of the witch at bay. *Sine gloria et laude, officium nostrum in tenebris*; without glory or praise, our honourable duty in the shadows."

They believe in what they're doing. They see it as honourable and righteous. What a crock of shit.

"Before we start the ceremony, I must thank you all for the ongoing support and dedication to the cause. Many of you are more family than friends. In fact, some of you stood where you are now forty years ago as Hitler battered these shores and my father stood right here and spoke on that night of tribute." He clears his throat and taps the surface of the podium.

"Our mission is not an easy one, but it's essential to the ongoing well-being – nay, survival – of humanity. We are the ones who keep the evil at bay. The people up there wouldn't understand the challenges we face. In a modern world where right and wrong is black and white, they would not understand this process of tribute where we must commit one act of horror in the interest of preserving our way of life and protecting our children. Moving in the shadows, we know there are many shades of grey in between. One man's murder is another man's saviour. Put simply, the realities of the world can rarely be viewed in terms of black and white; good and evil."

His voice quivers as he says the word 'horror', and he turns his head up and looks across the people in the gallery. He's struggling with this. Is that why he sleeps with a bottle of whisky next to his bed?

"As always is the tradition, before we walk to the site of tribute, we will relive the story of the witch and how the Custodians came to be and play the role we do."

He nods to someone on the side of the area and the small actor dressed as a witch dances across the stage.

"In the early seventeenth century, a dark cloud hangs over the town of *Nant-y-Llyndu* – as it was known then. A witch by the name of Mari Evans troubles the townsfolk. Infant mortality is high, animal and livestock disease is common, and the crops frequently fail."

The witch taunts the other two, one being a villager and the other, the Lord Robham of the time. There are titters from the gallery above. The witch now disappears, and the townsman appears to be telling the one dressed as the lord something.

"The peoples of the town come together and decide this cannot go on any longer. They visit Lord Oliver Robham to beg for his help. Knowing who is behind the darkness that has befallen the habitation, the men of the town raid the witch's house late one night."

The townsperson and the lord chase after the witch – running around the current Lord Robham and his podium. After a few laps, they grab the witch and pretend to tie him up using a rope. There is further laughter in the gallery.

"They catch the witch and take her away. At her house they discover she has a son and Lord Robham takes him into his care."

The small lord picks up a doll that is meant to be the boy, and he hugs it. He holds the doll as he pretends to be a judge and has a wig on his head, and he stands on a box. They are acting out the trial. The witch looks stern-faced, while the other is making dramatic gestures with his hands like he's demonstrating the different crimes she committed.

"At the trial, the case against Mari Evans is presented and the evidence is indisputable. Lord Robham presides and is given no choice but to find her guilty and he sentences her to be hanged. Strangely, the witch appears to accept her fate without much concern. However, she tells those present that if she dies then so must her son. He must join her in death, or the town will suffer."

Little Lord Robham holds the doll tightly. The witch tries to take it off him, but he pushes her away.

"Lord Robham refuses the witch, but as the time of the hanging nears, she maintains her demand. The boy meanwhile becomes more upset and stops eating, starving himself. The witch tells them that if the child is not allowed to join her then pestilence will be rained upon the children of the town from here on in, and each generation will suffer terrible illnesses. Still, the lord refuses the witch, and she is put to death."

The witch now stands next to a cardboard tree. The rope is used as a noose, and the actor does a very dramatic performance of her death. There are more chuckles from the gallery. The audience above could be watching a comedy show – it's sickening.

"After she is executed, the town is fearful for what might come next. However, as is the tradition with executed criminals, her body is taken up to Plum Mountain where it is thrown into the black pit. This is a deep, dark hole inside the main cavern that many believe is directly connected to hell."

Damn it, I think. Plum Mountain is important to this story. I should've known.

The lord and the townsperson drag the witch to the side of the stage and then return to the centre where the lord picks up the doll again and holds it even tighter than he did before.

"Not long after her death, the children of the town start to get ill and many die. It becomes apparent that the curse is coming true. The townsfolk beg the lord to allow them to give her the child, but he refuses. He tries to hold off for as long as he can. Mari Evans's boy meanwhile still won't eat, and he becomes thin and unwell. Eventually, Lord Robham realises that his only option is to allow the child to die."

With a gravely sad look on his face, little Lord Robham hands the doll over to the townsperson, and he consoles him somewhat before throwing the doll away in the same direction as they took the witch. This results in more laughter from above. My jaw drops as I realise what comes next.

"The weak and sickly child is taken up to Plum Mountain. But upon realising what is happening, the gaunt and emaciated child starts to panic. He fights for his right to live and not die with his mother in the darkness. Those present are shocked but they throw him into the black pit anyway and a horrendous howl is heard as the boy dies in the hole. As soon as the screaming ceases, it is said that the black clouds that hang over the town lift, and the sun begins to shine. Sick children regain their health. Crops regrow and livestock stop dying. The witch's curse fades away. For this generation at least."

The lord and the townsperson appear to go back to their usual day-to-day business but the actor playing the witch returns – now covered in a sheet to make her look like a ghost.

"Forty years later – a generation according to the Bible – children in the town start to get ill again. Many fail to recover. Those who remember the curse of the witch remind the new lord and the townsfolk of what happened. They try different methods to stop the curse. They throw a recently deceased child's body into the pit, but that doesn't work. They try a sick boy who had fallen into a coma after an illness but that doesn't work either. The only thing that works is the sacrifice of a living boy. An orphan is chosen from a local workhouse, he is starved and then thrown in, and the curse lifts and the clock stops once again."

Another doll is thrown, and the lord and the townsperson sit down and look like they're having a serious conversation. This is how it all started.

"This time the lord and the town elders sit down after the sacrifice. They realise the curse will come again in another forty years and they must be prepared for it. They set up a group funded and led by the lord – who on behalf of his family takes responsibility for instigating the witch's curse after his father's actions forty years earlier. The group is tasked with taking charge of this terrible burden. They must act decisively and ensure the traditions and truths of the time are handed down over the years to enable future leaders to protect the town and its children from the curse of the witch. Everything must be done in the same way as it happened the first time. The child must be starved until weak and thin, but he must be strong enough to live and fight. He cannot go willingly into the hole."

The lord and the townsperson shake hands and appear to reach an agreement. They disappear for a moment and then return with small animal skulls over their faces – smaller versions of those worn by the people in the gallery. There is a loud applause from above and they both bow. It's like being at a stage show and the whole thing makes me want to vomit. They've turned a murder into a bloody comedy routine and the reality of it is disgusting.

Robham continues. "Of course, it has not been an easy path. There have been attempts to change course and find alternative means of avoiding the needful. In 1743, half of the town's children died of smallpox before they realised there was only one way to stop her. Over the years, we've also learned that preparation is key, and things must be done in a specific manner for the tribute to work. If the boy is too healthy, then it won't have the necessary impact. The child must be starved and weakened for the witch to recognise him as her own. In addition, we have had to wait and watch until the sickness starts before we act decisively. The tribute cannot be made too early. We must be sure that the curse is active before the boy is given. As always, we thank our members in local healthcare who ensure we have good oversight of the health status of the town. This year, they were able to alert us promptly about a new viral strain circulating that has proven to be deadly among our little ones."

Healthcare? That must mean some of Mum's old colleagues are members of the Custodians. I wonder if she knew. The depth of this thing is mind-boggling.

"Many in our wider community know what must be done when the pestilence comes," he says, "and this year – as per tradition – the announcement of the postponement of the *Gŵyl Awst* festival is our message to the townsfolk that the curse has initiated and that a boy has been selected and is being readied for the tribute. When we know the time is right then we confirm the festival will go ahead and the date is set for the tribute. Some years, the curse has come earlier, some years it has been later; but as a rule, it has been every generation since 1623."

Jesus. Everything that's happened has been planned as such. These Custodians have been one step ahead of us from the start. They run things like a military operation. What hope did we have of stopping them? It's hard not to be impressed with their efficiency. Robham looks up from his notes and scans the gallery then he stares in my direction.

"This year, however, has been challenging. The hospital is full, and we've already lost some of our children to this virus. There have been other obstacles along the way as well, which have necessitated decisive actions by the Custodians. And we express our gratitude to our faithful members for their dedication in the face of adversity. But thankfully, we are now ready to end this for another generation. It's time we make our tribute."

There are cheers and clapping up in the gallery followed by chattering and discussions. The way those in the gallery respond blows my mind. This is a bloody murder, you bastards. You're celebrating the killing of a child. You may be saving others but you're doing that by allowing one boy to suffer at the hands of evil. Tears are streaming down my face, and I want to lift my hands up to cover my eyes, but I cannot. I'm stuck and tied up in this cage, forced to watch this horror show and listen to these sods cheer.

Lord Robham lifts his arms into the air. "Please, may I have your attention. We will finish our final preparation in a moment. In the meantime, you will see that coffee and tea is served in the adjacent rooms. We will call you when it's time for us to make our journey to the mountain."

My heart is racing. So that's that. Terry will be thrown into a dark pit of death, and me? What will I be? A bonus tribute? An extra? We will both disappear into the dark history of this town like all the other children. The sacrificed few who allow the majority to live on? There must be something I can do. I need to think. But I'm struggling. I've no options left. I fall to the ground as the realisation of my fate hits me. I hear jangling – someone is approaching with keys. The tribute is imminent. I'm all out of ideas. What the hell else can I do?

CHAPTER 71

A person wearing a skull mask is at the door and I recognise the man's stature and shape – it's Gatsby. I wish I could speak but all I can do is growl from my throat and rattle my chains like some old-fashioned ghoul. I hear the door being unlocked and it makes my blood go cold. Gatsby opens the door slightly and stops. Someone behind him is speaking to him.

"She's missing?" he says. "How can she be missing? We've been preparing for this for years."

He turns his ahead again as the other person speaks. "We must go ahead without her. And yes – whether he likes it or not – he'll need to take charge of things. It's his duty as Grand Master."

Do they mean Mrs Astley is missing? And the lord is expected to run whatever happens next? Sounds like he doesn't want to be doing this after all. Maybe this is my chance. Maybe things aren't lost yet.

Gatsby enters the cell and unlocks the chains that I have attached to my wrists. I swing for him and hit his chest, but he grabs the bridle and twists it, thrusting a bolt of pain through my head and directing my reach away from him.

"Ned, I know you don't want to be here," he says. "But you should be proud. You get to play a very important role today.

A historical day of great significance to our wonderful town and heritage. I'm almost envious of you."

He's jealous? Of me? What the hell? Let this fucker wear the rusty birdcage around his head and die at the bottom of a dark cave. I try and reach again but he twists the bridle and I shriek as I'm battered by the pain. He has complete control over me.

"I'm leaving this on for now. You do as you're told, and I won't hurt you again. We'll take it off when we get where we're going."

Where we're going. The Black Pit, where they'll kill me and Terry. I stop fighting and I go along with his direction. I need ideas and I need them now.

Gatsby pulls me out of the cell. On the opposite side of the stage, Terry is being taken out as well. He is barely able to walk. He is dressed in rags and looks like an old empty sack. His face is grey, and he could pass as a *Night of the Living Dead* zombie. The lord has hold of his hand, but Terry is resisting, and the lord is struggling.

"Hold him," Gatsby says to the maid, and she grabs my bridle as he rushes over to help Robham. Gatsby uses more force with Terry, and he is now unable to resist. He gestures for Robham to take over from the maid and he slowly steps over to me and takes hold of the metal frame around my head.

Gatsby leads Terry out of the stage area, and Robham and I follow. The maid steps up to the front carrying a lantern and she lights the path ahead. We follow the route back from where I came. I see the steps where I descended from the greenhouse and wish I could leg it back up there now. I try and pull away, but Robham still holds on like he's walking his dog.

We go past the steps. We're now heading in the direction I wondered about when I arrived. It's still not clear to me where this route takes us. If we're heading to Plum Mountain, Ogyn Lake is in the way. Could the tunnel be going under the lake? It does feel like we are going downhill, and the air is becoming colder. The ground is rough and covered in pebbles and loose stones.

Behind me I hear voices. I can't turn my head to see but it sounds like a group of people whispering and murmuring. I think it's the audience from the gallery who are following us down this route. One voice becomes louder and speaks the words, *Mari Evans hath her dispute; hither we join with our tribute.* The others chime in, and they repeat the words in unison. The voices echo along the inside of the long, empty tunnel.

I can't look up at Robham, but I try and get his attention by tapping on his hand. I point in the direction we are going and hold out my hands like I am asking him why.

"I'm sorry, boy," he whispers. "I'm sorry. This is just how it must be."

I can't see his face, but there is regret in his voice. How can I use that?

I try and see past Terry and Gatsby, but all I see is a pitch-black void – into which we keep walking, deeper and deeper. Terry stumbles and falls to the ground. They've made him so weak and thin. He must have been tied to that bed for the whole time he's been captive. They starved him so he's skinny and sick like the witch's son. It's horrifying and his fate up ahead is even worse.

Gatsby pulls Terry up to his feet. He handles the boy like he's a flimsy little doll. Terry falls again and the man starts dragging him along the ground.

I tap on Robham's hand and point to Terry. He moves over to Gatsby, pulling me with him, and gives him some instructions. Gatsby lifts Terry up and carries him in his arms. I try looking up at the lord by moving my eyes and can see flashes of Robham's face beneath the mask. There are water droplets on his chin, and I wonder whether they are sweat or tears. Wait, I can hear him sobbing. This whole thing is really getting to him. He needs Mrs Astley here to ensure the job gets done but she's gone missing.

I reach up and grab his hand as it lays on the top of my bridle. I try and squeeze it. He pushes my hand away. I tap him on the back and try to look up at his eyes. If I could only make eye contact with him. This man isn't a killer. He no more wants to be here than I do. He pushes me forward and keeps hold of the metal frame around my head at arm's length so I can't touch him. I twist my body, but he easily controls me with the bridle. I try and make noises with my throat, but the chanting of the Custodians is too loud for anyone to hear me.

Our path now appears to be turning uphill. I can feel myself getting out of breath and my legs becoming tired. We must be coming up on the other side of the water. I try and picture a map of the area in my mind's eye. Robham House is on the edge of Ogyn Lake. Ogyn Lake is then separated from Plum Mountain by the main road. We've never really explored Plum Mountain. It was always off limits. Not only because it was private property (owned by the Robham family) but because it was dangerous. Apparently. After all the mining there, the place was said to be full of deep holes and land ready to collapse at any moment. That is what they always told us, at least; lies to keep kids and hikers away.

I try and think how long we've been walking for. Half an hour, maybe? Half a mile underground? That would make sense. I start to hear periodic rumbling. What is that, I wonder? I notice running water flowing past me along the ground. I realise it's a storm. The hot summer weather above has finally come to an end like they said it would. The rumbling is thunder, and the heavy rain is pouring water into these holes. If there is water getting in, then there must be holes. I am still hopeful there is a way out of this. Although I'm not sure how we get away from these people.

The echoes around us are changing. They become deeper and wider. Up ahead, the tunnel grows. After we walk between three or four boulders, I can no longer see the sides of the tunnel. We have entered a large open space, and it is completely dark. Gatsby turns and yells something.

He repeats himself. "Lights. Need more lights."

Someone passes us holding two large lanterns. It's a man, I think. He looks familiar but I cannot fully see his face. I think it's

Robham's butler. He stops next to Gatsby who has Terry in his arms and the maid that walks along with him. They look down at something and then walk more carefully.

Gatsby turns again. "We're here. This is the Black Pit."

The people behind us cheer and the chanting stops. The three adults and the child up ahead appear to move to the side now. Their lanterns briefly light up areas inside the cavern. I can't see the insides of the space, so I assume the cavern is very large. I can hear the thunder more clearly now. Also, there are flashes of lightning from outside meaning there must be gaps in the rock. I can hear a lot of running water and dripping.

We follow those up ahead and Robham's lantern shows that we have reached the edge of a large black hole. The whole group is now treading carefully along the edge. I hear whispers of excitement coming from the audience that walked with us. I try to understand their perspective but struggle. They are here to celebrate the murder of a child. Or maybe two children. I take a deep breath through my wide-open mouth.

"We're here," Gatsby yells. He gestures with his hand for Robham to join him. Robham is frozen and does not appear to want to move. Gatsby lets go of Terry and asks the maid and the butler to grab hold of him. Terry is weak but he shakes his body like he's trying to get their hands off him. He's resisting as best he can. It's what they need to happen so the tribute works.

"Your Lordship now needs to commit the boy to the pit and make the tribute final," he calls out manically.

"I'm not sure if... Still no sign of Mrs Astley?"

"No, Your Lordship. This is up to you now. Let me take this one. The tribute must go first." Gatsby takes hold of the bridle from Robham. *Go first.* I am to be thrown in as well. I need to think of something right now. This is my last chance.

"Now, sir. It must be you. Please. All you have to do is push him in. It'll take the smallest of efforts. The boy is so weak – just a nudge is needed."

"I don't know if I can…"

Gatsby leans in, and his voice drops. "If you don't, then the sickness will continue. It will spread. Your boy will get it eventually as well. We'll make sure of it."

Robham is now crying his heart out. Reluctantly, he steps over to Terry, who stands next to the pit with a fearful look on his face, his arms gently flailing like he's trying to defend himself from some invisible force. The flickering light of the lantern lights up his pale, sick face, and that's when I see it. The dark halo of *Cysgod Annwn* surrounds his whole body. Oh fuck, oh fuck, it's coming. There's no turning back. I reach out again, but Gatsby twists the bridle hard. Behind Terry stands another Custodian, his body covered in a cloak and his face hidden by the horse skull.

Lord Robham stands next to Terry and his head drops.

"Speak the words, Your Lordship," yells Gatsby.

Robham clears his throat, but his voice continues to quiver and rattle as he fights the tears. He closes his eyes and starts to speak like he's reciting a poem.

"Mari Evans. Mari Evans. Hither is thy son. We answer thy dispute, thy child is returned, hither is thy tribute." He stops and takes a deep breath. "Hither is the boy, not with thou at death; hither is the boy that left thou bereft. As we return him to thee – much as thou craved; we bid that thou let our town children be saved. Release 'em from infirmity, free 'em from pain; bring an end to the pestilence, break this drought with the rain."

Is the heatwave connected to this whole thing – linked to her rising power and the curse? Maybe the energy of the spirits on the other side as well? Perhaps that happens each time? Not important right now, Ned. You're about to die. Think.

Lord Robham stretches out his hands. At the same time, I notice Gatsby has started to open my bridle. He unlocks the mechanism that holds it in place at the back of my head and then lifts it up. The metal comes out of my mouth, and I cough and start biting and licking the air as I feel the relief.

A lightning strike above ground sends a flash of light into the cave and the thunder makes everyone jump. I get a sense of the size of the cavern and it's huge. Behind Terry and Robham, I see the full dark form of *Cysgod Annwn*, and I feel sick.

"Now, Lord," Gatsby yells again.

"Free 'em from thy pestilence!" Robham yells, and he pushes the boy hard into the hole with a howl. Terry disappears and I reach out wanting to help him, but I slip on the wet rocks beneath and topple over into the darkness as well. I feel myself drop and I reach out trying to grab whatever I can to stop my falling, but I am unable to. I am not dropping fully, I'm sliding and tumbling down a steep rocky surface, my body being battered by the stone as I roll and slip down, and I can hear my voice scream out as my legs and arms bash the hard surface. The shin of my right leg takes a hard strike against a jutting rock. I flip over and unexpectedly hit a flat surface where I stop rolling. My body aches. The pain in my leg is horrendous and I've almost certainly broken it. From above I hear cheers and I see the lights of the lanterns as three silhouettes look down at us. I watch – motionless – as they stare. Don't move, Ned, I tell myself. Play dead. Let them think you're gone. I remain still and try and regain some calm. The whole of my body quivers with pain but I survived.

After a short while, the cheers fade like the crowd is leaving and the people watching appear to step away. The lights and their illumination of the cave disappear as the group retreats the way it came. The cavern becomes dark and silent. I can only hear rainwater seeping in and the odd clap of distant thunder as the storm moves away. It's just me alone in the dark, but what about Terry?

I hear something – Terry's whimpering in the dark. The fall didn't kill him.

CHAPTER 72

"Terry?" I clear my throat. "Terry, are you okay?"

He groans a response. "Where... Where am I?"

"Inside Plum Mountain. You've fallen down a hole."

"Hole? What hole?" he says.

"The Custodians threw you into a hole. They hoped the fall would kill you but you're okay. You're going to make it, Terry."

"The who?" he says. "Why did they do that? Where's my mum and dad? Have you seen them?"

"The Custodians took you away from your mum and dad two weeks ago. Don't you remember?"

"Oh yeah," he says, and he starts gently sobbing.

"I want Mummy and Daddy," he mumbles through his tears.

I take a deep breath and listen to him. "Terry, I'm going to get you out of here, but I need you to calm down and help me."

"I just want Mummy," he says again.

As I listen to him cry, I try and think of a plan. I touch the rock wall again and grab a part that seems to stick out. I pull myself up so that I am sat upright. I move my hands over it. Aside from the odd ridge or hole, it feels like a cliff wall. There's no way I can climb up it – not right now at least. I turn to the side and lean my back against the rock. The ground beneath me is flat – but there is an edge and a further drop. I was lucky to have landed on this little ledge.

I wonder how deep the cave is and I reach around in the dark until I find a pebble which I drop over the side and I hear it bounce down into the depths of the cavern; it takes a good few seconds to stop falling.

Jesus, it's deep. I wish I could see what the surrounding cave looks like. I have no idea how far I need to climb to get out or how far Terry has fallen. All I know right now is that he's below me. But I can't tell how far below. His voice doesn't sound too distant, but the echo of the cave is confusing what I hear so it may not be accurate. I must try again.

"Terry," I say loudly. "Terry. You need to be quiet. I need to talk to you."

The uncontrollable sobbing eases off but he continues to sniff and whine.

"Terry, do you remember me?" I ask.

"I can't… see you," he says. "I didn't see you before. I can't remember if you were there at that place. Where was I before?" He sounds really out of it.

"I'm in the year above you at school," I say.

He pauses for a moment. "Ned?"

"That's right, mate. It's Ned." I can't see my own hands in front of my face, but I rub them on my cheeks in the dark to know they're still there.

"Do you remember what happened to you?"

"I – er – I don't know," he says. "I'm confused."

"What's your last memory of being outside?" I ask.

"I was on my bike. It was hot. I was on my way to *Nain*'s house. I remember waving to the policeman."

"The policeman?" I can't help but spit. That bastard. "And then?"

"And then… I'm not sure. It all went dark. I remember flashes of being in a jail or a dungeon or something."

"Were you awake during that time? What do you remember?"

"Not much. I remember this woman visiting me. She tried to calm me down when I got upset. I wouldn't stop screaming. I told her I wanted my Action Man. She asked me where it was, and I said in my school bag, and I'd lost it when I was taken from my bike. I screamed and screamed and then she brought it to me, and it was wet, but I did stop screaming."

"Your Action Man?" That's what was in his bag. They wanted to calm him down. "Was it just the woman who visited you?"

"There was a man with her sometimes as well. But he didn't say anything. He just stood by the door watching."

"Did they do anything to you? Anything strange?"

"I don't know. I don't think so. The woman told me things. Crazy things. She said she needed for me to be calm so that I would listen. So that I would understand what they were doing. They kept trying to play soothing music to calm me down, but it didn't work. I just couldn't do it. I got so angry. Even when I had my Action Man. I got so angry. Who were they, Ned?"

"They're called the Custodians. A secret group that steals children."

"Steals children? Why would they do that, Ned?" His voice quivers and I fear he may start bawling again.

I sigh. "It's a weird tradition. It happens every forty years and ends with them throwing the child into a dark hole."

"I don't understand."

"It's not easy to explain. Just understand this, they took you and all the town has been looking for you the whole time you've been away."

"How long was I away, Ned?"

"Over two weeks," I say.

"Oh God. What about my parents? What happened to them?"

"They haven't given up on finding you. Neither did I, Terry. My friends and I turned this town upside down trying to find you."

"You did, eventually."

"Hmm." A fat lot of good it was to find him at this stage when we're both stuck in a deep dark bloody cave inside a mountain that everyone steers clear of.

"Ned, are we going to get out of here?" he asks in a desperate, shaking voice.

"Yes, Terry, absolutely." Honestly, I don't know.

I listen to the dripping water. I can feel my spirits slowly sinking lower and lower. No, I think. Can't give up now.

"Terry, tell me about where you are now."

I hear struggling and huffing.

"I think I'm on my back, Ned. But my body feels crooked like it's lying on top of something. I'm not sure, Ned. I don't think I can move my arms or my legs. Ned, why would that be? Ned, I think I was hurt in the fall."

Shit, it sounds really bad.

"It's okay," I say, lying through my teeth. "It's probably the shock."

"I don't know. I'm scared, Ned. I can only feel my head and my head really hurts, Ned. It's wet and sticky. I can feel it on my lips. I think it's blood."

"It's probably water," I say. "Cave's full of holes and the rainwater's been pouring in. We're probably both soaked."

"I can't feel anything. The water, the cold, nothing. Ned, I think my body is broken." He starts to sob again. "I just want Mummy. Where's my mummy…?"

All at once, Terry stops crying and he lets out a blunt scream.

"What is it?" I yell.

"Ned, something touched my face."

"Probably the water again," I say.

"No, it feels different. Oh God, it's happening again. Ned, there's something here with me. No, *someone*. Someone's stroking my face. Who's that? Who's there?"

I stretch my head out and try to look down but it's no use, I can't see anything.

"Ned, it's a woman. Can you hear her?"

"No, I only hear you," I say.

"She's humming something. Ned, she's singing to me. No, don't do that. Don't touch me."

"What is it? What's she doing?"

"She has my head resting on her chest. Oh shit, who are you? Urgh. Oh God, this is weird. Ned, help me. Help me, please."

Oh fuck, she's here, and there's nothing I can do for him. In the dark, my head drops, and I bite down hard onto the back of my hand.

"Don't worry, Terry. She won't hurt you. She's there to help you. She'll make sure you're safe."

There's no response. "Terry? Are you there? Speak to me."

I can hear muffled groans and sounds like a hurt animal struggling.

"Terry, are you okay? What's happening?"

There's a sudden whimper, and the noise stops and the only sound in the cave – aside from the dripping water – is my voice.

"Terry? Are you there, Terry? Terry?"

I call out to him, but inside I know he's gone. I am alone in the cave.

"I'm sorry, Terry," I whisper. "I failed you."

CHAPTER 73

Despair swells up inside me, and sharp pains fill my chest like I've been stabbed by a hundred knives. My head feels light and the darkness around me seems to twist. I can't tell which way is up or which is down; I could be hanging upside down right now for all I know. My body begins to shake, and my breaths become short gasps of air. I try to regain some control, but the panic overwhelms me and the only movement I can accomplish is to lie down on my back and allow the tears to come.

I failed Terry. I tried my hardest, but it wasn't enough. I failed. Failed to rescue him, failed to keep him safe. I'm useless. I tried to keep us all safe, but I couldn't, and Terry is dead, and soon, so will I. There was never any point fighting so hard. I was just one little boy fighting the monsters, fighting the Custodians – but for what? Nothing. To end up dead in the cold dark of this fucking cave, alone. Away from those I love. I thought I could keep them safe by defeating the monsters. But I had no chance. What I thought were monsters were just shadows of death. The real monsters were people I knew, and they were the ones who killed Terry. They were the ones who've killed me. I give up. "I tried, Terry. I tried." My words dribble out in a mixture of tears and snot, but I don't care. I don't care about anything any more. I am a failure.

My uncontrollable sobs echo across the vast empty space. Listening to my own cries bounce off the rocky insides of this place sickens me further but it's also stark and hearing it stops me in my tracks. My whimpering slows and focusing on the sounds helps, briefly, until, that is, I hear something else.

From below I hear rocks moving. "Terry?" I call out but I get no response. Then there is the sound of scurrying like an insect is crawling up the rock wall. It gets louder as whatever is out there gets nearer.

"Terry?" I say again, knowing full well it's not him.

Something reaches the ledge, and my nose picks up a foul, disgusting smell – worse than anything I've encountered in any of the old buildings we've investigated or even the foul stench of the witch bottles. I hear it breathing heavily through its mouth then it reaches out and strokes my leg. I pull back and retreat as close to the rock wall behind me as I can. I hold my hand against my mouth, and my heart goes wild as my body trembles uncontrollably. Something touches me again and I change position to try and keep every part of me away from it.

Instinctively, my eyes close and immediately I can feel this thing that is near me and it's not what I expected – not fully at least. I can sense she is there; the sad, angry mother, betrayed and killed by cruel townsfolk but her slight presence hides in the shadow of an overwhelmingly vindictive and rageful force. A disgusting, bitter and hateful force that needs to destroy and spoil the innocent for its own survival. It's an entity without heart or direction – a malevolence as old as the mountains that has fed on the suffering and pain of countless souls.

This thing has entered my mind, and it grows and attempts to take control. I can feel it reaching in and trying to feed off my misery and fear. My thoughts move away, and I find myself thinking of my mother and as I try to stay out of its reach – both my body and my mind – something occurs to me. When it kills me then at least I'll be with her. Here, I'm alone in the cold, sickening dark but beyond I could be with her, surrounded by her glowing, warm love. I try and imagine her face and I can see her smiling at me. Her eyes glisten and her long brown hair shines. There is pure white light around her – not the horrible dark halo. The shadow that follows her that night is gone. She is now only surrounded by the gentle sunshine of love and life. The realisation fills my body and I feel a strange acceptance of my fate. I take a deep breath and stretch out my body. I'm not a hero. I never was. Mum loved me regardless because that's what parents do. I'm just a boy. A boy who's about to die. I've stopped caring. "Take me," I say. "I'm done fighting. I didn't keep anyone safe. I give up. I'm ready."

I expect pain and an end to everything, but a curious thing happens. Rather than move in and finish me off, the entity stops and remains still. I hear it breathing and then it makes a sound like a woman muttering her frustration. Like she – it – is disappointed. I sense that – yes – it's lost interest. It doesn't want me, for now, at least. Maybe I'm not close enough to death yet. Maybe it's the memory of my mother's love. Or wait, maybe it's simply that I no longer give a shit if it kills me or not.

There is a moment of silence before I hear it moving and I sense it leaving – down into the depths of the lower reaches of the Black Pit. As it descends, the air in the cave starts to lighten, like a heavy mood is lifting or a poisonous gas is leaving the room.

"I'm still here," I yell. "Come back here and finish it. I want you to. It's my fucking time, damn it. Be done with it." I scream and realise it's not coming back. I turn on my side and start to cry and slam my hand repeatedly on the rocky ledge. I yell and shout and roar until my voice is nothing but a croaky mumble. The tears stop and the raging, sad voices and bitter, hateful thoughts fade away leaving nothing but empty space and silence; peace and a calmness I haven't felt since before I can remember. There is no voice pushing me forwards, searching for revenge, or egging me on to complete the mission at all costs. The mission is over, and the raging waters have stopped, leaving only still, crystal-clear waters.

Is that it then? The curse fades and leaves us for another generation. All thanks to the little lad from the year below me who was sacrificed to keep the town safe.

I turn onto my other side and feel my body become heavy, as a blanket of tiredness is draped over me. Without any light, my eyes don't know if they're open or closed, and as I lay on the cold stone, I feel them become more closed than open, and I drift off into a deep, peaceful sleep on the ledge.

When I wake, up above, I see something. I'm not sure what at first, as my eyes have become used to seeing nothing. But after a moment of staring, I realise what I see is a thin sliver of light that stretches out from the roof of the cave. It forms a bright line in the darkness that cuts across the darkness and travels down to the area beneath my ledge where Terry had fallen into. I quickly move my body over to the edge and look down. The line of the light does not appear to illuminate much below but what it does show is a small pool at the bottom of the cave. I can see no sign of Terry – or anyone else for that matter – in that area, but what I do see takes my breath away. The rocks at the bottom of the pool make it look like a bunch of eyes are staring back up at me. Their colour is a deep, reddish hue. Red eyes. It's the red fucking eyes. I don't believe it and my laugh echoes across the empty cavern. I tried to warn myself about this moment and this place. I sent myself a message and my younger self didn't do the needful and figure out what it meant. Had I, might we have known where this journey would end? Where would my journey surely end as well? There was no way I could climb back up that rock face with my broken leg. This is where my body would rest. I would join the other boys who died down here. I would join Mari Evans and the rest of them.

I turn around and lie back down. I stare at the hole where the light is coming from. Red eyes, I mouth, and repeat it over and over in my head. Perhaps if I try again then another version of myself in a parallel universe – if that is how it works – may do something differently and not end up like this at the end of it all stuck in this bloody cave. I can save another version of myself, somehow.

Suddenly, I hear something. At first, I think it's in my head. But no, there is a noise up above. Voices. Familiar voices.

"It should be here. There. Down there."

"Rebecca?" I whisper.

"The Pool of the Red Eyes." Another voice – was that Rhys?

"He must be around here somewhere." Dad's voice.

Beams of light are flickering across the cavern as torches shine in every direction and search across the big, empty space.

"Oh God. I can see Terry." Gwyn is here as well.

"Help," I call out, but my voice is weak. "Here."

"There he is." I look up and see Rebecca with a headtorch shining down at me over the edge of the cliff. She's immediately joined by Dad.

"Oh, my boy, my boy. Are you okay?"

I nod.

"Give us a second. We have rope. We'll come down and get you out of this damned place."

"Good," I say. "Good. I'm done."

CHAPTER 74

I'm back at the hospital with my leg in a cast. Dad is on one side, Hannah is in a wheelchair on the other, and Auntie Val sits on the end of the bed. Dad has hold of my hand and he hasn't let go since I woke up. Hannah looks pale but she's in good spirits and keeps smiling. They've told me it's Monday afternoon. I was found in the morning, half conscious in the cave. I needed food and water, and I was overly tired and had a broken leg. Another day and the witch – or whatever that was – might have taken me as well. My brain is cloudy as they have me on strong painkillers, after having to set the bone when I arrived earlier. The break was very bad. I'm trying to get my head around what happened after I went into the hatch at Robham House but I'm struggling with the details.

"Tell me again," I say to Dad.

Dad glances over at Auntie Val and then Hannah and back to me. "When you didn't return home on Friday night, we called the police."

"Gave us a right scare, you did, Ned *bach*," Auntie Val chips in.

"We thought whoever had taken that Rowlands lad had got you as well," Dad says.

"They had," Hannah says.

"Right," Dad says.

"I phoned the police," Auntie Val says, "and got a crappy response. They said lots of kids were out late because it was the eve of the festival. They told us to get back in touch after you'd been missing for twenty-four hours."

"We didn't believe them though," Dad continues. "We knew something was up. I came back from the hospital and Val and I searched everywhere. All around town and up into the *Cewri*."

"We were up all night," Auntie Val says, yawning as if to emphasise her efforts.

"We phoned the police again in the morning," Dad says. "They told me they would investigate, but I really wasn't convinced by their enthusiasm." He stops, shakes his head, and blows out through his lips. "I could have been reporting a missing cat – not a missing child."

"We called your friends," Auntie Val says. "The Bowen boys. Your dad even went looking for the Travellers to see if the Gypsy girl had seen you. Of course, none of them had."

"Later in the day on Saturday," Dad says, "we tried the police again but there was no answer, so I decided to head down to the station to see what they were doing. Gatsby and the others were out and there was just some clueless young constable there managing the place while the others were out watching the town during the festival. The young idiot had no idea that we'd reported you missing. I was furious."

"We didn't know they were involved in this thing," Auntie Val says.

"No one did," Hannah says.

"I told him I needed to see some action." Dad drops his fist on the bed. "He went into the back office, and I could see him on the phone. It was weird. He was all flustered. Didn't have any idea what to do."

"Go, Dad," Hannah says with a proud smile on her face.

"Then while I'm waiting, Gatsby's little sidekick runs in. He doesn't see me but yells to the lad on the phone to say there's been an attack at Robham House."

"What?" I say. "In the house? When was this?"

"Late evening, I think. Just before the storm came."

"They say it was Horse," Hannah says. "Horse bashed the housekeeper over her head with a rock."

"Mrs Astley? What the hell?"

Dad nods. "Yeah, they found her half-conscious outside."

"How did they know it was him?" I ask.

"She was still alive," he says. "But died on the way to the hospital."

"Jesus," I say. "That's why she wasn't there underground."

"She was supposed to be where you were?" Hannah asks.

"Yeah, I heard them say she was missing," I say. "What happened to Horse?"

"He legged it," Dad says. "Disappeared without a trace."

"Wow." I am in shock. Horse probably saved me. "What happened after that?"

"It gets weirder," Hannah says.

"I came home," Dad says. "Val and I decided to keep looking. We got a few people together and went out again, searching everywhere we could. We went back to places we'd already been in the hopes we might find something we missed. If the police weren't going to help, then we'd do the job ourselves."

"But Saturday night was hard," Val says. "We were struggling to keep our spirits up. When the storm came, we hit rock bottom. It all seemed so hopeless."

"We had to call off the searching by Sunday lunchtime," Dad says. "We came home. I went into your bedroom and started looking through your stuff. That's when I found your notebook. You'd written *RED EYES* again and again all over it."

"You knew what it meant?" I ask.

He shakes his head. "But I phoned the Bowen boys. Gwyn didn't know but Rhys did. He said it was the name the miners working in Plum Mountain gave to the pool next to the Black Pit. A place they said was haunted and they always steered clear of. He said we should go there. Both came down with their dad. They picked up the Gypsy girl on the way saying she could probably help."

"When we got to Plum Mountain, she took out this skull and started talking to it," Val says with a look of awe on her face. "Never seen anything like it. But it worked. She guided us to an old entrance that'd been hidden by corrugated iron and slates."

"Don't know how," Dad says, "but that Gypsy girl and her skull showed us the way into the mine and then along a route through old tunnels to the cavern where we found you."

"We were so relieved, Ned *bach*," Auntie Val says, welling up. "But then we saw little Terry's body at the bottom of the hole."

Dad takes a deep breath. "And he was surrounded by skeletons. Lots of small skeletons."

He places his hand on my arm and tries to smile calmly. But his eyes can't lie – they don't hide the horrors they've seen.

My head drops and I don't know what to say. My mind is a kaleidoscope of crazy pictures, feelings and memories. On the one hand I am lucky to be alive but on the other, I failed Terry.

"There's more," Hannah says.

I glance across the three of them, not sure of what else there could be.

"Lord Robham," Dad says. "Whatever he did underground caused him to snap."

"Maybe he finally saw sense," Hannah says.

"What?" I ask.

"He hanged himself," Dad says.

"No, how?"

"In his bedroom." Dad leans over in his seat. "But before he did it, he got in contact with some people in London."

"London? Who?"

"We don't know exactly but last night the town was inundated with Met police officers and national news people."

"Our town is famous, Ned," Hannah says.

"What do they know?" I ask.

"The stories are crazy," Auntie Val says. "Secret cults. Child sacrifice. Conspiracies and murder. Who's to know which are real."

I rub my eyes, checking I'm not still asleep. I can't believe it's true. I failed Terry but at least people will know his story.

"They reckon some of the skeletons were very old," Dad says.

"What about the detective?" I ask. "The lady who came to our house. They got to her as well, didn't they?"

"It's been mentioned," Auntie Val says. "But they're cautious about the claims. Everything must be investigated. No one's proved anything yet."

"They're investigating all of it?"

"Sounds like it," Auntie Val says.

"There's a group of detectives outside who want to speak to you as soon as you're ready," Hannah says.

"They're piecing everything together," Dad says. "But before they come in, let me ask you first, what were you doing in that cave? Did those people take you?"

I sigh. "Sort of. I went after them and then, yes, I suppose they took me."

"And they threw you into that hole?" He frowns and his hands become fists.

"Kind of," I say. "I toppled in before they could push me. Guess that's what saved me. Had I been pushed into the pit where Terry fell, I doubt I would've made it."

Auntie Val puts her hand to her mouth. "That poor boy. His family must be heartbroken. And to know he was alive all this time…"

"Ned tried to tell us," Hannah says. "We should've listened."

"I know." Dad brings his face close to mine. "I'm sorry, Ned. I should've listened. I've been too caught up in my own nonsense. I don't know what we would've done if we'd lost you as well."

"It's not worth dwelling on now, Gethin," Auntie Val says. "Our Ned *bach* is safe."

There's a knock at the door and a nurse sticks her head in. She looks to Dad and Auntie Val. "Sorry to disturb but these detectives are desperate to speak with Ned. Is he okay for a quick chat? Ned, do you think you'd be okay with that?"

Dad, Auntie Val and Hannah turn to face me.

"I can talk for a bit," I say. "It's important they hear the truth."

CHAPTER 75

My night is restless. My sleep is full of mad dreams and frightening nightmares. I wake up repeatedly in the dark thinking I'm back in the cave. At one point I must've made a lot of noise because I wake to find a scared nurse staring down at me. She calms me down and then the cycle starts again.

Late in the night – or early in the morning – I wake to see a shadow in the room that was not there before and it's not a nurse. In the mad frenzy of my dreaming-waking state, I'm not sure what is real. I almost fall out of the bed when I see the figure moving but then he steps forwards with a knife in his hand and a finger over his mouth. Horse.

"Are you really here?" I whisper.

"Jesus, lad. They've got you on the strong stuff, haven't they? You looked like you were fighting someone in your sleep."

"You were watching me sleep?" I ask. "How long were you there for?"

"Not long," he says.

I nod to the blade he holds up. "You don't need that."

He glances at the knife, grins and drops it to his side.

"What are you doing here?"

"I wanted to know what happened before I leave town."

"Leave? Where are you going?"

"I can't stay here after what I did. You know what I did, don't you?"

"The Astley woman?" I say hesitantly.

He nods. "I told you it would be dramatic."

I try to find the words to respond. "I'm not sure but… But I think you may have saved me."

"By doing that old hag in?" he says, pulling a dramatic, surprised face.

"Did she look sorry?" I ask.

He shakes his head. "She sneered and bled heavily. She bled a lot actually. I hit her so hard, her eyeball popped out."

"She was the one driving the rest of them," I say. "Without her there…"

"Robham lost his bottle, didn't he?"

"Kind of…" I say, unsure of how to explain it.

He sits down on the edge of the bed.

"Where will you go?" I ask.

"Away from this shithole," he says and breathes out loudly through his nose. "Cousin is waiting for me outside. He'll take me to a mate's place in Liverpool."

"Risky for you to come. You can't have come to hear my story? You must know what happened?"

"Yeah, it's fricking everywhere. You're famous, soft lad," he says. "But there is one thing."

"What?"

"Is she real? The witch. Did you see her in there?"

"I didn't see her, but she's real. Or something in there is real. I'm not sure if it's a woman or a witch or something else."

"Something else? Is that what you were fighting in your sleep?"

"I don't know. Whatever it was has been there for a long time, and it's nasty. Really nasty and bitter and twisted. God, I could feel the anger and the hatred like it was heat from a fire." I swallow and wipe the sweat from my forehead with my arm.

"And that's what killed the missing lad?"

"Yeah, guess they don't mention that on the news?"

"Nah. Fucking cult gets all the blame. Although I got an honourable mention as well. *Lad who saved dog murders cult leader.* How's that for a headline?"

"Did you really save the dog?" I ask. "Some people reckoned you tied it up and tortured it."

"That would be telling." He glances over and gives me a devilish smile. "But we're getting off topic. What happened with the witch or whatever it was? How did you get away?"

I sigh. "After it took Terry, I sensed it nearby. It came up close like it was sniffing me, checking – checking to see if I was near death."

He cocks his head to one side. "And why didn't it finish the job?"

I shake my head. "I don't know. Maybe I was too strong. Maybe it was because I had given up and didn't care any more…"

Horse smiles and claps his hands together. "Our little victim gives up on life and the monster loses interest?" He looks down at his blade and grins. "The curse is real, isn't it?"

I nod. "They say the sick kids started to get better after the festival."

"Jesus. Despite the blood on their hands, the Custodians did keep this place safe over the years." He stands up and rubs his face. "What do you think'll happen in forty years when there's no one here willing to do the necessary?"

"I don't know," I say and reach over to grab a glass of water on the side.

"I may have to come back here for that," he says, clicking his tongue. "Might be a good laugh." He turns away, walks to the door and taps his blade against the wooden frame. "Anyway, you little turd. I'd better go before my cousin thinks I've been abducted. Toodeloo, shithead. Stay safe."

"Bye," I say faintly, and I watch as he pops the knife in his jacket pocket and gently opens the door before stepping out into the shadows of the dark corridor.

CHAPTER 76

It's one week since the night of the festival. The days since have been a strange carousel of odd experiences. All of it is nuts, like I'm watching myself on television in a detective programme. I've spent hours talking about what happened with police officers and a counsellor. Everyone wants to hear my story. They all want to help. Are they able to? I don't know. Do they believe all of it? Who knows? I take each day as it comes and try and focus on the positives but it's hard to move on. It's hard to leave the cave and Terry behind. Part of me will always be trapped there in the dark like the souls of the boys. And the witch.

Dad and I are visiting Mum's grave at the churchyard. Last time I was here, I was gathering soil for the witch bottle. I wonder if they're still above the ceiling of the toilet in the hospital. Not sure if they helped much in the end. But even if they saved one kid then it was worth the effort.

Things feel very different now. For me, my family and – I guess – the town; everything has changed. The war is over and we're still counting the casualties. I should feel lucky I survived but I'm not sure if I do. It's hard to explain. My rage and need to fight has gone but what I'm left with is a sad, empty feeling – like I miss the anger. The counsellor tells me to talk about what happened with my family as much as I can but it's not easy. Dad certainly tries and he barely leaves my side most days. It was his idea to come and see Mum's grave. I didn't want to at first but now that I'm here, I'm glad I came.

He places some tulips in the stone flower vase at the base of her headstone.

"How often do you come here?" I ask.

"Varies," he says. "For the first few weeks I was here every day. Then I became distracted, focused on the writing, and I didn't come here so much."

"I've not been here for a while either," I say. "I've been to the churchyard. Just not to see Mum's grave."

"Why's that, do you think?" he asks.

"I always had things to do," I say. "My investigations and the mission."

Dad places his hand on my shoulder. "Maybe we were both trying to avoid it, eh?"

I look up at Dad. "I knew something was going to happen to her," I say.

"What?" His eyes narrow.

"I woke up when she came into my room that night. It's difficult to explain but I saw a darkness that clung to her. I knew something bad was going to happen. I tried to warn her, but she wouldn't listen."

"Ned *bach*," he says. "It was her heart. Probably a fault that she was born with. A time bomb that she had lived with all her life. Even if you did know what was coming, there's nothing you could have done. It was a small, subtle fault that resulted in a catastrophic failure in her body that ended her life. There's nothing any of us could have done."

He turns his head and looks down at me with a sad face. "You didn't tell me this… Has it been on your mind since she died?"

"I don't know. I just think that maybe I should've done more. Stopped her going to bed. Sent her back to the hospital."

"It's unlikely they would have found anything, to be honest. It was very well hidden, and she was otherwise fit as a fiddle. Please don't dwell on it. There's nothing you can do to change anything now. All we can do is remember the time we had with her and be thankful that we had her in our lives."

I sigh and think about what he says. "What do you think she would've made of all this nonsense with the Custodians?"

"Knowing her, she would have been furious with you for going up against them alone and me for allowing you to do that."

"Right," I say, clearing my throat.

He puts his hand on my shoulder. "But also, she would have been proud of you for trying to save that boy. For pushing ahead and trying to do the right thing when everyone else had given up."

"But I failed," I say.

"Sometimes, all that matters is the intention. That you try your hardest. The rest and the stuff you can't control will happen whatever way it will, anyway. The important thing is you play your part – to the best of your abilities."

"Hmm." I don't know how to respond. I certainly tried my hardest, but I'm not sure if that makes any of it feel better. For now, anyway. I stare at the grave, and we stand there in silence.

"How's the writing going?" I ask him.

"Good, now that I've got the old typewriter back. The ideas are flowing again." He sees my face change. "Don't worry. I'll be taking it a bit more slowly this time."

I give him a wry smile. "Have you worked out how the story ends? What happens to the King?"

"There's still a lot to write but I have the story worked out. It's complex – as life often is – but I think eventually the King learns to live with his decisions. Sometimes big decisions involve sacrifice. Realising that you can't have everything and that some things must be given up for the greater good. The King made the hard choice in the short term but in time it became clear that what he did saved many more lives."

"I hope it does," I say.

CHAPTER 77

I sit alone in the Jungle on Horse's tree stump next to the Eagle's Nest. Dad dropped me off after we visited the churchyard. I can hear footsteps. I have arranged to meet my friends here. I haven't seen them since the hospital, and I didn't get much time with them then because of everything else going on. Gwyn rushes towards me first and he is followed closely by Rebecca and Rhys.

She is carrying her satchel and I sense the fifth member of our group is with her in the bag.

Gwyn sits down quietly on the stump next to mine and reaches his arm around me.

"Here's the hero of the hour," Rhys says. He leans over and ruffles my hair with his fingers. I laugh and shake my head at what he calls me.

Rebecca gives me a big smile.

"Are you okay?" Gwyn says.

"Yeah," I say. "Bit more mobile now."

"You look tired," Rebecca says. "Are you sleeping?"

"It's not easy," I say. "The nights are when I remember things most clearly."

Everyone goes quiet for a moment.

"Still no sign of Horse?" Rebecca says.

I shake my head.

"I heard he was in Liverpool with his cousin," Rhys says.

"Right," I mutter.

"Can you believe the coverage the Custodians are getting?" Gwyn says. "It's on telly and in the newspapers every day."

"Gerald Edwards is doing well from it," Rhys says. "He was on the radio this morning saying he's writing a book about them."

"The whole thing is unbelievable," Rebecca says.

"Their membership was nuts," Rhys says. "Town councillors, that scumbag Chelmsley, business owners..."

"Policemen," Gwyn says, shaking his head.

"What's the latest with your uncle?" Rebecca asks.

Gwyn drops his head and Rhys crosses his arms.

"They've charged him with the murder of the detective," Rhys says. "He'll probably get it for Terry as well."

"With Robham and Astley gone, he'll likely be at the top of the pile," I say.

"What does your mum make of it?" Rebecca asks.

"She's being weird about it," Gwyn says. "Like the problem is the town – not him."

"Maybe it is," I say.

"So many key people here have strong connections with the Custodians," Gwyn says.

"It's no wonder they were so powerful," Rebecca says.

"They won't be getting away with it this time," Rhys says and kicks a tree stump.

"They had it coming," Gwyn says. "What they did to Terry and those other boys over the years was monstrous."

"Right."

"Yeah."

I take a deep breath. "They did keep the witch at bay though, didn't they?"

"Don't tell me you're sympathetic after all this?" Gwyn asks.

"I'm not, but I saw what her curse did. Hannah was one of

them. If the Custodians hadn't done what they did, she probably would've died."

"There must be another way to stop the curse," Gwyn says.

"Maybe," I say. "But I sensed her – it – in that cave. I felt the presence nearby. It came up to the ledge to see if I was ready. I felt the wickedness and the power of the witch or whatever it was, and it scared me more than anything ever has before."

Everyone is silent for a moment, but I know the next question is coming.

"What stopped her, do you think?" Rhys asks.

"I don't know," I say. "Thought about it non-stop and whether it was due to my state or how I focused my thoughts, but honestly, the presence only retreated once I'd resolved myself to my own fate."

"Meaning you gave up?" Gwyn says, frowning.

I sigh. "Basically, yes. Everything had got to me, and I no longer had any fight left. I realised I was just one little boy battling against a world of evils and I had no hope of winning."

Their expressions all drop, and I try and do something with my fidgety fingers.

"Honestly," I say. "It felt good. I'd been fighting so long; I'd almost forgotten what was driving me. To finally realise it was not my job to save everyone was a massive relief."

"But you know you did save the day in some ways," Gwyn says. "Maybe not for Terry but you certainly saved many more boys in the future and stopped them from being killed by the Custodians."

"Did I, though?" I say. "Only time will tell."

Rebecca reaches over, rubs my arm, and gives me a sad look that I've seen too many times since the cave. I'm tired of it.

I clap my hands together. "But you know, it was you guys who saved me. I would've been a goner had it not been for you finding me."

"And yourself," Gwyn says. "Red eyes? You passed that message on to yourself across time and space. Pretty impressive."

"I don't know how…" I say.

"Uri Geller, eat your heart out," Rhys says with a beaming smile.

"You've definitely got some *klewmeirw* in you." Rebecca smiles.

"Maybe." I blow a raspberry and push on my crutches to get up.

Rebecca scans the surroundings. "It's weird being here without Horse."

"Yeah," Gwyn says. "Say, why did you want to meet here of all places?"

"Seemed like a good place. There's something I wanted to do." I take out the copy of Terry's missing poster that I had in my pocket when I was in the cave. All the others around town had been destroyed in the storm.

"Poor lad," Gwyn says, gazing at the paper.

"I was with him until the end," I say, "but there was nothing I could do to help him. Knowing that is hard." I blink back tears.

"You did everything you could," Rebecca says. "You went much further than anyone else in this town did."

I shrug and sigh. "Anyway, I thought that because there's no mention yet of when his funeral will be, we could bury this poster instead. Maybe take a moment to remember him."

I'm not sure what everyone will say to this, but no one seems to object.

"Where shall we do it?" Rhys says.

"I dug a small hole just there," I say, pointing to a spot near the camp.

I hobble over with the others and place the paper down in the hole so that Terry's face looks up at the four of us.

"Who wants to go first?" I ask, glancing around at the others.

"I will," Rebecca says. "Terry, you were in my class, but I didn't really talk to you much. You were always nice to me when you did and for that I thank you."

"You were a great goalkeeper," Gwyn says. "You always played well for the school team."

"Very moving," Rhys says.

"What?" Gwyn says.

"Okay," Rhys says. "Terry, I didn't know you, but you're now famous and your name will live on forever in the history of this town, and probably this country."

It's my turn and there's a pause.

"Terry," I say, my voice cracking. "Terry, we tried. I tried so hard to help you. I came close but failed. I was with you until the last moments of your life, but in the end, I could do nothing to stop the darkness from taking you. Terry, I'm sorry. I'm so sorry…" I am sobbing and I cannot hold it back any longer. My tears fall like a waterfall onto his paper face in the hole beneath us. My three friends step closer and put their arms around me.

"Okay, enough," I say. "Can you…" I nod towards the hole and go to sit back down on the stump.

Rhys moves soil onto the poster with his hands, making sure the paper is fully covered. There is a moment of quiet as everyone seems to gather their thoughts. I wipe my face and feel like a little bit of the weight has been lifted.

"You okay?" Rebecca asks with her hand on my shoulder.

I nod and give her a half smile. Gwyn comes over, grabs my crutches, and starts to hobble about. Rebecca chuckles. Then his face becomes serious. "What do you think will happen?"

"When?" I ask.

"In forty years, when another generation has to face the curse. The Custodians are done for. Robham's dead and his wife and son want nothing to do with the family name. There's no way their legacy will live on." Rhys wipes the soil from his hands.

"Someone will have to step up and take her on," Gwyn says.

"Hopefully without resorting to murder," Rebecca says.

I can sense all three of them are staring at me.

"I'm not doing it," I say. "I'm done with the fight."

Gwyn nods and smiles. Rhys and Rebecca glance over at each other.

I look at my watch and have a thought. "How long have I got you guys here for?"

"Well, I'm here for the rest of the year," Rebecca says. "Dad decided it was safe for us to return now that the Custodians are out of the way."

"Great," I say.

"We've got a few hours," Gwyn says. "Parents are sorting stuff out at the old house."

"What've you got in mind?" Rhys asks.

"Investigation?" Gwyn suggests, wide-eyed. "Old asylum's just up the road. We could go and find out who that crazy spirit was that attacked us."

I breathe out heavily through my lips and shake my head. "Oh God, no," I say. "Let's – erm – play something or we could go and watch a film."

CHAPTER 78

Dad picks us up in his transit van and the three of them sit in the back on some boxes while I sit up front.

"You want dropping off at the cinema?" Dad asks.

"No thanks," I say. "Leave us at the newsagent. I want to get a bag of penny sweets. Can't stand that popcorn they serve."

"Righty ho," he says. "Will you be alright getting there from the High Street?"

"Yeah, I'm getting pretty nifty with these things." I tap the crutches resting on my legs. I hear chuckles from behind and turn my head.

"What was that?" I say, trying to push in on the joke.

"Rhys reckons we could do more investigations if we had a van like this to get around in," Rebecca says.

"Ha, right," I say. "Maybe we could paint it blue and green and write *The Mystery Machine* on the side – what do you reckon, Dad?"

"I may have the right paint back there if you look carefully." Dad winks at me.

"We'd need another girl," Rhys says. "We need Daphne and Velma."

"Hannah could join us," I say.

"We have three guys, though – one of us will have to be a dog," Rhys says.

"I'm not playing the role of fricking Scooby-Doo," Gwyn says.

"Well, it's him or Shaggy," I say. "I have to be Fred."

"How do you work that one out?" Gwyn says.

"I'm the leader of the group," I say. "So, I have to be Fred."

"Well, that means Rebecca must be Daphne. Because Fred and Daphne were boyfriend-girlfriend. Hannah can't be your girlfriend…" Rhys says.

Gwyn closes his eyes, purses his lips and makes smooching noises. I can feel my cheeks warm up and redden. "Oh. Are they supposed to be a couple?"

"Of course," Rhys says. "Have you never noticed that?"

"Guess I never thought about it." I see Dad is smiling at me. "Yeah, maybe we can have a rethink about who does what in the group."

The van turns up onto the High Street, and the three in the back topple over from their boxes. Dad looks into the mirror. "Sorry, guys," he says. "Maybe should have taken that a little slower."

Gwyn appears a little alarmed while Rebecca and Rhys laugh loudly.

"Reminds me of riding on the back of your dad's bike," I call out to Rebecca.

"He's been asking about you," she says. "Wants to know how you're doing after… everything."

"He helped me a lot," I say. "Tell him I'm alright."

At that moment the van brakes again and we stop. I look outside and see we're outside the newsagent.

"Are you sure you don't want me to wait for you and take you to the cinema?" Dad asks.

"We'll be fine," Gwyn yells from the back, lying on the floor, covered in paintbrushes and wallpaper rolls.

The other two giggle and I shake my head. "It's alright, Dad. Thanks. After the movie is fine."

"Four thirty?" he asks.

"Four thirty," I say.

While the others wait outside, I hobble into the newsagent. Gwyn holds the door open for me and I enter the shop on my crutches. The bell above the door rings and I enter to see Mrs Jones leaning on the counter with a broad beaming smile like she's been waiting for me to enter.

"Well, look who it is, the hero of the hour," she says. "How are you, Ned *bach*?"

"Erm – good, thank you." I can't help but glance over to the newspapers on the stand. I see headlines like MURDER AND MACHINATION IN THE MOUNTAINS and CULT RED-HANDED.

Mrs Jones sees my eyes wander. "There's no avoiding it, I'm afraid," she says. "It's all over the papers and news programmes right now."

I nod slightly and carry on to the counter.

"Ned *bach*, I can't imagine what you went through in that place." She smiles gently. She sees me spying the penny sweet trays in front of her. "Such a shame things had to end up like that." A *shame*, I think. Odd word to use. Why would she say that?

"Usual?" she says, and I nod. She lifts the glass and reaches in. "Oh, I've run out of paper bags. Just a second, Ned."

She gently drops the glass lid back down and then grunts as she bends over behind the counter. I lean to one side, placing more weight on one crutch than the other and then lift my arm and rub under my armpit where the crutch has been rubbing hard against my skin.

"They're here somewhere," she says, digging through the cupboard. I can only see the silver hair on the top of her head, shifting about on the other side of the counter.

"But you know, life is often about difficult decisions. Sometimes we all must make sacrifices for the greater good." She stops and glances up. I start to feel uncomfortable.

Then she's back into the cupboard. "For many years, the Custodians protected the children of this town from the evil powers of the witch. They had to make the greatest sacrifice of all to keep the rest of us safe. That is something these newspapers and outsiders just don't understand. We're the ones who must live here. We're the ones who must exist with this terror."

I'm uncertain of what to say. My mouth has become dry, and I try and use my tongue to make the inside wet. "But they killed a boy," I say. "They killed lots of boys."

"To save the lives of countless more, Ned *bach*. Did you ever read Kings in the Old Testament? It tells of King Mesha of Moab, who sacrificed his son, the crown prince, to defeat an alliance of invading armies. Are you familiar with that story, Ned?" My jaw drops and I turn my head to see the road, but Dad has now gone. "Yes," I say weakly and clear my throat. "Yes."

"That is what the Custodians had to do. Their task was brave and frightening. Imagine having to take responsibility for offering up a boy in exchange for the life of countless other children in the town and maybe even beyond this area, and doing that every forty years? Can you imagine inheriting that burden knowing you'll have to pass it on to your child when their time comes?"

Maybe it's one of her jokes. Maybe she's trying to wind me up.

"Ah, here they are." She groans again as she straightens up. In her hand is a small packet full of paper bags and she has a sardonic smile on her face. I'm ready to leg it from the shop as quickly as my crutches will allow me or to scream and tell my friends, but I take a deep breath and remain where I am.

She takes one of the paper bags and lifts the glass panel. "Now what would you like, Ned?"

"Erm – just a mixture for a pound, please."

"Ah yes, Ned *bach*. I know what you like, don't I? And you're one of my best customers. I'll give you a fine selection."

She reaches in and grabs a good load of cola bottles and fried eggs and does the same with a few others. It looks like well more than a pound's worth.

"I'm not sure if I have enough money," I say.

"Oh, this is my treat, Ned *bach*."

"Erm – thank you."

The bag fills up and she weighs it up in the air. "That is a good load, Ned. Jelly babies – sorry, I forgot the jelly babies. You always like your jelly babies, don't you?"

I nod and she reaches under the glass panel and pulls out a few more sweets from their compartment before placing the lid back down and twisting the end of the bag. She holds it in her hands and glares at me, but the smile is now gone, and I feel the shiver down my spine again.

"Now look," she says. "The leadership of the Custodians is decimated. The group's existence, its purpose and its resources have been exposed. The Robham bloodline will no longer ensure continuity of the practices and rituals. But what you must realise is that the Custodians were far more than just the small collective of people that ran the group. The Custodians were made of beliefs and shared objectives. The Custodians also had deep roots in this town." She leans onto the counter and her head comes close to mine. "Very deep roots, and it would surprise you how far they reached."

She points to the newspapers. "All this fuss and drama will ease off in a few years and the story of the Custodians will just be another legend, like the *Cewri*. Like the witch."

I can smell her minty breath and step away, but I can't stop staring at her wrinkled face.

"But come another generation, the needful will need to be done once again."

"No," I say.

"Yes," she says. "It must. The alternative is far too horrifying to consider. The evil that exists here must be contained and suppressed, and that can only be carried out by ensuring another tribute is made. Another child must be given to the witch. If we don't, the children of this town will suffer. And who knows how far that evil will travel if allowed to escape the confines of this space."

I turn my head and hope that one of my friends will come in, but they don't; it's just me and the shopkeeper.

"I know it wasn't all your doing," she says. "The Robham line had been weakening over the last couple of generations and it was inevitable that this time would come. But you must share your responsibility for what happened. You played your part, and you and your little friends' interference made sure the Custodians' time – as currently structured – could not carry on. And for that reason, it's you that must step up."

"Me?" I say. "No way. Never. Custodians did horrible things."

"Yes, the Custodians did horrible things. They did terrible but incredibly brave things to stop the evil from overcoming the town and hurting our children. In a generation, someone will need to do that again. Ned *bach*, you will need to do that again. It must fall on you to take on that burden."

She stops for a moment, licks her lips, drops the sweets on the glass counter and places her clasped hands next to them. "If you don't, the darkness will win. That is how we defeat the monsters and that is how we keep everyone safe."

"It's not my job to keep everyone safe," I say. "It's too much for me. I'm just a kid. Someone else will have to do it."

She gestures to the sweets next to her hands. "Take them. These are yours now."

"I don't want to. I didn't pay for them."

"Oh, you did, Ned *bach*. You don't realise it, but you paid a great price for these sweets and now they are yours to take."

A million thoughts are flying through my mind. The next tribute is forty years away. I could be on the other side of the planet by then. I could be rich and powerful and free to do whatever I wanted. But what about the people here in this town?

Who would be here? What if Hannah lives here? Would Dad and Auntie Val still be here? Would they still be alive? And what about the children? What would really happen if the tribute failed?

I close my eyes, reach over, and take the heavy bag of sweets.

"There's a good boy," she says, and I lean on my crutches and turn to leave the shop.

ABOUT THE AUTHOR

After gaining a Ph.D. in Molecular Epidemiology, **R H Williams** soon realised he'd rather write about science than do it. His day job involves teaching doctors worldwide the latest developments in medicine. He lives with his wife and two children in the Welsh countryside. His debut novel, *The Madness of the Faithful*, was published by Troubador in 2022. *Don't Let 'Em Take the Children* is his second novel.